THE INFERNO OF PROMETHEUS

TAPESTRY OF FATE
BOOK 3

MATT LARKIN

INCANDESCENT PHOENIX BOOKS

The Inferno of Prometheus: Eschaton Cycle
Tapestry of Fate Book 3
MATT LARKIN
Editors: Sarah Chorn, Regina Dowling
Cover: Felix Ortiz, Shawn T. King
Map: Francesca Baerald

Incandescent Phoenix Books
mattlarkinbooks.com

TITAN ERA
OKEANUS
THULE
HYPERBOREA
KELTIA
ILLYRIS
SALON
RASSENIA
MNEMOSYNIA
THRINAKIA
OLMECATL
TARTESSOS
KARKHEDON
KARTH
KEMET
MEMPHIS
TIWANAKU
TIWANAKU
INUMIDEN
OSIRION
THE GREAT VELDT
KUSH
HY-BRASIL
KONGO JUNGLE
KGALAGADI DESERT
AZANIA

KER-YS
NYXLANDS
ISSEDONIA
XIRONG
YAN
WAKOKU
ARIMASPIA
JINYANG
YINDAI
HYLEAN WOODS
XIANYANG
YING
XIAO
YAMATO
KIMMERIA
GEBI DESERT
XIANG
BO
WANGGEOM
PHLEGRA
THEMISKYRA
KOLCHIS
DANGUN
OLYMPIAN MOUNTAINS
AXEINOS SEA
KOLCHIS
ELLADOS
IOLKOS
PHRYGIA
KUNLUN MOUNTAINS
PHAEAKIA
ILIUM
YUESHANG
DELPHI
THEBES
ARAD MOUNTAINS
BYBLOS
PHOENIKIA
VYADHAPURA
ITHAKA
ARGOS
KORINTH
SLESVOS
PHOEBA
NUSANTARA ISLES
KROKYLEA
SKYROS
NERITUM
KRONION
LYDIA
TYROS
AEOLIA
NAXOS
KHIOS
HELION
HAWAIKI
ATLANTIS
KNOSOS
THALASSA
ATATI
ATLANTIS
NUSANTARA
OGYGIA
UGART
NESHIA
MUGEDANG
BADIAN STEPPES
NINEVEH
DREAMING DESERT
ASUR
BABILIM
DREAMING LANDS
BULU
EMPTY DESERT
BABILIM
KISSATU
RAPAI
PURANIC MOUNTAINS
MU
NYSA
SHALMALI
SUMERU MOUNTAINS
TAKHKHASILA
HURU MOUNTAINS
BARBARIKON
PATALIPUTRA
HINDUSH
DHANYAKATAKA
KUMARI KANDAM

THE WHISPER

It starts with a whisper, a haunting intimation of a World askew. That we are, in the end, caught in a death spiral, time nearly played out, whilst entropy tugs ever harder upon the Wheel of Fate.

Looking now into the dying embers, we at last apprehend Truth, and in it the revelation that the vaunted tales of old were not what we thought ... And neither, in fact, were we.

For if we have lived before, might not all we've dreamt be but our souls' memories of Worlds become dust ...

A QUICK NOTE

For full colour, higher-res maps, character lists, location overviews, and glossaries, check out the bonus resources here:
https://tinyurl.com/hw52dzss

And if you liked this book, be sure to check out my offer for a free novella at the end.

PROLOGUE

2386 Golden Age

In the last days of the Time of Nyx, Prometheus—under another name—had taught the Titan forebears, the uriași, the Art of Fire. In his desperation to break the hold of the Elder Goddess of Night, he had given a gift to some few who little understood what he offered. It had, in soul-crushing fashion, consumed too many of those to whom he had given it, the Fire spirits they had borne in their breasts claiming them.

They had become living infernos, unleashing their conflagrations upon the Mortal Realm, caring naught for friend or foe. Even now, in the recesses of Prometheus's own soul, the spirit growled at him to burn. Burn it *all*. But his disciples had, after all, broken the hold of Nyx. Night had ended, even if the price had proved dear.

And now, with another great war drawing nigh, he found himself forced to repeat his teachings. In time, he would pass the Art of Fire on to Mankind, but for now, his first student was the Titan Hestia, daughter of Kreios and Eurybia, who cared for Man as he himself did.

In a cave south of Korinth, above the rampaging waves of the Aegean, the two of them stared into the flickering remnants of a rectangular fire pit that had dwindled to crackling embers. Crimson splotches bled through the bandages wrapt around Hestia's feet. Those had been the worst of her burns, though in passing through the flames, fire had licked her shins as well, and those too remained rubescent and peeling.

While no doubt in pain, she hid it well. The slight tremble in her fingers as she reached for the embers, that was probably more trepidation at further injuries than pain at her current wounds. Everyone feared a recurrence of agonies once suffered, yet when she mastered this, naught would ever singe her again.

But there were always those first, terrible burns.

No Firewalkers could rise without walking through fire.

Such was the way of it.

Hestia's fingertips brushed over a tongue of flame and she started. When she withdrew her hand, sprouts of fire lingered upon the back of it, flowing over her fingers, swaying as if to unheard music. A gasp escaped the Titan. Despite her centuries of life, childlike elation lit her face as she looked at him, and Prometheus couldn't stop the smile from rising in him as well. Unabashed joy was, after all, catching, not least for its precious rarity these days.

Hestia huffed, still shifting her arm before her face. "I can hardly believe this real." Fire spilled down over the crook of her elbow, only to swirl back toward her wrist as she shifted her arm once more.

"After all you endured, I should hope it would prove so." But he wasn't really looking at her.

Within the flames, silhouettes shifted, patterns beginning to shape themselves. The complexities of its rhythm threatened to pull him inward as fire so oft did. "Rest yourself now," he said, barely aware of the Titan.

His mind fell into the burning maelstrom ahead, and mummery formed up from the shadows about him. Voices broke through his haze slowly, first seeming to drift in through thin walls, then rising until it seemed he eavesdropped on those but a few feet away.

Hekate and Zeus, and Zeus's brother Hades, naked in the dark of the woods, painted with sorcerous glyphs. *This* ... Prometheus fell deeper into the flame as the scene played out around him.

The World bucked in cringing revulsion as Hekate sang of times she did not understand, invoking nostalgia none who had lived through the woes of Dark Faerie would ever have felt. Her whirling dance bent the cosmos in time with her profane intent, the likes of which Prometheus had never before witnessed. Invisible presences seeped inside Hades, driving the Titan into convulsions. The grisly ruination of flesh and soul unfolding within the flame churned Prometheus's gut, left him desperate to deny that his daughter could conceive such obscenities.

"I didn't know this would happen." Zeus's inane complaints seeped from the flame into Prometheus's mind and were rejected by Hekate as much as by Prometheus.

When Hades's torso imploded, Prometheus shut his eyes with a wince, blocking further display of his accursed Sight, which so oft condemned him to witness things he might rather have not. The temptation always lurked just out of reach, an overwhelming desire to turn aside from the course the Moirai had saddled him with.

Allowing himself a grimace, Prometheus opened his eyes. Of course, he had known for so very long the war would come. Zeus would battle against his father and win, and pitiable Kronos would be cast down into Tartarus for his failings. And this moment would serve as the catalyst, would it not?

Faint snores from the corner of the cave drew his gaze to Hestia, curled up in a ball and, he hoped, at peace.

But peace did not last, and she too would invariably find herself swept up in the coming war. Could he avert it? Could he take any action that might forestall Kronos's terrible Fate?

But he knew better and had told Pandora as much. They could not risk any action that might unmake their own pasts and thus destroy their child, and besides, his greater plan required a strict adherence to the Fates' design. He had agreed to become their avatar, had set the whole of history upon its course with a singular aim, and no matter how vile the path, he could not lose sight of the end because of events along the way.

No, Zeus's profane ritual was inevitable, as would be Kronos's response. In fact, to truly play his role, Prometheus would need to *ensure* Kronos learnt of this at the right time.

Repining, cursing his Fate at having to tread such paths, it was a self-indulgence he would not permit himself. Not given all he had already sacrificed and the greater pains ahead. No, the future impended.

And Prometheus must dive back into the pyromantic trance to ensure he knew exactly what steps would uphold the timeline. Such was his role, and no other choice lay before him. History was merciless.

PART I

... The Gigantes are the broken Titans. Those rejected, grown misshapen by their need to devour Man-flesh. Pushed to the fringes, they were long primed to move against their Olympian oppressors, needing but a single spark to launch them into the frenzy of war. Demeter gave them that spark.

— Kleio, Analects of the Muses

1

PANDORA

715 Bronze Age

Given that Herakles's farmhouse had lain outside Thebes, it might have proved the perfect place for Pandora to sit and contemplate her course. Might have, save for Herakles's pressing need to flee from the scene of his crime. Pandora had checked in on his wife to ensure she would recover on her own, then sent word to neighbours that she thought something dire might have unfolded here. Herakles assured her that his brother's son lived close and would check in soon.

Before that could happen, Pandora and Herakles made their way into the woodlands. The hulking demigod sat against a pomegranate tree, his head in his hands, fingers clutching at his skull as if he considered crushing it beneath their might. While Pandora had given him a semblance of hope, it could not outweigh the torment of guilt that wracked the man. In the abortive whimpers that escaped him, Pandora imagined she could hear the voices of his slain children, accusing him. A dark fancy, of course, but then, worse must now plague the demigod.

Pandora's gaze shifted from Herakles back to the Box she held in her hands. Though Nemesis had interrupted them, she had encountered Prometheus in Byblos, in the time of Perseus, many decades before now. Which meant Herakles must free him *before* that time. She had never tried to take another person with her using the Box. So far as she could tell, Prometheus had not tried to use it himself, either. But unless she brought Herakles with her into the past, how could she fulfil Prometheus's future as she had already experienced it? Or his past, rather, as the implication remained he must already be free now, in this time. Free perhaps, though she had no idea where or how to question him on what to do.

No, all that came to her at the moment was that she must send herself and Herakles back, as close as possible to the time when Zeus had first bound Prometheus.

"What is it?" Herakles asked.

Pandora hadn't noticed him look up from his torturous self-reflections, but now he stared hard at the Box.

"Is that a toy?"

"No." That one should call the Box thus left her torn by laughter and despair. "Rather, it makes playthings of us all, I think." With each use, Pandora's understanding of the workings of this thing became more refined. She had seen Prometheus set it to bring her here, to the point when she could save Herakles. And while her lover may have relied upon pyromantic insight to determine those settings, from them she could still glean her own lessons.

Grim-faced, Herakles crawled over to her side. Under other circumstances, the dubious look he gave the Box might have drawn a chuckle from Pandora.

It must be possible to bring him along, for how else could he have saved Prometheus in the past? "I want you to hold on to my shoulders." Physical contact might, with luck, be enough to draw him into the bubble the Box created. "This is going to allow us to reach the person who needs our help."

"How?" he demanded, though he did place his fingertips upon her shoulders, his touch so light she imagined him afraid. Frightened, perhaps, at the idea of the least connection with another woman, given what he'd done to his wife.

"Grab hold," she instructed. If he was left behind in this time, she could not be certain of returning to this moment. Thus far, she'd never managed aught exact with the Box.

He did so, and she popped the top, welcoming the distorting bubble of light that enveloped them, though a gasp escaped Herakles. The big demigod fell backward and Pandora spun, wrapping her arms around his knee in the bare instant before the growing haze at the edge of her vision filled it.

Blinking away the disorientation, Pandora rose, finding herself sprawled atop an unconscious Herakles. Given he must have many times her fortitude, she had to assume it was the mind, rather than the body, that the Box strained. The more she used it, the more she became inured to its effects.

They lay upon a hilltop, amid tall grass, a blue sky above them, with what looked to be a town in the distance below. More than that, she couldn't say. The hope remained that she'd managed to bring them to just after Zeus had cast Prometheus into Tartarus, but even if so, she didn't know *where* the Box had sent her.

After giving him a moment of blissful ignorance, Pandora shook Herakles awake. Maybe she ought to have told him more about what the Box would do, but then, she could not have afforded to take the chance he'd have balked. She *needed* the demigod, and he had proven himself unstable enough with his crimes already.

His hand shot out like a striking snake, caught her wrist, and squeezed until she felt bones grind against one another. Her sudden yelp of pain had Herakles releasing her, though, and scooting back on his arse, casting about himself in bemusement. "What ...?"

Rubbing her wrist, Pandora scowled at the murderous demigod she'd thrown all her hopes into. "Tell me about your father," she said.

The man continued to look around, as if wondering where the woods past his home had fled to. "Amphitryon, son of Alkaios." The hitch in his voice revealed a half-truth Pandora had no patience for.

"He's not your real father."

Herakles folded his arms over his chest like a petulant child, his glowering making plain what he thought of her knowing the details of his life.

How to phrase this? If she gave away too much, she might lose her chance at his aid. "The prophecy says only a son of Zeus can free the Titan from his torment."

"Which Titan?"

Her mind whirred with possible answers or evasions. Deceiving him might help her get him into Tartarus, but what if he then betrayed her when he inevitably learnt the truth? "Prometheus." Speaking his name left her almost breathless. "My lover."

Herakles snorted. "My lady, Prometheus escaped his torment ages ago. It's a common enough bard's tale. I guess my father forgave him his crimes, or at least they became somewhat reconciled. Either way, you're centuries too late."

Sitting upon the hilltop, she looked hard at him. How much trust could she afford to place in the man? How *little* could she? "He was freed by you, a son of Zeus, who saw the inequity of his father's actions."

A raised brow in answer. "I think I'd have remembered a trek into Tartarus."

"It hasn't happened yet, for you." She held up the Box.

"I told you, it happened long before I was even born."

"This brought us backward in time, into the past, where you will fulfil your destiny and save Prometheus from Tartarus."

He cleared his throat, then looked about the hill a moment. "I knew I'd gone mad." Once more, he moved with surprising speed, snatching the Box from her hand.

"No!" Pandora lunged for it, but Herakles caught her arm and shoved her down into the grass, even as he himself stood, examining her one hope. He turned it over in his hands, then began prodding at the panels. "Don't!" Pandora implored, scrambling to her feet. Again, she swiped for it, and again, he held her back like she was a child.

"This thing, whatever it is, rendered me senseless for a time. I cannot imagine how you dragged me up this hill, but you've made a jest of me and my grief." The look he gave her froze her, killing her struggles at once. "Were you a man, I'd beat you bloody for it." Some emotion crossed his face, perhaps the realisation he had beaten a woman bloody too, this past night.

"Please ..." Pandora began.

With a scoff, Herakles let the Box fall at her feet, then turned, tromping down the hillside toward the town, muttering obscenities under his breath.

While Pandora's skill in Phlegran had atrophied, she recognised the speech of the locals in the small city the moment she entered. Of course, these people no doubt also spoke some Elládosi, but as the language came back to her, she decided she need not bother asking anyone to switch. It never hurt to practice as many tongues as possible.

This place, she soon learnt, was Iolkos, Phlegra's sole polis, a site ruled by Ares, at least in name, though she realised the Olympian did not oft come out so far. In her studies in Atlantis, Pandora had heard tale that Ares had set his sights upon the town ages back. Iolkos had no wall, and in three days of bloody slaughter, he had installed himself as ruler of this place, demanding the populace raise a temple for him on the acropolis and worship him as their god.

From the look of the landscape, she gauged Iolkos must have lain not far from where Athyras had stood in the Golden Age. Did that town yet exist, or had it fallen into decay in the passing of years? Well, such things mattered little to her mission, she supposed, though sooner or later she'd need to return to the Golden Age to deal with the Nike issue. If her daughter needed Nike's help to survive the Titanomachy, Pandora would damn sure find the other Titan.

First, though, her oath to save Prometheus. That came before all other things. It must.

Beneath a colonnade abutting the forum, she found Herakles, the demigod having all but finished a large amphora of wine. He'd laid his sword and shield beside him, and now, seeing them in the light, she realised she knew them. Had helped Perseus find those adamant arms buried in the Garden of the Hesperides. She could not help but shudder at the memory of the cyclopean presence of the drakon Ladon brushing against her mind.

Part of her wanted to let Herakles wallow in his self-pity, but her situation would not permit such a thing. Thus, selecting a step before the column he leaned on, Pandora settled down, folding her legs beneath herself. "Who is king of Iolkos in your time?" she asked the hulking demigod.

The man snorted, wiping his lips on the back of his hand. "Uh ... Pelias, I think."

"Because I heard the locals speaking of King Kretheus. The demigod son of Aiolos. Which would mean, either your knowledge of Phlegra is somewhat lacking, or we have moved in time. Either way, Herakles, you can well enough see we've come to Iolkos. You imagine I carried you hundreds of miles whilst you slept? I'd have struggled to have moved you a few feet."

Glowering, the man chucked the amphora, which shattered against the cobbles beyond the colonnade, causing a great many passersby to shout in alarm, and earning him no few glares. "I don't know how you've done any of this, but your claims reek of absurdity."

"Then how would you explain our present circumstances?" A faulty argument, of course. That Herakles did not know how they had gotten here did not actually prove her claims true, but he was drunk, and she was too desperate to try to sway him using logic while deep in illogical situations.

His frown only deepened.

"Come with me," she pleaded. "Come with me to Olympus."

A scoff answered her.

"Atop the mountain lies a gateway of some sort, a passage into Tartarus. I beg you, Herakles, help me. Prophecy ..." She hesitated. She wanted him to believe in time travel? Then perhaps she must dispense with pretences. "I encountered Prometheus already freed in the time of your great-grandfather Perseus. He told me you saved him from his torment. That's why I know you, and you alone, can and will do this."

The flush of wine in his cheeks seemed to have drained. "You promised me redemption." His voice had become the broken whisper of a man who feared to even speak of his last chance.

Pandora scooted closer and took his hand. "This is that redemption. I swear to you, what I have told you is the truth, Herakles. This is your path." It had to be. She *needed* it to be, and maybe he did too.

For a long time, he watched her face. Pandora could scarce imagine the weight of his crimes upon his soul, or how fragile the hope she had given him must feel within his breast. "If we are in Iolkos," he said at last, "then many miles of rugged terrain separate us from the Olympian Mountains. Terrain I do not know in the least."

Oh, praise any gods who listened, he would do it. "I've come through here before, in another time. I think I can find my way back."

"We'll need supplies. With a bow, I can hunt for us."

She nodded. "I've some drachmae. I can arrange it."

The demigod gathered his adamant sword and shield, dour and resigned. "Let us be to it, then. Far be it from me to stand in the way of Ananke."

2

———————

ARTEMIS

2392 Golden Age

Not even Artemis's oft garrulous twin brother spoke as their ship moored in Helion. The weight of their mission had mired limb and tongue, perhaps, and Artemis found it easier to hold her silence and ignore his presence beside her. His own sullen reticence meant he felt the same, and her golden-eyed brother had avoided meeting her gaze since they'd left Athyras.

Without a word, Apollon vaulted the gunwale and leapt to the dock, not bothering with the gangplank the bireme's crew had begun to set in place. Frowning, Artemis followed in the same manner, trailing behind her brother as he made his way toward the acropolis and Father's palace.

Despite the sunlight overhead, the bear inside her stirred. Less a conscious thing—at least not one she could communicate with—and more a sensation, a prickliness arising in her own soul. The intervening centuries since this thing had taken residence inside her had granted Artemis an awareness of its influence, even if she could not always separate the bear's emotions from her own. Once, in those early days, she had beaten a fishmonger for haggling too parsimoniously. The snap of his shoulder crunching pulled her out of the red haze that had claimed her. Sometimes, in the days that followed, she wondered if he had spent the rest of his life lamed. She'd left him every drachma she had on her and fled in horror, afraid to ever look in on him again. Shamed by her fear.

Some months later, she had backhanded a servant girl who tried to clear away a bowl of soup that still had a few dregs left in it. Another senseless victim of the bear's cantankerous nature.

A scent came to her on the breeze, well before they reached the acropolis, and Artemis grabbed Apollon's shoulder. For the first time in days, he looked to her, the strain in his eyes evoking cracked ostraka, ready to fall to pieces with the slightest nudge. How much more could either of them take?

"Phaethusa," she said. Another sniff. "Lampetia's with her."

The hint of joy at seeing their half-siblings warred on his face with trepidation for the reception they would find here, after spending a year helping Zeus and his rebels subvert the Ouranid League. "It disrupts my digestion, thinking you can smell people."

"I can smell that, too."

Apollon favoured her with an irate smirk. Soon, sure enough, Neaera's girls came into view—flame-haired Phaethusa, and flaxen Lampetia, each radiant and beautiful as the sun. Like Apollon. In them, as in most of Helios's children save Artemis, the Heliad genos shone clear, with those aureate irises and fair features.

Though both Nymphs smiled, Artemis could not help but note a whiff of tension in their scents. That, and that Phaethusa wore a gilded breastplate, her palm resting light upon the hilt of a xiphos strapped to her hip.

"You're home," Lampetia said, drawing Apollon into an embrace. Artemis wanted to refuse when her turn came—being embraced put one in the perfect position to get a knife in the back—but demurring would further sour relations. And her quarrel had never been with her siblings, regardless. She returned her sister's warm hug, patting her on the back, then Phaethusa stepped in to repeat the gesture.

"Papa has grown rather vexed with you," Phaethusa said once she pulled away. "If I had to guess—only a guess, mind—I'd assume it relates to the treason and the taking up with people who have murdered his servants."

Artemis frowned in answer. "We must speak with him."

"Indeed, you must," Phaethusa agreed, the threat in her voice not half so subtle as courtesy would have suggested. Phaethusa had spent years honing her sword skills and she had, Artemis knew, blindingly fast reflexes. Still, she fell just short of earning the title *Titan*, which meant the Nymph had received less Ambrosia than Artemis. Could Artemis defeat her in a fair fight? Almost certainly. Could she do so without risking severe injury to one or both of them ...? She'd rather not find out.

Their sisters guided them the rest of the way to Father's golden palace. Within the courtyard sat their aunt Eos, along with Kirke, another half-sister. Given that Kirke's mother had joined Zeus's cause, Artemis might have expected Kirke to come over, though the witch Nymph didn't have so very much to offer, having never trained at arms.

Kirke watched her and Apollon with a heavy stare, not rising to extend any greeting the way Neaera's daughters had. But then, she had never been close to Kirke. As far as Artemis knew, *no one* was close to Kirke.

Phaethusa and Lampetia escorted them right up to Father's megaron, but Helios was not upon his throne, though their mother Leto sat on hers, staring at them with trembling lips. Their father paced about the hall, seeming to fill the space with his presence, the clop of his sandals echoing loud upon marble. As he drew nigh to one side or the other, courtiers and servants filling his hall shrunk away, all refusing to meet his gaze.

When he spun at their entrance, Artemis could understand why. Father's eyes seemed to blaze like the sun, flashing as he took in first Apollon, then her.

"Perfidious swine," Father snarled at them. "The very stars quake at the ambit of your hubris in daring to show your faces in my lands after all you have done. I'm of a mind now to see the both of you handed over to Kronos. Were you not my own blood, I'd have you staked out to bake beneath the sun." He fixated upon Apollon now. "I might have expected such duplicity from *her*—she's not even a Heliad —but from *you*?"

Artemis had long moved past flinching at his casual snipes. Banal cruelties and pervasive disdain defined the whole of her life, after all.

"Father," Apollon said, and Artemis imagined a twinge of regret in his voice. "We have taken Thebes. Tethys has foresworn the Ouranid League. Zeus's influence has spread from Phlegra into Ellá-dos, and in time, even Kronion will fall. You can join us before it is too late."

Their father turned his back upon them, rubbing at his brow with one mighty hand. When at last he returned his gaze to them, his face had gone slack. "You ask me to betray the Ouranid League that has reigned for over two thousand years? To betray mighty Kronos, who fought alongside Ouranos to guide our world out of the Time of Nyx? You are no children of mine."

"Helios," Leto whispered, rising from her throne.

He whirled on their mother. "Maybe they never were! Did you spread your legs for some other man, wench? Are these false Heliads the get of a lesser Titan?"

"Father!" Apollon protested, plodding forward, perhaps intent to reach Leto.

Father roared at him, however, closing the distance between them in two mighty bounds. Caught off guard, Apollon had no time to avoid the haymaker his father threw at him. The impact seemed to shake the whole of the hall, sending Apollon hurtling through the air dozens of feet, flying from the room.

Flooding Pneuma into her Pneumatikoi, Artemis launched into motion, racing for her mother. Helios surged for her, a flash of speed and fury. With the Pneumatikoi of Potency and Alacrity, Artemis leapt over his head, flipped through the air, and landed by her mother's side. Helios bellowed and jumped himself. Artemis jerked her mother's hand, yanking her to the side an instant before Helios crashed onto the dais. His fist smashed the throne to kindling and cracked the marble beneath it.

Artemis just had time to flood Pneuma into Steadfastness before his rising blow smacked into her. With herself between him and Mother, the both of them went careening backward. Her Pneumatikoi kept his strike from shattering bones, but the blow still winded and unbalanced her, and by the time she had righted herself, Helios was upon them once more.

Shoving her mother aside, Artemis braced. When next he attacked, she caught his wrist in a pankration hold, swept his ankle, and flipped him over her shoulder. With her Potency and werebear strength, she sent him flying into the shrieking cluster of servants. Not waiting to see the impact, she snatched Mother's arm once more and took off running, dragging her behind.

In the courtyard, Apollon had risen and faced off with Phaethusa, arrow nocked to his bow. He was going to kill her.

"No!" Artemis shouted.

Her brother loosed. Phaethusa twisted aside so fast her form seemed to blur. Artemis increased the flow of Pneuma to Alacrity. If Phaethusa could move that fast, she needed to be able to keep up. Another arrow flew at Phaethusa as she charged Apollon, xiphos in hand. The blade batted the arrow out of midair, their sister not missing a stride.

From the abrupt way Apollon began to fall back, nocking once more, he had suddenly realised he might have underestimated the Nymph.

"Take Mother!" Artemis shouted at him and dashed to intercept Phaethusa. "Get to the harbour!"

She managed to get a dagger free the instant before Phaethusa closed in. The xiphos darted past Artemis's defences, a striking serpent that punched through her left shoulder. Searing pain hazed her vision, lancing through her with every beat of her heart.

"Submit," Phaethusa hissed at her, driving her backward with pressure on the xiphos impaled into her.

Artemis shifted some of her Pneuma from Potency, readying to flow into Steadfastness the next time a blow got through. Her arm hung uselessly at her side, but she could already feel her shifter nature knitting the wound back together. "I don't want to fight you."

"Then you ought not have betrayed the Heliads." Her next slash, as she jerked free the sword, came lightning quick. Artemis parried with her dagger, but Phaethusa twisted the slash into a thrust that darted in. Only having Alacrity drawn gave Artemis the reflexes to flood Pneuma into Steadfastness. Phaethusa's blade struck her collarbone but clattered off Artemis's hardened flesh.

She wasn't going to win this with a contest of blades, just as she couldn't have overcome Father in a match of pure brawn. But then, Phaethusa probably couldn't match *Artemis's* strength, either. When her sister moved in to attack once more, Artemis flooded all the Pneuma she could into both Steadfastness and Potency and dove right into the blow. The blade scraped her cheek, even through her hardened flesh, tearing a gouge out of it. But Artemis shoulder-slammed into Phaethusa's gut and bore her down, the pair of them crashing into the lip of a fountain.

The Nymph had Potency, but not enough to match Artemis's. Phaethusa wriggled and twisted, trying to worm free. Artemis rained blow after blow upon her until her fist caught the other woman full in the mouth. A block tore free from the marble fountain when Phaethusa's head hit it. That her skull hadn't split—praise Thoth— meant she had some Steadfastness herself. Artemis reared back, fresh pains shooting through her wounded left arm, and landed three more blows upon Phaethusa's face until the fountain gave way, drenching them both as waters washed down over them.

A wave of dizziness raced through Artemis as she rose. She'd burnt through too much Pneuma. And she needed more still to escape. Forgoing everything else, she focused what little she had left into Lightness and Alacrity and made a mad dash for the wall.

Before she reached it, she found Lampetia fallen, hands wrapt around one of her brother's arrows jutting from her thigh. Poor Nymph. Artemis leapt to a column in the courtyard, ran up it and bounded to the rim of the balcony on the upper level. From there, she vaulted onto the roof and raced across the slanted tiles.

Arrows clattered against the spaces she had just left, but she was moving too fast for mortals to draw a bead on her. Which meant she couldn't let up on the Pneuma, though it had grown hard to breathe and black haze tinged the fringes of her vision. She dashed across the rest of the palace and made a running leap to next closest building.

Another leap, and her Pneuma faltered. She missed the lip of the third building and crashed onto the cobbled street, landing with a thud.

Then her brother was there, grabbing her left elbow and heaving her up. The motion tore a scream from her, all senses blurring with the pain. "Move!" Apollon shouted, unaware or uncaring about her injury.

They ran through the polis, Mother in tow, Artemis's chest feeling apt to burst, her arm a searing agony. The struggle against Father and Phaethusa had taken far more out of her than she had expected. Maybe she was due for another drought of Ambrosia, though Zeus's supplies had begun to dwindle. Only her shifter stamina kept her moving at speed now, and even that would give out without Pneuma.

Pushing her ahead, Apollon turned, loosing arrows at whoever pursued them now. The whole of Helion would be after their heads soon.

But when they reached the docks, Poseidon was there, beside the boat, ushering them onboard. Crewmen had already begun untethering the bireme, no doubt at Poseidon's command, and the gangplank teetered. Artemis ushered Mother up it first, then scrambled aboard. The crew pulled the plank up. An instant later, Apollon took a flying leap off the docks and landed on the deck with a roll.

Poseidon dove beneath the waters. A sudden surge of waves hefted the ship, flinging her out to sea and crunching the dock into driftwood. Artemis clutched the gunwale with her good arm and gaped as the sea churned. Poseidon could move their whole boat thus? And what did such an act take out of *him*?

Then, Mother moved to stand beside her, hand to her mouth, trembling. "I was with him so long ..."

Artemis cast her a sympathetic smile. "It wasn't meant to go this way." She had let Zeus convince Apollon they could sway proud Helios to their cause.

What vanity. All they had achieved here was costing their mother her marriage and making a true enemy of the rest of the Heliad genos.

Huffing, Artemis sank onto the deck, trying to catch her elusive breath. They had been fools, as they so oft proved.

3

HERAKLES

1600 Silver Age

All his life, Herakles had heard tale of Cyclopes, those towering one-eyed Gigantes whom all the others feared. Now, crouched behind boulders beside Pandora, watching the Gígas march against Olympus, he could not reconcile the monsters of story with the reality playing out before him. Rather, the sense of having stepped into a dream settled upon him, with all the numb acceptance that entailed.

Amid dozens of Gigantes, he spotted at least three Cyclopes standing eleven or twelve feet tall, each hulking grey masses of muscle ripped from nightmare and given flesh. Voices so deep they seemed to billow from the mountains themselves, the Cyclopes urged on their brethren. The temptation arose to think of the other Gigantes as lesser, and many were smaller, if perhaps more deformed. A great many had serpent tails for legs, and some few had extra arms, or even two heads. The Gigantes ranged in height from seven feet tall to a handful who might have reached fourteen or fifteen feet.

In the midst of this wretched horde strode an ebony-skinned Titan, and—though tall herself—she seemed tiny next to the slavering monstrosities she travelled amongst.

"That's Demeter," Pandora said, voice shaking, perhaps as much in shock at the Olympian's betrayal as in horror at the sick panoply marching against their gods.

And it was true—all Pandora's mad claims of having sent them back in time. For this was, without doubt, the Gigantomachy, the great war that had ended the Silver Age, centuries before Herakles's birth. Demeter had betrayed Olympus indeed, and Zeus had drawn the other Olympians closer under his watch, reducing their interaction with Men.

"We have to do something," he said, nocking an arrow to a bow.

"You want to fight an entire army of Gigantes?" Pandora had procured a spear for their trek across Phlegra, and though she seemed to know how to use it, he could not blame her for her hesitance to engage these foes. "We have to sneak up the slope. The tumult of this battle can prove to our advantage. The Olympians will be busy fighting against their enemies and may never notice us breaking into the Throne of Zeus."

Herakles frowned. How quickly the woman's mind worked, turning tragedy and devastation in her favour. That she was right did not much obviate the sting of harnessing suffering around them. Grimacing, he crept forward, toward the southern slope of Olympus.

Oft enough he had imagined seeing the halls of his father, of coming to call upon him—in temerity, perhaps, but fancy was like that—to demand his birthright. None of those daydreams had involved creeping up the escarpments like thieves while war raged about them. But then, what in his life had ever turned out the way he might have wished?

IT WAS NOT, in fact, possible to avoid all conflict with the Gigantes. They moved upon the gods, not as a united army, but rather like a pack of wolves converging upon prey from all directions, mad and vicious with hunger. And wrath.

These creatures flowed over the foothills in a wash of chaos. Though he and Pandora hid on several occasions, on others, he was forced to launch arrow after arrow. His missiles took Gigantes in throats and groins and brows. One Cyclops he shot in its mighty single eye, sending the creature pitching over backward, screaming as it clutched its face, somehow yet alive.

Running the adamant xiphos through its chest proved mercy, Herakles thought.

Pandora, too, charged in, finishing off those he shot with simple, efficient thrusts of her spear. Halfway up the slope, and the both of them were drenched in sweat and blood.

They paused, sipping at what remained of the water they'd filled in the river well below, and he fixed her with a hard gaze. "Are you certain you are up to this?"

The look she gave him would have shamed obdurate mountain slopes.

With no further answer, Pandora rose, then yelped an instant before Herakles felt the tremors in the ground. A bellow shook the escarpment, sending pebbles skittering. The creature that rushed them stood fifteen feet tall, at least, its every hurtling step a quake upon the land.

Herakles snatched up his bow, nocked, and loosed. The arrow took the beast in the throat while between steps. Its momentum carried it forward, but it fell face-first against the scree, skidding in their direction, but its weight sent it tumbling down the slope to crash against an outcropping ten feet below them.

Pandora huffed a sigh of relief, and Herakles offered her a nod. Then her eyes widened, and he followed her gaze.

The Gígas Herakles had shot had risen to its knees. With a meaty hand, it plucked the arrow from its throat like a splinter and cast it aside. Its torrent of blood had a golden tinge to it, almost ichorous.

Before Herakles's disbelieving eyes, that blood ceased to flow, the wound he had inflicted sealing itself.

The Gígas's next bellow was more wheeze than roar, but still its wrath saturated the land, sending Herakles's skin crawling. It loped toward them, using arms like forelegs, hurtling itself forward with animalistic fury. Again, Herakles nocked and loosed, this time aiming between the creature's eyes. The Gígas jerked its arm in the way and the arrow smacked into flesh. The monster did not even falter, tearing free his missile and tossing it aside while continuing its loping charge.

A snarl as the monster heaved itself aloft, and Herakles rolled to the side, just avoiding its impact. The beat of its fists cracked stone and sent scree flying. It spun, faster than something of that size ought to have managed, and Herakles barely had time to flood Pneuma to his flesh to toughen it. The backhand caught him full in the chest and sent him hurtling through the air, wind whooping past him. Only his Pneumatikoi kept him conscious—or alive—and still, the impact of the mountainside blurred his vision. Over and over he tumbled, momentum and the incline claiming him.

Then he managed to slam Pneuma-enhanced fingers into the rock. The sudden stop jerked at his shoulder, but Steadfastness kept it from being yanked out of socket. Still, a groan. Blood seeped over his brow, stinging his eyes, blinding him. Grunting, he yanked himself up to his knees and wiped at his eyes.

Above, Pandora jumped over a lower precipice and landed on loose scree, skidding down the slope in a desperate attempt to evade the Gígas. The creature took one look at the incline, but rage seemed to overshadow caution, for it leapt, its shadow passing over the woman's head.

Shit.

Herakles had lost his bow and his sword both somewhere above where they now stood. He pooled more Pneuma into Potency, the strength of his legs sending him surging forward like a charging bull. The Gígas landed with a crash in Pandora's path, and she could never have altered her momentum now. An instant before she reached it, Herakles plowed into its back, caught it in a pankration hold, and bent over back-ward. Never had he tried such a manoeuvre with a fifteen-foot-tall Gígas. Never had anyone, so far as he knew, but Pandora was dead otherwise.

All the Pneuma he could muster flooded into Potency, he heaved the Gígas airborne, arcing it back over his head to slam it down upon the escarpment. The echo of cracking bones reached him.

That had to have broken its back and neck.

He looked to Pandora. "Are you all—"

Pale, she pointed behind him, and he turned to see the Gígas rising again. Its head was twisted around backward. With sickening pop after pop, it yanked it back into position.

Herakles's stomach dropped.

Wasn't there a story from the Gigantomachy ... some Gígas that could heal from any injury, so a champion of the gods had drowned it? Far down the slope, a stream cut through the mountainside.

Ares's arse.

Still holding Pneuma in Potency, Herakles bellowed his own war cry and charged. The impact sent him and the Gígas both careening toward the precipice. A scraping, bouncing, wild tumble, then they were free-falling for a gut-gnawing instant. A moment of utter terror before the ground surged up to smack them down. The Gígas was beneath him and took the brunt of the blow, though Herakles flew free, spun end over end, and crashed down, into the stream.

The water's shock drew him from the daze, and he sputtered to the surface, gasping, then stumbled to shore, hands on his knees as he panted. "I'm going to kill you ..." he managed.

A primal roar answered him, and the Gígas charged. Herakles ducked a great swiping blow, and then another. The creature's lunges brought him lower than necessary, each strike hurling up mud from the riverbank. After dodging another, Herakles countered with an uppercut to the Gígas's jaw. The blow sent the giant reeling, and Herakles used its daze to seize its knees and heave, sending it sprawling into the mud.

Maybe he could have dragged the creature straight to the stream, but relying on so much Pneuma was draining him, and he couldn't risk the thing matching his strength. Instead, a leap carried him onto the Gígas's chest, then he stomped a sodden sandal upon its throat. Its windpipe collapsed into pulp, the creature flailing limp, pathetic hands around in panic.

A twinge of pity shot through him, but only a twinge. Hopping down, he grabbed the Gígas by one bulbous arm, then pulled it down to the water's edge. Already, the collapsed throat had begun to reform, as if the Gígas siphoned the very strength of Gaia herself. A heave sent it into the stream, and Herakles knelt upon its neck, hands shoving its head into the silt. Flailing giant hands slapped at him. Even the ill-aimed blows carried enough force to sting, though the Gígas could not leverage itself from this position.

This was taking too long. Did its lungs too try to reform, to keep it alive even while drowning over and over? At last, though, the struggles abated and the Gígas lay still beneath the river.

Herakles held it a while more, before huffing and stumbling to the bank to land on his arse. Using so much Pneuma took a toll. Perhaps it was the Kroniad blood in him, but he found it easiest to redraw the precious breath of life in storms. A thundering tempest, as ever, raged above the peak of Olympus, but they were quite far below that. Still, lounging upon his back, he stared at the rumbling dark clouds encircling the summit of his father's home. Breathing in and out slowly, only half aware of his surroundings, he heard the scuffle of Pandora's sandals when she at last managed to join him.

Without a word, the woman settled beside him. What did she think of him, having witnessed such a display? Did she think him akin to these creatures they fought? Herakles found he had neither the will nor the strength to ask such a question at the moment. Rather, he lay there, hoping to reclaim enough Pneuma to push on, knowing every moment he passed here, the battle above grew more dire.

But then, the Olympians won the Gigantomachy. Perhaps the only fear was missing their chance to sneak into Tartarus in the strife.

Huh. Sneak into Tartarus. Never would've thought he'd hope for that chance.

"Can you carry on?" Pandora asked.

Of course he could. Herakles was not the sort to leave things half done nor to back away. No, that wasn't one of his weaknesses. Not that.

4

———

HEKATE

2393 Golden Age

Not for the first time, Hekate found herself pondering just who had first recorded the grimoire she now pored over in her manse in Athyras, reclining upon the floor of her bedchamber. The flickering lamplight spilled over the pages in a dance of shadows, a reminder of the disquiet this tome engendered, even now, after so many millennia. Oft, when she dove too deep inside, she found her dreams—even her waking fancies—haunted by ponderous, empty spaces, teeming with unseen presences. The pervasive sense of insignificance such intuitions evoked oft left her drawn into bouts of melancholy, staring insensate into the haunted corridors of her own mind for hours or days.

Whence had the book come? If Raziel had scribed some fragments of the Ontos—and thus, these spells—from whom had *he* learnt these truths?

And beyond, whose hands had further amended and annotated, who, besides herself, had expanded upon this book of secrets? From the dark of prehistory, from a time before Man had dreamt of binding books thus, Raziel had created this beauteous, obscene tome. No matter how many times she read through the grimoire, she always seemed to discover new meaning, new potential hidden within, as though the authors had built layer upon layer of mystery into its crafting.

A promise, of the unfathomable depths that lay beyond, not merely past the Veil in the shadowy Penumbra, but *deeper*, to outer reaches of the Spirit Realm. Perhaps even beyond *those* unknowable spaces.

"Watchers ..." Hekate's fingers brushed over a note she herself had scribed into the margin of one section. She flipped forward, toward another section that referenced winged "psychopomps," beings that, nigh as she could tell, could fly not only through this world but into the Underworld—or those far reaches she sought and feared.

And what, exactly, did they watch? The very World itself?

Desperation and devouring need for answers, in equal parts, drew her always back to the tome. As now.

Though Zeus had sacked Thebes and overthrown Tethys, Kronos seemed forever a step ahead of them. His forces outwitted ambushes and appeared to protect supply lines as if with prescient insight. Though Zeus had claimed Thebes and left Ares as warden, Kronos had driven him out, forcing the rebels back into Phlegra. Papa said Kronos had hidden devices, Oracle Mirrors, he used to spy upon past, present, and future. But what if Hekate could give the rebellion a means of spying of their own?

Further along in the book—not that it had a linear order—a spiralling diagram might have referenced psychopomps. "Through flesh and metal banded in shadows forever to soar ..."

In her mind, Mormo cackled, though Hekate couldn't shake the intuition the wraith's forced mirth masked a nameless unease, as if even the hateful ghost feared the import of the spell. For wraiths were, in truth, the rotted souls of dead sorcerers, and perhaps Mormo recalled enough of the Art to apprehend the danger of such a spell.

Not that Hekate would take advice from a wraith, most twisted of all eidolons.

"Flesh and metal ..." And only one metal held any import toward sorcery: orichalcum, that most precious of all materials. Banded. Like a ring? A ring to turn a person into a psychopomp?

Though midnight had come and went, Hekate needed answers now. She paused long enough to yank up a loose tile in her floor and tuck the grimoire beneath it. While it seemed unthinkable that anyone might intrude into her sanctum here, she would take no chances with this tome. Morpheus and others would pay their very souls to claim it, she had no doubt.

Satisfied it was well hidden, she peeked inside Athene's room. The child slept with her mouth open, head lolling to the side, blanket twisted about her tiny feet. Treading with care, Hekate made her way over and shifted her daughter into a more secure position, then tucked her in once more. Should she wake, Eileithyia slept in the next room over and would no doubt hear her.

Content, Hekate made her way from her home and out into the light of an almost-full moon. Her manse lay beneath the acropolis, and she had to take a winding path to reach the slope that ascended the hill. Once she made the climb, a glint of moonlight upon bronze drew her eye and she found herself wandering off to a small spruce grove outside the acropolis proper.

Within the heart of the grove, Artemis knelt before the body of a stag, blood from its throat staining the grass darker, though the moon's pale gleam blunted the colour. The Titan dipped her fingers in the animal's blood and then drew them along her cheeks, leaving smeared trails.

"A nigh full moon, and still you seek me out?" Artemis said, staring up at the night sky.

Animal, Okypete hissed in Hekate's mind. *Moon-tainted* beast!

Yes, a spirit had taken up inside Artemis, and unlike those Hekate had bound inside herself, the bear in Artemis was not contained. Sometimes, it took her, and so little of the woman remained. And somehow, that was Hekate's fault, for having asked her to go to the Lodge of Whispers so long ago.

"I shouldn't have come," Hekate said, backing away.

Artemis grunted and rose to her feet. "Wait." She took a hesitant step toward Hekate. "You said ... once you loved me as a sister."

Hekate inclined her head in acknowledgment. She had said that, yes, when Artemis had attacked them on Khios. When Keuthos had died protecting her. In the two years since then, she had tried, a few times, to bridge the gap between them, but time and pain had turned it into a chasm so wide one could not so much as glimpse the far side.

"I ... saw several sisters, not so long ago, in Helion. One of them tried to kill me, and the others would not have shed a tear had she succeeded."

"I would have," Hekate said, wondering if it was true. She wanted to believe it was, though delving into the Art had flensed away pieces of herself until such emotions seemed the stuff of half-remembered dreams. The Art abraded the soul until sorcerers, in death, became what Mormo was. A terrible price—the sacrifice of humanity in life and eternal damnation in death—and yet she, and no doubt Mormo, paid it willingly for the power sorcery bestowed. Either way, her words seemed to be what Artemis needed to hear, and she strode closer, taking Hekate's hands.

"This struggle, this damn war, it seems to cost us all so much. So many of our kin we lose, even if they yet live."

Hekate struggled to keep the pain from showing on her face. Some grief still managed to worm its way through to the surface. Was it stronger for seeming so solitary? When Pandora had come to her, when she and Papa had left the manse that night, Hekate had beaten her fists against her thighs over and over until her flesh bruised. Until strength fled her and she'd tipped over, wrapping her arms around her legs and wailing, desperate for tears that refused to fall and offer any release from that pain.

Some agonies burnt bright enough to scorch even her abraded soul.

"Did ... did you see Kirke in Helion?" Was she one of the sisters Artemis spoke of?

Artemis dropped her hands. "I saw her, though we did not speak." Something heavy lurked unspoken behind those words, and Artemis offered no further answer.

Hekate nodded in acceptance. So many frayed relations, indeed. "I may have a way to help us gain an edge, or negate one of Kronos's advantages, at least."

Only a half-smile answered her, as though Artemis could not imagine this war ever ending. Maybe, neither could Hekate.

THEY HAD RECOVERED a small deposit of orichalcum ore from Thebes, one Zeus had stored within his own manse on the acropolis. Hekate had expected him to have found sleep long since, but the king instead lounged in his courtyard, drinking with his son Hermes, and Eris, the three of them seeming to have drained a half dozen amphorae of wine.

"Join us, witch!" Zeus commanded on spotting her, wine sloshing from the bowl he hefted in her direction.

Hekate frowned. "I've just come for—"

"Get that honey-sweet cunt of yours on the floor, bitch," Zeus shouted, snickering at his own poor attempt at humour, though Eris broke into a guffaw, then choked as she snorted wine out her nose.

Enodia had assured Hekate that Zeus would rule Elládos and the better part of the Thalassa world. That the future would lie at his sandals. For that reason, and that alone, Hekate had seduced him, born him a child, and joined his rebellion. Not for the first time, she found herself wishing the old sorceress had instead advised her to follow the wretch's father rather than Zeus himself. Would that Fate had allowed her to cast her lot with studious Kronos, a man steeped in ancient wisdom instead of churlish fury.

Her frown now a scowl, Hekate sank down upon the floor before the others and accepted a bowl of wine.

"Hmm," Hermes said. "Just how sweet is it, after all?"

Hekate levelled her gaze upon him. With a bit of care, she could slip into a person's dreams, lace them with nightmares that would leave them whimpering, and slip out without anyone realising she lay behind it.

While she doubted he could guess her intent, Hermes must have perceived some threat in her visage, for he sputtered, looking away. "The wine ... I was asking if the wine was sweet enough ..."

Hekate ignored him, looking back to his father. "I've decided upon a use for the orichalcum we recovered from Thebes." Zeus might have objected, wanting to insert his own inane ideas for it, demanding a sword or some equally phallic frivolity, and thus Hekate plowed forward before the king could think aught up. "Using it, I can craft rings that might transform some few of our warriors into winged emissaries who could move through shadows and act as perfect spies."

"Spies?" Zeus asked.

Eris perked up, no doubt envisioning the mischief she could cause while invisible. The Nymph delighted in turmoil. Just the other night, she'd gotten Apollon and Epiphron—even otherwise temperate Epiphron!—uproariously drunk, stripped them naked, and left them asleep in one another's arms in the agora.

"The more we learn ahead of the Ouranid League," Hekate said to Zeus, avoiding Eris's gaze, "the sooner we can break them." It was, of course, the phrasing he needed to hear.

A smirk had begun to crease his mouth.

"But rings?" Hermes asked. "How can rings help?"

"A ring is a band, its very shape symbolic of binding. That symbolism lends itself toward sympathetic magic."

"Uh?" Hermes asked. "Why would we want to be sympathetic?"

She almost rolled her eyes. "Sympathetic magic means like attracts like. You don't need to understand the principles." *Asinine cur*, Tithorea snickered in Hekate's mind. "What matters is the ring will serve as an anchor for the power I will endow into these soldiers."

"Give it to me," Zeus said, pushing himself up off his elbow to sit. "I want the power."

"To be a spy? This particular ability will avail us more if bestowed on those who might gather intel, rather than those who will fight in the thick of the war."

"Ooo," Eris's moan of desire echoed so deep anyone outside might have thought her in the throes of lovemaking.

Zeus glowered, folding his arms across his chest and huffing. This morning, Athene had adopted the same face and posture when Hekate had told her she'd had enough honey and couldn't have more until after supper.

"How many rings can you make?" Hermes asked.

"With the ore we have? Perhaps three," she said. "I cannot afford to stretch it too thin."

"So choose me and the twins," Zeus's son blurted. Twins. He meant Iris and Arke, his lovers. "We already serve as scouts. Any further power you can grant us will only improve that function."

"But ..." Eris moaned.

A slight groan escaped Hekate at the thought. While Hermes's words made sense—far more than giving the power to Zeus or Eris—it would mean she'd need to bed Hermes and his paramours, and she had no desire to give him any such satisfaction, much less after his earlier comment.

Still, a small sacrifice for ensuring she came out on the winning side.

"I'll need time to forge the rings first, then a soul to prime each of them."

"Souls?" Hermes asked.

Zeus, though, understood well enough. "If you hadn't lost control of my brother, we could have demanded he offer up souls." If she hadn't lost her hold over Hades, the dead Titan could not have claimed Keuthos, either. Little Zeus could say would sting half as much as Hekate's own self-remonstrations, the haunting failures that left her restless long into the night. "Eh, fine. We have some prisoners from the battle at Lésvos. Use them."

"Souls?" Hermes asked again. "Prisoners? What does—"

Hekate ignored him and rose, stalking off to find the ore. If Hermes thought one could touch the Art and remain untainted, he would soon find his naiveté flayed from him. Magic, when it worked, was the stuff of blood and pain, of agony and damnation. The willingness to sully herself was what would give Hekate the edge they needed to win.

❦

GIVEN that Hekate had no particular experience with metallurgy, she had no choice save to call upon Pallas's son, Hephaistos, their master smith. Unlike his father, Hephaistos had not tasted Man-flesh, and thus remained a Titan rather than a Gígas. Perhaps that explained the queasy look upon his face whenever his gaze drifted over the three bound and gagged prisoners fettered to hooks pounded into the smithy wall.

Hekate seized his chin, forcing him to look into her eyes. "Without Soulforging, orichalcum lacks potency. Their sacrifice, their blood, and their souls fuel the forge of our creation."

The smith Titan glowered at her, jerking his head free, not well-pleased with being castigated by a woman, she supposed. She could almost see the loathing as it welled behind his eyes, the desire to put her back in her place and reclaim his affronted pride. As if Hephaistos had aught he could do to her. Hekate met his gaze without flinching, imagining ravaging his mind with nocturnal torments.

Abashed, Hephaistos averted his gaze first, returning once more to hammer at the rose-gold bands they crafted. Once the shape had taken, he set to etching the glyphs she had drawn into the surfaces. One had to admire his craftsmanship, whatever one thought of the Titan himself.

At last, he finished. "Now leave," she commanded. His brows rose. Perhaps he intended to object, remind her they stood in his smithy. "Or stay to watch if you wish, though you must not move or speak."

Her tone had him scrambling away, grumbling, yes, but fleeing out into the moonlight.

When he'd shut the door behind him, Hekate paused to check the circle she'd painted upon the ground. The packed dust didn't hold the colour as well as she might have liked, but it should do. At last, she stalked over to the prisoners, all males. Each of them wriggled against the back wall as though they might squirm through it and out of her presence. She could offer them empty platitudes, she supposed. Claim their sacrifice would mean something.

The truth was, though, she would damn them, bind their souls into the rings, and condemn them to eternal servitude. Would aught of their minds endure the forging of their souls within the orichalcum? She dared to hope not. In her mind's eye, she could see herself releasing them, letting them scramble far from here, return to whatever lives they might yet claim. She could see herself being other than the wretch who must so wrong them.

No one touched the Art and came out clean, she knew well enough. They paid with their souls, and she, for this act, would carve out yet more pieces of her own.

Mormo's cackles in her mind answered in perverse promise of the madness-laced future that lay before her.

Three swift strokes of a knife opened three throats, spilling their lives into the dirt. Hekate's cants reverberated in her skull, thrumming against the Penumbra, even as she scooped up the three rings. Her words became a beacon to souls cast adrift, compelled and cajoled them into their new vessels. She refused to embrace the Sight, refused to watch the spectacle and bear witness to what she had done. Even so, a moment of Otherworldly disquiet rushed through her, a dawning horror accompanying the sense of something filling up the bands in her palm. A hint of warmth, perhaps. An intimation of voiceless screams.

ARKE BIT her lip as Hekate slipped the ring over the girl's finger, even as she had with Hermes and Iris. The four of them all knelt in Hermes's room, their garments strewn to the fringes, the air trembling with impending concupiscence, candlelight writhing in erotic gyrations.

Hermes had nigh danced in anticipation when she'd revealed the binding would require her to bring release to each of them. He leaned in now, reaching for her even while her hand remained on Arke. Hekate pushed him down, hand upon his chest. Perhaps he thought she would mount him, but she could not resist claiming a perverse glee in denying him entry to her body after his vexing leers and boastful words.

It mattered little how he climaxed; all she required was the release of Pneuma that would accompany it and bind him to her. That she would, in fact, gain some mastery over his will, she saw no need to explain.

He shuddered as she wrapt a hand around his manhood, the fingers of her other hand streaking down Arke's body to tease at her sex as well. Iris rose up behind Hekate, her own hands tracing Hekate's abdomen and sliding down to her nethers in a not unpleasant manner. Her release didn't matter, but neither would she deny herself a moment of pleasure.

"Speak the words," she commanded.

"We are yours, body, mind, and soul," the three intoned.

It took only a few strokes for Hermes's hot seed to spill over her fingers, leaving her to wonder what the twins saw in him as a lover. Either way, she felt a pressure build in her mind even as she wiped her hand clean. An awareness of him, almost akin to the presences of those spirits she had bound within herself, if smaller, weaker.

Hekate twisted around so she could attend to Iris as well, but the other woman insisted on squirming until she could put her tongue against Hekate's own sex. Not … unpleasant at all.

THE THREE NEW psychopomps knelt now, the wings jutting from their backs large enough to brush the ceiling. They kept craning their necks, trying to better look at the new adornments that bedecked them. The wings would mean they could cross the Mortal Realm with ease, yes, but the true power would come from their ability to shift into the Penumbra and move unseen. Time dilated outside the Mortal Realm, which meant less would pass for those on this side of the Veil, allowing their spies to cross the shadows with unprecedented speed.

Of course, they would need training to learn to master such abilities, and she would need to prepare them for the breadth of dangers beyond the Mortal Realm. Eidolons drifted amid the caliginous reaches, any one of which could devour an unwary soul.

Her eyes hurt, though, and lessons would keep for another day.

There is more ... in the dark ... than light can dream ... Mormo's warning sent a chill through her.

Exhausted and aching, Hekate slunk back to her own manse and collapsed onto her bed.

THE TWIN STONE gates that rose into towering edifices each bore reliefs depicting a writhing mass of bodies. At a glance, one might mistake the mounds of flesh for a scene of prurience. A second look, however, revealed visages wracked in torment, eyes wide in terror. Given yet closer inspection, Hekate saw—as she had in nightmare—the more violating truth that the chiseled forms here moved in indolent gyrations, their writhing a pitiable attempt to draw themselves out of a prison that would never release them.

Colossal stone imposts framed the portal of tormented souls, rising up to a gable that bled shadows. Within those recesses, eyes watched, scouring down to her soul, judging, perhaps reporting the depths of all who came back to Hades.

An effort of will alone allowed her to remain steady, unsquirming, beneath the penetrating observation. Whether it judged her worthy, or Hades welcomed his chance to confront her at last, the groan of separating stone preceded a widening crack between the two doors. With agonising lethargy, a dark abyss opened in the space before her, beckoning Hekate into the necropolis.

ZEUS SHOOK HER AWAKE AND, when she lurched up, caught her wrist before she could lash out at him. "I want it."

"Want what?"

"*Power* of the Otherworld."

Sleepy fog clouded her mind, made it hard to parse what she had beheld, to name it nightmare or Oracular prophecy. She had dreamt of the Underworld before …

Zeus's tightening grip drew her back to the moment.

Hadn't they already addressed this and decided Hermes better suited for it? Besides, she had used all the orichalcum and wasn't sure she wanted to make more of these messengers even if she could. Not with the sensation the rings had carried, the eternal torment locked in cold metal. She was not like to forget it, even in the passing of ages.

"They say storms run through Kroniad blood, coruscating through our veins. Give me that, witch. Give me the power to command the skies."

Hekate peered into his ice blue eyes. He was dead serious. And when Zeus set himself upon some course, she doubted the Moirai themselves could have shaken him.

All she could do was grunt in agreement.

5

PERSEUS

625 Bronze Age

Given that fidgeting while being crowned would have perhaps soured his heroic image, Perseus endeavoured to hold still while the priestess of Hera laid the diadem upon his brow. Still, kneeling before her on the cold, marmoreal temple floor would have discomforted the most pious of Men, and Perseus was, at best, the second-most pious. Third maybe, assuming the contest only between himself, the priestess, and Andromeda kneeling beside him.

Once the golden crown settled in place—and some acolytes waved peacock feathers about in vain attempts to fly around the temple—the priestess spoke. "Rise, King of Argos." She motioned for him to stand, though poor Andromeda remained stooped. The woman would need a massage, he suspected. Alas, a hero's sacred duties never ended.

The acolytes produced another diadem, and this they placed upon Andromeda's head. "Rise, Queen of Argos." Though she made no protest, from the corner of his eye he could have sworn a slight wince creased his wife's face when she rose.

The temple was freezing, in fact. Dustings of snow had drifted down on them while they made the climb to the acropolis. Rare this far south, and Andromeda had questioned whether Perseus's father Zeus would have sent the winter chill in honour of his son's ascension. Perseus suspected Zeus would not have bothered breaking wind on his son's behalf, much less summoning up snowfall, but he'd offered Andromeda a smile in answer.

They'd arrived in Argos to find King Akrisios had vanished, slipped away a few nights before, perhaps having had forewarning that his grandson now arrived. Prophecy claimed Perseus's mother's son would undo her father, and he supposed he had, because a few months later he wore the crown, and Olympus alone knew where Akrisios had gotten off to. It suited him well enough, though, as it meant he need not decide what to do about a grandfather who'd cast him and his mother into the sea in a *chest*, of all things. That would have made for an awkward conversation with Grandpa.

The Olympians may have frowned on kinslaying, but Perseus suspected they would excuse him beating Akrisios around his own hall with a muddy sandal. Perhaps he might even accidentally step in horse dung beforehand.

The gathered aristoi cheered as the priestess escorted Perseus and Andromeda out amid the temple's peristyle. Grasping Andromeda's hand, and squinting at the winter sun, Perseus reached for the sky. Sunlight had, in fact, begun to settle upon the rooftops here on the acropolis, only enhancing the glare.

The revelrous adoration of the crowd carried them back down to the forum, where commoners and even slaves waved and clambered atop one another for a better look at their new rulers. Perseus beamed at them, nodding and raising a hand to as many men and women and children as he could manage, and a few more besides.

When at last they returned to the palace, shivering and wet from the weather, Perseus shut the door to his chamber, leaned on it, and winked at Andromeda. "Zeus! I can't wait to get you out of those damp clothes."

His wife favoured him with an enticing upturn of her lips. "Is that what you were thinking on whilst becoming king of one of the great poleis of Elládos?"

"Ah, my dear, one must have priorities."

SPRING at last broke the grasp of a too-harsh winter, and though Andromeda was thick with child, when the invitation came from Thebes for the annual festival games, she insisted they attend. And, of course, trying to convince her to remain at home while pregnant proved about as effective as trying to breach a city wall with a live trout.

Overland offered rough roads, the path winding through hill lands and snaking between the lesser peaks of the peninsula, so instead, they chose to sail.

Most of the voyage, Andromeda clutched the gunwale, watching the turquoise sea. Or perhaps trying not to retch. He wasn't really sure and expected asking would have earned him a glare and maybe an elbow in the ribs.

Either way, once at Thebes's harbour, welcomed by those towering cliffs, he helped her down the gangplank, and Andromeda heaved a sigh of relief, hand on her abdomen. They followed the path up the cliffside, and there his wife paused, frowning at the endless stretch of marble stairs that rose up, past a waterfall, and on, to the cliff on which Thebes proper stood.

"Want me to carry you?" he asked.

"Ugh." Sometimes, Perseus wondered whether all women had that special way of looking at you as if you had the brains of a burnt loaf of bread, or if his wife had a unique talent. "Didn't you say it's seven hundred feet up?"

"Indeed." Perseus looked the stairs over once more, then folded his arms across his chest. "You're right. You ... should probably carry me."

"You know what, *demigod*," Andromeda said. "Go ahead, carry me up *that*."

And he did.

The Pneumatikoi of Potency made her feel as though she weighed no more than a babe, though when he deposited her on her feet outside the great city walls, Andromeda couldn't stop staring at him rather than the polis. Perhaps it had proved too much reminder of his not-quite-mortal nature. True, she well knew of his parentage, but knowing it and apprehending it were different things.

He felt his shoulders hunching inward in self-consciousness and hurried her along toward the gate, almost afraid to hear aught she might have to say about his display. It had seemed, when contemplating it from down below, heroic. Now it felt something else.

Perseus ... He didn't want to be a god to his wife. Not to her. He wanted to be a man, a husband.

Oh, she'd seen him slay Ketus, true, but perhaps her vantage, chained to the cliff—or the rush of terror—had not allowed her to witness or dwell upon his demigod abilities.

Would it help if he started breathing heavily? No, that was absurd. He ought to have done so before reaching the top, not moments later.

And the king of Thebes had asked Perseus to compete in the athletic contests. Should he withdraw now rather than reveal his strength?

"You're going to win every event you compete in, aren't you?" Andromeda asked, her mind having followed the same track as his own.

"Should I ... forfeit?"

She drew up short. "Why would you do that? Why should you pretend to be less than you are? Perseus, the reminder of gods in our midst can discomfit Men, I know. But it is not your burden to ensure the masses are comforted by allowing them to wallow in self-deceptions. Be true to yourself or you'll regret it forever."

Huh. "I should have married you years back. Would've saved me many a childhood debacle. You know, a little wife my own age to keep toddler me running in a straight line."

Andromeda rolled her eyes.

WHEN PERSEUS HAD FIRST ENTERED the field for pankration, none of the spectators had known him, though once the herald named him king of Argos, men had watched with eager eyes. After seeing him pin opponent after opponent, their enthusiasm had swelled until their whooping applause obviated the need for any herald to announce him.

Only a few challengers, perhaps other demigods, had given Perseus the slightest difficulty, and still he won the laurel for the event. Now, discus in hand, he raised his arms, and the onlooking crowd erupted into roars.

Their adoration allowed him—almost—to forget the inherent irony of men so praising someone for excelling at games, when in truth, he had done naught to better their lives. They lauded him, rather, for the distraction he offered. But then, bards told tales of these festivals, too, so Perseus could not complain much.

Flashing his best smile—naked, as such things went—Perseus whirled around, dancing from one foot to the next as he spun. He opened the floodgates of his Pneuma, allowing it to well within the Pneumatikoi of Potency, fortifying his muscles. At the apex of his whirl, he released, the discus hurtling from his fingertips like a missile from a sling.

It whistled through air, flying farther even than Perseus had suspected, soaring into the onlookers on the far side. From so far off, the shrieks sounded muted, but he saw a man drop, a dead weight after the discus struck his brow.

Oh ... Oh, no. The Pneumatikoi of Alacrity sped his steps, wind tugging at Perseus's hair as he crossed the field in the space of a few breaths to come stumbling to a stop. The throng had surrounded a man, his skull split. Amid shards of bone and pools of blood, bits of grey brain oozed free.

Though he could not say why, could not have done aught for the man, Perseus found himself reaching for a hand already no doubt cold and clammy.

"That's old King Akrisios," someone behind Perseus said.

His hand fell limp at his side as the noose of prophecy closed in around him, suffocating and inescapable, until dark clouds hazed his vision and he could no longer catch his breath.

ANDROMEDA OFFERED no words of comfort when they sailed back, the shroud-wrapt body of his grandfather in the ship's hold. Rather, she held him, arm about his waist, head upon his shoulder. Sometimes, the weight of silence itself became a bedrock upon which to steady oneself. Sometimes, the held hand amounted to more than a thousand platitudes.

Later, in the candlelight of her room, reclining upon her divan while he sat on the floor, she fixed him with her entrapping gaze. "The Oracle's prophecy revealed the future."

"If not for that prophecy, none of this would have happened. Had Akrisios not imprisoned his daughter, story of her beauty might not have reached Zeus, and I would not have been born. Had he not cast her into the sea, I'd have grown up in his court. Had he not gone into hiding upon learning I lived, he would not have been in Thebes to die. At every step, the prophecy caused itself and Fate made mockery of our lives."

"Maybe," she said, her tone making clear she refused to join him in his dolors. "But if the future exists, even accounting for the existence of prophecy, then that is the future the Oracle saw. We do not know that she apprehended the full scope of the how and why."

"So blame not the Oracle, but rather the Moirai."

A frown creased her face. "Did they engineer a tragedy, or does their weave but record one that already exists?"

Perseus snorted. "Ah, my dear, *that* is a question fit for philosophers clogging the colonnades in Athenai, not kings who must bury their grandfathers." And then there was the piercing thought that had plagued him all the long sail back to Argos. "I cannot rule this city, Andromeda."

Her sad smile told him she had well garnered as much. How was he, having slain the last king, his own grandfather no less, to reign here? His days would be forever stained by his unwitting crime, and he could not imagine aught save ill fortune would unfold as a result. "Our child will be born by summer. Wait at least that long to name a successor."

Of course, she spoke wisdom. Finding the right king to take his place would need time, and neither could he uproot his wife so late in her pregnancy. "This isn't ... it is not the home I promised you when we left Byblos." He'd brought her to Neritum only to find his uncle had betrayed him, forcing him to respond with death and chaos. Now, he'd come to Argos and, in less than a year, found himself ready to abdicate.

"Am I to hold you responsible for the vagaries of Fate?" Andromeda groaned, shifting on the divan. "We'll find our place, Perseus. I believe in you."

I believe in you. Perhaps the kindest words a person might ever utter to another.

Despite it all, a smile tugged at his lips.

6

KIRKE

625 Bronze Age

The hill-strewn island of Thrinakia seemed slashed from the coastline of Rassenia by the Strait of Messina, a dangling triangle Kirke's father had long ago snatched up from Mnemosyne in a trade deal. Far from the Elládosi world, the island hosted Father's prized cattle as well as offered the occasional Heliad refuge from the tumult of politics.

In the waning sunlight, she strolled alongside flame-haired Phaethusa, one of her two half-sisters Father had gotten on the Nymph Neaera who ruled Khios in his name. The other sister, Lampetia, tended to a farrowing sow, and Kirke saw little need to watch.

In truth, perhaps, she had little need to be here at all, but Kirke, of all people, found the unabating internecine politics of Elládos wearisome. All her efforts at perfecting Nectar, at overthrowing Olympus, had amounted to little more than the ephemeral vestiges of dreams banished by the harsh light of dawn. She could make monsters, she could drive Men to fits of madness, but making something to mimic Ambrosia? No, the Tree of Life tolerated no rivals in its bounty, and the Olympians might well press their sandalled feet upon the throats of Men until the end of time.

"Those centaurs roam the breadth of Phlegra, I'm told," Phaethusa said. Kirke's sister, on the other hand, never seemed to tire of hearing of the politics of Elládos, perhaps because ruling this idyll saw her so very removed from them. "I don't think Father overmuch cares as they cannot reach the islands, but I hear Themiskyra suffers unending raids."

Oh, Kirke damn well knew all that. She'd lain low for decades after that mess and whispered prayers to Hyperion no one ever realised her part in all that. Some six hundred years after creating the monsters, and now they'd become a race unto themselves, a blight haunting the wilds and preying upon the very Men Kirke had once sought to save.

"Yeah," Kirke admitted, "Father worries about monsters on the mainland about as much as he worries about a flock of harpies descending on his palace and opening a brothel on the roof."

"Uh ... what?" Phaethusa quirked a brow.

"You know, because harpies would make awful ... you know what, never mind." She waved that away. "Helion feels little concern over the plight of Men *anywhere*."

"But you do."

Sometimes, Kirke could forget Phaethusa was a bit more astute than Lampetia. A bit more, perhaps, than most Titans with whom Kirke oft dealt. "I ... well, yeah. I mean, people suffer and die." And it was Kirke's fault. "And I empathise with them. Just because most Titans wouldn't offer Mankind a runny shit without charging for it doesn't mean we all have to act like constipated donkeys."

The woman snorted. "Maybe we should hunt these centaurs, then, if they so vex you."

"Yeah, that would end with me spitted on seventeen spears and rotting away in a nameless wood while my shade waited for someone to weep over me."

"I can do it," Phaethusa objected.

"What, weep over me? Kind of you."

"Slay the monsters." Maybe she could have, too. The woman had Pneumatikoi *almost* strong enough to have avoided the title Nymph, and no doubt rankled because of it, always wondering if Father had spited her by not naming her Titan instead. Wondering, perhaps, too, if she got just a bit more Ambrosia, could she transcend her limits? Did she then want to hunt centaurs for the sake of Man, for her own glory, or merely for the chance to escape her tedious island prison? Helios had made them governesses of Thrinakia following his submission to Zeus during the Titanomachy, damn Artemis and Nike for it. Or maybe it was punishment for Phaethusa failing to stop Artemis when she had the chance.

"You think Father would grant permission for such an expedition?"

Phaethusa didn't answer the question because they both well enough knew the answer. Whatever her gifts, Phaethusa was a governess of this island, watching over those precious cattle, and Father would have blazed with searing rage if she left without his consent.

No, the centaurs would remain, breeding and spreading, and Men, as ever, would suffer and die for the crimes of Titans.

A while more they walked in silence, coming to the beach just after sunset. The moon speckled the waters, glinting like a silver field, peaceful enough to almost allow Kirke to deny her burdens and forget her own impuissance. To pretend, if only for a night, that she had not failed in her aim to break Zeus and his ilk.

From the waters, in silent silhouette, rose a glinting form, a mer approaching the land even as Phaethusa stiffened beside Kirke, aware that whoever this was, was intruding upon her island.

"Are we having guests for supper?" Kirke asked.

"Glafkos," Phaethusa addressed him when the merman had plodded close, sloshing through the shallows to stand naked before them. Water streamed off argent scales, beading upon fins running along the creature's arms and legs. Despite his alien appearance, this

Glafkos had a somewhat noble bearing, and his onyx eyes settled upon Kirke with such heavy regard her breath caught.

"This is her?" the mer asked.

"Oh. So we were expected, huh?" Kirke shot a perturbed look at her half-sister, who refused to meet her gaze. "Guess it wasn't quite a causal stroll in the moonlight so much as a clandestine audience."

"You are the famed witch Kirke?" Glafkos asked.

That drew a snort. "Yeah, sure. Infamous, maybe."

"May I walk with you?"

Huh. Quite a polite parasitic alien fish god, wasn't he? She spared a glance at Phaethusa, who nodded, her face betraying a quiet hope Kirke couldn't understand.

"Give me your word I'm in no danger," Kirke said to Glafkos. Spirits lied, oft, sometimes for no reason save the perverse joy they took in misleading mortals. They did not, however—perhaps even could not—break their words.

"I give it," Glafkos said, eyes a smidge wider. Admiration, perhaps.

"Sure, then," she said, motioning him to follow beside her as she started. "A walk in the moonlight along the beach sounds pleasant. You know, with a creature who stalked up out of the deep. For, um ... Yeah, I mean I don't know why you're here."

For the thrill of it, Kirke pulled off her sandals, luxuriating in the squishing wet sand between her toes. She cast a glance back at Phaethusa, who had remained where she'd left her and now offered a single wave in acknowledgment. Did someone like her, someone without knowledge of the Art and the Otherworld, find spirits like Glafkos more intimidating or less, for not knowing how perilous they could prove?

"I am here," Glafkos said at length, "because even in Pontus tale reaches us of the witch whose potions can affect such changes as never before seen in the Mortal Realm. Because whispered rumours claim a woman, beauteous and grand, created a new race that now roams the wilds."

They knew. A gulf of terror opened in her chest, bored down into her gut, and threatened to hollow her bowels. They knew, they knew

… And she would at last have all her crimes laid bare. "Beauteous and grand, huh?" Kirke said, almost managing to keep the stammer from her voice. "You … Ahem. Flattery's sure worth a listen. I mean, I'm listening. Continue." Heat flushed her cheeks. Could he see it in the moonlight?

"You do not deny it, Lady Kirke."

Oh, shit. "What? Pssh. I deny everything. I'm a fair mistress of denial, you know. I … uh, I deny even my denials. So." Would he tell Olympus what she had done? Did he know *how* she had done it? "Nice moon tonight. Wow, we should have brought some wine. I could *definitely* have gone for some wine—do you drink wine? I'm sure they probably don't have it in Pontus. Talk about watering down the wine. I mean, with the whole damn ocean. That's … um, a lot of water."

A cold, webbed hand fell upon her upper arm. "Lady Kirke, I mean you no harm. I've no intention to reveal your secrets to those on land, and I do not think my father much cares."

"Your father?"

"I am a younger son of Poseidon and Amphitrite."

Oh, well, good thing it was only the *son* of an Olympian who knew she violated the laws of Olympus. Why in the depths of the Underworld had she not brought wine when she went strolling with Phaethusa, and what had she ever done to her half-sister that necessitated the woman setting up this meeting?

"Your disquiet sits taut upon your shoulders, though I mean you no ill," he said, withdrawing his hand. "Would you prefer I leave?"

Yeah, without a doubt. Save sending him away thus might well earn his spite, and if he knew about the damn centaurs, that spite could go a long way.

"No, no, of course not," she said, chittering. "I love talking. I'm a talker. I talk to, well, right now I'm talking to you, and it'd be rude to leave while someone's talking to you."

Glafkos laughed, the sound more human than she expected, and motioned her to sit on the sand with him. Taking in the invitation, she sank down onto the beach and watched the waves in pleasant silence for a moment.

"There are parts of the human host that survive," Glafkos said. "Vestiges of personality, perhaps, that saturate our consciousnesses." Did that make possessing a body better or *worse*, she had to wonder. "Remnants of such lead us to value moments a mortal would have cherished. A quiet night of conversation. The massaging sound of waves breaking upon the shore." A pause. "Next time, I'll arrange for wine."

"Yeah, do that."

Another too-human laugh, making her wonder, indeed, how much of the original mortal host lingered beneath the surface. "I know I engendered some unease within you, though I did not intend it. For that, I apologise."

Kirke rubbed her knees. A spirit apologising to a witch. Huh. Sure, that was about as likely as spotting mermaids flying through the sky, trying to catch rainbows. "Pssh. I'm fine."

"Perhaps a song to soothe the nerves?" Glafkos settled back, leaning on his palms. Mer—called sirens by some—were famed for their singing voices. Maybe she ought not indulge, but how oft would she have a chance to hear such songs, and from a mer who had promised no harm would come to her?

When his voice burbled forth, it washed over her like a lover's caress, setting her mind and skin atingle, leaving her drifting in untethered wonder. His words, in some lost tongue, seemed a lament, and as the song soared up among the stars, Kirke found that, while she did not know his meaning, still a tear had welled in her eyes.

Because the sorrow Glafkos evoked contained within it all sorrows, the very essence of loss, perfect and wistful. In flowing panoply, Kirke saw the fall of the Golden Age and the decline of a world, along with the deaths of so many during the fateful Titanomachy. A decay of time, and with it the withering of her own heart as she passed unending millennia alone.

As the song ended, shudders wracked her. Glafkos stroked her hair, murmuring soothing nonsense she didn't hear.

Only later, when he had slunk back into the sea, did she realise she had never asked why he'd sought to meet her at all.

When she slept, his voice tantalised her dreams, dancing through her memories like a mountain wind.

THE NEXT NIGHT, Glafkos came to her again, this time bearing an amphora of wine, though no glasses. Sitting once more on the sand, they sipped straight from the decanter. A pleasant aromatic vintage out of Rassenia, one she had to assume the mer had picked up from Phaethusa, though her sister had spoken little of why she'd arranged their meeting.

After handing back the amphora and wiping her mouth with the back of her hand, Kirke looked to the mer. A pleasant warmth spread through her. Not watered at all, this wine, and its strength coursed within her. "Will you sing for me again?"

Perhaps she ought to have asked about his purpose here, but from the moment his last song had ended, the need for his voice had plagued her, waking and sleeping. Like ants crawling along her flesh, she could not shake off the tingling it had engendered, nor the shuddering despair and relief it had drawn from her. The song had unlocked something buried so deep within her breast Kirke had almost forgotten it lurked there.

Glafkos flashed a smile, exposing pointed shark-like teeth that, under other circumstances, would have had Kirke scrambling away, though his expression seemed one of pleasure rather than predation. He broke into song once more, in the same unknown tongue, and this time his melody carried more energy. Its vivacity coursed through her, lancing out the compounded weight of millennia like poison drawn from a wound.

Rapture embraced her, had her wrapping her arms around herself and weeping for sheer relief at the shredding of burdens.

"Kirke," Glafkos said, hand on her cheek. She didn't know how long ago he'd stopped singing, or how long she'd wept.

Her sniffles must have left her seeming pathetic to him. "Memory has weight, piled upon us like stone after stone until we cannot help but begin to crack beneath it."

Though he said naught, his expression revealed a keen understanding of her words. After a moment, he leaned forward. "Spirits struggle to retain memories. The Lethe feasts upon our distant pasts until all that remains for us is the haze in which your kind perceives your early years. We are left in a muddle of emotion and half-remembered dreams."

His words triggered a new crack of the dam within her, her emotions spilling forth in lachrymal waves. What he described seemed a horror, the utter loss of self, and yet, too, almost a relief from the unabating weight of piled memories. So beset with a maelstrom of grief and ecstasy, she didn't even know when she had lain down on her side.

Some forty-five centuries of life, and they had choked her.

Later, when she had risen once more and downed all save the dregs of the wine, she turned back to him. "You sought me out, it would seem."

"I did," Glafkos admitted, the mer now turning his gaze back to the sea as if overrun by anxieties of his own. As if afraid to ask what he'd come to ask. "Your fame ..."

"As a witch?"

A stiff nod. "We are not, as I said, as divorced from our hosts as some spirits would make it out. Mmm. I find myself ... besotted."

Kirke swallowed. Was he saying ...?

"It is a strange thing, for my kind, who are more oft driven by lust than love."

"And now?" Her voice stuck in her throat. Her palms had begun to sweat, her heart to beat faster.

"Her name is Skylla, daughter of Krataeis and Triton, the most radiant of Nymphs."

Kirke shut her eyes for a moment. Stupid. Stupid, stupid, stupid. Of course he didn't mean her. He'd first met her only to gain such aid, and once more, an excess of wine had made Kirke into an utter fool.

"She ... does not accept me, though, so I must turn to a tonic to win her affections."

"You want a love potion." A needle wormed its way through her veins and into her heart. Kirke the witch. Always the witch, never the woman. A thought rumbled up to her. "Triton ... is also a son of Poseidon. That makes Skylla your *niece*."

Glafkos shrugged. "Relations among my kind are complex and not always linear." He looked so deep into her eyes. "Will you do it?"

Though she could not have said why, Kirke found herself nodding. Even when he had left, she sat there, by the sea, watching the waves. Perhaps not even his song could draw out the sum of her melancholy.

7

HERAKLES

1600 Silver Age

In the distance below, a war chariot raced among the seething horde of Gigantes, leading one branch of the Olympian defence. Unless Herakles missed his guess, its rider, with his blazing shield of bronze and streaming horse-hair helm, was Ares himself, God of War, son of Zeus. In a sense it made the god half-brother to Herakles, though he had never met the Titan and doubted the god would hold to any bonds of kinship.

The war god slew Gígas after Gígas, cutting serpent limbs out from beneath his foes, riding them down with a manic delight Herakles could see even from the slope well above the melee. At the least, his brother seemed to have drawn the better part of the Gígas army away from this south slope.

Climbing up, Herakles had shot several more Gigantes, though no more had regenerated from their injuries like the brute he'd drowned, Zeus be praised. Would they acclaim Herakles for this? But how could they, for none of the tales of the Gigantomachy mentioned him, fought as it was, centuries before his birth. Herakles tried not to think on such things overmuch. Pandora's Box had wrought a savage violation of the natural order, and it churned his gut to muse upon it.

When a Gígas drew too close, Herakles sidestepped a swing of its mighty club. The impact shattered stone and could have pulverised even his Steadfastness-infused bone. The creature had swung with savagery but no control, however, and given Herakles the chance to step in and open its gut with his xiphos. Its blood sprayed him, mingling with that of so many of its kin.

For a moment, as the creature collapsed in a heap, Herakles considered the club itself. The weapon had enormous reach and power, and with his Potency, Herakles could wield such an implement with as much force as any Gígas. Well, but for now, his bow proved the most useful, keeping the monsters at a distance. He sheathed the sword and snatched up his bow. They had to trek on.

Mopping the blood from his face—or smearing it, rather—Herakles pushed onward, sparing only a glance back to ensure Pandora followed. The woman may not have had demigod stamina, but sheer tenacity kept her trudging on when Titans would have faltered. They had forded streams of viscera and blood and ichor, sandals squelching in shit as they fought time and again, and though her chest heaved in obvious exhaustion, she did not stop.

One had to admire that.

When he glanced back, he saw Athene standing upon the slope above, watching him climb. For a moment, Herakles could only gape at his adoptive mother. Of course she would be here, defending Olympus, but still, he hadn't considered ...

A Gígas crawled on the rocks above her, walking on all fours like some lizard, neck twitching at angles that had Herakles wincing. The Olympian didn't seem aware of the creature, so Herakles unslung his bow, nocked an arrow, and sighted the giant. He loosed and Athene darted to the side, perhaps thinking him shooting at her, at least until she saw the lizard-giant tumbling from the rocks, clawed hands clutching at fletching jutting from its throat. Herakles's arrow had punched clean out the other side, no doubt severing its spinal column.

Her gaze shot to the fallen Gígas, then settled back upon Herakles. What was he to say to her? She had reared him, made him the warrior he was, even given her these very arms he now wielded. But nor could he avoid contact with her now. Not while she clearly watched him, waiting for some explanation.

Beset by apprehensions he could not quite name, he trudged up to meet her but stopped a number of paces away.

"Athene," he rasped.

"You are Herakles," the goddess said. She knew him. She knew him nigh seven hundred years before his birth. Of course Athene was a famed Oracle, but this …

Herakles looked back to Pandora, but her expression looked as tension laced as his own.

"I am," he admitted, turning back to look at the goddess who had meant so much to him.

"What are you doing here?"

"I have to reach the summit of Olympus," he said and again looked to Pandora. He had sworn to her to do this, and she had promised him it was a step toward his redemption. He had to believe that. How could it not be, with him helping save Olympus itself in the process? "I will slay any Gigantes who try to claim it."

Athene swallowed and nodded. "Go then, and be blessed, ally of Olympus."

Herakles bowed his head. He wanted to thank her. He wanted to call her *Mother* though he dare not. And this, this blood-drenched version of the goddess, centuries younger than the one he knew, she had more wildness to her, that much he could see.

Despite all he wished to voice, he and Pandora pushed up the slope in silence, reaching the steps Athene had guarded. These must lead to the summit and to the acropolis where the Olympians had their palaces.

When he looked back down, he saw Athene well below, caught in the melee, cutting down Gigantes with fluid grace even Herakles had to admire.

"We have to keep moving forward," Pandora said, her hand alighting upon his shoulder.

And they did.

THE HIGHER THEY CLIMBED, the more the air grew chill until their breath became mist and Pandora shivered against the cold, unpossessed of Pneumatikoi for Tolerance. The air thinned, too, but as he drew closer to the eternal storm, Herakles found it easier rather than harder to breathe. While Pandora wheezed, for him, each inhalation carried with it the energetic tang of excess Pneuma, refilling and sustaining Herakles.

They soon reached a waterfall pitching down from the peaks. Was that the source of the stream in which he'd drowned that Gígas? The dark-haired Heliad paused, hands on her knees, panting and shuddering, until he had to wonder if her reaction was a response to more than cold.

"You've been here before."

"Once." A wispy answer, her voice all but swallowed by the roaring fall.

Far, far overhead, islands of rock orbited the summit, expanding upon the agora. Had they had a pegasus, they might have flown up to the Olympian palaces, but not even demigods received such blessings, so far as he knew. Titans alone warranted the magnificent steeds, and only those most in favour of Olympus.

"Can you continue?" Herakles asked.

The Heliad huffed, making an ill-fated attempt to corral her windswept hair into a tail. "Naught in this world ... nor any other ... will keep me from him."

"What does a man need do to earn such loyalty from a woman?" The question escaped him before he thought better of asking it aloud.

It did not seem to offend, however, and for a moment, she considered it. Or perhaps exhaustion slowed her answer. "Loyalty, like love, is a circle, compounding upon itself with every revolution. As long as it's returned, the wheel spins and outside pressures only serve to reinforce the structure, not crush it."

Even when they resumed their climb, Herakles found her words rang through his mind, themselves a circle as well. If he wasn't careful, he'd one day find himself looking into pellucid waters, staring at a reflection of himself, and forced to ask where any falterings in his own circles began. Or perhaps Pandora would have claimed that the very point—that circles have neither beginning nor end.

Further up, flurries of snow whipped about them, wind tugging at their cloaks and hair, invigorating Herakles even as shudders wracked Pandora. They came to a column-lined agora, the place desolate, with all its defenders now upon the lower slopes, engaging the besieging army. In the shadows of civic buildings, he spied people watching them, fear seeming to radiate off them though he could see little. They knew, if the Olympians fell, the whole of this place would be torn down in fire and slaughter, swallowed by Demeter's rage and the spite of the Gigantes.

Beyond the agora, he spied temples for each of the twelve Olympians, Demeter included. Surely Zeus would have it torn down after this, though Herakles had never heard tale of it.

"This way," Pandora said, pointing up toward the towering palace in the distance. The Throne of Zeus, crowning the summit beyond yet another marble staircase, soaring above the whole of Gaia.

Part of him expected the mortal woman to give out any moment, collapse from cold and fatigue and the despair of circumstance, but Pandora pushed onward without complaint or pause, drawn forward by forces he could not see or understand.

The true acropolis was broken by several canals that fed the cataract they'd passed below, with bridges spanning those canals to reach the manses of different Olympians. He received his first clear look at his father's palace, and it left him gaping in awe and wonder. For it was not just a palace upon the mountain. Rather, great buttresses joined the structure to many of the flying rocks, creating wings of the palace held aloft by invisible forces. The palace itself rose up in several tiers, each ringed by peristyles and decorated with reliefs and frescoes depicting raging whirlwinds and bolts of lightning. The lord of all storms resided here.

Enormous double doors stood open, allowing a dusting of snow to colour the marmoreal floor inside the vestibule. An honour guard watched the entrance. "Hurry up inside," one of them snapped, having judged them not Gigantes and thus no threat.

Sparing a glance at Pandora, Herakles complied, passing columns larger than ancient trees. At the heart of the vestibule, Pandora took his hand, pulling him past a courtyard and onward, only to pause before a set of closed doors he assumed led to the great hall.

"Where now?" Herakles asked.

"I don't know. I wasn't with him after this point. I ... I should have asked where they took him, but I never seemed to have enough time to plan these things. Shit."

Well, that proved somewhat inconvenient. Herakles cast about until he spied a lone guard emerging from a side corridor. He scrambled to the man's side, drew upon his Potency and, before the guard knew what was happening, slapped a hand over his mouth. With his Pneumatikoi, it was like dragging aside a struggling toddler.

Of course, if anyone saw them, an alarm might draw too many protectors, but he had to take a chance. They might not have so much time. So he hurled the man into an empty room, then dropped down beside him before the guard could recover his senses. Behind them, Pandora slipped inside and shut the door.

Herakles raised a warning finger and, from the way the man's eyes fixated upon it, he knew well enough the implied threat should he shout for help. Even if any came, it would prove far too late for this hapless soul. "Zeus has a gateway into the Underworld beneath this mountain."

"T-the Tartarian Gate," the man said with a helpful nod.

"Where is the passage?"

"It ... it's down the stairs."

Herakles seized him by his khiton and hefted him to his feet. "Show me. And if you lead us into an ambush, I'll break every bone in your body."

The terrified guardsman guided them round a series of corridors until Herakles guessed they were just behind the great hall. Then, indeed, they came to stone stairs descending into the depths of the mountain.

"F-follow the tunnel to the end," the man stammered.

"Good." Herakles jerked his head in dismissal. The moment the man tried to flee, he grabbed him once more, this time with his hand clamped over mouth and nose both. "Sleep." The struggles didn't last long, though long enough for Pandora to frown. "Can't have him warning others while we're down here." He allowed the unconscious guard to slump to the ground. "He'll wake in a while with a headache."

The woman didn't say aught, though, just grabbed a torch from a sconce and started down into the gloom. They passed doors banded in orichalcum, deeper and deeper beneath Olympus, until at last they came to a great open cavern.

Pandora hissed as though in pain, though Herakles suspected it was more pain of the heart than aught in the present. As though caught in a dream, she drifted across the cave, drawn inexorably toward an archway cut into the far wall.

A fell gleam emanated from sigils carved into the stone blocks, a light that induced a bilious churn in his gut to look upon. Beyond the archway, the air rippled, thick and distorted.

Herakles found it hard to swallow looking upon this wretched thing.

The very gate to Tartarus.

INTERLUDE: AUTOLYKUS

765 Bronze Age

Twilight began to stretch its fingers when the boy came tromping down the foothills, gaze sweeping over the escarpment of Mount Parnassus. The mountain lay just north of the Minyan lands, overshadowed by the greater Olympian Mountains that rimmed northern Elládos. Owing to the pugnacious tribes of the Minyan highlands, few approached Parnassus, which meant it had long served as an ideal refuge for Autolykus.

Here, in caves burrowing through the timeless slopes, he had secreted away his spoils from countless thefts and swindles. Here, with rivers of drachmae diverted from gullible aristoi, Autolykus had raised a private manse for himself and his wife, hidden in a valley created by a cleft within the peak.

But the boy made for Autolykus's estate like he knew well enough where to look. No lost Minyan lamb, this one, and given his aspect, Autolykus judged him Antiklea's boy, come at long last. Perched in the boughs of an oak, Autolykus watched young Odysseus for a time, curious how much of the family's keen intellect the young man had inherited. How many years did he have under his belt now? Fifteen, perhaps, though like so many demigods, time tended to slip by Autolykus unmarked. He himself had passed something close to a century already and felt less than half that, if he did say so himself.

Of course, he might—once—have pilfered a tiny draught of Ambrosia for himself and Amphithea, with his wife's mulish grandfather left scratching his own arse wondering if he'd downed it and forgotten.

As Odysseus drew nigh, he slowed, looking about as though he sensed something amiss. Astute enough to realise someone lurked close, but not quite clever enough to find Autolykus when he wished to hide himself. But then, Autolykus had managed to sneak onto Olympus itself, nab some of Hera's jewels, and even sneak a peek at the goddess whilst she slept in naught save a gossamer shift. One couldn't expect a Man with but a trace of divine blood to—

Odysseus's gaze abruptly rose to the tree, scanning the branches.

Well, then.

Before the boy could locate him, Autolykus dropped beside him. Odysseus concealed his sudden fright well enough a drunken fool might not have noticed. Something they'd have to work on, Autolykus imagined.

"Grandfather."

Autolykus took the opportunity to give the boy a thorough looking over. "Got my eyes," he said.

Odysseus folded his arms over his chest. "You knew that when you named me." Defiant and proud. All good things. "And Mother claimed you had gifts for me when I should come of age."

"Did she, now?" Autolykus allowed his gaze to pointedly sweep the boy once more. "And have you?"

"I'm stronger than most." Still that haughty look. Was it possible, even after several generations, the young man had some hint of Titan Pneumatikoi?

Either way, Odysseus might have *too* much pride. If it rose higher than it ought, one risked taking a painful tumble. Autolykus might have suffered a few of those too, though he made damn certain such tales never spread. "Oh, is that what makes you a man, then?"

That chin rose higher. "I've known women. Four. Four different women. Honeyed words spilt from my lips and had maids sneaking off to join me in fields beneath the moonlight many a time."

Autolykus watched the boy's face as he spoke, measuring every twitch of muscle and flitter of an eyelid. "You're a good liar, boy, but not good enough. Not yet." Unless he missed his guess, Odysseus had no moral compunction against lying. He probably even enjoyed it. No, his problem was, he was a little too desperate for Autolykus to believe his bravado. "One girl, was it?"

Now the boy lowered his eyes, flushing.

"Mmm, yes. Not quite so pleasing for her as she expected?" He clapped a hand on the boy's shoulder. "A little practice clears that issue."

Given the boy's uncomfortable shifting, Autolykus barely restrained his chuckle. But to laugh at a teenage boy thus might have shamed him beyond endurance and destroyed Autolykus's nascent relationship with his grandson.

"Come," Autolykus said. "Your grandmother's making venison stew, and I've a few amphorae of decent Delphian vintages on hand. Good food and spiced wine tend to soothe even bruised pride."

WHEN THEY HAD EATEN WELL and were deep into their cups—the boy held his better than Autolykus had expected—he took Odysseus to the terrace where they could gaze upon the stars punctuating Nyx's abode. Thoth was a pale crescent hung overhead, adding a pleasant glow to the night.

Amphithea had doted upon her grandson with all the earnestness Autolykus had known must flow from her, and it had taken hours before she'd let him steal Odysseus away again. Laertes, the boy's father, might have been a king, yes, but he was an impoverished one. Autolykus could ensure the boy had a decent fortune to build

Ithaka up into something respectable, and he would do so. But his real gift for his grandson would not come in drachmae, but rather in honing his native wit into a razor.

Autolykus sniffed, sloshing the dregs in his wine goblet. Even now, so many years later, some tales came tinged with pain, like splinters that had wormed their way through blood and into the heart.

"You know we are of the line of the Olympian Hermes, yes?" Autolykus said at last.

"Mmm, Mother said he was your father, and that his cunning is in our blood."

"Cunning, yes, and wickedness too." Autolykus set his goblet upon the marble balustrade that rimmed his terrace and fixed his gaze solidly upon Odysseus. Some stories were wretched enough that to embellish them was a profanity. In such rare instances, only the unvarnished truth would do. Ugly, brutal, and dripping with blood, and all the more human for it. "Well." He cleared his throat. "Hermes has a long rivalry with his sister Athene, you know. I cannot guess how it started, but my father clearly mislikes the way the goddess gives aid and counsel so oft to mortals.

"I think, perhaps, for this, he seeks to strike at her, time to time." Autolykus could understand the—admittedly petty—need to punish those who vexed him. Some of his trickery served him little gain, save revenge. "Do you know of your great-grandmother, Khione?"

"Uh, some legend about a snow Titan, before the Titanomachy?"

"Named for her, yes, but not the same one. This one was, in fact, a daughter of one Daedalion, son of Hesperos, himself a son of Eos. Perhaps this Khione was named for the other out of Daedalion's sense of irony, given that the first Khione had besieged Helion long ago. Or perhaps he didn't even realise it and just liked the name. I cannot say I ever met him. He was, however, favoured by Athene, who had long aided him.

"I have oft suspected it was this connection to Athene that drew Hermes's eye to Khione. Or maybe it was her beauty alone, for she drew a hundred suitors, all of which bid for her hand. Whilst Daedalion considered his options, Hermes, however, sought the man's treasure for himself. But not to wed, no. Hermes snuck into her chamber in broad daylight, drugged her, and took what he wanted from her."

Not so unlike the tales of Hermes's father, Zeus, either.

Autolykus watched Odysseus's face when he voiced the crime, watched those eyes narrow, just a little, in wrath at his great-grandmother's fate. "My mother, after I was born, she took her own life. In despair at the loss of his beloved daughter, Daedalion, my grandfather, cast himself from this very mountain. There is a legend that Apollon took pity upon him and turned him into a hawk that he might fly away and live forever in the sky.

"Do you think that probable, boy? Do you think Apollon would have bothered to offer a mortal a three-day-old fart? Olympians oft think they can take aught they wish. They think it their due, caring little for the damage left in their wake. We Men, Odysseus, we have to be better. At least in this. Priests and kings may purify you for murder, but you cannot absolve yourself of rape. So, if you want a woman, you win her. By truth or by lies, by deeds or trickery. But I ever hear you forced yourself on a woman, my next theft will be of your stones, boy."

Odysseus shuddered at that, his hesitation making plain he considered whether Autolykus spoke in earnest. "Such things hardly need speaking aloud, Grandfather."

Oh, but they did. In a century of life, Autolykus had seen well the way of the world. The things that happened in war. The vileness that lurked in the hearts of Men was the same as that which poisoned Titan souls. The only difference was, Men thought themselves less likely to escape consequence. But they had to be better. Virtue upheld solely for fear of punishment lost all meaning.

Still, he trusted he had made his point and all that remained was a sour taste upon his tongue. "Go down and fetch us another amphora, boy. There's more to tell."

When Odysseus returned, Autolykus poured them each another goblet. After downing a long swig, he settled upon a divan and kicked his feet up on the balustrade.

"So, I was a babe, bereft of immediate kin, and mostlike to starve and end the pitiable story of my existence. Rather, though, Athene learnt of her brother's actions and took me under her protection. She brought me to my great-grandfather Hesperos, who saw me reared and educated, though in his eyes I was a burden thrust upon him by an Olympian.

"For Athene's part, she checked in on me every few years, but always seemed drawn toward Mykenai. I was born, you see, not long before great Perseus abdicated his throne, and the goddess directed ever so much of her attention to protecting his line. I cannot much complain, given she saved me when she owed me naught at all.

"She never asked much of me, save once to train Perseus's great-grandson Herakles in the arts of wrestling."

"Wait, *the* Herakles. You knew Herakles himself? You claim to have *taught* him pankration?"

"Hmm. He was just a boy then, and I was already a man grown, married to your grandmother."

"I don't believe you. You did *not* train Herakles."

Autolykus grinned, glad the boy had some incredulousness in him. Even if, in this particular instance, he happened to speak the unadulterated truth. "Well, regardless, it's of no import to what I want to tell you. I left Hesperos's care as soon as I could. He was, in truth, a bit of a prick, though not half so bad as his uncle, Helios, who manages to elevate himself to the esteemed title of cosmic arsehole. Hesperos had lived upon Aiaíā, a useless island ruled by his mother, Eos. Not wanting to linger under their gazes, I came first to Leukophrye—now called Tenedos—a small, sparsely-populated island off the coast of Helion. Its most significant virtue was that no godsdamned Titans lived there.

"That was also, in the end, how I first encountered Amphithea and her brother Tenes. I'm going to tell you a different story now, boy. It's your grandmother's tale, and it serves, mostly, to prove the gods are bastards on whom you cannot rely. Amphithea and Tenes, you see, are the twin grandchildren of Apollon. Whom they have never met and who has not once bothered to pull his shiny thumb out of his glowing arse long enough to lend them the least aid. My wife and her brother, their mother was the daughter of Laomedon—"

"Who?"

"Erstwhile king of Ilium—the local folk sometimes name it Troy —and father of Priam, who rules now. Ilium's not of much import, so I wouldn't worry over it. Attend to this, though, boy: Their father, now, he was King Kygnus of Kolonai, a minor polis under the authority of Ilium and thus under Laomedon. Kygnus was also Apollon's son, for all the good it did any of them. So, Kygnus thought to improve his fortunes by marrying Laomedon's daughter, Proklia, making his line kin to the lords of half of Phrygia.

"Didn't work out that way, though. Proklia died birthing the twins. So, some years later, Kygnus, weary of taking slave girls to bed, figures he needs somewhere new to stick his cock on the regular, and Laomedon isn't about to give up another of his daughters. What does that old prick do? He cosies up to one of his fellow petty kings of Phrygia, one Tragasus, and makes a bid for his daughter. This girl, Polyboea, well she is but a girl, young enough to be Kygnus's daughter. I don't imagine she took well to being married off to that grizzled old fuck.

"Polyboea does take a liking to Kygnus's children though, them being only a few years her younger, and spends her free time with them in the gardens. Can you guess what happened next, boy?"

Odysseus shrugged as though he had not the least idea in his head, but something in his eyes belied such innocence.

"Eh, well. A few more years, and Tenes is grown tall and broad, a worthy prince of Kolonai. Polyboea takes a fancy to him as a ... different kind of playmate. Tenes, though, he's either too pure or too stupid to take what's being offered freely and spurns his stepmother."

"I feel I've heard this story before."

Autolykus raised a finger to acknowledge that. "Bellerophon, right?"

"Somewhat about Theseus and his son, too."

Huh, Autolykus hadn't heard about that. "Well, people fight with what weapons they have, I suppose. And as you've guessed, bitter Polyboea is probably affronted and certainly scared shitless that Tenes will tell his father, so she preempts the whole thing by claiming Tenes assaulted her. If I believed that, I'd have his stones upon my trophy shelf, boy. You're welcome to check if you see any stones there. So. King Kygnus, being furious and almost as much of an arsehole as his father, summons Tenes and glares at his son.

"'So oft did I watch you playing at being legendary Perseus in the gardens, chasing after Medusa, or rescuing Andromeda.' Kygnus sneers at his son first but turns his scorn also upon the boy's twin sister, standing behind him in solidarity. Oh, she had been his Andromeda in those games, saved from the rocks. Hades, maybe Polyboea hated Amphithea for that, too. Hated that she was never asked to be the princess. 'So, then, I shall allow you live out another of your idol's much vaunted adventures.'

"Of course, Kygnus probably never imagined how close Tenes and Amphithea's tale would follow Perseus's. The fuckwit king, he orders his own children locked in a chest and thrown into the sea, thinking Poseidon will have them, just as Akrisios did with Perseus. And just like then, this chest instead washes up on an island."

"Leukophrye," Odysseus supplied, and Autolykus nodded, pleased the boy paid that much attention.

"So, I'm wandering the island, wondering what to do with myself and if anyone's purse is feeling too heavy for them, when I spy this giant chest and assume I've just made my fortune. It must have washed up from a shipwreck, I think, and hurry to claim my prize. Only, before I even reach it, something inside starts banging on the lid, making the box shudder.

"I rush over and—being me—have no difficulty picking the lock. The lid pops open to reveal a pair of waterlogged teenagers, legs all tangled together. They reek of brine, almost enough to cover the stench of piss. Neither of them has the strength to heft themselves up, but the girl looks up at me through a mat of hair plastered over her face, such relief in her eyes just to be alive.

"'Who are you?' I ask once I'd gotten them loose and built a fire for them to warm the chill out of their bones. They've got Apollon's blood in them—not that I knew it at the time—so they recover quick as rabbits loosed from snares.

"Before they can answer, the boy's stomach growls, and I remember I may not have attended to all their needs. 'Hold here,' I tell them, 'but I'll expect a tale or three when I return with supper.'"

"Some bit later, sunset scorching the sky, I came back with fish for the spit. Whilst it cooked, Amphithea introduced herself and her brother, and gave me their story, more or less as I gave it to you now."

"More or less?" Odysseus asked.

Autolykus flashed his grandson a grin. "Telling a story is an art, boy. One you'd do well to learn yourself."

"Hmm." Odysseus rubbed his chin, clearly as proud of his first wisps of beard as any boy. "And then?"

"Eh. Me, I felt sorry for Tenes and his sister, so I offered to marry the girl. Convincing the Leukophrians to name Tenes their king took only a little effort. They were subject to Helios, as I said, so it wasn't a far step for them to want to name an heir of Apollon—and thus Helios—their ruler. The key in the best tricks, boy, is making the marks think your plan is their idea in the first place.

"More than that ... Well, what say we go for a hunt tomorrow? I've a good many things more to tell, but the hour grows late, and your grandmother will be wondering what keeps me out in the cold rather than in a warm bed."

Odysseus rose and stretched. "But tomorrow you'll finish the tale?"

Autolykus poked a finger in his grandson's chest. "See? You've already learnt a lesson in the telling of tales, boy."

PART II

It is the thing we fear. The phantom we sense and yet doubt, even as it lurks ever at our senses, and we wonder if we push so far we might cross into nightmares. Thus we believe, at the furthermost fringes of the World, beyond even the outer edges of the Spirit Realm, lie the walls of Tartarus. If any ever understood the nature of that place, I wager it is Kronos himself. For he controls a gateway to the absolute extremities of the cosmos, a place not even Oracles dare ever to look.

— First Chronicle of the Circle of Goetic Mysteries

8

———

PANDORA

1600 Silver Age

The air wavered before Pandora, viscous, stomach-churning, reflecting the light of her torch in a way air ought never to do. Dread mingled with desperate hope as she pushed a hand through the Tartarian Gate. It pushed back, too thick, and Pandora jerked her trembling arm back, staring at it, trying to suppress the shudders wracking her. A place beyond the Underworld. A Realm of torment and Khaos and darkness. But then, her beloved lay within, suffering such agonies, and if she did not brave them, he would face them for eternity.

They had made it this far, breached the very Throne of Zeus thanks to the tumult engendered by the Gigantomachy. Had the hand of Ananke guided her to the one time in history when she might cross this threshold? And would she falter?

Never.

Herakles's hand landed on her shoulder. "I'll go first."

"No." No, this fell to her, for it was Pandora's promise to

Prometheus, to *herself*, that she must fulfil. All her steps had brought her here, and if she demurred now, then all she had done amounted to naught. History could not be denied.

A feeble attempt to swallow the lump in her throat, and Pandora stepped into the boggy air. The strain lasted but a moment, then she found herself within the same tunnel. The same, only a change in pressure had her ears popping, and something about the air here had her skin crawling, possessing her with the sudden urge to tear off her flesh with her nails.

The need to collapse to her knees and beg for mercy rose of its own accord, a stifling weight upon her chest. She refused to break now, though. One foot forward, and then the next, her torchlight failing to do more than adumbrate the fringes of the passage, the dark seething as if vexed. Herakles's gasp and grunt behind her told her he, too, felt the horrible unnaturalness of this Realm. Ought that to have comforted her?

"Where do we find him?" Herakles asked.

Once again, Pandora had no idea. How large was Tartarus and how would she find her beloved in its massive gloom? Perhaps she should have claimed more than one torch. Though she cast a pensive look over her shoulder, she already knew she'd not go back. Not now, not with her feet already upon this path.

Behind her, Herakles had drawn his adamant sword and shield, the hand holding the blade twitching in agitation. Or perhaps an aching need for something to strike at. The urge to sweep the torch at the creeping dark filled her too, as if she might bludgeon shadows into submission, force them to withdraw.

To avoid obscuring her vision, Pandora held the torch out to her side, pushing forward, deeper into this subterranean world. After a time, a faint luminance spread out ahead. Was it better … or worse to think some source of light lay beyond the end of this tunnel? Her steps faltered, but only for an instant. They delved on until, at last, they emerged into a boundless cavern, and Pandora stumbled, dropping to her knees in innominate horror at the panoply spreading out before her.

Above, the sky had become a void of mist and storm, flashing with iridescent lightning, and beyond, an expanse somehow darker than pitch black. Burning tornados swept across a landscape composed of jagged rocks illumined by incandescent rivers of magma and yet obscured by vents of billowing ash and sulphur. The reek of putrescence choked her, clogging her sinuses. In the distance lay a wall of onyx, and from this jutted curving thorns and spiked chains, that, if she could see them from here, must be massive beyond imaging.

Tears welled in her eyes as she turned, beholding one vision of wretched damnation after the next. This ... was where Prometheus had lingered, suffering for she knew not how long. How much time had passed between his imprisonment and the Gigantomachy? She had no way of knowing, nor even if his mind and soul would remain intact after his imprisonment here.

"Fuck," Herakles rasped.

And, indeed, it was rather the only thing to say.

The demigod used his shield arm to place a hand under her arms, guiding her back to her feet. "We have to keep moving."

Scrubbing away tears, Pandora sniffed and nodded. Whatever Prometheus had suffered, she had come to save him, and she was going to do it. A moment, she turned about, trying to gauge the best direction. To one side lay that onyx wall, and every time she looked at it, it seemed to move, twisting into impossible geometries that sent her mind reeling. To the other lay the greater expanse of chaotic flame and darkness, where reality itself became nebulous. Zeus had ordered Styx's children to bind Prometheus "over the black walls of Tartarus."

"This way," she said, no longer holding the torch high, for it provided little more illumination than the flaming twisters or magma flows.

They pushed onward, Pandora clenching her jaw in a desperate attempt to keep the whole of herself from spilling out. For this place wanted to swallow her, body and soul, she had no doubt. Screams and wails and whimpers sometimes cut through the cacophony of thunder and raging winds. Most such sounds seemed to emanate from all around them, but one sounded close enough, Pandora turned toward it, drawn by the cries.

A few steps and she beheld a man, bound to a stone slab set amidst a putrid bog. Lazy bubbles arose from dark waters, lingering before breaking. A petrified tree protruded from the shore, its branches stretching over the waters. From one dangled an impaled golden apple, just out of reach of the man's mouth when he strained his neck up for it.

An involuntary gasp escaped her as she drew closer. The fetters that bound the victim to the slab bore rusty spikes that pierced his flesh deeper the harder he strived for the apple. After a futile attempt, he collapsed, whimpering, head banging back against stone.

What was the point in setting it so close to him and yet ... Pandora sucked in a sudden, ravaging breath. Oh, gods. She knew him. That was Tantalus. Her grip around the torch tightened until her knuckles popped. This man had bought her as a slave. Beaten her and, when she began to bleed, forced her into his bed. In him, in his pitiless eyes, her World had collapsed, sucked into a swamp of despair until hope had seemed just an ephemera of phosphorus, forever beyond *her* reach. Here, chained in a bog, lay the very instrument of the ravishing of her soul.

Kelaino had said she had handed him over to Zeus, blamed him for Nectar, probably having no idea her own daughter was behind it. Or maybe she knew and used Tantalus to draw attention away from Kalypso and Kirke. Either way, it had inadvertently led to Pandora's freedom, when Zeus's forces had made her master disappear.

So ... Zeus tormented Tantalus with a golden apple from the Tree of Life, a tease of the real thing. Had he ever, in fact, taken Nectar? Probably, but it mattered little. How did he yet live, though? Did Tartarus itself keep him alive?

Not knowing why, Pandora waded into the murky waters.

"What are you doing?" Herakles demanded.

But she had to see him now. She stalked up to his side until Tantalus looked up at her, emaciated, eyes hollow and pleading. His stomach had sunken until she could make out the spine behind it. Maybe … maybe he was not alive at all. Maybe his soul remained bound here in torment for as long as Zeus's cruelty persisted.

"You want me to free you?" Pandora asked.

From the empty way he looked at her, maybe he did not even recognise her now, a grown woman. Maybe she little resembled the squirming, weeping child he'd trapped beneath his weight. He seemed so very close to breaking and managed only a pathetic nod.

She leaned close to his face. "I wanted you to free me, too."

The silence lingered until his eyes widened in broken recognition. He knew her *now*.

Herakles said naught while Pandora sloshed back toward him, despite her weeping once more. The tremors that shot through her threatened to shake her in twain. A part of her knew she ought to go back, release him from this eternal torment. Another part revelled, wanted to call it *justice*, for the life and innocence he had helped steal from her. She would not look back at him. She would never look at him again.

In silence, they strode together toward the wall until Herakles pointed at a chain that ran from a soaring, twisted pillar of onyx toward the lip of the wall itself. "That's our route to the top."

Words, she thought, could never express her gratitude to him at that moment, for holding his peace. Sometimes, the quiet held its own condemnation, the air pregnant with unspoken judgments. But at others, times like this, the quiescence was *compassion*, the utter admission that another person could not begin to fathom someone else's travails.

They approached the chain and Pandora stood, grimacing at the column. At irregular intervals thorns the size of swords punched out the sides of the edifice, some in perilous proximity to the winding stairs encircling the pillar. From a distance, she had judged it onyx, like the wall, but now this structure seemed more like black bone, twisted into unnatural spirals.

In the distance, beyond the haze of smoke, she could just make out the silhouettes of more such pillars, like a broken rib cage running the circumference of the wall, which itself sometimes seemed to bend in a convex arc to enclose the cavern. A vagueness saturated this Realm, the very air tingling with inchoate energies. Or was it entropy? The fall of order into Khaos. For, after all, according to Polyhymnia, the Time of Nyx had spawned from the infinite dark of Khaos. Perhaps even Gaia herself had arisen from the black.

And here, in this place of collapsing potential, Pandora imagined the beginning and end of existence. It crept over her with the sensation of a serpent slithering over her in her sleep, with the compounded dread of all the intangible fears of a childhood spent without the comforting arms of a mother or father.

Another shudder, and she placed a sandal upon the stone stairs rimming the bone tower, careful to avoid any thorns that began to form. Their protrusions came without warning, but not so quickly she could not step around them. Up they climbed until her lungs hurt, and not least from the putrid, ashen air. Still, she dare not pause upon the stairs, and thus she forced herself on, past the pain, steadying herself with one hand upon the wall. Moist warmth seeped out from it, and Pandora jerked her hand away in disgust.

By the end, she found herself gasping for breath and swaying with vertigo. If she pitched over backward from this height … Like a fool, Pandora glanced down, to a fall hundreds of feet. Herakles's steadying grip caught her, easing her up those final steps.

"Help me," someone gasped as Pandora crested the rise to the top of the tower.

The pillar had a diameter of perhaps twenty feet, and at its centre, bound in orichalcum, knelt a naked woman. Crusted vestiges of what might have once been wings jutted from her shoulders and Pandora winced to imagine what had torn them from her. Hadn't she seen this woman, too?

Pandora knelt beside her. "Who are you?"

"Arke." Her voice was raw, almost destroyed. From screaming …

Right. One of Hermes's lovers, back in Zeus's camp at Athyras. Pandora had made it a point to avoid contact with any of the Titans, especially Zeus himself, but she had seen twin sisters back then. "Why did he put you here?"

"Because I ..." A pained, broken chuckle. "Because I saw him for the madman he was."

She had betrayed Zeus. Pandora glanced back to see Herakles too watching the woman, expression grim. "Help her," she pleaded.

A grunt answered her, though he did look to the rings pounded into the pillar, holding her chains. "We did not come to Tartarus to free every prisoner my father bound here. You have asked me to defy him to release *one*."

"She's been here for centuries. Surely having chosen a different side in war does not merit further punishment than she has already endured."

Still glowering, the demigod knelt beside one of the rings binding Arke, then wrapt his meaty hands around it. "I have my doubts about this."

"You want redemption ..." And yet she had left Tantalus to rot. Wasn't that different? He had enslaved and raped her. How could anyone expect *her* to provide his salvation? It had to be different. It had to be. And yet, even speaking it flensed her soul. "Maybe redemption lies in helping as many as we can down here. Maybe no one deserves eternal torment for transitory crimes." Nor was Pandora much convinced betraying Zeus was a crime.

Another grunt, and Herakles heaved. The ring screeched as it scraped over the bone tower, then the spoke burst free, showering dust as it did so. Arke drew in a shuddering breath, then rose, her knees trembling as she did so. Pandora wished she had something to wrap around the naked woman, but without her cloak, the cold outside might kill Pandora, and Arke was a Titan.

Though the woman did not speak, she levelled a look of gratitude at Pandora. Relief so profound no words could express it. When Arke turned, Pandora thought her going for the stairs, but the woman leapt into the open air, plummeting into the darkness without so much as a scream.

Yelping, Pandora rushed to the edge. Given the cavern's gloom, perhaps the stain she thought she saw was her mind providing the imagery it knew must lay below.

"Sometimes death is release," Herakles said, though he too looked shaken.

Was it? Arke's death punched Pandora in the gut. It was a physical blow that stole her breath and made a muddle of her thoughts, and all she could do was steady herself against Herakles. But then, maybe he had the right of it. Maybe, for Arke, even dying seemed better than another moment in Tartarus.

Would her soul escape this place or remain trapped here, as Tantalus's seemed to be? Pandora had no answers to such questions.

The great chain that spanned the gulf between tower and wall swayed, just a little, disturbed perhaps by the winds of the burning tornados in the distance. Enormous links composed the chain, which, in fact, rose to a wall that actually stood higher than the tower. Herakles had sheathed his sword and strapped the shield to his back. One hand out to steady himself, the other he wrapt around Pandora's wrist. If she fell, would her weight pull him off too? Best not think on such things.

She mirrored his pose, far less confident of her balance than Herakles seemed of his, and they plodded out onto the chains together. Though she had thought them metal, the links seemed pliant beneath her sandals, almost alive. A thought that drew a whimper of disgust from her.

Far off, the gloom gathered, a miasma of darkness and smoke rising from lava flows. And beyond it, the onyx wall of Tartarus.

9

HEKATE

2393 Golden Age

Gigantes such as the Cyclops Steropes fortified their Pneuma by consuming the flesh of Man. They feasted, growing wretched and puissant, and, unfortunately for Steropes, that meant they themselves fair surged with Pneuma. Using the very orichalcum chain that had once tethered the Sefer Raziel to the pedestal in the Lodge of Whispers, Hekate had bound the Cyclops within the cave.

The one-eyed Gígas's bellows reverberated against the confines of its stone prison, but they were too far removed from Athyras for anyone to hear him. Still, Zeus paused his pacing long enough to land a blow against the Cyclops's jaw, sending the massive creature stumbling to the floor. The orichalcum blocked it from using Pneuma, meaning that strike landed with full force. Given the trouble Zeus and Hekate had gone through to capture Steropes—they had found him gorging himself on a hapless farmer—Hekate had little pity for him.

Madness compounds upon itself, Tithorea repined, *until aberrant schemes glitter in aureate splendour.*

Gritting her teeth and trying to ignore the dryad, Hekate turned back to the circle she'd drawn using blood from gashes cut in Steropes's thighs. Indeed, it seemed every spirit within her soul objected to her plan, though she had but extrapolated from spells within the grimoire.

Naught save mastery of the Art of Storm would sate Zeus, that much he had made clear. Okypete had, of course, suggested she summon a harpy inside Zeus. Even if Hekate could have managed a binding inside another, similar in kind to how sorcerers bound eidolons within themselves, she could not have avoided the reality that the more Zeus called upon that power, the closer the harpy would come to possessing him. Knowing him, Zeus would find himself enslaved to a spirit's will in a matter of days.

Part of her thought he deserved it, she had to admit. Already, violence and pettiness ruled him, lust and cruelty, making him not so different from a spirit.

We are the truth of all souls, Okypete crooned. *Unbounded by the insipid contrivances of societal mores.*

Maybe. Maybe all that separated Man, or Titan, from spirits was an ingrained, and perhaps fragile, artificial, sense of honour born from the expectations of society. Perhaps human nature, without the necessity for cooperation, would too have devolved into the solipsism that drove spirits. If so, however, Hekate would have named that force conscience, even while it ever threatened to slip between her fingers.

Either way, she'd not loose a free spirit upon the Mortal Realm, much less in the body of a Titan destined to rule half the world. No, she needed a solution whereby a harpy's entire essence could be consumed and absorbed by Zeus, and for that, she would need to call up greater powers than she had ever before touched. For the grimoire made reference to beings older than time, older than the World, lurking beyond its fringes, beyond even the far domains of spirits.

Tartarus ... Okypete's voice held true fear.

Old Ones, the book called these timeless entities, though Hekate could not say for certain whether the term applied to all the beings beyond the World, or a specific subset of demons. Nomenclature mattered little enough, she supposed. Though ... long ago, Themis had termed Python an Old One, and perhaps Ladon was too. Were dragons also spawned in the dark before time? Or did she attempt to apply rigid classifications to nebulous conceptions refusing constraints?

Your mind wanders as if to flee the fear and culpability for unhinged paths. Now, even Khione had joined in the tirade of voices demanding she change her course. But Zeus had insisted upon this power, and besides, Hekate had the grimoire. If she refused to call upon the arcana given to her, she would never attain the greatest possible power. She wanted the answers to everything, every secret of the World and beyond, and she would never hold those secrets if she refused to look into the dark.

With the circle finished and midnight drawing nigh, she looked to Zeus and nodded. The Titan grinned as he stalked closer to Steropes, knife in hand. Apprehending his fate, the Cyclops strained against his chains, seeking refuge in the recesses of the cave, though it was not deep.

Zeus seized a horn jutting above that single eye and jerked Steropes's head down. "You will give me the gift of thunder, brute." A swipe of the knife, and blood spurted over the cavern floor.

Hekate had positioned her circle with care, though. Steropes's spilling life would not run into her designs and disrupt them.

"Aello," she called. She needed an elder harpy, the strongest she could find, and the grimoire had given her the name. "Aello, I summon you." She fell into Supernal cants, stalking toward Zeus.

Evoking it would not suffice here, nor even peering into the Penumbra with the Sight. Snatching the Titan's wrist, she called upon Mormo, and the wraith squirmed within her soul. The cloying shadows rushed down her throat and choked her, the sensation of wading through tar as Mormo pulled the pair of them bodily through the Veil.

Color leeched out of her vision, replaced by the writhing, blue-grey shadows of the Penumbra. The world shifted, twisting itself as if bent in torment. The back of the cavern itself fell away, vanishing into a caliginous recess that bored deeper than in the Mortal Realm, while a chill mist wafted in and clung to her legs.

Beyond the cave, she saw the hints of iridescent lights that comprised the Ethereal firmament of this Realm.

This time, she was prepared for Mormo's brutal assault. The wraith swarmed over her mind and body like a cloud of locusts trying to crawl its way out from beneath her skin. Hekate dropped to her knees and wrapt her arms around herself, hissing in agony even as she focused the whole of her will on pressing the ghost back down into dormancy. At the fringes of her being, the wraith *gnawed*, slurping upon tiny morsels of Hekate's Pneuma and soul.

When at last the barrage abated, she remained kneeling, trembling. It took a great deal of willpower to hold back whimpers that would have shamed her before Zeus.

"What the fuck is that?" the Titan demanded, thrusting his finger at some momentous shifting in the darkness beyond the cavern.

Following where he pointed, Hekate rose and drifted to the threshold, steadying herself against cold rock. Indeed, out there in the shadowscape version of the wood, an entity lurched between the trees. Though it resembled a bear, even on all fours, her head would not have reached its shoulder, and gloom seemed to drip from it like runoff from the rain.

Further back, she beheld more incipient shapes drifting about the Etheric forest. A handful of shades, listless and tormented, wandering as if guided by the nether winds that wafted the mists. Peering eyes from within the trees that she dared to imagine a dryad. Somewhere, in the dark of the chasm where the ground fell away, a squamous bulk swimming through shadows as a crocodile through a river.

"Do not stare," she warned. "Do not draw the attention of aught passing through this space."

Thunder rumbled above, a herald announcing the harpy an

instant before she heard its mind-shredding screech and felt the tempestuous surge of its descent. The gale hurled her and Zeus aside even as the harpy streaked into the cavern, landing in a crouch and turning to regard them with its avian visage.

Blood without apparent source seeped from its wingtips, and crackles of lightning coruscated along its talons when it took a single, threatening step toward them.

Zeus rose to meet it, fists raised, while Hekate fell back into her Supernal cants. Aello had not entered the circle that might have bound it. Had she made some mistake? It should not matter though. She should be able to—

When it lunged, the creature moved so fast it seemed a bolt of lightning. Zeus managed to interpose himself between the harpy and Hekate, only to be sent slamming into the floor. The creature's bloody talons had punched through his thighs. Towering above the Titan, it spread its wings and raised its head, looking right at Hekate in bitter mockery, daring her to stop it from dropping that beak and biting out Zeus's throat.

"Aeshma!" Hekate screamed, invoking the name of the Old One from the book. "Aeshma, grant me your power! Bind my enemy in your name!"

Though naught changed in her vision, Hekate felt her stomach drop out from under her. Vertiginous waves sent her spilling onto her hands and knees, even as the sensation of sinking redoubled, as if the whole world had fallen away beneath her, exposing her to the depths of an endless abyss.

A flicker in her mind's eye, a colossal, skinless hand reaching out of the dark, grasping, blood oozing from exposed veins. The inchoate phantasm vanished in the blink of her eyes, and she could not be certain what she'd seen.

Only that Aello had frozen in place, paralysed, save for the faint flutters of its wings, feathers rustling in the nether winds. Roaring in pain, Zeus heaved the harpy off himself, growling as ichor-stained talons tore free of his flesh.

"Aeshma," Hekate's voice trembled with a nameless fear, a sudden, nascent apprehension that perhaps the now-silent spirits in her head had been right to warn against this course. Too late, too late ... "Grant us the power to claim this soul and its puissance."

A flicker again, a shadow towering over her, not seen with the eyes but felt for an instant—a darkness perceived without senses —nonetheless.

"Consume its heart," Hekate commanded Zeus, though her words held the force of a weeping child.

When he glanced at her, Zeus licked his lips in sadistic glee. With his wounds, he had to crawl over to the creature, pulling his still-bloody knife as he did so. The tremors that had seized her prevented her from watching—not that she'd have wanted to, regardless—as Zeus set to carving away at Aello's ribs.

Whimpers of agony ripped from the harpy, though it seemed unable to form a full scream whilst held in the grips of the Old One's power. Blood trails dribbled down over stone, claiming Hekate's gaze while she tried to still the shaking in her core. As if something deep inside had taken a chill, she could not stop her shaking. She wanted to beg forgiveness, though she could not have said to whom she might plead.

Papa, maybe, who so long ago had implored her not to delve into the dark.

"You must turn back from the path you have set yourself upon. The Art has broken entire civilisations. It has rendered death on a scale you cannot conceive, blanketing the land in night."

Now, his words came back to her clear as the day he had spoken them, thousands of years prior.

Cackling, Zeus ripped a still-beating hunk of grisly muscle from the harpy's chest, hefting it like a laurel crown won in a festival. His precious prize. When he bit down, crimson imbrued his platinum beard, seeping through it so completely Hekate imagined it forever dyed thus.

Oh, Gaia, what had she done?

They needed to return to the Mortal Realm. They needed to quit the foul dark of this Realm ... this *truer* reality that encompassed the whole of their fragile world.

BLOOD-DRENCHED *bone spurs the size of trees jutted from an obsidian wall in the background, a structure so high the fulgurations in the darkened sky above threatened to brush over it. Ash from a thousand fires and billowing volcanoes mingled with roiling storm clouds, the sky choked and thickened.*

And from the dark, a tremendous foot descended, skinless, streams of blood dribbling down like sweat, muscle and bone exposed to the foul air. The foot crashed down into the stone before Hekate, sending tremors running beneath her.

She needed to scream, but it welled up in her throat and refused to escape, allowing her no more than an inarticulate moan of complete impotence.

Another leg, and her gaze was drawn helplessly upward, over a desiccated abdomen, toward a flayed chest and great arms a hundred feet in the air. Behind one dragged a club—no, a mace—seeping blood. And finally, hidden within the murky shadows that filled this place, its head of bones. Not a skull, at least not of any creature Hekate knew, but rather an osseous maze of horns, within which pulsed some incandescent light. With every beat, fresh streams of blood drizzled down its neck and over its torso.

That gargantuan mace rose, a sanguine cataract falling from it, streaming over her, stinging her eyes and filling her mouth. Its shadow drifted above her ...

TEARS STREAMED from the corners of Hekate's eyes, and for the life of her, she prayed she was awake, though still she had not managed to free the scream that had lodged in her throat. A choking cough loosed her, and she curled over onto her side and wept.

Oh, Gaia, what had she done? What had she invoked?

A foulness rankled her nose, and it took her a moment to even recognise it. Like a babe, she had soiled her own bed.

Had she thought herself incapable of weeping not so long ago? Now she could not stop the lachrymal convulsions that had claimed her.

***

Zeus, being Zeus, had insisted upon testing out his newfound power, brushing aside any attempt she made to urge him to train with it or practice caution. The king instead marshalled his forces to assault Ilium, a polis in Phrygia ruled by Menoetius, loyal brother of Atlas.

Should they slay Menoetius, Zeus claimed, their alliance could overrun Phrygia, laying open the path for an assault upon Phoeba. That he would have rationalised any excuse to unleash his lightning mattered little, Hekate supposed, though indeed, seizing Ilium would help swing the war in their favour.

Thus had they ferried troops across the strait and now marched upon the towering walls of Ilium. A part of her longed to remain in Athyras, clutching young Athene to her breast, striving not to whimper the night away, though she had not dared close her eyes in days. No, but Hekate needed to see for herself what her Art had bought them. Whether a price so steep could have *any* justification.

So they came to war, and Menoetius's scouts must have seen them crossing, for he had well prepared.

The great throng had gathered before the cyclopean walls of Ilium, Menoetius standing a head above the rest of his forces, clad in full battle panoply, his breastplate glinting in the morning light. The Titan lord strode forward, his ranks parting around him like the sea around a ship, clanking his long spear across his bronze-banded shield.

His burnished helm concealed all but his eyes, but still, Hekate saw the challenge there, even before he pointed his lance at Zeus, his throng unleashing a collective *whoop* in time with his movement.

Her gaze fell on the prince beside her, a malevolent smirk curling his lips as his eyes clouded. The air grew pungent, crackling with energies that had the hair on Hekate's arms standing on end. A clean taste filled her mouth as Zeus thrust his arms skyward, his sudden cackle so rabid as to silence both armies, drawing all eyes upon him.

They could not know, though Hekate's gaze rose to the gathering dark above, the roiling clouds, the fulgurations that coruscated among them in forewarning of what impended. A bellow escaped Zeus, primal and mad, melding into the roar of thunder that, at once, issued from the storm above and the chest of the Titan at Hekate's side. Instinct had her falling back, away from him.

Menoetius must have apprehended the danger at last, for the Titan lord charged forward, sandals slapping stone, spear primed to impale Zeus. He made it a dozen steps before the blinding effulgence ripped down from the firmament, a streak of such bitter whiteness it sent afterimages skittering over Hekate's vision.

The blast of lightning streamed into the Titan, and he jerked to a stop, seized by convulsions. The galvanic river did not abate, but continued to flow into Menoetius, leaping in arcing chains into his forces. Waves of acrid stench washed over Hekate, the scents of charred flesh as Man and Titan cooked beneath the current of Zeus's power.

Bands of lightning shot through the throng, the roar leaving a ringing in her ears, the radiance becoming a play of afterimages. Then the stillness settled in, a sudden cessation of violence that only served to reinforce the harrowing she had just witnessed. Motes of light flitted across her vision, leaving the part of her mind yet functioning to wonder if the display had damaged her eyes. Probably men screamed and moaned, but all she heard was a high-pitched whine. When she tried to move, her legs trembled, her equilibrium shattered.

You gift what Man ought not receive. Okypete's voice in her head seemed no more than a susurration borne down from a far-off mountain, rasping, impotent.

The smouldering field of charnel and molten bronze gave

credence to the harpy's claims, though. Khaos manifested upon Gaia now, and culpability for what ensued would forever lay at Hekate's feet. Much as she wanted to retch, she found herself falling in behind Zeus as he continued to advance upon soaring Ilium, sparks still leaping between his fingers.

Amid the field, patches of men rose now, some dragging themselves free of the carnage, others weeping over massacred comrades. Not one warrior sought after weapons. No thoughts of vengeance darkened them now, for who strove for vengeance against a force of nature?

Though Hekate still could not hear, the gaping grin Zeus cast her way told her well enough he cackled, revelling in the scope of his power, drunk upon blood. Before the great gate, the prince curled his fingers into a fist, then thrust them out. A fresh arc of lightning burst from his own body, slamming into the barrier. Wood darkened and burst, flaming cinders hurtling in all directions. Zeus's lightning continued to flow from him in a torrent that skittered along the cyclopean wall, charring it, leaping up to hapless defenders upon the ramparts and sending them careening backward. Coruscating fulgurations wormed into the masonry an instant before ponderous blocks launched themselves outward, the very towering walls blown apart under the stream of fury, and Hekate could do naught save raise a hand to her mouth.

A storm of dust and debris raged about them, and Zeus waded into it, so enthralled with his own glory as to think himself inviolable. Perhaps—though the thought horrified—Hekate had indeed rendered him thus, creating a living storm against which neither Man nor Titan could stand. Faced with the implacable rage of the heavens, one took shelter and prayed, or one perished.

The prince waded through the slaughter, chest heaving from the drain of his power, yet showing no sign of abating his wild wrath. Lesser bolts leapt from his fingertips, sending men and women flying backward to land in convulsing, smouldering heaps of ruination.

Slowly, Hekate's senses returned, though she did not welcome the shrieks of terror that had begun to pierce through the whine of her damaged ears, and less so the visions she now beheld. Tendrils of smoke rose from the corpses of street dogs cooked alive whilst entire apartment buildings had burst into flames that now raced through the city fast as bitter gales. Heaps of bodies lined the alleys, and not just warriors, but tradesmen and housewives, children blown apart by the indiscriminate whims of a prince she had made into a living god.

Your paltry sentiments little avail the dead, Khione mocked.

"Zeus, stop this!" a woman shouted, rushing out into the street, tall enough to be a Titan or Nymph.

Another bolt leapt from his hand even before his gaze fell upon her, its blinding light ripping through her even as it hurled her away. In the half instant Hekate had seen her, she thought …

"Mother?" she heard Zeus say.

Rhea, Kronos's lover, mother of Zeus.

A sudden stiffness replaced his shocked concern. "You betray me with your presence among my enemies!" the prince bellowed.

Smoke rose from the blackened flesh and singed clothes of the fallen Titan, yet she managed to heft herself up onto an elbow, staring at her son even as golden ichor oozed from ruptures along her face.

Zeus gagged at the sight of her. Hekate expected him to rush to the woman, help her, but instead, a second stream of lightning escaped him, immolating the Titan, reducing her to naught but ash.

"Traitor!" he shrieked. From the way he said it, he must have been screaming it over and over, though the ringing in Hekate's ears had prevented her from hearing before now.

Throwing his hands into the air as if rejecting the whole scene, the prince pushed on, deeper into the city, to continue the slaughter of all loyal to Menoetius. Hekate, though, broke away, suddenly gasping, ravaged and trembling.

What had she done?

You know too well … Mormo taunted.

Gaia forgive her for what she had brought forth. Unbridled

madness. Solipsism given the force to realise its self-aggrandising delusions.

How will you live with yourself now? Khione demanded.

She couldn't. The weight of her actions settled upon her, a crushing mountain pushing all breath from her lungs, dimming her sight until her vision narrowed to a tunnel. A pinprick of light, along the ground, and she was on her knees, wailing, digging through ash, though she could not have said for what.

Her fingertips scraped over metal, a cut she barely felt. The still warm bronze of a xiphos. Bereft of conscious thought, she grasped the hilt. An easy escape, offered up by the dust, by Gaia, giving her the chance to abrogate the devouring guilt consuming her. All she could see now was the pitted point of that blade, the dark circle of her vision driving it closer to her throat.

A drifting, encircling gloom rising up to swallow her whole.

The sound of a heartbeat in the dark. *Thump, thump. Thump, thump.*

Bones crunched beneath the weight of the flayed colossus, and she lay within its palm. With claw-like thumb and forefinger, it reached for her, dug into her chest, and tore free her beating heart.

Thump, thump.

Ichor streamed from it, even as the demon hefted it to the maze of bone that formed its head. Inside the impenetrable dark within the maze, she heard the gnawing mastication. *Felt* it, despite the organ having been ripped bleeding from her, as it devoured pieces of her.

The slowing, final abating of the agony. The final *thump* came upon her ...

The peace of oblivion would swallow her now.

Then, once more, thumb and forefinger descended upon her, punched through her chest, and ripped out her beating heart. *Thump, thump.*

"HEKATE!" someone was calling her name, rocking her back and forth.

The dark fell away, but not the weight nor the pain that lanced through her chest with each fervent beat of her heart now. Devoured over and over in defiance of logic, an eternity of consumption that awaited her the moment her soul left the fragile cage of her body. She had plumbed the darkest depths of the cosmos, and it *saw* her now, apprehended her in a primal way beyond all words, beyond expression of thought. It knew her to the pith of her soul and awaited its unbreakable claim upon her.

Such was the inevitable end that lay before her. If all sorceresses doomed themselves to become wraiths, Hekate had invited yet greater torment upon her soul.

Hekate wailed, knowing, in truth, what little she had beheld in her moment of weakness was but a foreshock to the quake of damnation that would open beneath her. It fed upon *souls*, and her mind struggled to parse a bare instant of such agony as would stretch down through ages.

Tears streamed down her face, even while she was dimly aware someone cradled her.

"Hekate ...?"

Oh, Gaia. What had she exposed herself to? This was what lay behind the furthest reaches of the cosmos? This fathomless, consumptive Khaos out of Tartarus, ever clamouring for souls to feast upon and savage?

Rough hands shook her. "Wake up!"

A ravaged breath tore through her chest, and Hekate focused, at last, upon the face of the woman so desperate to tether her to the Mortal Realm. For which Hekate ought to express more gratitude than could be shown in a thousand lifetimes. For she now knew what awaited her when death finally closed its icy claws around her.

Aidos, though, had seen none of it, and perhaps thought the whole of Hekate's catalepsy brought on by her horror at the fall of Ilium. As if that had not been enough.

"You're here," Artemis's cousin said, stroking Hekate's back. "You're here with me, still."

The woman must have brought her outside the walls, Hekate realised, for they were now in Zeus's camp, in one of the tents. A crackling brazier offered transitory warmth, almost enough for her to pretend the abyss of darkness did not reach for her, grasping up from shadows to brush against her soul.

Almost.

10

ARTEMIS

2394 Golden Age

*T*he lush green of the lower mountain Artemis trekked along had begun to yellow with the autumn, the scents of the changing season undeniable to her enhanced senses. Hints of decay, animal spoor, and the muddled reek of Man emanating from a village down in the valley. Out there was Lydia, lands under the authority of her grandmother.

With Zeus having appointed Apollon a general, Artemis found herself in charge of scouting her brother's enemies in Phrygia. No doubt Apollon and Zeus had thought Phoeba would fall just as Ilium had, but their advance on Grandmother's polis had faltered on finding the Ouranid League had now enlisted Gigantes of their own. So Artemis stalked the mist-laden hills and snow-capped mountains of Phrygia, seeking out clusters of Ouranid-loyal troops.

Atlas and Phoebe had combined their forces here in an attempt to drive Zeus's alliance from this peninsula and, thus far, had succeeded time and again. Despite the new spies Hekate had created, the

League remained a perpetual step ahead. Artemis dared to hope Mother safe in Athyras, but sooner or later, the Ouranids would learn of the rebel refuge.

The moon would rise within a few hours, then she could pass without risk of detection. She'd need to scour the village for hints of Gigantes or any other sign of Atlas's war bands.

A sudden sense of wrongness pressed in upon her, prickling her flesh and sending her baring her teeth and nocking an arrow to her bow. Beneath the long shadow of a boulder, the air rippled as a hand pushed through an empty space, stalling upon a membrane for an instant before a face joined it. Instinct—and a bear's ire at surprise—demanded she loose her arrow, but Artemis pushed that desire down. She would never grow accustomed to their new spies or their flitting about between the Earth and the Underworld.

The moment of seething wrongness abated as Arke materialised, tremors shooting through the winged Nymph as though she'd emerged from the Axeinos Sea in the dead of winter. Arke dropped to one knee, her expression haunted when she gazed up at Artemis.

Artemis put away the arrow, then helped the spy rise.

"They're not down there," Arke said. "Atlas's forces gather north of the Arad Mountains, in the Katpatuka highlands."

Rugged, rocky terrain with not enough water to supply an army, or so the thinking went. "They plan to move on our garrison in Ilium." Artemis's cousin Aidos was there, helping administrate what remained of the local populace, though Morpheus ran the garrison.

Arke nodded. "If we move fast, we could intercept them in the highlands, before they reach the ruins of Menoetius's city."

Artemis could only grimace. Her brother was too far off to bring his forces around the Arad Mountains. Was that part of Atlas's plan? Had they been lured south out of the way, or had Apollon's own eagerness overcome him? Either way, their best chance to stop the Titan lord of Atlantis lay in ambushing him before he was expecting battle. "Get word to Aidos and Morpheus. Tell them to send what war bands they can muster and meet me at the edge of Katpatuka."

Another nod, and Arke stepped backward, seeming to dissolve into the shadows.

Artemis shuddered at the sight of it.

WHEN SHE ARRIVED IN KATPATUKA, Aidos awaited her, along with a force of two hundred warriors. She might have hoped for more but had expected fewer, what with so many of their fighters away with her brother.

Biting her lip, she took stock of those here. Perhaps a third of those that came were archers, though, which would well suit her plans to rain arrows down on unsuspecting Gigantes and Ouranid troops.

Her cousin's sudden embrace shook Artemis from her calculations. Artemis returned the hug.

"Morpheus did not come himself?"

Aidos affected that too-innocent smile she had mastered as a child. Her cousin forever smelled of openness, both the least guarded and the least prideful of any Titan Artemis could ever remember meeting. "Guess he wanted a nap. The man makes sleeping an art."

Artemis snorted at that. "Fine, it doesn't matter. We have enough if we find the perfect location for an ambush. Somewhere Atlas has to move his forces below us. I sent Arke out to locate such a place."

"Creepy little—" Aidos began an instant before Artemis felt herself cringing from the approach of the Otherworldly.

Shadows bent backward as Arke pushed into their world once more.

"Oh, Arke!" Aidos blurted. "I was just missing you, darling."

Could Arke hear them speaking here, in the world of the living, whilst traveling in the Underworld? If so, the only indication she gave of realising Aidos had spoken ill of her came in the form of a slight scowl directed at Artemis's cousin. "I found a place like you described."

"Good," Artemis said, then looked to Aidos. "Get your people ready. We march immediately."

ARKE'S CHOSEN location fit almost perfectly. To move a large force toward Ilium, Atlas would have to pass through a gulley some sixty feet below, while Artemis and her archers hid in scrub and behind rocks on the cliff above. The landscape here looked almost like an empty sea, full of rounded mountains and jutting rock spires, and not a tree in sight. Beautiful desolation, and she could not help but imagine what the full moon would have looked like above, flanked by a blanket of stars.

Depending on how fast Atlas could move his people through Katpatuka, maybe she would get the chance to see the moon and stars. Not the full moon, though, and she supposed she'd have to consider herself lucky on that count. Even after all these centuries, Artemis could not control the bear on the full moon. It ripped out of her flesh, and she had no choice save to become the animal and run wild, little aware of her actions.

In the shadow of a rock, Artemis crouched, and Aidos settled in beside her. "Word came Ares fights with Kreios, north of Thebes." Artemis's cousin grunted. "Probably over by now, I suppose."

It took Artemis a moment to realise why Aidos should take special care over that. While her mother was Asteria, Leto's sister and thus Artemis's aunt, her father was Perses, son of Kreios. "You think your father fights against Zeus's son."

"Probably. They disowned me once they heard I joined Zeus, you know."

Artemis hadn't known, but then, the same fate had befallen most of the rebels. So many had turned against their parents.

"All these years, I was just a Nymph, a prize to be traded off when need arose and naught more. My father arranged barely enough Ambrosia to keep me immortal, never enough to grow strong. But somehow, this is my fault, for wanting what everyone else has." The scent of her shame saturated the night.

"Not everyone."

Aidos scoffed. "You do."

No arguing with that. Artemis had shown early promise, so Father had made sure she got more Ambrosia to develop her Pneumatikoi. If a girl didn't demonstrate power early on, well, men had other uses for her. Artemis remembered visiting Aidos in Helion during the Ambrosial War and hearing they had named her cousin *Nymph*.

She wanted to believe, if Zeus won, all that would change. But having spent some time around him, Artemis had her doubts. Zeus saw *only* one use for females, and he took that use as his due any time he wished.

Artemis squeezed her cousin's hand. "When they come, I'll handle Atlas myself. Get the archers to rain arrows among them and, above all, make sure none manage to climb out of the gulley."

A time they waited in silence, the sun dipping below the horizon, painting the sky the colour of fresh apricots. A clamour in the distance told her Atlas's forces approached down the path below, and Artemis nocked an arrow to her bow, ready to rise the moment she spotted Atlas himself. Famed for his size and strength, Atlas would prove an implacable foe—unless she lodged an arrow in his throat before he realised his danger. Few enemies posed a danger with arrows in them.

While the bear spirit inside gave her an excellent sense of hearing and an even better sense of smell, it did little for her eyesight, so Artemis flooded Pneuma into her Perspicacity Pneumatikoi, enhancing her vision. The moment she did so, a sudden awareness of the Pneuma of those around her flared. She so rarely relied on this sense anymore because of the bear, but ...

Artemis turned, all but certain too many strong Pneuma signatures drifted in from the fringes, beyond where Aidos had stationed her troops. Before she could issue a warning, the first arrows fell in a killing rain among her people. They streaked from all directions, pouring down from the rocky hills leading up to Artemis's carefully selected ambush spot.

She flung herself aside, trying to grab Aidos. An arrow punched through her cousin's skull, its fletching quivering as Aidos dropped in a heap. The moment froze for Artemis, paralysed her, left her choking upon a scream. A drawn-out instant passed before she could even drag herself over to Aidos, stare into beloved, vacant eyes.

Time and hope were ripped from her.

Another arrow grazed Artemis's bicep, the pain hurling her back into the moment. Adrenaline surged through her. Centuries-honed reflexes sent Pneuma flooding through her limbs, strengthening and speeding them, and Artemis scrambled along the ground, out of the path of more falling arrows. Dozens upon dozens of archers had closed with them, caught Aidos's troops in their exact hiding spot, though Artemis had no time to think on how such could be possible.

A phalanx of spearmen closed in upon her even as the arrows continued to fall. With Pneuma flooded into Alacrity, those arrows seemed to slow in midair, just enough for her to dance aside from one after another. But she would never dodge them all while fighting so many foes. Not with her allies already broken, dying.

Instead, Artemis glanced over her shoulder, gauging the distance across the gulley. Fifty feet, maybe. An almost impossible jump, but with Alacrity for speed, Potency lending strength to her legs, and Lightness reducing her effective weight ... Quick breaths, and she broke into a run, casting aside her bow. All that mattered now was escaping this ambush. Wind raced past her, tore at her clothing, tugged her hair. Her sandals brushed the edge and she leapt, streaking skyward as her limbs flailed in empty air.

She'd duck into a roll and then—

The instant before she landed, towering Atlas himself rose from behind a boulder to greet her, in the very spot she had selected to land. For a heartbeat Artemis gaped at the impossibility of him knowing where she would choose to jump. Sheer bad luck on her part, she supposed. With little choice, she made her roll, coming up beside him and narrowly dancing out of Atlas's reach when he lunged for her.

Another man rose up, catching her arm. Artemis's elbow took him in the mouth, shattering his jaw and sending him careening backward. A dozen men now closed in around her, each bearing a spear or xiphos, all ready for her. Atlas lunged, a mountain of muscle, fist a descending meteor, even with Alacrity slowing her perception of the blow. She couldn't imagine how fast it would have seemed otherwise.

Artemis bent backward, twisting under the blow, then rolled between Atlas's legs. The Titan's fist splattered the head of one of his own men in a rain of gore, the mortal's body not even slowing his momentum. Artemis kicked her legs into both of his knees, sending him stumbling as she yanked free her knife and went for his jugular.

Incoming spear thrusts forced her backward before she could finish the job. Artemis twisted aside from the spears, caught one by the haft, and jerked it forward, slamming the wood into the man's helmet. More and more men closed in, thrusting and slashing at her with spears and swords. Even with Alacrity, it took all she had to dance among them, evading blow after blow, knocking a few aside with her palms. Her knife bit again and again, severing hamstrings, snaking into armpits, and finding gaps between breastplates.

Blood drenched her. The thundering beats of her heart threatened to shatter her ribcage.

Atlas snared one of his own men between himself and Artemis and hurled the man over his shoulder like dirty laundry. Artemis lunged in, intent to wedge her knife into his gut and spill his bowels over the dust. Her blade clanked off his abdomen as though she'd struck solid rock.

Realising her mistake, she leapt backward. Not fast enough. Atlas's fist clipped her shoulder, even as she flooded Pneuma into Steadfastness. The blow spun her around and sent her tumbling to the ground.

Roaring like a lion, Atlas jumped into the air and slammed both fists straight down toward her. Artemis kicked off the legs of another of his men, sending herself skidding over rocks, toward the precipice. The Titan landed with the force of an earthquake. Stone shattered beneath his blow, a spiderwebbing of cracks the only warning before the cliff crumbled, sending the lot of them tumbling down into the gulley.

Flailing as she fell, Artemis bounded off a chunk of falling stone the size of a horse, flipping away from the landslide. Even with Steadfastness, the impact jarred her. A torrent of dust and debris rained down upon her, choking her, blinding her. Her Perspicacity alerted her to an approaching assailant, though she saw no one and the smothering cloud clogged her sinuses.

Had Atlas somehow known the cliff might collapse and planted ambushers *here*? It was impossible. And yet, a spear darted past her head, a hair from her face. An instant later, she recognised Pleione, Atlas's wife. In other circumstances, Artemis might have tried to reason with her. One more Titan whose presence might aid either side in this war. One more family torn apart.

Just like she'd lost Aidos.

Pleione lunged with that spear once more. Artemis caught the shaft and stepped in, her blade disemboweling the Nymph in a stroke. Pleione toppled to her knees, even as more warriors closed in on Artemis.

Not bothering to fight further, Artemis dodged backward, then broke into a mad sprint, dashing amid the carnage through the darkening wasteland.

How could he have planned all this so perfectly?

Lightness allowed her to jump onto the cliff and run up it far enough to leap topside once more. She crested the rise, landed in a roll, and flooded all she had left into Alacrity and Lightness, racing off into the dark of night. Thoth lend that Atlas had no further traps laid for her.

ALL THAT NIGHT and for days more she trekked, pushing hard to make for the garrison at Ilium. And trying—failing—to not imagine Aidos's face, the arrow jutting from her brow. A thousand childhood memories of her cousin mingled into an indistinct ocean of sentiment. Death would forever tinge the sea of joys with shadows of despair.

When at last she came nigh to Ilium, she spied it from too far off, heralded by dozens of plumes of smoke mingling in the sky above. Though she knew what she would find, Artemis pressed on until the breached wall came into sight.

Great chunks of the cyclopean barrier lay in piles of debris, and beyond lay fields of ashes where homes and markets had flourished not long ago. The stench of charnel hordes suffocated her long before she spotted the heaps of bodies thrown into the pyres. Ouranid archers patrolled what remained of the broken walls, while others had posted watches at the breaches.

Phoebe's—her own grandmother's—flag crinkled in the breeze.

With a groan, Artemis cast a last look back at the smouldering ruin of Ilium. Twice in two years it had fallen, and the dead went uncounted, crushed beneath Titan heels. Had any of Morpheus's garrison escaped the slaughter? With Phoebe's forces occupying the ruins—and others yet hunting her—she could afford no time to investigate.

She had to get back to Athyras. At its narrowest, the strait was only a couple of miles across. Filled with Pneuma, Artemis could make the swim, though it was wider here in the south. Maybe she could have still managed it, had she not so depleted her reserves engaging Atlas. To have any chance now, she needed to rest, preferably beneath the moonlight to breathe in more Moon-tinged Pneuma.

How had they fallen so completely into Atlas's trap? How?

No answers came to her as she slunk through the woodlands, keeping well back from Ilium. She needed to find the point closest to Athyras on the far side of the shore. Low and silent, she crept on, for hours, her stamina returning with painful lethargy.

At last, in the dark, she settled in, planning to await the rising moon. A familiar scent wafted from upwind, though it took Artemis a moment to place it. Prometheus? Here?

She'd had few interactions with Hekate's father before, but she knew his scent. Keeping to a crouch, she edged forward, and sure enough, a shape in a small rowboat beckoned to her, even in the darkness.

A surge of relief shot through Artemis's veins, leaving her light-headed. Had an ally really come for her? Desperation won out over caution, and she rose, breaking into a trot to reach him. As she drew nigh, Prometheus hopped over the edge and set to pushing the boat back into the water. Artemis's sandals splashed in the shallows, then she was inside, and Prometheus vaulted back in as well and set to the oars.

"What the ...? How did you ...?" She grunted. Her mind refused to settle upon her abrupt change in fortunes. Everything had gone so wrong and now, hope dangled in front of her, unbelievable. Ephemeral, certain to flit away if she blinked. "How did you know I'd be here?" she managed.

"I'm an Oracle."

Artemis chewed on her lip a moment, mulling that over. She *had* heard about his pyromancy but hadn't really considered it would provide him such accurate information. "Why are you helping me?"

The Titan's sapphire eyes glinted in the moonlight. There was something strange about him, no doubt, an alienness to his scent, a disconcerting air to his manner. And those eyes held wisdom beyond Man or Titan, she had no doubt, though she could not have explained it. "Centuries ago, you saved my daughter from a terrible fate when no one else was there."

Had Hekate sent him to her now? Had her dreams revealed Artemis's plight? "Did you know what would befall Ilium?" Would befall Aidos?

"Prescience is never perfect, Artemis."

As their vessel pulled further from the shore, she dared release a pent-up breath. Had she made it after all? "All this is gratitude?"

"You are one of the finest warriors on our side. Perhaps it is necessity. Perhaps Ananke."

"Then why not rescue me sooner?" Why not save her cousin?

The silence deepened as he watched her, taking on an almost physical weight. Did he see something within her? Her skin crawled as though he glimpsed the periphery of her soul. "What do you know of Oracles?" he asked when the quiet had grown so painful she'd been about to speak without having even formed a question.

"I ... My brother studied with Themis at Delphi, but I have no gift for such things. My grandfather, Koios, though, is an Oracle and ..."

Oh. What a fool she was. If Prometheus could locate the exact spot along the strait in which Artemis would shelter, perhaps Koios too could have known where Artemis would plan her ambush. Where Apollon would send his troops. Even where Artemis would flee the ambush. Every move they made, Phoebe and Atlas seemed ahead of them. Because Grandmother's husband saw the future, and Artemis had not accounted for such things. Apollon's gift, such as it was, did not avail him in war, and so she had not even considered that stronger Oracles might outwit them thus.

The wonder then became not how well Atlas had planned his trap, but that she had slipped it at all.

Prometheus nodded, seeming to read her thoughts off her face.

Thoth's moonlit cock! Artemis punched the deck, rocking their little boat. "Hekate says Kronos has Oracle Mirrors that let him see things, too. She thought it was only a matter of time before he found our refuge, and so she's been seeking out other potential bastions we could occupy, but his forces oft strike at them before we establish a significant presence. They see where she plans to go before her people ever get there ..." Artemis paused. "So why haven't Kronos or Koios found Athyras?"

"Think it through."

She wracked her mind, but naught came, and she spread her hands.

"Oracles see the shape of time, a glimpse of the Tapestry of Fate." Prometheus paused in rowing, hands resting on his knees. "Thus, we cannot behold aught that might change that Tapestry—it would be paradoxical, seeing a future that might not exist."

"A possible future," she said.

He shook his head. "The pleasant lie to smother the unpalatable truth, that our actions were writ, not even from the moment of our birth, but from the first breath taken by the first Man to ever walk beneath the endless sky. Gazing into the future or looking at the past makes no difference. Perhaps the whole of the Tapestry was woven at the very moment Man emerged from the dark."

Artemis shivered. It was just the chill autumn breeze over the waters. Certainly not his intimations that her actions were all written, that her will accounted for naught. "Suppose I believe what you're saying. Suppose I grant that there's only one future and you see it." It made sense, she guessed, given the abilities Prometheus and Koios had demonstrated. "What does that have to do with my grandfather not finding Athyras?"

"If two opposing Oracles beheld the same events, one might manage to take steps to change those events. Both Oracles would have then foreseen a non-existent future and unleashed a paradox. It doesn't happen because it cannot happen. At best, only the stronger Oracle can bear witness, and only seeing a future already accounting for their having beheld it."

In the moonlight, she watched him, understanding creeping up on her. "You're the stronger Oracle. They can't see Athyras because you're here, and they cannot spy on you. None of their visions reveal *you*, and thus nowhere adjacent to you." Now, she glanced over his shoulder, toward Athyras. What if he had gone too far out? What if, in coming to save her, he had exposed Athyras?

"It's just over the water," he assured her, having once again read her thoughts with stomach-churning ease.

One worry soothed, at least. "We can't beat them." The words tumbled from her, and she knew them for true the moment she spoke them. "We cannot defeat the Ouranids because my grandfather will forever remain a step ahead ... unless you were with our troops.

And you cannot leave Athyras, for any length, because doing so exposes us to our foes."

Prometheus said naught, but then, what was there to say? She knew well enough they had reached an insurmountable impasse. Maybe, if Apollon was a stronger Oracle, they could have thwarted their foes, but it mattered little now.

Did Hekate know what they faced? Did Zeus? Would the prince even care?

"You have much to think on," Prometheus said.

Oh ... Artemis had only one thing to think on: death. Sooner or later, they would all die.

11

PERSEUS

627 Bronze Age

Once, in their long voyages across the Thalassa, Pandora had told Perseus how Akrisios's brother Proitos had helped her, if only out of loathing for his twin. Still, the man was Perseus's uncle, and so it was to his son, Megapenthes, Perseus's cousin, that he left the kingdom of Argos. Fitting enough, he supposed, given that Akrisios had driven Proitos from Argos years back.

Thus, with carts laden with a share of the Argosian treasury—only what was fair, Perseus was certain—he and Andromeda and a few retainers had headed inland, among the slopes of central Elládos, into the unclaimed wilds between Argos and Korinth. The way Perseus saw it, if Fate had spoilt his claim to Argos, well he would see Andromeda a queen of elsewhere. Only, most cities he knew of weren't, in fact, taking auditions for the roles of king and queen, more was the pity.

So, he'd picked out a tall hill surrounded by woods and bounded by a wide stream and set his people to building a fortified wall. Ah, he wished he could say the wall was but to protect the livestock from wolves, but in truth, their new home lay not so far south from Minyan lands, and he'd rather discourage raids with a show of strength.

"Mykenai," Andromeda said when he asked what they should name it. She had their newborn son, Sthenelos, cradled in her arms while she surveyed the work alongside Perseus. "After the abundant mushrooms that sprung up alongside the stream."

"Ah," he said. "Hmm. If I'd known you wished to live in a mushroom, I'd have rather built a hut in the woods instead of founding a citadel for a palace."

"Maybe I want a palace *and* a hut in the woods, depending on my mood."

"Sure. Sometimes I want trout, sometimes grouper." He shrugged. "I can't much argue with it."

No, and Argosian drachmae paid workers aplenty, while others flocked to his new town perhaps seeking a fresh start themselves. Fate, or life maybe, made fools of many, it well seemed. And Perseus could offer them refuge. Or at least mushrooms.

A DECADE LATER, and the walls of Mykenai were among the strongest in Elládos, or so Perseus told anyone who asked—and a good many who did not. The grand palace he had built for Andromeda housed their many children, and now he and his wife reclined before the sacred hearth, watching those children chase each other about the four fresco-painted columns of the megaron. Well, all save Sthenelos, who watched over his younger siblings like a guardian spirit, silent as he drifted around the fringes.

Elektryon and Alkaios dominated the games, as always, with Heleios, Mestor, and Gorgophone giggling, attempting to follow the lead of their big brothers. Laughter, pure and untrammelled, rang through the hall, and Perseus could not have imagined a greater blessing.

"No, no," Elektryon said, wagging his finger at them. "Mestor and Heleios are the Argosian phalanx! Gorgophone is the abducted queen they have to rescue."

"But I wanna rescue them," the five-year-old girl whined.

"You can't rescue boys, you're a girl!"

"They're smaller than me!"

"*Papa!*" cried five voices all at once.

Perseus started to look to his wife for help, but Andromeda's hands shot up. "Oh, I can't rescue you. I'm a *girl*."

With an affected shrug, Perseus rose, drew upon his Pneumatikoi, and raced forward like the wind, snatching up his three youngest in his arms and spinning them around. "Now you *all* need rescuing!"

Twice more he spun round, then faltered on spotting the Titan watching from the shadow of one of the columns, her grey eyes assessing everything in the palace, her expression unreadable.

Setting the children down, Perseus took a knee. "Goddess Athene."

"Walk with me, Perseus."

A twinge shot through him, a sudden fear she would again ask him to undertake some grand quest, as if the slaying of two monsters had not made enough story for one man. Any more, and it would start to seem like bragging, and he'd have to worry on people thinking his tales embellished. Ah, the burdens of heroism.

But one did not deny a goddess.

While they walked, Athene eyed the frescoes bedecking the walls. Perseus had hired Athenian painters for the designs and, naturally, took great pride in their epic depictions, ranging from his own slaying of Ketus to the famed Gigantomachy, which, in fact, showed Athene fighting Gigantes. Only a slight hesitation in her step indicated she had noticed her own presence on the wall, and then she led him out, past the vestibule, and into the gardens.

A flock of doves had settled upon the olive trees, and a peacock roamed the yard, strutting with understandable pride in its plumage. If Perseus had a rainbow coming out of his arse, he'd prance a bit too.

"Time has blessed you at last, Perseus," Athene said, eyeing the peacock as though it might charge her in defence of its territory. "Your children shine radiant and your wife looks on you with genuine love."

"Requited, I assure you." Andromeda's smile had become the measure by which he judged his life. With a look, she could still send his heart soaring or plummeting.

"Then you must count yourself among the most fortunate of Men." Ah, he did at that. "Now, Mykenai has begun to earn itself a name amid the poleis of Elládos."

"I cannot help but fear the sweetness of your lure, Goddess. I'd prefer not to swim straight into the trap and find it shut behind me."

The Titan lady drew up short. "I'm not trying to trap you. I've come to offer you advice. A prophecy, if you will."

Ah, and Perseus wanted another prophecy about as much as he wanted a mule with runny shits traipsing about his bedchamber. "Do tell."

"Choose your son Elektryon as heir to your kingdom, Perseus."

"Err, my second-born? That ought to sit well with Sthenelos. Should I actually instruct them to make war upon one another or just let nature take its course?"

Now, Athene levelled her heavy gaze upon him, its weight paralysing. "If I said they would fight, would it prevent you from following my counsel?"

"It might," Perseus admitted. "Not that I am not grateful for all you did for me, Goddess, but I cannot see my own children at one another's throats."

"And if I will guarantee Sthenelos will never raise hand or blade against Elektryon?"

All he could offer her was an overwrought shrug, spreading his hands. A part of him—one he'd never dare show her—wanted to demand by what right she came here, intent to meddle in the destinies of his children. While he might owe his life and that of Andromeda to her aid, did he bequeath such a debt to another generation? "Why does this matter to you?"

The worn, almost battered, expression that overtook her made her seem too human. To behold an Olympian thus, wracked with doubt and disconcertion, sent his stomach burbling. "The future is not always clear," she admitted, voice far away as though she spoke to someone else. "Not always, but I can say, along a certain path, Elektryon will marry a descendant of my own bloodline, and their line will culminate in the birth of the greatest hero in the history of Elládos."

Perseus rubbed his hands together as if wiping away the whole thing. "Ah, well, that won't do, now, will it? I can't have my descendant outdoing me. I've worked rather hard to earn my way into the bards' tales, you know."

"Do this thing for me, Perseus. That, and return to me the adamant sword and shield that I might bestow them upon the boy when he comes of age."

Of course, in the end, he'd not deny her aught, nor deny the land a hero. How could he think to do so? How, when he did owe some much of the life he'd won to her? Without Athene, he'd not have defeated Medusa, much less found and rescued Andromeda.

But, behind the foppish bravado, a niggling fear did remain. "Will I be forgotten, then?"

Athene laughed at that. "Men will tell stories of your deeds for as long as the stars glint in the night sky."

Ah. That, he supposed, would probably do.

12

KIRKE

625 Bronze Age

"*B*ecause he drew something from within me," Kirke said to Phaethusa while they lay atop a grass-dappled hill, watching the cavalcade of clouds swirl overhead. "Because, for millennia, I have wilted, and for a moment, with Glafkos, I felt I could bloom."

"You sound as if you would define yourself by the affections of a man. Or male, rather, given the creature isn't even a person."

Kirke huffed. "It's not about defining myself as aught, Phaethusa. I don't need to define myself because I don't owe anyone a definition of me. It's ... it's about having spent so long alone I have plumbed the depths of myself and thought I knew all that lurked there. And then, in the mirror of another person, I saw something *more*. I mean, have you never loved someone for how they made you feel, even if they did not return your feelings?"

The silence stretched until the other woman sighed.

"You have, I know," Kirke said. Even now, she to ask herself if the other woman had a point. If her supposed love for Glafkos arose not for the mer himself, but for the emotions his voice had wakened within her. But did it matter? "I'm no expert on, love, Hyperion knows. I've had lovers enough, men and women, but none who ..."

"Endured?"

"Erato once said something about it. I mean, I don't remember her exact words." Kirke's days at the Muses College seemed so long ago. "But something like 'love feeds itself.' Right? So then what matter whence it originates? Maybe it starts with lust for lots of people, but then it becomes something else, and if it's reflected—"

"It's not reflected," Phaethusa cut in. "That's the problem. Glafkos loves Skylla, he came to you for a love potion for her."

A knife driven into her flesh. "Yeah." It was, after all, an infatuation she ought to let slide. But, by Hyperion's shining arsehole, was Kirke tired of losing. Sometimes, it felt like she had lost everything she'd ever wanted in her life. Everything she had striven for had come up a failure. Or maybe her true downward spiral had come that day when Artemis and Nike convinced Helios to surrender his throne to Nyx-damned Zeus. "I want him. Skylla doesn't."

And Skylla truly was a haughty bitch; Kirke had met her once, and the only thing she'd been able to think was, now she understood what Athene had done to Medusa.

Phaethusa whistled. "Then the only thing for it is to tell him. If you think your honest regard for him enough, if it can engender love in return, then tell him how you feel. If he refuses you, you will still find yourself no worse off than you are now, and at least you'll have your answer."

She was right, of course.

AT THE MOMENT, *she and Medea—who shared her Heliad eyes, though with dark hair—knelt in the Qulha Palace garden cultivating herbs, as they so oft had done in the past two years. That the girl had already appre-*

hended the potency of moly boded well—or perhaps ill—for her future as an alchemist.

"With this we could brew something to change shapes," Medea mused, fingers shaping loam up around the root to ensure its ideal environment. "Could we become birds?"

"Changing your own shape?" Kirke almost laughed. "I have no idea what that would do to your mind. Suppose it became that of an avian? Would you know enough to be able to change back?"

"There are legends of wizards and witches taking animal forms."

"Yeah, true. And maybe they could, or maybe they were shifters merged with Moon spirits. But if the former, we don't know how it was done. Do you want to test such a question?"

Medea huffed, pushing her hair from her face with the back of her wrist. "I wanted to fly."

"Better to brew a drug that makes you feel like you're flying. Yeah, I've had my share of those."

SOMETIMES, the dreams meant naught. Times and places cast in the shadowy haze of sleep, faces she could not recognise. Now, though, she knew the spot, if not the person. And it seemed she must one day return to Kolchis, where her brother had built Qulha.

The dread of it, of facing what she had wrought in that polis, it shot through Kirke, leaving her ragged and worn thin. Even here, beyond the Elládosi lands, still, her past haunted her, her failures stalking a hairsbreadth behind her fleeing sandals. The reminder that she would have naught for herself, for the Moirai offered her no succour.

When Glafkos next visited, appearing from the sea at night, water streaming down his silver flesh, it was Kirke who hefted the amphora of wine. The mer sloshed his way to shore, cocked his head at the decanter, then plopped down onto the sands in a heap.

Settling down beside him, Kirke took a sip of wine. Well, another sip, as she *might* have indulged in a few to settle her nerves while awaiting his arrival. Maybe a few dozen. Was the amphora feeling light already? She passed it to him, hoping he wouldn't notice.

The mer threw back a quick swig before setting it down to fix her with his onyx gaze. "Did you make it?"

"Uh, no. But, I mean, I wanted to talk to you about that first." A clamminess had built up in her now, had her shifting in discomfort. There was sand under her khiton. How did it always wind up under her clothes? "What if ... eh, shit."

"What if shit?"

"No, no, no shit. Um ... fuck."

A smile creased his lips. "Which is it? Shit or fuck? Most find one more pleasant than the other."

Kirke huffed. "Now listen here, fish god, I'm trying to manage something profound, yeah? Shut the gills and just let me ..." She threw up her hands. "Look, Skylla doesn't even care about you, yeah? But I wouldn't spurn you. I would choose to be with you without need for any draughts to bemuse my mind. Wouldn't you rather have the woman who chooses you of her own free will?"

Glafkos's eyes nictitated in silent reminder of the alien nature of the creature before her. But Kirke didn't care. By every last Primordial, she wanted something real, something hers. Something ... The mer worked his shark teeth a moment, the incipient grimace rising on his face making his answer plain.

Damn it. The urge to dive into the sea and let it swallow her rose up in Kirke. Running now might only redouble her shame, but damn, it was tempting.

"You may speak truth, Kirke, and yet, trees would grow upon the seabed and seaweed upon the mountains before I could turn my heart from Skylla. The heart bends to no master save its own whims, giving little care for what is good for it."

She doesn't love you! Kirke wanted to scream. The noxious Nymph cared for no one save herself, but Fate had given her such beauty Glafkos could not see past it.

"Will you help me?" Glafkos implored, dark eyes shining in the moonlight. "I must have her. I long to caress those breasts, to dive between those thighs."

Must have her? For all his protestation of love, that sounded more akin to unbridled lust to Kirke.

Ravaged, she answered. "Come back tomorrow."

DESPITE ALL THAT HAD HAPPENED, despite having given over her attempts to elevate Man using Nectar, Kirke always brought the ingredients along with her. A small bit of dried moly, the other herbs and reagents, just in case she needed to brew something essential. Not that she'd imagined using it for love potions.

But then, the moly, mixed just so, would have an additional reaction.

A punishment for one born with too much beauty, who stole from others even without trying, and a worse punishment for Glafkos, who would rather force love than accept it given with open arms. If he used drugs to draw an otherwise unwilling woman to his bed, did that make him a rapist?

Such thoughts rumbled around in Kirke's mind whilst waiting for him by the seashore. The ceramic phial at her side felt hot, as if her own perfidy could sear through her satchel and scorch her treacherous flesh.

Didn't he deserve this?

Didn't they both?

Maybe they did. When Glafkos came, she gave him the phial, then turned from him without a word, lest her face give her away.

She was doing it again, giving in to spite and bitterness, even after what had transpired with Pikus. But Hyperion, did some men not *deserve* it?

HANDS SEIZED her as she passed around the bend of the Thrinakian manse. With strength Kirke could never have matched, Phaethusa hefted her up by her biceps and shoved her against the marble side of the building.

The Heliad leaned in close enough her breath warmed Kirke's face. "What in Tartarus have you done?"

"You'll have to be more specific," Kirke said, squirming though it little availed her. "I mean, just now I was picking violets in the meadow. Perhaps I was a bit rougher than strictly necessary, I admit, but I figured, if you're going to yank something out by the roots, it's a bit late for tenderness."

"You turned Skylla into a monster!"

"Oh. Hmm, I think she was already rather a monster, what with walking around with her nose so high in the air she seems to want to sniff the clouds."

Phaethusa rolled her eyes. "She grew to the size of a colossus, her legs turned into sea serpents, and giant dog heads popped out of her crotch."

That might have been a larger change than Kirke had sought. "So ... no one's diving in between those thighs then, huh?"

Her sister released her but raised an accusing finger in front of Kirke's face. "You have turned a Nymph into a monster one would assume born from Echidna herself, and you make light of it."

Kirke decided it best to avert her gaze, her shame real, even if it brought with it a guilty thrill at the sheer expanse of her power. In creating the centaurs, she had made monsters with enough control to ensure they did not destroy a city. Now, without bridling her Art, she had created something legendary. A monster bards would sing of to inspire dread in generations to come.

Worse, perhaps, than Skylla deserved, true, but still, a part of her tittered at what she had done.

"What is wrong with you?" Phaethusa demanded, apparently having read some of those thoughts upon Kirke's face. "Setting aside the *how*, Kirke, what would possess you to take such steps? Jealousy?"

When she looked back at her half-sister, it wasn't rage that limned her face. Wrath she could have weathered. Instead, she saw such honest bemusement Kirke found herself stammering, unable to form any coherent excuse.

Such regard broke her, and Kirke ducked under the other woman's arm and fled. Because Phaethusa was right, and *Kirke* was the greater monster than Skylla. So she ran and ran, all the way to the small harbour.

Thrinakia had become a prison, a cell forcing her to peer into reflections of her shame within the eyes of those around her.

Kirke was ... broken.

13

ARTEMIS

2398 Golden Age

*H*aggard and worn, blood still crusted upon her knuckles and imbruing her khiton, Artemis slunk back into Athyras. In the four years since they had lost their foothold on Phrygia, she had lost more friends than she could count. Epiphron was the latest, fallen not fifty miles from here in a pointless skirmish over land Apollon could never have held.

Maybe Epiphron had not been close with her—certainly not as close as the man seemed to want, though he'd never said it aloud—but Artemis had shared wine with him around a hundred campfires. She had listened to his counsel so oft ignored by her twin, had heard his stories of his home in Knosós and his travels in Kemet, and had known him well.

Perses, Aidos's own father, had split Epiphron's skull with an axe, spilling the sum of his life along with blood and brains. A death that had bought them naught, had amounted to naught, save a body interred beneath a nameless hill.

Eris, one of the other survivors of the battle, shouldered past Artemis as they passed through the gate in the palisade. "Time to find a man," the Titan said with a salacious, if unconvincing, wink. Eris always insisted on drawing married men into affairs, said the fear of getting caught enhanced the experience. Artemis couldn't say she much approved, but then again, this was a woman who thought a scorpion in someone's bed counted as a 'prank.'

Artemis would have bet a talent or more Eris was the one who'd painted that giant cock on the side of Ares's tent, along with the words, 'send more.'

Either way, Artemis didn't offer any response to the woman's suggestion, instead making her way toward the edge of town. Prometheus maintained a house on the far side, just inside the palisade, with a modest yard. In that yard, little Athene studied beneath a cypress tree, hunched over a sheet of vellum.

The eight-year-old girl looked up when Artemis approached, fair leapt to her feet, and flung her arms around Artemis's waist heedless of the dried blood. "Auntie!"

Artemis patted the girl's hair. "Your mother is inside?"

"Yup. But I was bored, so Prometheus gave me something to read." From the way she spoke, the child didn't seem to realise Prometheus was her grandfather. "It's about birds. I like birds. My favourite bird is an eagle. My stepmother likes peacocks, but she said I can't have one. That's all right, because eagles are magnificent. If I'm good, maybe I can have an eagle."

Artemis kissed the top of Athene's head before disentangling herself. "What about bears?"

"I think those smell bad. Don't they?"

Artemis shrugged. After going to war, everyone smelled bad.

Inside, she found Hekate and Prometheus sitting upon a rug before the hearth, cast in writhing shadows by the undulating flames, each giving the impression of a perfect sculpture. Both their eyes glinted in the firelight, his crystal blue, hers lambent gold.

Though neither Hekate nor Prometheus invited her, Artemis joined them on the rug, legs folded. "We're going to lose."

"Perhaps a subject for Zeus," Hekate said, voice laced with the unspeakable weariness of a woman haunted. How long had she seemed thus? Was it sometime around the sacking of Ilium? Hekate had withdrawn into herself, the dark circles rimming her eyes now a permanent aspect of her visage.

"We're losing because my grandfather sees every move we make before we even form the plan. Our troops face unending ambushes, morale fractures, and we lose nine out of ten engagements. That they have not discovered this place is the only reason our rebellion yet endures, and still, skirmishes grow ever closer to Athyras." While she spoke, she kept her gaze fixed upon Prometheus.

Only the slight crease of his face revealed any change in his expression, but she had little doubt he followed her implication. Four years since Koios had begun lending his Oracular insight to their enemies, and in such time, they had lost again and again. While her grandfather could not have personally overseen every encounter, she could not otherwise explain how things had turned so dark for them.

"We're all going to die soon," she said when neither Prometheus nor even Hekate spoke.

"I have naught more to give to this cause," Hekate said with a shudder. "I gave Zeus the lightning, and you cannot imagine the price I paid for it."

Perhaps not, though Artemis had perceived that something haunted Hekate in the days that had followed. A shadow had settled over her, an impression of a woman wasting away, despite her immortality. "You're not the one I need to act now," Artemis said, looking back at Prometheus.

"I suspect you do not understand the cost of what you seek," Prometheus said at last. "That I side with his son against him at all must rankle Kronos almost beyond endurance. Should I raise my hand in direct opposition to the Ouranid League, he will take the betrayal as so complete we cannot predict how he might react."

What was this? "You *already* completely betrayed the Ouranid League, years ago. If you do not act to counter Koios now, we will lose all we have left. You fear they will find this place without you here, blocking his visions? Perhaps that's truth, but they'll find it sooner or later, regardless, and at this rate, we shall have no one left to defend it when that happens. Even blessed with lightning, Zeus himself has lost battle after battle. We cannot overcome a foe who sees the future." She hesitated. Something she had not thought of for so long forced itself to the front of her mind. "Koios told me, centuries ago, that one of us would kill the other. It has to happen now, Prometheus. If I hunt him down and slay him, maybe Zeus and my brother can still turn the war back to our favour. But the time for such things grows thin. And I cannot catch him unawares on my own."

The older Titan turned his gaze to the hearth, silent for a moment that stretched too long for Artemis's comfort. "You'd have me accompany you on a mission to assassinate a man I have known for long years."

"We. Are. Losing this war. No other choice remains to us, save perhaps surrender and throwing ourselves upon the mercy of the League."

Hekate scoffed, the sound emotionless and faraway. "They will have no mercy." A shudder wracked her. "Papa ... Go with her. This has to end. After all we have paid for it, it must end."

Prometheus frowned. "So be it."

Though Artemis had feared Prometheus would not share her aptitude for stealth, the way he clung to the shadows as they stalked the periphery of Delphi bespoke one well familiar with such arts. Hekate's father, as always, remained brimming with surprises.

Having learnt Koios had taken to dwelling in Delphi, Artemis's brother had insisted on coming to watch her back. Unlike Prometheus, his skills as a scout had profound limits, and Artemis rounded on him well outside the city. "Keep to the wilds and watch for us, in case we need retreat from heavy resistance."

From the sullen look he shot her, Apollon knew well enough why she didn't want him accompanying her.

Themis ruled here, and while she had remained neutral in the war, if she harboured Koios, that neutrality had faltered. If her forces discovered them before Artemis got her shot at her grandfather, all of this was for naught.

"He must have come here to rarify his Sight," Apollon said, voice leaving little doubt he wished he'd bothered to do the same.

"How?" Artemis asked.

"The Old One, Python. The drakon oozes a potent liquid that expands the mind."

Prometheus grunted. "There is a price for that, as well, Heliad."

Apollon paid him no heed. "I always knew Themis held back from me, but until now, I had not thought she would have given to our foes either. This has to be how Grandfather's Sight became so strong as to thwart us at every turn."

Which left Artemis wondering, if Koios consumed enough of this drakon essence, would his Sight overcome the blind spot Prometheus created? Did he already know she was coming for him? The thought sent a chill shooting through her. "Let's get this done."

Apollon snatched her wrist. "Be careful, sister."

His outburst of emotion left her speechless, able only to nod in acknowledgment. This wasn't how they related to one another. Not ever. Had the loss of so many immortals gotten to him?

She pulled away and, along with Prometheus, crept forward toward the mountain slope upon which the settlement rested. The Firebringer had assured her Koios would spend the night in Themis's palace above, not down in the catacombs carving through the mountain. For which Artemis offered silent thanks to Thoth. She quite did *not* want to encounter ancient drakons, given the choice.

Cyclopean walls surrounded the city, well watched from above the path leading up, but less guarded from among the nigh-impassible rocky escarpment overhead. It was toward this rugged terrain she led Prometheus, the other Titan climbing with practiced ease. Full of surprises and mysteries, indeed.

"How old are you?" she whispered. "Is it true you saw the Time of Nyx?"

Prometheus paused, his eyes glinting in the moonlight. "Old enough I had other names before this one. Old enough to have seen things I might rather have not. Old *enough* ..."

Artemis blew out a breath. "The way you spoke before, it sounded almost as though you considered Kronos a friend."

"That did not sound a question."

It was, but his tone and scent both made clear he had little wish to answer it, and Artemis could not press. They each pursued these paths for their own reasons, she supposed. She climbed on until at last coming to a precipice that jutted out over a declivity on the back side of Delphi. The gap between here and the wall was maybe forty feet.

She turned to Prometheus to ask whether he could clear it, but the Titan nodded before she could give voice to the question. In the distance, on the cyclopean wall, she could see braziers burning, with a handful of warriors huddled close to them, drinking in warmth and light. And spoiling their night vision.

Once certain no one would see them, she flooded Pneuma to her Pneumatikoi and took a running leap, soaring over the open air. A weightless moment she flew before tumbling down atop the wall. An instant later, Prometheus dropped down behind her. She spared him a glance, and he pointed ahead, to a small palace upon the acropolis.

Keeping low, Artemis scurried to the edge of the wall, vaulted it, and dropped into a shadow-drenched alley below. Her ursine senses made a simple matter of avoiding those few inhabitants still awake, so she crept forward until she reached the acropolis slope, then scrambled up it.

A peristyle rimmed Themis's palace, watched by a pair of languid warriors. A burst of speed carried her to the back of a column, and she pressed up flat against it, listening for any sign the men had noticed her. When none came, she darted to another column, then another, and finally around the bend. Windows forty feet up let light inside and might be just wide enough for her to slip through.

Prometheus pressed close to her to whisper in her ear. "Do not harm Themis."

Who was she to him? An old lover? A friend? "I only want Koios." For now.

"He is ... in her bedchamber."

It took a moment for that to settle in, then Artemis glowered. Grandmother would grieve to hear her husband died in another woman's bed. Still ... maybe such a shame befitted the crime, and either way, Artemis could not afford to waste the chance.

"You are not to kill her, Artemis," Prometheus warned once more.

A grim nod, and she flooded her Pneuma to Lightness, then dashed up the wall, grabbing the windowsill. A heave pulled her into the gap, and from up there, she scanned the megaron. A handful of simmering braziers lit the room, and beyond, moonlight spilled in from the courtyard. The relief-carved door ahead must have marked Themis's own chambers.

A handful of dozing men reclined below, so she didn't drop down. Instead, she bounced from the wall to an interior column, kicked off it to another, and thus crossed the courtyard to land feet from Themis's door.

She tried the handle and found it unlocked, then slipped inside, a ghost in the shadows. Two Titans slept side by side, both naked. Pangs of doubt and regret shot through Artemis as she crept up to the bedside, pulling her knife. Her grandfather ...

Someday one of us, my dear, shall cause the death of the other.

And how many had died because he turned his visions toward murdering Zeus's rebels? She tried to conjure up Aidos's face to steady her hand, but still, it trembled. Themis shifted, groaning. Artemis lunged, caught Koios's forehead with one hand, and jerked the blade over his throat with the other.

Golden ichor gurgled from the gouge as he shot awake, flailing.

Themis, too, tried to leap up, but Artemis hopped atop her, pressing the knife to her throat. The Oracle stiffened, dead still, her eyes watching her lover bleed out two feet away. It was not fear Artemis saw before her, but resignation.

Prometheus had begged Artemis not to kill Themis.

"When Tethys lost Thebes, she quit Elládos forever," Artemis said, unable to stop her own shaken gaze from drifting to her dying grandfather. "Your oath now, to do the same. Leave these lands, and you can keep your life."

Something unreadable passed over the Oracle's face, as though she had foreseen this moment but not apprehended its context until just now. Perhaps that was the burden Oracles always bore.

"I swear to leave Elládos and never return," Themis said, voice stiff, though her eyes held only resignation.

"Swear not to send anyone after me."

"I swear."

Artemis rose, looking once more to Koios. Now still in eternal repose. One moment, an immortal Titan, her own blood, and now, he had become a weight soiling the bed.

"Kinslaying comes with a price," Themis warned, perhaps judging Artemis's thoughts.

"Everything does." There were always prices.

She fled back into the night.

14

PANDORA

1600 Silver Age

When at last they crested the onyx wall, gasping for breath and hacking out wet coughs, Pandora and Herakles found the wall itself too seemed alive, fleshy beneath their sandals. The top of the wall stretched out hundreds of feet more into a gloom that seemed cloying, leaving a sickening aftertaste in Pandora's mouth. Her body ached to pitch onto her knees and retch, but the thought of touching the pliant ground with her hands only further disgusted her.

No doubt the demigod felt the same, for he gripped her arm, steadying her once more. "Let us ... have done with this." The man turned, spitting out a wad of ash-blackened phlegm.

In the dark ahead, a figure rose up, chained to the wall and concealed by the shadows.

Prometheus? Exhaustion forgotten, Pandora dashed for him, paying no mind to her faltering stumbles. Her torchlight sent the dark skittering away like a nest of agitated serpents, albeit only by a few feet. It ought to have illumined further, but the caliginous expanse refused to retreat more than it had to. Was it, too, alive?

The paltry hints of light fell upon the man's face. He was a hair taller than Prometheus, with platinum hair and ice blue eyes. Only once had Pandora beheld this Titan, and only from a distance, and yet she knew, skittering to a stop before him.

"Kronos."

The Titan lifted his agonised gaze, eyes taking a moment to focus upon her own, as if his mind had detached itself from his body. A swallow. A shuddering breath, then Kronos whimpered, the sound so pathetic it compelled Pandora to kneel before him in silent acknowledgment of the torment he had suffered. How many years had he dwelt thus? Zeus had condemned his father to Tartarus at the end of the Titanomachy, so ... many centuries, at least.

"Pandora ..." the Titan wheezed.

"How do you know my name?"

The Titan's focus sharpened. "So much has not yet unfolded for you, I take it."

He would know her in his past? But then, it made sense, for she already knew she must return to the Golden Age. Her own future self had commanded it, invoking Pyrrha's very survival, and Pandora could not argue with *herself*. But this Titan, he knew things. He had known of the Box, even at the dawn of the Ambrosial War, and had known she had it. How was that possible? "Help me understand the shape of all this."

A chuckle escaped him. "You've a thousand questions, burning through your core, consuming you in flames you would do aught to quench."

Herakles's hand on her shoulder shook her from herself, and she glanced back at him. "This is ... my grandfather?"

Pandora nodded, looking back to Kronos. "Tell me."

He hefted his manacled wrist. "Release me from this eternal prison."

"If I do?" Herakles asked. "Will your war return to trouble Elládos once again?"

A bitter laugh answered that. "The whole of the Ouranid League failed to stop my perfidious son's uprising. You think I will risk a return *here* by further confrontation with him?"

Pandora looked to Herakles once more. "He knows things I must know." After all, how was she to challenge Fate if she could not understand the whole of the tapestry the Moirai had woven? How was she to make any choice while so much remained muddled and concealed from her? There had to be a way to fix all this, to save her family and the World, and bring even Ananke to heel. For if she could not, then what was she but a castaway, clutching driftwood on the storm-tossed ocean of past and future?

Grim-faced, Herakles grasped the spoke binding the chain to the wall. His muscles bulged as he heaved. Pandora imagined she felt the wall groan and convulse as the spike lurched free. A putrid black film oozed forth from the wound left behind, a filth from which Kronos scrambled away on his hands and knees before looking back, a man dazed by his sudden freedom.

The demigod cast aside the spoke, gripped his grandfather's forearms, and hauled him to his feet. "Answer her questions lest I pound that stake back into the wall and leave you here." Of course, Herakles had heard, all his life, of tyrannical Ouranids whom Zeus had overcome. That his father was *worse* must have been too hard for him to swallow.

Kronos grunted in acknowledgment and took a stumbling step from Herakles, toward Pandora. "Ask, then, and I will provide what answers I can."

"How do you know me?"

Kronos sneered. "You would waste your inquiries upon questions for which you well know the answers."

"You knew me even on Ogygia, in farthest antiquity."

A cocked head. "Farthest? As if the dawn of this Era were the dawn of all time? If this winding road of Fate had a beginning, if it is not all but an endlessly constricting circle, perhaps for you, I might have said it began ... in Vulgeth."

An endlessly constricting circle? Kronos, too, felt the crush of the ouroboros that so choked Pandora. The serpent devoured its own tail and trapped the whole of the World, but there had to be some way free of its coils. And ... Vulgeth. Had she not heard that name before? Her mind whirred, struggling to place the strange word. "Prometheus used that term ... Said something about a Time Chamber."

"Did he indeed?" Kronos shook himself, already beginning to recover his strength.

His earlier words tickled Pandora's mind. "You imply the Time of Nyx was more than a fathomless dark of prehistory."

"It was *history*."

"Vulgeth ..." Pandora swallowed. "It was a place in the Time of Nyx." The idea of that, of *knowing* aught about the mythical past, it seemed some primal violation of all accepted conceptions of the past. When one spoke of the Time of Nyx, one imagined Khaos and night and Man struggling to rise from the dark.

Kronos stepped closer, face contorted in a wicked smirk. "You begin to apprehend."

"This ... isn't the first iteration of our World."

"Yes."

"And you and Prometheus, you knew each other, even back then."

Kronos grinned, pointing now into the distant gloom further down the wall. "Ask him."

Maybe she ought to have lingered, questioned Kronos more, but his words had broken a dam in her, and her legs broke into a run of their own accord, sandals slapping the fleshy surface of the wall. He was here. He was truly, truly here, and she could not endure another moment without him. Could not abide his torment for another breath.

A few easy strides brought Herakles up beside her as she ran. The torchlight seemed to lag a step behind her, leaving her perpetually pushing further into the tenebrous reaches of Tartarus, but she didn't care. She had to find him.

Prometheus.

Prometheus.

At long last, after so much, after the ouroboros had nigh pulverised her, she would ...

A momentous shifting in the atramentous depths beyond the wall had her tripping over her own feet, pitching forward. Herakles's arm shot out and caught her, and there, dangling in his grasp, she peered into the dark. And it into her, for it swallowed her soul at a gulp, leaving her powerless to avert her gaze. The wall of Tartarus encircled the World and shut out this ... this shifting, writhing blackness, within which roiled a thousand, thousand alien intellects. Or, perhaps, a single multifaceted, monstrous mind, in an amorphous sea. Within the dark, she could make out only hints of nascent, blasphemous forms.

Shapes that arose into limbs and phalluses and mouths and eyes and tentacles, only to collapse back into themselves, unable or unwilling to hold together or remain bound to single forms. Amid the entities, one lurched out of the dark just enough for her to perceive a hundred arms all jutting from each other, compounding on one another in mockeries of human form, cast onto a spider the size of a mountain.

Those intellects brushed her mind with chilling tendrils that flensed away fragments of her soul, leaving her a weeping, quivering mess. Herakles jerked her away from the edge, and the pair of them tumbled down atop one another, his arms around her.

"What? What did you see?" His voice was so far away, barely breaking through the haze of abject horror, the trembling, wracking sobs that had seized her. "Pandora?"

For that instant, she saw her mind settled upon a precipice, ready to pitch over and collapse into gibbering madness if she could not deny what she had beheld. An insane sea of prurient darkness, clamouring, seeking ingress into the World, held back only by this sickening, damning, essential wall.

Khaos lived. It sought after her.

"I ... I ..." Words refused to form within her mind, much less reach her tongue. The glimpse of incipient horror defied the fixture of language even as it defied coherence in shape—or perhaps the two were intertwined.

Herakles pulled her back, drawing her into the paltry shelter of his arms. As if the man thought a mere embrace could shut out the knowledge that now assailed her. A Truth that the World was so very fragile. That just beyond the sight of Man lurked an ocean of consuming wills clamouring to devour the cosmos.

Tears were streaming down her face, and still she could not manage to form any means of conveying what she'd seen to the demigod. He broke away from her, striding for the edge himself, intent now to see what she had beheld. And his fragile mind might well break at it. Pandora caught his wrist, and pulled him up short, shaking her head in answer. No, he ought not to look. No one should see that.

Prometheus ... He remained bound out here, subjected to this madness for Gaia-knew how long. Primal instinct demanded she drop to her knees, curl into a foetal ball, and implore all the powers in the cosmos for this to be over, for it be a fleeting nightmare. But none of them could afford that. Pandora forced her feet to move, one plodding, aching step at a time.

Forward, deeper into the depths of this place. Had Zeus understood the Khaos that lurked here when he condemned his father and Prometheus to this place? Had these same visions deepened the Olympian King's madness?

Overhead, thunder rumbled, and brighter flashes of lightning illumined the dark sky. Something about them had Herakles drawing up short, unshouldering his bow.

"What?" Pandora asked, finally finding her voice.

A flash above them, and a screech, something streaking across the tenebrous firmament. Growling, Herakles nocked an arrow. Was that ... an eagle?

No.

The winds whirled around the half-concealed bird, carrying it in shifting loops. Lightning coruscated along its wings, enough she caught a glimpse of a blasphemous mingling of avian and human features. A bird woman—a harpy. The spirit banked into a dive, shooting down toward the wall, though farther away from herself and Herakles. It had another target.

Prometheus.

"No ..."

Herakles loosed his arrow. A heartbeat later, a shrieking wail ripped through the darkness, assailing ears and mind, forcing Pandora to try to block the sound with her hands, even as she stumbled forward.

Another arrow whooshed by her, drawing forth another wail.

Giving over her attempts to dampen the sound, Pandora broke into a run. There, chained to the edge of the wall, drenched in shadow, lay another figure.

Him, it was him, it *had* to be him.

Before Prometheus lay the fallen harpy, the fletchings of twin shafts quivering in its flesh as the abomination attempted to drag itself toward Pandora's lover. Shrieking herself, Pandora lunged, caught one of its taloned feet, and yanked it away from Prometheus, beating at it with the torch she held in her other hand. The spirit wheezed, snarling back at her with perverse avian features and an eagle's beak. Its fingers dug into the wall, fighting her grip.

Then Herakles was there, his hand shooting out to seize the creature by the back of the neck. The demigod hefted the spirit over his head and flung it right over the side of the wall, into the pit of amorphous Khaos that still haunted Pandora's mind.

Tossing the torch aside, Pandora scrambled over to her lover on her hands and knees. The auburn-haired Titan gasped, hand pressed against his abdomen. Stains of dark blood plastered the lines of his muscles, soaked his thighs, and welled beneath him. His sapphire eyes darted about unfocused, brushing over her without seeming to see.

A sob wracked her to see him thus, as though his every torment had been wrought upon her flesh as well. She crawled to him, clutched his hand in her both of hers. "Prometheus ... Prometheus ...?"

His listless gaze swept over her face twice before it seemed to lock upon her eyes. "Is it … real?"

"I'm here."

"Pyromantic visions …" His voice seemed scraped raw, parched yes, though no doubt also from screaming.

"No," she answered, wrapping her arms around him, drawing him close. "It's real. I'm here."

"You always … say that …"

Oh, gods. Had he endured this torment by dwelling within his own mind, living out the moment of his rescue over and over, until he could not separate the vision from the present? "Herakles!"

Already, the demigod gripped the spoke that had bound Prometheus's fetters into the wall. Groaning, he heaved. With agonising indifference, the chain lurched free, metal squealing in protest.

"Y-you're really here?" Prometheus asked.

She pressed a kiss against his brow. "I am. I swore I would find you."

"I always … knew." He wavered as she eased him to his feet, scarce able to stand, so she drew his arms about her shoulders. With his hands bound, it had to be both of them. While Pandora was taller than most women she knew, Prometheus was taller still, and the position of leaning on her must have been awkward for him, especially like this. Maybe almost as awkward as bearing his weight proved for her.

Herakles moved to take him, but Pandora waved the demigod away. This was for her to do, and naught would deter her. Naught she could ever imagine would get her to release him now.

Her beloved took one pained step after another. The Titan paused, however, before an onyx spike lined with jagged ridges, this one more wicked looking than most upon the wall. Her lover eased himself off her, then sunk to his knees before the thorn, which from there, rose well over his head. A heaving, pained breath, then he placed the fetters upon the spike and began to saw at them.

"I thought ..." Pandora began. "Aren't those unbreakable orichalcum chains?"

"Zeus does not understand what this place really is," Prometheus answered without pausing in his work. "He does not apprehend the least of the Ontos."

"Isn't orichalcum unbreakable?"

He cast her a grim look. "It is rendered so by the forging of souls within it. And here, parts of the very wall can feast upon souls. It is what holds back the demons bound within."

The scope of his words churned in her mind, and as his meaning settled in, her hand went to her mouth. Creations of orichalcum ... were made ... from *people*. Souls bound in eternal servitude, even as she had been once made a slave. Did they retain awareness of their enslavement? She hoped not but feared otherwise. And now, Prometheus would allow those souls to be freed—albeit by feeding them to this abominable wall. That itself held back Khaos seeking to feast upon the World.

She wanted to weep once more, though her tears felt all spent.

Had Zeus bound him here, thus, mere feet from potential freedom, just as he had done with Tantalus? But Prometheus had said Zeus did not understand this place, so perhaps the king could not have imagined aught could have broken those chains.

A hiss of steam and a hint of greenish vapour escaped the fetters as Prometheus sawed. Her lover rocked back on his heels, drew in a breath, and jerked his hands apart. The chains snapped liked dry kindling, a reminder of the strength within him, denied to him by the orichalcum.

At last he rose. Though he said naught, his eyes made plain his desperate need to be gone from this place. A need they all shared.

"I CANNOT fathom how you endured such a thing," Herakles said, as they emerged from the Tartarian Gate, back into the depths beneath Olympus. "I cannot imagine retaining my mind ..."

And perhaps, even now, his thoughts drifted back to his murdered children. Though the demigod had seemed sane enough in her presence, Pandora found her own mind had oft returned to his crimes. What had possessed him with such a bout of rage? Perhaps neither of them would ever know.

Prometheus did not look at Herakles, but rather sank to the ground and pressed his cheek upon the stone of the cavern, seeming intent to reassure himself he had, at last, returned to the real world. A ravaged shudder wracked him, and Pandora dropped to her knees beside him, hand upon his back.

"It's over." His agony had ended. "We ... we have to bring down Zeus now. What he has done cannot be allowed to stand." Arke and Kronos and Prometheus and how many others? The murders, tortures, rapes, and virulent cruelties compounded to form a life of solipsistic depravity that must be ended.

Herakles balked, taking a step back and shaking his head. "I agreed to help you free prisoners from Tartarus. Not to raise arms against my own father, Pandora. That is not ... Kinslaying is not the redemption you promised me."

Much as she wanted to object, perhaps she could never have expected otherwise, and it would have been *her* cruelty, had she tried to force the issue, no matter how much she could see the conflict raging within the demigod. Yes, he had witnessed the aftereffects of his father's malignancy, and yes, must have known him now for a despot. And still, the demigod could not turn his back on his blood.

"We must be reconciled with Zeus," Prometheus said, lifting his tear-stained face from the floor. The Titan looked shrunken in upon himself, harried by his ordeal.

"Reconciled!" Pandora blurted. "With the man who did *this* to you!" She waved her hand to encompass the wretched cavern and thus her point.

"I gave him a prophecy that Olympus would fall unless his son fought at his side."

The memory of it smacked her like a blow. The very day Zeus had condemned him thus, Prometheus had uttered that, but she had been so broken by the whole affair she had given it no further thought. But he had *known*, even back then, that the Gigantomachy would come. That Herakles would be here and aid the Olympians.

"Olympus deserves its fate," she retorted, hating the petulance in her voice but unable to suppress it. Was she not, after all this, entitled to a hint of bitterness?

A sadness in his eyes, her lover rose and took her hand. "History does not, as rule, show overmuch concern for who deserves salvation or damnation." Prometheus's gaze darted to the demigod beyond her.

Because, of course, Zeus was still in power, nigh seven centuries later, when he sired Herakles. Who would come back here and free Prometheus.

"Whatever your anger at Olympus," Herakles said, "you cannot believe having a horde of Gigantes overrun the land would behoove the common Man."

Pandora rounded on him. "You imply the choice is between enslavement to despots or being *eaten* by slavering monsters? Can we not even aim for a third alternative?"

"We do aim for it," Prometheus said. "We always aim for it. But time is not an arrow, as most imagine it, rather a maze we navigate in darkness, feeling our way toward an uncertain centre."

Dammit, the two of them made her feel all the more the petulant child for her objections. But this ... "So, Herakles will help his kin before I return him to his own time."

"Not only him. You and I will, as well, and thus earn ourselves some reprieve from Zeus's ire."

Pandora snorted. "Me? What would you have me do against Gigantes? I barely survived the ascent while avoiding conflict as much as possible."

His eyes, as he squeezed her hand, had that hooded look he so oft bore, the one that bespoke hidden burdens. "There was ... a legend, Pandora, a thought I chased after for ages until, at last, I realised I must create what I sought myself, even as I created the Box. All for you."

"What are you saying?"

"As best I reckon it, I spent some three decades bound in Tartarus. And in that time, I kindled a flame … an ember broken off the First Flame."

She felt the colour drain from her face. "You want me to become a Firewalker, like Hestia."

"No, my love. I want you to become something *more*. The flame I will give you will burn like a sun compared to the candle Hestia bears. And it will …" Emotion choked him and he fell silent a moment. When he spoke again, his voice had become a whisper. "It will burn in you. Through you. With more Pneuma than you can ever imagine—if you can but harness it. For I stole this Flame from Agni, when the world was young and I was another man. It is brighter, *scorching* hot, Pandora." The trepidation in his always implacable visage made her stomach lurch. This scared even *him*.

"But … why me?" Why would he want to bestow such power as he spoke of on her? Why not use it himself?

"Because you know your journey has not yet ended. Because you will need it, and I would see you protected, armed and armoured against the ravages of time that will still befall you." Another pause. "Or deny it, Pandora. I would never force such a burden upon you. If you take this spirit within you, you will not be the same. It will burn and burn, and you will have to struggle to keep yourself against the conflagration."

For so long, she had sought a way to take control of her own destiny. To be able to change time and fate and the World for the better. To fix everything, to give hope to everyone crushed by the weight of the apathetic weavings of the Moirai. "I will take the flame." Though she felt she had whispered, her words seemed to fill the silent cavern.

Perhaps feeling he intruded, Herakles backed away to the threshold as Prometheus laid his hands upon Pandora's shoulders, guiding her down to her knees while he knelt in front of her. "Pneuma," he said, "is breath. And I will breathe the Phoenix into you."

"Phoenix?"

"Your favourite uncle, you once said. Named ... for the legendary bird. For you, I think."

"I ..." She could not swallow. Could not think.

His open mouth pressed against hers, his sudden kiss full of need and trepidation and centuries of doubt and regret. Full of, she dared to imagine, *hope*. His warm breath seeped into her, filled her lungs. Warm at first, then hot. Searing, as though an inferno surged forth from his chest and unfurled within hers. His fingers were tight upon the back of her skull even when animal instinct had her trying to jerk away.

A breath longer, until smoke and embers filled her mouth. Then he let her go, catching her in his arms and easing her to the ground. For indeed, the strength had gone out of her.

"You can survive this, my love," he promised.

But the heat had become an erupting volcano inside her breast. Its fury exploded, turning her insides to ash. Pandora opened her mouth to scream, but only steam billowed out. Agony, unlike aught she had ever imagined, shot through her. She held her hands up before her face. They burst into flames, flesh charring away, sloughing off in wafts of drifting ash.

"Pandora?" Prometheus exclaimed. He sounded far away, but even from the distance, she could hear the sudden fear straining his voice. "Pandora!"

Blackened bone in her arms crisped and tumbled to the ground. The throes of torment beyond description seized her, her whole being, body and soul igniting, burning away.

It welled up inside her, a rage, the manic frenzy of a wildfire, alive and euphoric to *burn*.

Her eyes melted and her body gave way with the final thought— she had failed.

INTERLUDE: PROMETHEUS

Asura Era, Bronze Age

The awful, soul-rending knowledge of the Ontos shadowed Matarśivan's footfalls, even as he passed through the nebulous shadowscape of the Roil. Knowing what lay behind it, *beyond* it, only redoubled the horror of this place, yes, but for now, it was but a transitory space on his road to confront his erstwhile master.

If all the Fates had shown him was true, he had been lied to and betrayed from the moment of his birth. The Elder Gods had deceived him, but he would not be fool enough to take the revelation at face value without confirmation. No, he would never again be led by blind trust in any authority. He would see for himself and look the Ever-Burning One in the eye. He would demand his answers and confirm the Truth.

Above him, the iridescent sky fulminated with hidden lightning, and before him, a river of sputtering magma demarcated the boundary with Phlegethon, the World of Fire. For a moment that seemed to stretch on into eternity, Matarśivan stood upon the bank, feeling the merciless heat as it washed over him. The air scalded and left him wondering that his tunic did not burst into flame. Even through his sandals, his feet baked.

If not for his status as a Watcher of Agni, his skin might well have begun to cook.

He could still turn back ...

No, that was a lie. He needed confirmation, one way or the other. After what the Fates had revealed, he'd never again know peace without certainty. Was the master he served the beauteous divinity he had once beheld? Or was he, were all the Elder Gods, something eldritch and alien that stood in mockery of life itself?

Matarśivan crouched and leapt into the air, a beat of his powerful wings hurtling him up onto nether winds. The river's swelter increased as he flew overhead. He passed through a curtain of shimmering heat and found himself landing inside in an ash-choked cavern. Above him, hidden in shadow and half-concealed by billowing smoke, the roof glowed in incandescent fury.

Every so often, geysers of sulphuric vapours or spouts of magma burst into sudden violence, while the cavern itself seemed a caldera bifurcated by a river of lava. Great clouds of soot billowed and rumbled in mockery of an atmosphere.

His flesh sizzled from the scorching air and his sandals began to melt. Fits of choking coughs seized him as he plodded forward, wending his way around plummeting rents in the ground. Tremors continuously wracked the cavern, threatening to send him tumbling down into any one of innumerable lava fields. He might have flown, but the ash and smoke would make seeing his way nigh impossible, even could he have breathed inside those clouds.

Though he had so rarely come here—and never without explicit summons—he recalled the way, pushing deeper into the caldera. A fresh billow of sulphuric gasses vented a hairsbreadth ahead of him, sending him stumbling backward. Flailing to regain his balance, Matarśivan stumbled. His knee hit the caldera and his flesh seared and blistered, the pain of it blinding, even as he lurched upward, screaming, arms waving about to keep from touching down again.

Then, after catching his breath, he forced his mind to stillness. Flooding Prana into his limbs allowed him to ease the pain and increase his resistance to the ever-present burning in Phlegethon.

This was madness. Who was he, immortal or no, to *dare* question his gods? The Archons had given the Watchers their power and earned eternal servitude in return.

But try as he might, the dread revelation refused to leave his mind. Damnation refused to stop playing out in merciless finality, whether he woke or slept. No other choice yet lay before him, even if his temerity ended in his own destruction. Maybe ... maybe that would be a mercy. But then, the Fates had also demanded eternal servitude, and he could feel their grasp upon him now, claiming him from outside of time.

Grim-faced, he continued onward. Jagged rock outcroppings formed a ring of knives around a deeper crater inside the caldera, and Matarśivan eased his way between them. Agni's palace lay beyond, surrounded by a soot-stained bronze wall that stretched a hundred feet in the air. Spikes jutted from the ramparts of the wall at irregular angles, looking most ominous around the barbican that warded the gate.

Perhaps he ought to have plodded up to the gate in supplication and requested admission from his deity. But then, he had not come here to offer obeisance or respect. He had come here to confirm the Ontos his mind wished to deny no matter how much his soul apprehended its reality.

Growling, he launched himself into the air once more, his wings carried him up, over that burnished wall. What he beheld beyond, though, had him faltering. He dropped down onto the wall's inner lip and crouched, gaping at the panorama of madness that lay before him.

Instead of an ebony, Man-like form upon a smouldering throne, he saw a half-dozen intersecting, incandescent wheels whirring about one another in irregular gyrations. Multitudes of eyes rimmed each wheel, and twisters of flame connected them like spokes. Naphtha drizzled down from the eyes in burning streams that fed pools of flaming oil dotted around the palace floor. At the centre of this abomination pulsed a throbbing heart, itself engulfed in a conflagration.

In rapt horror, Matarśivan knelt, his whole body trembling from the confirmation of his worst fears. This *thing* had deceived them all. The whole of the Dodecadic Circle was built upon the lies of the Archons, and surely, given its true form, the Fates had shown him the Ontos indeed.

MATARŚIVAN! The voice reverberated through the cavern, though it seemed to come from all angles, not only the burning wheels that lay before him. It filled his head and the space around him with the force of a thousand discordant gongs, each syllable echoing long after it ought to have faded. *FOR YOUR TEMERITY, YOU SHALL FORFEIT YOUR VERY SOUL! I SHALL CONSUME YOU TO THE PITH UNTIL NAUGHT REMAINS EVEN FOR THE WHEEL OF LIFE TO SPIN OUT AGAIN!*

The power of its words turned his muscles into water. His head bowed of its own accord. No Man, not even an immortal Watcher, could defy the awesome authority of an Archon. Eldritch terrors or no, they ruled the World.

All he could do was submit.

Or ... or ... refuse.

If he was damned, let him earn that damnation. Slowly, he raised his head. These horrors feasted upon the souls of Man. So let him then become the advocate of Man. Let him stare them down in defiance. Perhaps whatever the Fates had done to him would preserve him. Probably not. Either way, he rose to his feet.

There was no more kneeling before the horror. Not anymore. Not ever again. No ... he would stand against the end he had foreseen. And he would use the very power of the abomination that had so deceived him, had helped bring about that end.

WRITHE IN THE CEASELESS INFERNO!

Matarśivan leapt into the air once more, hurling himself forward with a single beat of his wings. The revolution of those wheels accelerated, sending him hurtling toward a flaming twister. Matarśivan tucked his wings in against his body, allowing his momentum to carry him inward as a ring swept overhead.

Scorching naphtha dribbled upon his flesh, and even his Prana was not enough to block out the pain as his skin peeled away. Losing his momentum, he pitched downward, colliding with the outer wheel. Its impact sent him careening through the air, only to smack down, broken upon the burnished floor.

Tongues of flame erupted from the eyes covering the wheels, raking over him. His clothes turned to cinders. His wings burst into flame. His flesh oozed away until naught save bleached bone remained in his hand, and even that turned to ash. He screamed, but his vision faded as hot liquid leaked down his face from his melting eyes.

In squirming agony, he lay upon the ground and knew death had him. Knew it, and even that would not begin to abate the torment Agni would wrack upon him.

Then his vision began to return. The perverse sensation of liquid seeping back *up* his face. The inverted pain of eyes rebuilding themselves. Ashes from his hand swirled back into bones. Utter torture as flesh rebuilt itself, streaming up from the molten puddles that had covered the bronze floor.

WHAT BLASPHEMY?

Time reversed itself around him, even erasing the burns of that flaming oil upon his skin.

The Fates had changed him. In that moment, it struck him. A keenness of insight beyond or within prescience. He had agreed to give them *eternal* service. It meant he would truly serve for all eternity. No respite, no chance to escape his oath, no matter what befell his flesh. He could not die.

Horror and determination warred within him as Matarśivan glared up at Agni's revolving rings. Screaming, he flooded Prana into his limbs so he could make a forty-foot vertical leap. Prana in his wings sent him streaking forward with the speed of a peregrine falcon. He twisted around, darting between the spinning wheels, heedless of whether or not flames or naphtha scorched him.

Prana could block the pain, and what cared he for injuries now?

Matarśivan dodged a flaming vortex and landed upon the inner-most ring. The heat of it ignited his sandals and seared flesh from his feet. He shrieked, not even Prana able to block that much pain. But the pulsing heart of flame throbbed mere feet in front of him.

YOU SHALL SUFFER WITHOUT END!

"I know," he said.

And he drove his fist into that heart. It ought to have incinerated his flesh, but instead, he felt his hand close around an oscillating core. The kernel of Agni's unfathomable might. With a roar, Matarśivan ripped that kernel out, holding the trembling flame in his hand. It burned with fervid light, leaping around his arm in exotic whorls.

A mind-rending shriek erupted from Agni, and all the rings abruptly fell still. The sudden cessation of movement cost Matarśivan his balance, and he pitched back down toward the ground. A moment before impact, he managed to flap his wings, aborting his fall just enough to lessen the blow.

Far above, Agni dimmed, faltering and weakened by the power Matarśivan had taken from it. Most of the eyes clenched shut, as if in agony.

That flame coiled about Matarśivan, then began to bore its way through his flesh. Wracking, blazing pain scorched him as the blazing strength of Agni seeped into his soul. He felt the whole of his being lit aflame.

Before he could even catch his breath, some of the eyes above began to open once more.

Matarśivan needed to escape before Agni could reassert itself and attempt to reclaim the Flame he'd stolen. The power now burning in *his* breast.

Once more, Matarśivan took to the air and flew from the palace.

PART III

No two tales agree on exactly where or how Prometheus stole the First Flame, but one fact seems undisputed. In the days before the Titanomachy, the Titan lord gave to Man the Art of Fire and the gift of pyromancy, that they might have the power to challenge even Titans. The Olympians have long held this an unforgivable crime, despite Firewalkers helping Zeus overthrow the Ouranid League. To this day, cults of Fire-worshippers persist.
— Polyhymnia, Analects of the Muses

15

———

PANDORA

1600 Silver Age

A sulphurous expanse greeted Pandora as she lifted her head up from the foetal crouch in which she'd wrapt herself. Pulsing warmth ran through the ground—and small wonder—as rivers of magma flowed in the distance and volcanoes belched acrid smoke into a cavernous sky. Was she back in Tartarus?

No, this place seemed nigh to it, perhaps, but not quite the same. Less nebulous, more an entire world set alight, engulfed in ceaseless inferno. As she rose, she realised that while her clothes had burned away, her flesh here seemed whole, and the pain had fled, nor did the heated obsidian ground seem to harm her feet.

It began then, like a rupture in the sky, an opening lens boring down upon her with its trenchant gaze. Colossal, intersecting wheels of fire whirled about overhead, each rimmed with innumerable eyes, all intent upon her. Rage, beyond human ken, beyond the scope of imaging, welled within the beating heart at the centre of the flaming abomination. That wrath became a searing heat in her own breast, a consuming blaze not unlike the one that had devoured her beneath Olympus.

BLASPHEMY!

The voice assaulted her mind, so cowing she might have torn off her own ears had she thought it would silence it. The scorching fever within her exploded, flames leaping along her arms as she outstretched them. Streaks of fire shot from her fingertips, racing along the cavernous floor in dancing parabolas.

The rage this infernal deity directed at her, it was *inside* her as well, now erupting forth and setting her alight once again. A flash of memory, a compounding of all the torments of her life, it swirled up within her. Abduction and enslavement, beatings and rapes, loss of herself. The stripping away of her beloved and her child. The absolute impotence inflicted upon her by the merciless Fates. All of it became a maelstrom of seething wrath churning and searing in her core, threatening to erupt into the world. To let it share her lifetime of anguish.

The fires no longer burnt her flesh, they infused it.

SUBMIT, MORTAL!

A form within her stirred, waking from long quiescence. A sensation more than a vision, the intimation of a fiery fusion of eagle and peacock. Her rage given form? Unable to contain the explosive force any longer, Pandora jerked her arms out to the side further and leapt upward, her legs inexplicably carrying her twenty feet into the air. Wings of flame shot from her back, stretching out dozens of feet, hurtling her upward, screeching into the smoke-choked sky that swallowed her vision.

FLAMES ERUPTED around her once more, and again, Pandora found herself rising from a crouch, this time surrounded by a pile of ash.

"Pandora!" Prometheus exclaimed, sweeping her up in an embrace even as Pandora realised she was back in the cavern beneath the Throne of Zeus. Had it all been a dream?

She could feel her lover's heartbeat against her naked chest, his hand pressed against the back of her head, stroking it as if to reassure himself she lived.

"What in the dark of the Underworld was that?" Herakles asked from over Prometheus's shoulder. "Was that ... a Phoenix?"

Had any of that been real? Had *all* of it been? Pandora pushed herself back from Prometheus to stare into his sapphire eyes.

"I ... never imagined it would consume you thus," he said in answer to her unspoken question.

"I saw some smouldering caldera and a burning god ..." The memory of it scorched her mind, and even considering it, she felt heat and wrath rise inside her chest once more. The entity, the Phoenix, it lingered inside her still. That, at least, was real. The thought of it, this entity seething inside the depths of her soul, it left her flitting between euphoria and disbelief. How did one parse such realities? That she, who had been a mere hetaira not so very many years ago, should now house living flame within her core?

Prometheus blanched for a moment before his usual composure returned. "Phlegethon. You saw Phlegethon and its ruler, from which I stole the First Flame, long, long ago, when I was another person." And he had not expected her to witness it.

A flash of irritation shot through her at his omissions and careless use of power. It rose, ignited within her core. Before she realised what she was about, she'd stood and shoved him in the process. Prometheus flew five feet backward to land upon the ground with an *oomph*.

Herakles gaped, even as his gaze roamed her unclad flesh. How dare he? She hadn't realised she'd moved, but streaks of fire shot out from beneath her feet, hurling her toward the demigod. Her fist smacked into his jaw, the blow hefting him off his own feet and spinning him around sideways through the air.

Pandora screamed in wordless fury. Flames from the nearby torches swirled up into a flying maelstrom an instant before they surged to her hands, blazing orbs dripping with naphtha.

"Pandora!" Prometheus shouted.

Burn, burn, burn! She would burn them all! She would burn the whole fucking world for all that had befallen her.

"Pandora!"

A shriek, and she jerked her hands out toward the voice. The orbs fused and launched forward, streaking toward Prometheus like a meteor. He caught the conflagration between his own palms. For a heartbeat more it blazed, then he pressed his hands together and the flames winked out in a puff of smoke.

"I know it burns," he said. "It sears within you and wants to spread. But you can yet bring order from the chaos inherent in flame. Fire is consumption, yes, but it is also life. Burning, searing, *life*, Pandora." His crystal eyes held not anger nor even fear that she had flung fire at him, but a desperate hope. And love, deep and unwavering.

Gods, what had she done?

Herakles, too, had gained his feet, this time averting his eyes as he edged closer, holding out his cloak. "You can't really blame a man for noticing ..."

Her mind felt swept up in a riptide, torn this way and that, and just below the surface lurked a simmering fury so eager to burst forth once more. Had that lain within her all along? Did the Phoenix merely awaken it, or had it engendered her wrath? Oh, how she wanted to burn it all. To let chaotic flames purify the whole corrupt World.

"Now," Prometheus said, "*now* you can fight in this Gigantomachy."

Trembling as she wrapt the cloak about herself, Pandora looked to him. "By harnessing this ... implacable rage? By letting it spill forth to immolate all before me?"

His hand drifted up to stroke her cheek. "It's not about rage."

That burning roil of pain, of stolen moments and compounded torments, it still swirled within her breast. Because, for her, it truly, absolutely *was* about rage.

WAS THIS PNEUMA, flowing through her veins, kindling her awareness with its searing warmth? Every breath now seemed deeper. She could feel it, flowing into muscles, pooling within her flesh, granting her puissance mortals could not have dreamed of. Was she now a match for even a Titan? Was this what Prometheus had given her with the Phoenix?

Such thoughts ran through her mind when they descended the Olympian acropolis, now seeking out the battle. She had ransacked rooms in Zeus's palace until she'd found a khiton and sandals that fit, then claimed a spear as well. They made for the chaos of battle, Herakles shooting numerous Gigantes along the way.

Part of Pandora longed to surge into battle herself, but for the moment, she kept by Prometheus's side, reassuring herself he was truly free. She had succeeded after all, though it seemed hard to believe.

Below, she spied the Gígas Mimas, whom she had seen in Athyras. Here, he led a pack of misshapen Gigantes against the Olympians. One of the so-called gods charged by in a golden chariot, hurtling searing javelins into the monsters. A dart took Mimas in the chest, and his hair burst into flame even as he collapsed.

"That's Hephaistos," Prometheus told her.

While she knew her lover had the right of it, that the Olympians had to win this battle, part of her almost wanted to linger and watch the various Titans destroy one another. All of them, Zeus especially, had failed Man, and none of them deserved a throne. Within her, the Phoenix—the expression of *her*—exulted at slaughter wrought among her tormentors.

But Herakles pushed onward, his arrows lodging into Gígas throats and chests with uncanny accuracy. The demigod drew up beside a black-haired Titan woman, another archer. Her arrow took a Gígas in the left eye, even as Herakles's struck the right. The woman laughed, looking first to Herakles, then back to Pandora and Prometheus.

She gaped before dropping her bow, breaking into a wild lope toward them. Pandora started to heft the spear, despite the grin breaking across the Titan's face, so taken aback by the charge. Before she could decide if this woman presented a threat, the Titan had her arms around Pandora, drawing her into an embrace.

"Nike! By Thoth, we all thought you must be dead!" Another tight squeeze, and then the woman held her back at arm's length, staring at her face with silver eyes. She had seen this woman in Athyras and the sacking of Thebes, too. Artemis, the archer, twin of Apollon.

Nike ...? Pandora's gorge rose even as her stomach dropped out from under her. And the ouroboros tightened its coils once more.

"Where have you been all these years, Nike?" Artemis blurted.

Madness. Impossibility, like so much else that had befallen her. So many twisting, winding paths of Ananke that had resolved into focus, one after another. The shifting coils of the serpent encircling time.

"Are you well?" Artemis asked.

Pandora glanced back at Prometheus, who stood expressionless, arms folded over his chest. He may not have known who Nike was when she had asked him back then ... but this Prometheus had already known. Of course he had. The Phoenix. Nike, the winged Titan, had been associated with the Phoenix. Pandora had revelled in the beauteous phoenix fresco painted in the Nike Springs baths, while disdaining the Titan herself.

But sculptures of Nike had never revealed her wings were wings of *fire*.

"I'm all right," she said, struggling to keep her voice even while the World spun about her too fast.

"Good, good." Artemis punched her on the arm. "Then why on Thoth's dark side did it take you this long to come find me? I thought we were friends, Nike." Genuine hurt laced the Titan's voice, a fragility that belied her stature as an immortal goddess.

What was Pandora to say? That she had never met Artemis before this moment? Pandora had spent enough time playing roles and faking emotions to fall back into it without difficulty, cupping the other woman's cheek with her hand. "It's a long story and I think now is not the time."

Indeed, and a flash of lightning and clap of thunder drew her eye to Zeus. On the lower slope, the king had launched a coruscating blast at a Gígas. The monster fell, and Herakles leapt upon its torso, slamming bloody fists into the creature's skull. The blows rang out again and again, splitting bone even as the impact cracked rock beneath the giant. Nearby, Hera lay upon the ground, wounded, her dress torn and splattered with ichor.

Beyond, a surging mass of Gigantes vaulted over the escarpment, closing in upon the beleaguered Olympians, their fury redoubled by the fall of this most recent Gígas.

Well, Prometheus had claimed they needed reconciliation with Zeus by helping defeat his enemies. Then let Fate unfold and history play out. Pandora slapped Artemis on the arm, then stepped up to the edge of a precipice. Beneath her skin, Pneuma tingled, scorching and eager, ready to burst into flame.

If only she accepted the wrath. She released it.

Pandora leapt from the plateau, and fiery wings erupted from her back, hurtling her skyward, her hatred given physical form. Air rushing over her face, streaming her hair behind her as she screamed in a fresh paroxysm. Utter freedom of flight, setting free the rage that so long kindled in her breast, unacknowledged. Then she twisted, and another beat of those wings sent her careening downward into the mass of Gigantes.

Among them, Hekate fought alongside an unknown man, flinging shards of ice and summoning up vines to snare her foes. Pandora soared over her daughter and landed amid the monsters in a crouch. Flames burst from her in a swirling explosion, the conflagration leaping over a half dozen of the creatures, sweeping in a wildfire that left scorched skeletons flailing in the wind an instant before those too disintegrated and blew away. The fire was hers to command, and wherever she turned her vehement gaze, it danced to her call.

Burn!

Pandora rose, allowing Pneuma to pool within her muscles and bones. A great leap sent her lunging forward before the gaping Gigantes could recover their senses. Her spear punched through a skull, the shower of gore churning her stomach. How many sentient beings had she just slain? But the heat had her, the burning rush, and she could not focus on aught else.

A serpent-Gígas surged up to seize her. Pandora spun, faster than she realised she could move, her fist sinking into the creature's gut. Deep. The blow hefted it off the ground and felt as though organs had ruptured beneath it.

Burn, burn, burn!

She jerked her spearpoint free from the skull of the fallen Gígas and whipped it around, impacting the head of another Gígas. The shaft snapped even as the giant fell. Some distant part of her revolted against the chaotic violence, but the Phoenix rose up, choking her. Before she knew what she was doing, she had leapt forward again, covering a ten-foot gap in a single bound, only to ram the splintered haft of her spear through the eye of another Gígas.

On and on, spilling blood and ichor, spreading wildfire, until the whole of Olympus seemed ablaze. Yes, she would burn the wretched mountain to ash and make pure the World once more.

Lashes of flame whipped about her, dancing upon her whims.

Her gaze settled upon platinum-haired Zeus on the ledge above, watching, his face rapt with joy at the chaos she unleashed. He revelled in it, for it was his nature to drink in suffering like a second Ambrosia.

His nature. Not hers. Never hers.

BURN!

Rage, so unleashed, scrambled beneath her grasp, refusing to be fettered within her core once more.

When she looked, the Gigantes had broken, the vestiges of their horde scattering to the winds, fleeing a host of pursuing, vengeful Olympians. Arrows rained by the terrified giants, and aureate chariots scraped over the escarpment in unbridled pursuit.

Pandora pressed a palm to her brow, overcome with disgust at her own capacity for hatred, for the senseless violence of Titans she had so abhorred. The flames around her dwindled. Behind Zeus stood Prometheus and Herakles, her companions in this, and, without doubt, Prometheus had achieved his reconciliation on the back of Pandora's tempestuous display. How easy now to turn her fires on the wretched king. But even if her flames could conquer his lightning, she would unravel history. Without him to sire Herakles, to abduct Europa, to do it *all* … Just … fuck.

Crouching, she drew Pneuma and flame into her legs. A mighty, fire-fuelled leap and a beat of her flaming wings—the faint tapping of her barely bridled fury—carried her fifty feet back up to the precipice where her lover stood beside her greatest enemy.

"Nike," Zeus said, face broken into a cruel, manic grin. "You return to us at last, in our hour of greatest need. The Goddess of Victory who shows herself only in the greatest wars in history. Hmph." His eyes roamed her body with more deliberateness than his son's ever had.

Of a sudden, Pandora realised her flames had singed her new clothes, too, leaving them in smouldering tatters, exposing far more flesh than she might have chosen. But really, what difference did it make? Too many people had looked upon her body for her to hold much modesty now. Her sneer answered Zeus's leering assessment. "Only for Prometheus."

Zeus turned back to her Titan lover, and Pandora could not catch whatever look the king cast him. Prometheus cocked his head a hair to the side. The king grunted. "Yes, yes, I am magnanimous, of course. In exchange for your services, I grant you a pardon, Firebringer. Do see that you do not vex me in the future."

"I shall bear it in mind," Prometheus deadpanned.

When Zeus turned back to her, the look he *still* gave her made her wonder if he intended to try to force her to his bed. Part of her hoped he would try. Her fist clenched at her side.

Burn, burn, burn.

The creeping desire to unleash that rage once more seared her. Was she now stronger than him? The mental image of her blows knocking his teeth out deepened her sneer. She could see it, in her mind's eye, the charring of his flesh, her sandal crunching down upon his smouldering skull. For now, the future needed him. But she would find a time where that no longer proved the case, she now felt fair certain.

Something in her expression had him looking away. He was a man who wanted his women afraid. He wanted them helpless beneath him. And Pandora would *never* be helpless beneath a man again.

Burn ...

Prometheus's hand upon her shoulder was a balm, cooling her heart, smothering the fire that had begun to rise in her breast. "I believe you promised to return Herakles to his own time," he said once Zeus had stalked away, no doubt to brag about how he had single-handedly won this battle.

Turning back to him, she snatched his hand. "And *us*? When will it finally be time for us, for our family, for Pyrrha?"

"I don't know." His expression looked wounded, crushed, even. "Some people have to seize what moments of happiness they might from the hands of Fate, for moments are all we are afforded."

No. No, Pandora was damn tired of having to claim these ephemeral moments he spoke of. Always running from him, dashing off to uphold the course of history, to keep it from unraveling and unmaking all she was and all she loved. Was it the Phoenix in her, giving rise to this defiance? Either way, she embraced him with a fervour, holding him tight, even as his hand stroked her back. "I love you."

"And I you." He offered her another squeeze. In his arms, time slowed, stretched itself deeper as if the shelter of an embrace might deny the inevitable future that must tear them apart once more. And then he pulled back, and it was like pieces of herself torn away. "But you well know what happens if we balk, Pandora. You told me, if Nike does not fight in the Titanomachy, Pyrrha will die. You told *yourself* that."

The reminder stole the strength of her legs. In the tumult of the Gigantomachy, she'd had no chance to muse upon the revelation that was, had always been, Nike. That she had, in fact, instructed herself that she must continue to side with Zeus no matter how much she hated him. All her life, all she cared for was predicated upon what had come before, and because of the Box, even what would come after in her case. Kronos must fall and be imprisoned in Tartarus, the Silver Age, the Bronze Age, all of it coming together as it always had.

And she would *again* be torn apart, leaving behind the two people she loved most. Leaving was all she ever did anymore, her whole life transformed into farewells and faltering hopes that, one day, she might claim more than moments.

"This ouroboros will crush me," she wheezed.

Prometheus stroked her cheek. "You are stronger than you think."

"Because you have unbridled this rage within me," she accused, uncertain whether to revel in the gratification of her unleashed fury or dread what it turned her into.

"It's not about rage," he repeated.

"Then do tell, Prometheus, what *is* it about?" she demanded.

"Whatever burns within you."

But he didn't understand; whatever else burned in her, this finally acknowledged acrimony scorched her like wildfire. And he was right, she was stronger than she had ever thought. In the Golden Age, Prometheus was waiting for her. Pyrrha was depending on her. She was depending upon herself.

"So be it," she said. "I will go." She thumped her forefinger into his chest. "But do not think I will accept mere moments, love. In the end, I will have a lifetime, if I have to carve it out of the corpse of Fate itself. I swore I would fix this, and I will not give up. I will ... *never* ... give up."

Prometheus kissed her brow. "I know."

16

———————

HEKATE

2399 Golden Age

An atramentous expanse had swallowed Hekate, a darkness without end, writhing in unspeakable prurience. Desolate, she found herself wandering in a space outside of space, the silence broken only by distant moans where passion and pain mingled into indistinguishability. That, and the squelching sound her bare feet made upon whatever moist, fleshy surface on which she trod. The ground itself heaved in languid waves, as though she walked across the back of some gargantuan being in the throes of slow coupling.

The moans around her had her skin crawling, her soul recoiling, and yet her body responded. She realised she was naked only when she caught her fingers trailing over her abdomen, enticing pleasure from her own flesh in echo of the need that saturated the darkness. Disgusted, she jerked her hand away, casting about for sign of aught here.

But all she beheld was her own body, even that hazy in the absolute blackness. She could not have said why she plodded forward through the darkness, nor could she keep herself from pushing onward, seeking some-

thing, seeking aught *to relieve the growing strain within her soul. Then the rising shape in the gloom, a deeper dark within the dark, it came with neither suddenness nor warning. Rather, she saw, in a slow dawning of awareness, the creeping apprehension of an enormity towering above her, uttering a discordant chorus of grunting and groaning. A mountain of flesh peered down at her, a form vaguely Man-like, though composed of wriggling torsos of dozens of men and women, arms flailing, groping one another in ceaseless, insatiable lust.*

Choking on her own scream, Hekate stumbled backward, tripped, and fell on her arse. Much as she wanted to erupt into shrieks, only whimpers managed to escape her, her arms raised in ineffectual warding. The abomination bent double over her. Lurching hands from so many reaching torsos seized her ankles, hefting her aloft. Her legs were yanked apart, and tongues scraped the insides of her thighs.

Before the horror of it had time to settle, a massive vulva opened within the fleshy mass ahead. Next she knew, the entity jammed her feet inside itself, pumping her legs as though to use her whole body as a phallus. Crushing pressure engulfed her lower half, even as tears choked her.

Then she was inside, up to her hips, become one more of the writhing torsos comprising the demon's obscene shape.

HEKATE BOLTED AWAKE, jumping from her bed with a wild shriek, flinging herself upon the floor. Welcoming the pain it brought for the hope such meant she had only dreamt the nightmare. In centuries of oneiromantic wanderings, never had she found herself subjected to the utter horror that so oft crept upon her in the years since she had conjured the demon.

Never.

Weeping, she crawled along the floor, not even knowing what she sought after. *Something.* Some release from the torment. A knife in her hand ...

Except, except, except ... all she'd seen ... would come for her in death. No respite, not even in the acrimonious madness that claimed wraiths. Whether her nightmares held true prophecy of a literal future or a visited torment borne along the connection she had forged with Aeshma, either way, they carried the *flavour*. A taste of what lay before her, a fate without escape or hope.

The bronze knife toppled from her limp fingers to clatter on the floor. Moaning, Hekate pitched over onto her side, arms around her knees, whimpering, as her mind shredded. How long before waiting for damnation became equivalent to the torment of the damned itself?

Chittering laughter burbled forth from her chest. Her nails dug rivets through her bare shins.

Last year, she had seen herself carving up and eating little Athene. That was the worst dream, the one that had haunted her ever since. She had not slept for a fortnight after that, but even Pneuma-flushed Titans could not forsake sleep forever.

A door within her estate creaked, but Hekate could not bring herself to care about an intruder. Could not bring herself to bother rising, though she wore no more than a sheer shift.

"I cannot begin to fathom what you have done, that your mind should shriek in such abject terror, bleeding tinges of madness out into the dreamscape," Morpheus said.

Through an effort of will, Hekate managed to crane her neck around to peer at him as he stood silhouetted in the doorway, moonlight from the courtyard limning his figure. Her ... her dreams were polluting the town?

"Your mind has cracked, and horrors ooze out from the seams." Just how much had he seen? How long had he felt it, and did anyone else in Athyras know? The other oneiromancer folded his arms across his chest. "There is a temptation, I admit, to let you suffer in solitude. Hmm. Yet even I can bear witness to only so much torment before I feel compelled to intervene."

"I ... cannot block it out. I've tried." She had used every oneiro-mantic technique she knew to shield her mind, but she could not break a connection she herself had forged. Or perhaps, worse yet, such visions as plagued her came spawned from her own mind, from even the glimpse of the Dark beyond the cosmos she had beheld in calling up Aeshma.

Khaos, lurking.

A moment Morpheus held there, a silver shadow, then he pushed off the doorframe to saunter over and kneel beside her, bending his neck so his long hair brushed over her cheek. "Perhaps two might succeed where one has failed."

A momentous effort allowed her to roll over to look at him. "You would help me?"

A sadistic grin answered her. "*Beg* me."

Years of agony abraded pride even as they had worn away at her mind. Hekate grasped his hands. "I beg you." She pressed her brow to the floor in front of him. "I beg you, Morpheus. Help me."

A hand alighted on the back of her head. "I will try."

&a.

WHILE HEKATE SUSPECTED the mental exercises she had worked through with Morpheus would serve only to blunt the demonic intrusions into her dreams—that she would, at times, always find herself subjected to madness unfurling in never-ending layers—still, his efforts had bought her two dreamless nights of sleep in a row.

Two nights of true rest for the first time in six years. Such made it hard to cling to any remaining ire she might have held for the oneiromancer over wrongs done centuries ago.

Maybe all mortal grievances paled before the threat of damnation. Still, it did not keep Demeter from casting frequent glowers her way, whilst the two of them reclined upon the hillside. Given the choice, Hekate would not have whiled away an afternoon with the Inumiden Titan, but their daughters had formed a fast friendship, and now scampered about the slope, tossing a ball to one another.

Persephone was twelve now, Athene nine, and neither mother needed to oversee the girls, true, who oft played by themselves. But neither would it do for her and Demeter to hold grudges if their daughters were to be companions, and thus she had asked Demeter to join her. The easy camaraderie the children shared called up visions of her own youth—not that young, of course, but so young— walking the woods beyond Delphi with Artemis.

Try as she might, she had never quite rekindled the connection she had shared with the Phoebid she had once thought her closest friend. Oh, they spoke, in those rare times the scout came to Athyras. They talked the night away, drank wine, laughed and reminisced, toasting the fallen. But an unbridgeable gap had arisen between them, a distance that separated them, ever since they had first gone to Byblos. How different Hekate's life might have turned out, had she not insisted upon visiting the Lodge of Whispers, upon Artemis introducing her to the Circle of Goetic Mysteries.

She would not now stare into her own damnation, for one. And yet, despite it all, she had to admit, she *needed* the knowledge. She still found herself compelled back to the Sefer Raziel, poring over the grimoire again and again, seeking after yet more revelations. Maybe now, more than ever, *knowing* the face of Khaos in the dark, she had to understand what it meant. The implication of such seething madness lurking out of sight ...

Now, the afternoon had set and twilight clawed in upon the horizon. Once, Hekate had thought it her time, flourishing in the dark. Before every shadow became a predator, clamouring for her soul.

"I'm told Morpheus visited your manse in the night," Demeter said.

Hekate snorted under her breath. She was so far beyond such jibes now ... "He's not my lover."

"Oh?" That one word managed to mingle disbelief and disdain, but Hekate had little care for whether Demeter believed her, or even whether rumours spread of her taking Morpheus to her bed. In truth, the oneiromancer had indeed slept *beside* Hekate's bed that first night. While Hekate had given over her loathing of the man, she could not imagine ever again laying with him after all that had passed between them.

"Morpheus brought word from Korinth," Hekate said. "Zeus has slain Kreios and Eurybia, and the polis lies in ruins. The Ouranid

League falters. Soon, perhaps, he will move on Atlantis or Kronion."

Demeter clucked her tongue. "Will he kill his own father?"

Hekate had watched him kill his own mother, though he had not meant to, at the first. "He cannot leave him free to roam the world." She could not savour the thought of Kronos's death—how much one who lived the Time of Nyx might have to teach!—but nor did she want this war to drag on any further.

Once Artemis had slain Koios, the war had turned back to their favour once more, and Hekate had dared to hope the slaughter might soon end. Without Koios's Oracular insight, Zeus's galvanic power had proved decisive, and they had won victory after victory. Though Papa had feared Kronos would find Athyras, Zeus's unending assaults had given the Ouranid lord no time for a counterattack.

"Kinslaying is a perversion of the natural order," Demeter said. "An affront to Gaia."

Yes, but then, so were so many other deeds done in this war. The Titanomachy Men had taken to calling the unending struggle between Zeus and his father.

An uneasy silence settled between them, Hekate watching the last rays of sunlight vanish with a pang of regret. Or fear, perhaps, for the years of dreading sleep had implanted within her a force of habit not easy to cast aside.

With a sigh, Hekate climbed to her feet, intent to call Athene home and send for a servant to arrange supper. To her surprise, Demeter fell in step beside her, as if unaccepting their moment of reconciliation had set with the sun. Or perhaps something else weighed upon the Inumiden, for when Hekate looked to her, her mouth curled in the hint of a sneer.

"You would not have found lasting happiness in Zeus," Hekate said, knowing even as the words left her mouth, they would do more harm than good. But what was she to say? Apologise for pushing Demeter out as Zeus's lover? Doing so had given her Athene, and besides, Enodia had insisted the future demanded it.

"I suppose we'll never know, now," the Inumiden snapped.

Hekate considered what answer to make—or if peace between them was impossible—but something forestalled her. A vague sense of unease, deeper than that which so oft accompanied the gloaming these days.

A contortion bent the night air, an invisible perversion so intense Hekate held up her hand to silence Demeter. The Titan sputtered in indignation a moment, but then she too, though no sorceress, must have felt the violation of nature that so blasphemed the World. A thousand scorpions crawled along Hekate's skin as she strode toward the steps leading atop the wall.

The ground trembled before she reached them, lurching in protestation. A glance back, and Demeter had grabbed young Persephone, desperation having replaced loathing upon the Titan's face. To see that, to see her look to Hekate with such panic and the hope that Hekate, of all of them, might somehow save them from whatever impended—that more than aught else tied the noose around Hekate's throat. She couldn't breathe for dread of what might be coming. Had she foreseen this moment? It carried the tinge of oneiromantic dreams fulfilled, a sensation that only deepened her growing fear.

Blinking, in shaking steps, she ascended, having to steady herself as the tremors wracking the land grew more insistent. A roar of grinding rock. A convulsion of Gaia that alluded to pangs of birth, though Hekate knew, in truth, whatever lurched into reality was *not* born of the Earth.

Then she crested the wall and found herself clutching the rampart, wheezing weak, pathetic breaths through her nose at the panoply unfolding. The bucking, heaving of the land, as an abomination yanked itself free from Gaia's womb, grasping hands the size of horses latching onto rocks and hills, yanking a flowing, amorphous bulk out from a colossal rent splitting the hills. Hand after hand, a dozen hands. Two dozen. Three.

Arms bifurcated at elbows, each branch large enough to sweep away buildings, each acting as if possessed of its own fearful intellect. Arms acting as legs, dragging forth a flowing, shifting mountain. A chittering erupted, screeching over her brain, as dozens of Etheric heads formed and unformed upon a vaguely arachnid body, eyes bulbous wells of blackness.

And still, it continued to heave itself free, a bulk that would dwarf the hills around their town. A mass of limbs and heads and unspeakable, ever shifting revolution her very soul rejected.

Another nightmare. This, she had seen, in turbulent oneiromantic vision, and taken it for a nightmare. It had to be born of her own troubled mind.

The thought blared in an insistent chorus, and yet, she could have sworn this was reality, that she had been awake. Her gaze lurched between Demeter, sheltering the girls, and the demon crawling its way into the Mortal Realm. The impossibility of it, of something that ought to have lain beyond Tartarus breaching their fragile world, it ravaged the shreds of sanity she had so sought to patch together these past two days.

Hekate had no name for the hundred-armed monstrosity that had already begun to tower over Athyras's now flimsy-looking palisade, but she felt certain it had somehow crawled free of Tartarus. Its seething shadow began to occlude the moonlight as it rose above their settlement, a mountain of obscenity.

More than aught else, Hekate wanted to retreat within herself, to curl into a weeping, quivering ball and beg Gaia to wake from the unfolding nightmare. A gasping, breathless moment, she hesitated.

Then Persephone shrieked. Behind her, clutching her arm, Athene sobbed in unspeakable terror.

No.

Hekate wailed, drawing up Tithorea's power. Vines as thick around as her waist burst from the hillside, dozens of them, tangling and wrapping the demon in their thorny embrace. The explosion of flora tugged the abomination to a halt, giving her the chance. Feeding Pneuma to Khione, Hekate summoned ice crystals around her fingers. Boreal winds coalesced into frozen spears beside her.

"Pyrrha," she heard her father shout, even as gouts of flame scorched over the creature. He raced toward her side, gaze fixed upon the horror.

The demon jerked its limbs, unleashing a succession of snapping vines, tearing apart the land in the process. Torrents of rock from the shredded hillside rumbled along the ground, even as Hekate's ice lances shot forward like a hail of javelins. Those shards slammed into the creature, many clattering off chitinous armour in a cacophony, but some few punching clean into flesh beneath.

She might as well have launched her assault upon a mountain. The abomination roiled forward, unimpeded, leaving her to wonder if it had even taken notice of her.

Yes, she saw. It *had*, for Etheric heads swivelled at unnatural angles fixating upon her.

Hekate leapt from the wall an instant before a sea of limbs crashed down upon it. Some of the palisade spokes punched into flesh, but the demon paid them no more heed than it had the ice lances. The wall broke apart, so much kindling beneath a stomping foot.

Where had Papa gone? A sudden, sick fear, that he had fallen, crushed beneath that hand. But naught remained of the wall, and her daughter needed her first.

"Run!" Hekate shrieked at Demeter, then threw herself aside as a dozen crawling, probing claws skittered over the ground, seeking after her. The creature pitched over sideways, turning into a centipede-like horror, its Etheric heads melted away from what she had taken for a torso, only to form up along the back, an endless trail of them. Colossal limbs swept away houses and merchant stalls like toys, ever grasping. Hands pulverised stables, snared horses, and dragged the squealing animals beneath itself, toward concealed maws.

A spear flew over Hekate and lodged in an Etheric head. An instant later, that head melted away and reformed, the spear tumbling loose, then crunching beneath the ebullitions of limbs. Hekate scrambled backward, gaining her feet, to spot Eris, casting about for another weapon. Before the Titan could manage it, one clawed hand snatched her up by the legs, hefting her aloft. Another caught her torso, and the two yanked her apart, a shower of golden ichor raining down over Hekate, pouring into her screaming mouth.

Both halves of Eris vanished into the seething mass of the demon. Hekate broke into a mad run, chasing after Demeter and the girls as they fled. The demon skittered over the town, a flood toppling the paltry works of Man, sweeping them away in a moment of fury and madness.

More screaming then, a mad flight without direction or thought, her heart trying to beat its way free of her chest. Pneumatikoi leant her strength and speed, and she swept Athene up in her arms, charging onward. Anywhere, away from the abomination which none of them could dare stand against.

Behind came the crunching sounds of a devoured town, chewed up and vanished. An explosion resounded in the distance, a tornado of flame scorching the sky before winking out. A signal? She prayed it was and broke for it, trusting Demeter to follow with Persephone.

There, amid swirling ashes, stood Papa, arms outstretched. He must have leapt to the other side when the wall fell. His flames had blown open a fresh breach, creating a means of egress toward which he beckoned a stream of flowing townsfolk. Hekate had no time to check which of them survived, nor could she say whether escaping the town would spare them from the pursuing demon.

Only one thought had room in her head.

Flee. Run, run from this obscenity and the fate her death at its hands would bring her.

REFUGEES GATHERED in a cave ancient Phlegrans had used to bury their dead. The inscriptions had long since worn away, so Hekate could not have said whether this place housed kings or commoners, though she'd have guessed the former. Most of those here huddled around the flickering fire Papa had kindled, a concession to the demand for warmth and light despite their need to remain hidden.

Dawn could not be far off, then they'd need to smother the fire to avoid the smoke revealing their position. Cradled in the nook of Persephone's arm, Athene slept, wracked by fits and tormented by dreams Hekate feared to intrude into. Not that she could have slept herself.

How many other bands of refugees had escaped into similar hiding spaces?

Papa's hand fell upon her shoulder, offering a gentle squeeze, a pale comfort.

"What was it?" she whispered, not wanting any others who might remain awake to hear. For she knew the answer.

"I would term it the Hekatónkheir, though of it I can say little else, save that it is an Old One, released from Tartarus."

"*How*? She turned to look at him.

Something haunted lurked within his sapphire eyes. "The Old Ones are the spawn of the Primordials. As to how Kronos pulled one from Tartarus, I can harbour a guess. In the Olympian Mountains lies a breach, a passage between our world and the outermost reaches of the Spirit Realm. A place known to Kronos, and dreaded."

"Kronos called forth this *thing*?"

Papa's heavy gaze settled upon her. "Did you think one such as he would dissolve into frightened impotence? Did you think you could tap the darkest Art, transform Zeus into this perversion you have created, and no one would retaliate in kind? Where do you turn in your desperation, Pyrrha? How far would you go, facing the extinction of yourself and all you have worked for?" He hesitated, his posture revealing a ravaged weight upon him that did not otherwise show upon his face. "Artemis—and I—murdered Koios in his own bed. Zeus slew Kreios. The old order collapses, and Kronos, he has seen such things before, seen how bad they grow. And seen, too, in the Oracle Mirrors, ephemeral glimpses of his fate. Of the damnation he himself will face." The way his eyes held hers ... "What would you do to avoid an intolerable future?"

He *knew*.

An abortive sob escaped her. "Tell me it is not real." Her voice broke. "That we are not so precariously perched above this abyss I have seen. Tell me."

"I told you not to strive for answers in the dark." Profound sympathy tinged his recrimination and yet confirmed her worst fears. "Neither Man nor Titan welcomes the Ontos, once it begins to unfurl for them."

It became hard to breathe, hard to swallow. Even now, with thousands of years of life behind her, still she sat here, wanting her father to offer comfort. Desperate for a parent to shelter her from the World. But Prometheus never lied, so far as she could tell. Oh, he withheld information, misled, manipulated, yes, but she had never known him to utter an untruth. Not even now, when she'd have given away her last obol for the comfort of a reassuring delusion. For a word denying the utter damnation she had wrought for herself.

No, but he offered her, instead, the soothing of his hand stroking her hair, and she collapsed against him.

Quivering in the darkness.

17

PANDORA

2399 Golden Age

Despite her best efforts, Pandora had managed to return Herakles to a time some years after he had left, and yet, she dared not strive for more exact positioning and risk overshooting in the other direction. With the demigod consenting to remaining there, Pandora embraced him. Though she had not quite shed her instinctive revulsion at his crimes, the moments spent in his company —and the debt she could never repay—had forced her to look upon him with new eyes. A man, yes, and flawed, perhaps beyond repair. More than that, too.

Maybe everyone was more than one thing.

"What will you do?" she asked.

A visible weight tugged upon his mighty shoulders. "Redemption isn't one well-done deed cancelling one unforgivable crime." He clenched a fist at his side, setting his jaw. "But you, in the end, have given me hope it is something I can keep striving for."

Because striving was their one constant, wasn't it? With a nod of reassurance, she backed away and activated the Box once more, welcoming the bending light and momentary vertigo that accompanied her shifts through time.

The disorientation drove her to one knee, but she retained consciousness. A few blinks, and her vision adjusted to her new vantage, crouched on a hillside deep in the embrace of night.

A chittering screech ripped through the dark, fraying nerves, gnawing at the soul. Before her, an amorphous, gargantuan arachnid flowed over the obliterated ruins of a town wall. It took her a pained instant to recognise Athyras.

Torrents of refugees fled screaming from the dark flood of limbs. The creature had dozens of heads, each swivelling about on its own, acting with clear independence, a thought too obscene to dwell upon.

Caught aghast by the panoply of horror unfolding below, Pandora's hand went to her mouth. The presence of such perversion rooted her in place, left her paralysed with both nameless dread and damning recognition. For this vile, shifting maze of arms and inchoate heads could only have emerged from the writhing dark of Tartarus, now somehow present upon the surface of Gaia.

One of the fleeing townsfolk spied her, started for her, and Pandora caught sight of Styx rushing her way. An arm taller than a tree bent over backwards out of the rear of the creature and crashed down upon Tethys's daughter, the impact shooting tremors through the hillside.

Gaping, innominate dread.

No one, not even a Titan, could have survived the crushing blow.

Further agitation rippled through the ground with each slapping, grasping, lunge the abomination made, yanking itself deeper into Athyras.

This madness defied reason, drew a tear of denial from Pandora's eye, even as she watched civilisation vanish beneath it, swallowed as by a raging river.

Crunching, smashing. And ever that mind-breaking chittering.

"Get down," someone hissed behind her, then a hand seized her wrist and yanked her prone. A woman's face rose up across from her own, the woman's hair dark as night, her eyes glinting silver. Artemis. "There's naught to be done," the Titan assured her. "No weapons affect it, and I cannot imagine aught strong enough to do more than draw its ire."

"The people …" Pandora rasped. Prometheus and Pyrrha had lived in Athyras, last she had known.

"Whoever can get out will get out, and naught we could do in wading in there will help any of them." She pointed at the monstrosity swarming over what little remained of the town. "Athyras is *gone*." Still on their knees, Artemis drew Pandora away, around the side of the hill. From there they passed into woods Pandora dared to hope might shelter them from the countless eyes upon that thing.

IN THE FOREST, the Titan woman paused at a stream, washed her face, and filled a skin of water. Much as Pandora longed to sit on the loam, quivering, to surrender to despair and terror, she forced herself to crawl to the water's edge and drink.

In escaping Tartarus, she had thought she would never again behold such perversion of nature. Yet now, what felt moments after returning to the Mortal Realm, she found the Dark had crawled up out of the cracks, spilling Khaos into her home.

Too much.

This was too much. When would it end? She had sworn to Prometheus she would never give up fighting for a life with him, for a way to change Fate. Did the Moirai mock her insolent defiance by weaving in such circumstances as now beset her?

Burn …

The instinct seemed a mockery now, as if mortal rage could stand before the scope of cosmic obscenity now unfurling.

"Who are you?" Artemis asked when Pandora rose from the stream. "I saw you with Prometheus some years back, but not since then. Are you a spy?" While she did not reach for the knife at her hip, the dangerous pitch of her voice carried threat aplenty.

"I'm not a spy," Pandora said. "My name is ... my name is Nike."

"A Heliad?"

Probably. "Not every descendant of Helios has fair hair," Pandora said, looking pointedly at Artemis's own dark locks.

A slight frown. "They call me a Phoebid because of it."

Not knowing what to say to that, Pandora nodded.

When the silence had dragged on long enough to engulf them like a shroud, Artemis spoke. "What was that thing?"

Pandora almost laughed. The Titan was asking *her*? "Something that crawled forth from Tartarus." More than that she could not say. "I need to find Prometheus."

"He warned me ..." Artemis shuddered. "He said going after Koios, him leaving Athyras, it would come with a price. But I could not have imagined ..." Her gaze shifted to Pandora. "Caves litter these hills. If anyone survived, they'd have made for any number of possible refuge points. When we can be certain the creature has moved on from here, we can begin hunting tracks to try to find which cave." Something in her voice belied her words, as though she doubted to find any other survivors from the slaughter.

In truth, Pandora struggled not to give in to the same despair that so tugged at Artemis. The gaping void of it swallowed even the heat of the Phoenix, leaving only emptiness

"Prometheus warned you about whom?" she managed.

"Koios, my grandfather. An Oracle who had begun using his gifts to outwit our forces. Prometheus told me we could not overcome him without another Oracle." She said the last studying Pandora's face, perhaps gauging whether she already knew of Oracular blind spots. "When things turned dire enough, I begged him to accompany me so I could sneak up on Koios and ..."

"Kill your own grandfather."

"Mmm." It haunted her, Pandora saw, as well it should, not least because removing Prometheus from Athyras had cost so many lives. "I thought ... I thought we were winning. That this war might finally be ended. Yet, now, our brief victories seem paltry after the carnage we just witnessed, and I wonder if enough of us survive to even continue the struggle. Perhaps the war has ended after all, though not as I had hoped."

"Will the rest of the Ouranid League countenance such an abomination loosed upon Gaia?" Pandora asked.

"I don't know. If they did not, would they be able to make a difference against *that*? Kronos might sooner have harnessed Python or Ladon or some other Old One against us. Even one of those might seem easier to slay than whatever in Tartarus that thing was."

Easy to say, of course, but Pandora had felt the all-consuming intellect of Ladon pressing in upon her, when she had walked with Perseus in the Garden of the Hesperides. A lifetime ago, it felt, back when the omnipresent drakon seemed the worst incarnation of dread imaginable. Perhaps that was the Moirai's lesson for her—the World, like fear, always ran deeper.

FOR TWO DAYS AND NIGHTS, Pandora and Artemis stalked the hills of Phlegra, the Titan seeking after tracks well concealed by the carnage the monster had left in its wake. They passed the time in chatter, Pandora probing with subtle feints until she confirmed she had entered the ninth year of the Titanomachy.

Having heard no tales of the creatures Kronos had unleashed, she found herself drawn back again and again to an idea. A simple fear. For what if, despite it all, she *had* somehow changed the course of time, and Zeus would now lose this war? Despite the momentary rush, the titillating thrill at envisioning arrogant Zeus squirming beneath his father's sandal, Pandora could not allow such an end. Not when it would take all she had ever known and loved from her, too.

"I am my brother's equal in so many pursuits," Artemis was saying, "his superior in war and woodcraft, and yet, upon him falls all praise for any achievement. Was I to tolerate an eternity of snubs?"

Though Pandora could well appreciate the woman's justifications for turning on her own father, if she believed women would thrive under Zeus's rule, the future would soon disabuse her of those notions. She opened her mouth to raise the subject of Urania's Utopia, then shut it. Did the Muse even live yet? Certainly, she would not write her dialogue for centuries more.

"You seem well familiar with inequities," Artemis said when Pandora kept silent.

Oh, indeed, and Pandora could regale her with tales long into the night. Anecdotes of abuse—physical, verbal, mental—hurled upon her in her days as a slave and again as a hetaira. Then, worse perhaps, the tales of Io and Europa and the Pleiades and so many others shattered under service to the prodigious lusts of the very Titan she and Artemis fought for even now.

But doing so would burden Artemis and avail Pandora little, considering she still needed to keep true the course she had set herself upon. Zeus had to win this, and she could not begin to explain to Artemis her reasons. The woman made pleasant company though, warm in conversation, and seeming unbothered by hours of companionable silence.

When they found others at last, the refugees had taken shelter in a tomb cut into the side of the hill. Artemis crept up on scouts set to watch, tapped one on the shoulder, and smiled like a cat when the man nigh jumped out of his own skin. Once it was decided no one should catch an arrow, they found themselves greeted by a haggard lot. Men and women and some few children clad in filthy, tattered garb, faces gaunt from fear and hunger, eyes red from sleepless nights.

Hestia was among those first to recognise Pandora, though she did not rise. Both her legs lay bound in splints so extensive Pandora did not want to imagine how she had sustained such breaks. Where one leg poked free of her peplos, the skin had turned mauve, scars making plain that bone had not long ago jutted free of flesh.

Before Pandora could speak to Hestia, Prometheus emerged from further back in the cave, rushing toward her to wrap her in an embrace. The warmth of it stilled the shudders she didn't know had lain within her core. Would that this could go on forever. That she could shut out the procession of Ananke and the unending depriva-tions it visited upon them all.

But time was ever running from her.

Burn. A command to bring the inequities to ash.

After sharing a glance with Artemis, Pandora stepped outside with Prometheus for whatever passed for privacy in such circum-stances. Pain and hope and something unnamable lurked behind his crystal eyes when he looked to her, a glance brought the shuddering right back.

"I'm ... Nike," she said. It sounded absurd. Didn't she have a thou-sand other things to tell him, to ask him, to share with him? But her words spilled out, a breaking dam. "I'm the avatar of the Phoenix. And somehow, *I*, not even a warrior, have to fight alongside Zeus and ensure he wins, or else Pyrrha will die. And everything else I ever loved I'll lose too. I have no idea what to do or how to do any of this." Or whom to blame for it all, but damn, if someone did not need an epic castigation.

"I don't have all the answers ... Nike."

"You always have more than I do!" Her outburst drew stares from those within the cave. Glowering, she forced herself to lower her voice while dragging him a few steps farther away. "Just ... just tell me what to do, all right? Because every time I think I have a grip on all this, every time I think I can corral Fate to suit me, some fresh obscenity unfolds." It wasn't his fault, she knew. Ananke trapped him even as it trapped her, forced him to walk paths he'd have not chosen in desperation to preserve the things he loved. But he had made the Box, had left out so many truths his future self might have shared with her. Left them out—after having had *this* very damn conversa-tion. Because he had always omitted such details, because he dare not deviate and risk the Tapestry unraveling.

Taciturn, he watched her, no doubt reading the war raging within her upon the subtle shifts of her face. An instant of frustration rose, born of his very ability to so gauge her frustrations. This, too, she pushed down. Lashing out—and the Phoenix wanted to—at the one she loved the most would not change her situation in the least.

"How did Hestia sustain that injury?" Pandora asked, deciding it best to change the subject before her ire erupted and buried him.

"She led a group of Firewalkers to try to immolate the Hekatónkheir." That was what they were calling it? "They succeeded in wounding the creature, but Hestia says their efforts served to annoy rather than inflict lasting harm. We lost a great many ..." Prometheus's voice trembled, almost imperceptibly. These were people he had trained, Men to whom he had given the Art of Fire with a promise of a better future. Now they, and their future, were crushed beneath the Hekatónkheir.

"Pyrrha?" she asked.

"Resting within, taking care of her daughter."

Her ... daughter. Pandora and Prometheus's *grandchild* was within. Terrified and at the same time fair rumbling with excitement, Pandora worked her way within, and Prometheus guided her into recesses illumined by the embers of a fire. Beside it slept a girl, perhaps nine, her auburn hair a shade lighter than that of her mother nearby. Pyrrha—Hekate—looked up at Pandora's approach, her expression haunted. Pandora had dared to delude herself into thinking, this time, perhaps Hekate would look at her and want to connect.

But an ocean of pain and recrimination was too vast for any bridge to span.

Still, Pandora knelt in front of her daughter. "Who's this?" she asked, inclining her head toward the girl.

"Athene." Pandora had expected spite in Hekate's voice. She had hoped for an invitation to ask more. She had not, however, imagined the barren, emotionless answer she received.

That so struck her, staring at her daughter, that it took her a moment more to even realise Hekate had just told her she was grandmother to an Olympian. To ... to ... the same Titan who would one day aid Pandora and Perseus. Whom Pandora had encountered but a few days ago, upon the slopes of Olympus during the Gigantomachy.

Prometheus's hand on her shoulder kept her from drifting away, left as she was, untethered by the revelation. She wanted to say more, to say aught that might reach across to Pyrrha, but her daughter twisted around, turning her back on Pandora, refusing the least conversation.

When Prometheus had guided her away, to his own spot in the cave, he ran his thumb over her fingers. "Since you left, she has delved deeper into the dark, plumbing the shadows, despite my efforts to redirect her."

"What do you mean?"

"You, I think, have beheld the seething Dark and thus begun to apprehend portions of the Ontos. Having thus borne witness, you can, perhaps, imagine the weight piled upon one who bound herself to such forces."

Leaning against the cavern wall, Pandora clutched her fists, wanting to scream. For all the power the Phoenix gave her, she had failed to spare her daughter. Groaning, she slowly beat her knuckles against stone. What else could she do?

IN THE MORN, Zeus joined them, along with his son Ares, the both of them guided by Arke. At first, Pandora could not help but gape at the Titan woman, her resplendent wings folded behind herself yet still plain enough to see as Arke greeted the cluster of refugees.

"What is it, Nike?" Artemis asked, coming up behind Pandora.

Images of the woman casting herself to her death to escape Tartarus revolved in Pandora's mind. The relief on her face at being freed. The silent plunge into the gloom. If Pandora spoke now, she condemned Arke to that Fate. Yet, how could she hold her peace, knowing Arke might well have contributed to the massacre in Athyras by reporting to the Ouranids? Perhaps she had already betrayed even this location to their foes.

Much though it rankled, Pandora's lot remained with Zeus, and she could not change that, damn the Moirai for it.

"She's a traitor," she said, unable to look at Artemis as she spoke.

"What?"

"She's feeding information to the Ouranid League."

A sudden blur of motion rushed past her, then crashed into Arke, bearing her down, slamming her skull against the stone. "How many?" Artemis shrieked, now atop Arke. Her fist descended so fast that too seemed a blur, the speed as much a shock as the violence. Twice more, resounding blows retorted through the cavern. "How many died because of *you*! Aidos? Was that you, you bitch?"

Pandora had not had time to even think.

"What the fuck is this?" Zeus demanded, heaving Artemis off Arke with one hand. The Titan shoved her away.

From the look on her face, Pandora expected Artemis to charge back in, maybe even fight past Zeus, but she held in place, trembling with rage. "Arke has betrayed us to Kronos and the League."

By now, Hekate had emerged from the recesses of the cavern and knelt beside the winged woman. For whatever reason, she slipped a ring off Arke's finger, then rose, backing away.

"With her unconscious," Morpheus said, striding past Hekate, "I may be able to get inside her head to confirm."

Zeus's face had become a burnished mask of fury, inhuman in loathing, unspeakable malice lurking behind pale eyes. "Do it."

Morpheus had Arke dragged alongside the wall, then slumped down adjacent to her. Pandora had to admire his apparent ability to drift off to sleep almost the moment he shut his eyes. Not long later, he rose, cracked his neck, and looked to Zeus, offering a single grim nod.

"Get her up," Zeus growled.

When Ares and someone Pandora did not know hefted Arke, Zeus stalked around her. With a violent jerk, he tore the peplos from her shoulders. It seemed to bring Arke around, for she began to blink, to look about herself.

Oh, damn it. This would happen because of Pandora's own actions. She was going to have to bear witness to—

Grabbing a wing in each hand, Zeus planted his sandal against Arke's back and heaved. The sickening rip of flesh resounded through the cavern a single heartbeat before Arke's wailing agony drowned out all other sound. Golden ichor sprayed from her rent wings even as Zeus tossed the great feather hunks aside.

Bile scorched Pandora's throat and, more than aught else, she wanted to look away. To deny she had held any part in this perversion of justice.

The moment her captors released her, Arke crumpled into a heap, lying within the aureate puddle of her own lifeblood.

Because I saw him for the madman he was, Arke had said.

All Pandora could do was stand and stare, letting waves of horror wash over her.

18

ATHENE

1600 Silver Age

Fresh tremors shot through Athene's arms, ran down her fingers until she had to clench her fists in the hopes of concealing her condition. If she only had another dose of Nectar … But she had downed the last of it before the fighting had broken out.

Dead Gigantes lay strewn about the slopes of Olympus, the last of them at her feet in the very agora of her home. Another of those serpent-Gigantes writhed in death throes, her spear through its lung, pinning it to the cobbles. A jerk freed the shaft, and Athene paid the monster no more heed. Within her palace, she had another stash of Nectar, precious draught that could still the gnawing need fraying her.

"Athene!" a voice bellowed, Hephaistos tromping through streets imbrued with crimson and gold stains, the sheen of his armour obscured by gore. Blood painted his greaves, splattered his sandals, and trailed in his wake. In the thick of the fighting, Hephaistos had charged about on his chariot, but it would seem he'd engaged no few foes on foot as well. "I know what you have done, you odious bitch!"

Did he now? A grim smirk tugged at the edges of her lips, along with the welling desire to confess all, to pour forth the truth of her vindication. To let him recoil on seeing the depths of her loathing.

"I always believed you lay behind what befell Medusa," Hephaistos snarled, stalking closer. The Titan bore a javelin, its tip incandescent. Athene *revelled* in the look he shot her, his desire—impotent, for he dare not attack the child of Zeus—to fling the searing weapon at her. "I knew, though I could not prove it. But *this* ..." His delicious shudders bespoke just horror. His next words trembled forth through gritted teeth. "I beheld the flayed skin of my own *father*, strewn over the mountainside."

"Oh, *yes*," Athene said, closing in on him. The flavour of his despairing disbelief blunted the edge of her need for Nectar, so savoury, so sating at long last. "How he wailed as I skinned him." Laughter threatened to burst forth from her chest. "How he squealed like a pig."

"For what!" Hephaistos screamed, that javelin point drifting upward as though he thought he might really impale her with it. "What justifies this macabre violation of decency?"

"Violation ..." Athene sneered, her bout of humour smothered. "Your choice of words makes clear you already apprehend the course of justice, long delayed."

He had the gall to look surprised, as if the source of her righteous wrath was not so very plain. "What? Because we fucked, once? It was only natural, and you but too demure to admit your desires."

Askance, Athene cocked her head, not quite sure she had heard right. Dare he? The only answer she had left was to jerk her adamant xiphos free of its sheath.

"You would raise a weapon I crafted myself against me?" Hephaistos demanded.

When she continued to close with him, delectable fear dawned upon his face. He flung the red-hot javelin. Her Alacrity slowed its apparent flight just enough for her to bat it out of midair with her blade. Reversing her momentum, Athene jerked the pommel up into his nose. Cartilage exploded as ichor sprayed forth and Hephaistos stumbled backward.

An awareness that she had begun screaming in wordless rage settled on her, and she threw the whole of her fury into Potency. Her sandal connected with his armoured gut and sent him airborne for a single heartbeat before he crashed back down.

He must have managed the wherewithal to draw upon Steadfastness, for the blow didn't faze him, and he jerked free a kopis strapped behind his back. Adamant, like her own blade, of the finest workmanship. Athene deflected his first swipe, sidestepping around him. Her xiphos bit into his hamstring behind his armour, cut clean down to bone, driving him to one knee as his leg gave out.

His wild howling resounded off the palaces rimming the agora, delectable enough to savour for a moment. Then she caught the wrist of his sword hand and punched her pommel into the back of his elbow. Perhaps pain prevented him from calling on Steadfastness, for the bone snapped clean out the other side.

Growling, Athene jumped onto his back, pounding her fist between his shoulder blades. Broken and weak, he toppled to the ground face-first. At long last, her moment had come, and Athene felt her heart would burst from her chest with the surging relief pounding through her. With one Potency-infused hand, she shoved Hephaistos's face harder against the cobblestones, leaning close to his ear.

"Does powerlessness appeal?" And another thought.

She jerked away the armoured skirt of his pteryges, then his tunic and loincloth. The Titan, perhaps realising her intent, thrashed but could not dislodge her. Seizing his stones roughly in one hand, she purred, "It's only natural."

His shrieks, as her xiphos cut free the stones, dwarfed even the agonised wails elicited by his other injuries. The shrill blaring ripped through the summit of Olympus, so primal Athene's stomach dropped out from beneath her, her rage swallowed in a sinking chasm of horror at such suffering.

A distant part of her wanted to name it justice, but she could not quite push away the sudden disgust her own actions had engendered.

Whether mercy or the need to cling to the last vestiges of her fury, compulsion seized her, and she slid the xiphos through the back of Hephaistos's neck. At once, his thrashing abated, and a last, shuddering breath escaped him.

When she freed the blade that had slain both Demeter and Hephaistos, Athene could not help but stare, rapt and horrified, at dribbling streams of ichor tracing its length, seeping into the grooves of its pommel.

Oh, how she needed another dose of Nectar.

ATHENE'S TRIAL—FOR the way her father and Hera stared down at her from their thrones while the gathered remnants of Olympus looked on gave the impression of a trial—unfolded beneath the sullen silence of the king and the gleeful sneer of the queen. In truth, however, Athene, wracked by tremors and lost in the haze of slaughter and memory, felt the impression more of drifting through the proceeding than experiencing it. She recalled saying little in her defence, certainly not voicing her motivations for killing Hephaistos — such shame would never air. They had found her, bloody blade in hand, kneeling over the corpse, still as if cast from marble.

Her mother remained conspicuous in her absence. Perhaps because Hekate knew well the foregone conclusion of all this. While Hera droned on about the breaking of the Twelve Olympians, about justice, calling for Athene's head, Athene found her mind flitting, almost as if swept into Nectar-induced visions. Only, instead of glimpsing murky futures, she relived pellucid pasts, saw herself, fair choking on venom, plot three decades worth of vengeance against Hephaistos and the whole Kreiad genos.

Her father's abrupt rise from his throne, its legs scraping over marble with echoing screeches, forestalled Hera's bombast.

"Were you not my child, I'd indeed have your head for this."

Mighty Zeus stalked closer, pale blue eyes raking over the court in wild, simmering fury that drove her to sudden recollection. Before her death, Demeter accused Zeus of murdering Hades, his own brother, and in collaboration with Hekate, no less. Could Athene's parents have committed such a crime? Given the well of coiled wrath pacing around her, yes, Athene imagined it all too possible.

Coming to rest before her, her father flared his nostrils. "Demeter ought to have been brought before me, to face *my* judgment." Though she kept her face expressionless, Athene had to wonder: did Father object more to her slaying traitorous Demeter than loyal Hephaistos, for it had denied him his own vengeance? "You have struck down two Olympians and forever defiled the sacred order of this mountain. This leaves me no choice save to cast you from it and all the sheltering benefits Olympus bestows. You are no longer an Olympian, no longer owner of Athenai—though your line of mortal kings shall keep it, for now—and we shall ..." Her father swallowed, face contorted in apparent grief. "We shall no longer provide you Ambrosia."

Even through the miasma of her disorientation, that bit deep. For, unless other compassionate Titans chose to share their allotment, Athene would eventually resume ageing, one day to wither and die like a mortal. Or perhaps Father's sentence was calculated to remind her—and all other Titans—that their very lives depended upon his favour. That he could revoke their right to exist if they failed to abide by his rules. As an Olympian, Athene had thought herself standing astride Gaia, master of the world. Her punishment served as an admonition: that though Titans might dominate Men, still they too would be dominated by the very top of the chain. One who strove to climb too high, mortal or otherwise, must be cast down in ignominy.

Perhaps Father imagined the tremors now wracking Athene fear at her sentence. Either way, satisfied, her father dismissed her with a callous wave of his hand and a disdainful look.

Though she had expected her mother to meet her on the way from the palace, Hekate still did not deign to show herself. Had Athene disappointed both her parents? The thought might have horrified, but numbness and the desperate craving for Nectar forced it into the distant recesses of her mind.

When she reached her own palace, intent to claim some few supplies—and Nectar!—she found it barred to her, blocked by Hermes, who shook his head. Though she could tell he tried to keep his face impassive, he failed, a slight smirk creeping in upon the edges of his mouth. Perhaps her half-brother thought he might now become Father's favourite. Certainly, he had never well hidden his envy that she, a *woman*, should win more praise than he had ever received.

A perverse instinct rose in her, a sudden desire to rush him, to see if he'd dare fight her to stop her from claiming her precious Nectar. But then, if Hermes guarded her palace, Father had probably set him to it. Were Athene to slay him, her head would decorate an arch in this very agora.

And *still*, her voracious need made her consider it. The relief of even a sip might prove worth any price. To say naught of the grim satisfaction she'd get for impaling Hermes upon her blade.

"I gathered some supplies for you," a voice said from behind, and Athene spun, hand reflexively upon the hilt of her tainted xiphos. Of all people, Prometheus, her grandfather, stood there, an extra satchel hung from the crook of his elbow, crystal eyes sparkling. "Come." His open hand welcomed her in, offering her warmth now denied to her by every other Titan on this mountain.

Despite herself—or perhaps she had no strength left for bitterness or the accusation that her grandfather had never before taken the least interest in her life—she took his hand. "Why now?" she managed as they walked, knowing her question was opaque to the point of inaneness but capable of naught more at the moment.

Regardless, he answered, apprehending her meaning. "Our bloodline is blessed or cursed, so many of us wracked by prescient visions, yourself included. Witnessing such, you of all people should know Ananke sometimes demands paths beyond our desires or even understanding."

"You mean Fate itself forced you to ignore your granddaughters?"

He did not release her hand, even as they descended the stairs down from the agora. "I mean I have been remiss, and I hope to rectify it now, in ways I could not before."

❦

RAVAGED BY CHILLS, beset by foggy visions of slaughter and bloodshed, and wracked by occasional dry heaves, Athene lay beside Prometheus's fire and groaned. "I need it ..." She knew she ought to have hated the pathetic timbre of her voice, but she couldn't bring herself to care.

"This is the second time you've suffered these symptoms," Prometheus said, staring into the campfire. "If, after it is all finished, you truly wish to endure this again, you can find Kirke and ask for more of the stuff. I have none."

"Hades damn you," she moaned, squeezing her eyes shut as if it might somehow still the churning of her empty gut.

Prometheus poked at the flame with a stick. "According to old legends, in times gone, some ate the fruit of the Tree of Life whole, and thus extended their lives by thousands of years, reducing their ageing process so dramatically men thought them immortal. But few apples arise, a handful in a generation, and so was developed a process to distill it into a brew that could bestow limited immortality upon many."

Gaia, her head was breaking apart and he droned on about legends no doubt from the Time of Nyx. "Why are you telling me this?"

"Those first ones to craft the brew named it differently, but when Kronos restored the process at the dawn of this Era, he called it Ambrosia. Liquid gold, more precious than the metal by far, for the longevity and power it bestows, enough to elevate Titans so far above Men as to be called gods. Denied periodic doses, you will, of course, resume normal ageing."

"I know that, you gigantic arse-monster." Why would he not shut up? She caught herself wondering if boring her own skull open with a blade would alleviate the pressure, found herself dwelling on the macabre, satisfying mental image of it.

"Perhaps, though, if your words and deeds made you worthy, you might find some who cared enough to share with you. Those like Kirke, who might have more to offer you than poisonous Nectar."

She managed a weak snort. "Why would a Nymph share what little Ambrosia she receives with a half-sister she barely tolerated, when I was …"

"An Olympian?" Prometheus looked to her now. "Perhaps the question you ought to ask is, 'How can I become more tolerable?' Your arrogance, bequeathed to you by your father, has allowed you to think yourself better than Men. Or Nymphs. Your anger, however justified, has poisoned you to the pith of your soul."

Now, she forced herself up on one arm to glare at Prometheus. "Hephaistos made me into this!" He had turned her into this wretch who fed upon suffering, visiting it down upon the Titan and his kin.

"Indeed, he did. Violence propagates itself, the most virulent of all plagues. For it infects those who invoke it, those who suffer, even those who but witness it. It transmogrifies the soul, leaving all it passes close to blighted, changed."

His words cut, and Athene had no patience for even small wounds. "He *deserved* my wrath. He earned it a thousand times over."

"Did you deserve it?" That intense, sapphire gaze made it a real question.

"W-what?"

"Did you deserve your own rage?"

"I wasn't …" What in Hades's Underworld was he on about?

"Did you deserve the ruination of your own life? Did the decades of sleepless nights nursing grudges, reliving your torments, in the end, avail you? Did your rage, stoked fresh by your mind whenever it began to dwindle, give you a better life? Life is transitory, Athene, even for immortals, and being thus, we can measure our time in this world only by moments and memories. By the happiness we experience in our lives and that we can bring to others."

"Hedonism."

"No, not at all. The momentary joy of an overindulgence in wine —or Nectar—is oft outweighed by its cost, which may reach deeper than a mere hangover. The price becomes the life we might have led, the more meaningful moments we might have shared."

Still shaking, she managed to sit. "You imply I ought to have forgiven what that bastard did to me."

"Not that, either, for such was unforgivable." So he did know. Shame flushed her cheeks, though she hoped he could not make it out in the firelight. "Rather, I would have you consider whether you might have drawn more meaning from these last thirty years had you lived without seeping in toxins you yourself refilled. Perhaps, one day, I will tell you how *I* spent the past three decades."

"He deserved what happened to him!" she blurted, knowing, even as she said it, the lameness of reusing the same argument she had already relied upon.

Not deigning to repeat his answer to that, Prometheus turned back to the fire.

Athene groaned and slumped to the ground. Maybe she would hate him, before this was over. Maybe, but then, he was the only one still by her side. The only one in the World.

19

PANDORA

2399 Golden Age

"Nike was right," Artemis said, standing atop a hill, gaze locked upon the growing streaks of the rising sun. "Not all of the League will abide Kronos defiling Gaia with denizens of Tartarus."

Ebony locks fluttering in the morning breeze, the Titan cut an impressive figure, a warrior that, despite the Pneuma granted by the Phoenix, Pandora could only dream of matching. This woman had broken the siege of Helion in the Ambrosial War, saving Pandora back then, though neither had known the other at the time. Even now, standing on the hill with her, Zeus, Prometheus, and Hekate, Pandora felt the imposter. Did the name Nike alone carry with it weight enough to transform her into the legendary Goddess of Victory?

"Fuck that," Zeus said. "They're all fucking traitors." His capacity to reframe the whole of history to fit his internal narrative never ceased to astound. As if the Titan could not recall that, less than a decade ago, he had slain his own brother and rebelled against his father's authority, rather than the other way around. "Instead of coddling them, we ought to flay every last craven wretch of the League." He whirled on Hekate. "Get me one of those monsters for myself."

The very thought of Zeus in command of an Old One, *any* Old One, prickled Pandora's skin with goose pimples. The ravages he could visit upon Man played out in her mind's eye amid his cackles, the Titan aroused by his own perceived greatness. Pandora needed no hint of prescience to foresee the nightmare.

"We do not know whence Kronos brought it forth," Hekate said. Of course, Pandora knew the location, and she expected Prometheus might already know as well. Whether Hekate had lied or had not yet learnt where in the Olympian Mountains the Tartarian Gate lay, Pandora could not say. Either way, she blew out a faint sigh of relief at her daughter having denied at least this ambition of Zeus's. "Even if we did, we do not have the means to call forth or control such a demon. Concentrate instead upon surviving this one."

Artemis looked back at them. With the sun behind her, Pandora could not make out her face, but her voice conveyed strain enough. "My father may yet come to our side—if we can give him reason enough and a way to save face in process. With the might of Helion behind us—"

"You want me to entice him!" Zeus roared. "He owes me his loyalty! Helios is not fit to lick the mud from my sandals, and you want me to bribe him?"

To her credit, Artemis did not flinch beneath Zeus's tirade. "He controls a mighty navy and an army of Titans. I think likely that, were he to join us, Phoebe, too, would take our side, or at least abandon Kronos. That demon, as Hekate calls it, rampages through our forces, whilst our foes mount on all sides. If we dawdle now, we risk losing further position, making it impossible to sway allies to our cause."

Zeus rolled his eyes. "Fine, fine. Go. You want a gift for him to save face ... send your mother back to him. The chance to put her in her place ought to appease the Sun Titan."

The shifting of Artemis's weight made it seem like she might strike out at Zeus for such words.

Prometheus broke in before violence erupted. "Rather, perhaps offer him a new wife. Marriage alliances have long sealed pacts between allies, the bonds they form far more lasting than whatever transitory satisfaction Helios would derive from shaming Leto."

After a moment mulling that over, scraping fingers through his coarse beard, Zeus grunted. "Tethys has an unwed daughter. Hera's sister, Perse. The Titan can't much object to me sending my own sister-in-law." A snort. "At least not until he meets the bitch."

Silent, arms folded, Pandora watched Prometheus. Had he traded a woman's life in a political manoeuvre with such ease? The thought left a rumbling disquiet in her gut, a heat rising in her, demanding release.

"I'll inform Perse and make ready to sail," Artemis said, departing, followed by Hekate and Zeus.

The look Pandora cast Prometheus when they remained alone atop the hill, painted in spreading sunlight, must have made plain her displeasure, for the Titan sighed. "It is a fine thing to strive for a world better than the one in which we live. Less fine if we allow our current world to burn by pretending we have already achieved our desires."

"Small comfort to the lives sacrificed upon the altar of expediency."

Prometheus winced, the pain writ so plain upon his usually guarded visage Pandora had to wonder just how many lives he *had* sacrificed over the ages. "Do you imagine Perse's fate would have been more pleasant, crushed beneath a demon or executed by Kronos if we lose this war?"

"You already know we do not."

Now he frowned. "And you well know that any victory we achieve comes from our deeds, not from simply waiting for the inevitable. Prescience does not excuse us from acting, it accounts for those actions."

Was she being petty? Oh, but Pandora had seen women so oft

traded as chattel and counted herself among such wretched souls. *Burn them all!* Sometimes, the need for it seared all other thoughts, and Pandora had to struggle to form words. "In your prescience, did you *know*, on suggesting Zeus send a wife, he would select Perse without so much as consulting her wishes?"

"My prescience is stronger than most, Love, but I hardly forewitness every detail or result of a given conversation."

She scoffed. "Does anyone?"

His sudden, deepening silence caught her off guard. She'd meant to accuse him of abrogating responsibility for his words by claiming he had not known the full outcome, as if anyone did. But the pensiveness that claimed him now had her wondering—could some Oracle, perhaps the Moirai themselves—foresee greater depths of time than the glimpses Prometheus managed?

"Go with them," he said, his abrupt change of subject further throwing her off-balance. "You have a way with words and may help convince Helios to cast his full support behind an alliance, and too, you may soothe over any misgivings born from this. Because you are right, Perse was given no choice in the matter, and even in my haste to keep Artemis from assaulting Zeus, I ought to have considered he would consult no woman about her wishes."

Pandora was not the only one with a way with words, and though she wanted to say so, or to demur, refusing further separation, she knew he could not leave here without risking the Hekatónkheir discovering their hiding spot. Perhaps all she had to do was to keep pushing forward, striving for a way to work this out.

And wondering if the Moirai saw so *very* much of the future. If they accounted for her every word ever spoken. Every thought that would pass through her mind, even this one.

As it turned out, Perse had not the least objection to a marriage to a Titan she deemed one of the greatest lords in history. The Nymph claimed she would reign as queen over an island of sunlight, basking in the adoration of generations to come. That and golden palaces must have seemed all the more appealing after a fortnight spent in a draughty cave with no comfort and not enough food to go around.

They had trekked south over land, to the shores of the Thalassa, and bartered passage from a small merchant ship that stopped in a village on the way to Khios. A few tetradrachmae from Artemis convinced the captain to pass on from there to Helion.

As the bireme threaded the turquoise waves, the crew broke into a shanty. A bawdy tune about a winemaker's daughter seeing the world while entertaining a crew-full of men. Whether the sailors had forgotten three women now guested among them or did not care, Pandora could not say. Either way, she stood with Artemis at the stern, well behind the captain, watching the spilling wake.

"I've heard so many tales of you," Pandora admitted. Artemis had talked of the war, of joining Zeus because of a friendship she had once shared with Hekate, long ago. A stinging reminder of how little Pandora knew her daughter. Of lost time that, despite the Box, she could never reclaim. But the conversation lulled, and Pandora had other things to ask her. "They say you are the finest warrior on Gaia."

Artemis snorted. "Who says such? Were you to ask my brother, I think you'd hear I am, at best, competent. Admitting even that much might well so pain him he'd need to drown his sorrows with a dozen amphorae of wine."

"You slew Khione," Pandora said, smiling at the memory of a play retelling the event. A time with Prometheus before she could have imagined the winding currents of Ananke. "You drove off Kratos and his sisters. You hunted down and killed Koios and escaped to tell the tale."

The Titan flushed, turning her face to the side, unaccustomed to praise.

"Would you train me?" Pandora asked. "I've strong Pneuma, but only the most rudimentary of instruction in spear-work." From a demigod who would not be born for millennia.

The askance look Artemis cast her way implied Pandora had grown a second head, but as the shock wore off, she gnawed her lip in consideration. "Few women learn such arts, and I cannot say it will much improve your marriage prospects. Most men do not want a woman who might, if driven to it, challenge them."

"Yes, and I will surely base my life around what most men wish for."

That earned her a wry grin. "So be it. When opportunity presents"—a pointed look around served as a reminder they could not well train aboard the bireme—"I will teach you what I can, Nike."

Would she ever grow accustomed to that name? Either way, with Artemis's help, perhaps Pandora could at least become *worthy* of it.

THE COLOSSUS SPANNING the harbour greeted their arrival in Helion, its shadow sweeping over them a warning of how deeply they had passed into Helios's power. Last Pandora had visited this island, the statue had not yet existed, denying her the chance to gape at the wonder. A chance she now took full advantage of, not caring who saw her mouth hanging open while they drew into the sheltered harbour.

A herald announced their coming, and though Artemis intimated some fear her father would try to apprehend them, they received a royal welcome befitting peace envoys. Perhaps the Titan lord had heard already of the demon unleashed upon the mainland and thus sought after any means of escaping from his circumstance, or perhaps he wished to lull his insubordinate daughter into believing herself safe.

Either way, *another* female warrior met them, xiphos at her hip, golden eyes watching every move Artemis made while sparing a bare glance at Pandora and Perse.

"Phaethusa," Artemis said, one hand raised in an abortive attempt to embrace the woman.

"This way," Phaethusa said, beckoning them onward while keeping a measured distance away from Artemis at all times. Close enough to prevent any attempt at escape, far enough back to ensure time to react to any sudden move. The weight of history sat so heavy between the two women it filled the air.

Their guide brought them up to the acropolis, the golden palace Pandora had only ever beheld from below. With the Pneuma from the Phoenix, the climb didn't wind her in the least, leaving her free to absorb the splendour of caryatid-lined gardens, frescoes depicting rain-drenched jungles, and relief-carved columns, some plated in glittering gold.

They passed through a courtyard, where auburn-haired Kirke rose sharply from the lip of a fountain carved into intertwining mermaids. "They said you were coming," the Nymph said to Artemis, voice thick with apprehension. Though Kirke's gaze darted over both Pandora and Perse, she offered no sign of recognition.

Phaethusa paused, allowing Artemis to greet the woman, while Pandora folded her hands behind her back to keep from fidgeting. Of course Kirke would not encounter Pandora for centuries yet, and it would not do to make such an impression as to have her recognise her then.

"This is Kirke," Artemis said, looking at Pandora and Perse, "daughter of Helios and Hekate, and thus my half-sister. Kirke, I give you Nike and Perse."

Daughter of Hekate? It took the sum of all Pandora's will to keep from sputtering, to offer a simple nod in greeting. Kirke was Hekate's daughter? Which meant not only Athene but Kirke, too, was Pandora and Prometheus's grandchild. And he had never told her of it. Of course not, because Prometheus withheld most aught he could for fear of unraveling his precious Tapestry. The shock of it left her speechless, a hundred new questions worming their way through her soul as she wondered at the implications, at if Kirke *had* recognised her when they met in the Silver Age. If the woman had the least clue she had nigh throttled her own grandmother? Her mind struggled to parse the revelation, and she felt herself shifting to it, not unlike the sliding panels and gears of her Box.

A multitude of possible things she might have said to a grown grandchild, thousands of years her senior, and each she considered and discarded out of the same paralysing caution that afflicted Prometheus. What could she say? Her embrace, her words of intimacy and familiarity would fall unwelcome, seem unwarranted to a woman who did not know her. Any attempt to rectify that, to insert herself into Kirke's life here, risked *unmaking* that life by altering the course of time.

"Nike?" Artemis asked, motioning her forward and reminding Pandora that she stood there, staring at a woman she did not know and considering wrapping her arms around her.

"I sometimes think myself adrift through history," she mused, falling in step beside Artemis as the woman followed Phaethusa further into the palace.

"That we are swept up in forces beyond ourselves?" Artemis asked, thinking she could understand the life Pandora led. But only those like herself and Prometheus could begin to fathom the burdens Pandora bore.

The chamberlain bid them wait until the lord was ready for them, giving them a few moments more to stroll the gardens, Phaethusa ever trailing behind. With every passing heartbeat, the compulsion to return to Kirke, to spend even a portion of an afternoon in her company, it deepened. It echoed through Pandora's core, a primal need for a connection denied.

When the Titan lord at last readied to receive them, when Pandora thought she might burst from denying her instincts, Phaethusa guided them inside. Helios reclined upon a golden throne in a pose that bespoke such encompassing confidence Pandora felt tempted to name it hubris, even in a Titan. Here, in repose, dwelt a being that claimed these aureate halls, this city, the island, so *many* islands, in virtue of sheer, personal power. And indeed, puissance spilled from him until Pandora might, had she not known better, have sworn true sunlight radiated out of him. But she did know better, could see the masterful layout of the hall that limned the throne in afternoon brilliance, creating the appearance of a halo behind the crown, and would have gleamed along the form of any who occupied the position. Judging by the layout, the acoustics would have also cast the sun Titan's voice through the chamber like an amphitheater projecting the voices of an actor, giving the impression of divinity filling the whole of the hall.

Such things she studied, immobile, whilst Artemis relayed their suit, and the proposal that Helios should wed Perse, who offered the Titan a respectful bow and a coy smile.

"But why," Helios demanded, when Artemis had finished, "would I agree to ally against Kronos now that he has nigh smashed through the sum of your defences? What could possess me to turn traitor to my old friend when he appears on the cusp of victory?"

Artemis cast a glance to Pandora, who strode forward. "My lord," Pandora said, "you know well the dark forces Kronos has called upon to sway this war back in his favour. A Titan capable of such, driven to such desperation, is not likely to content himself with a mere return to a state of things as once they were. He cannot help but be warped by the power he commands, driven to think himself invincible." Or was she speaking of Zeus? Madmen and tyrants abounded, it seemed. "Do you believe such a ruler, one driven to paranoia by the perfidy of his own kin, will tolerate rivals? Whether Zeus wins this or Kronos, the Ouranid League as it was cannot endure. One or the other will come for your lands, unless your negotiation now, this day, preempts the need for it. This, to say naught of the more obvious concern: would you ally yourself with a man who could only win against his son by calling forth Tartarus itself to his side?"

Sometimes, for the sake of debate, a symposiarch asked guests, especially astute philosophers, to defend a position they did not even believe in. To make arguments, without lying, that only the keenest minds might refute. Pandora had watched it happen many a time, bitter that such rules forbade women from participating in either side of the debate, relegating her to playing a harp and seducing the guests. Never would she have imagined she would argue the merits of Zeus winning the Titanomachy.

Helios released an affected sigh that told her he, perhaps, wished only for a reason to turn from Kronos. The war had cost Helion, too, and the unleashed demon did not sit well with anyone, she had to imagine.

"I will marry Perse," he said. "I will swear to Zeus."

When Pandora left the hall, she saw Kirke there, on the fringes, tears glistening in her golden eyes, staring daggers at her and Artemis.

20

ATHENE

1 Bronze Age

In the first decade after Prometheus had saved Athene, after he had helped her purge the Nectar from her system, they had walked the breadth of Elládos and Phlegra, both. Though she could have found easy shelter in the palaces of aristoi, Nymphs, or other lesser Titans, Prometheus insisted they instead request guest-right from commoners and lesser nobles. They supped with merchants, feasting upon bread and cabbage. They slept in haylofts on simple farms and heard tale of village romances, forest folklore, and sometimes, vastly exaggerated stories of Titan deeds she had witnessed firsthand.

When she found a village's only road through the woods plagued by bandits, she had hunted the criminals down and distributed their stolen goods among the townsfolk. Though Athene had, at first, grimaced at the squalor and discomfort Prometheus forced her to endure, she could not deny the flush of pride at the beaming gratitude with which these people now showered her.

The casserole they offered her that night had bits of chicken woven within, the first meat she'd eaten in a month.

Later she learnt that her mother had sanctioned Prometheus's tutelage of Athene, and after a few years, Hekate had ensured Athene received a draught of Ambrosia from her personal stockpile.

She and Prometheus travelled every back road, every river way, every hidden route through lands she had ruled, in name, for centuries, and yet never known. In Atlantis, she had found Kirke living the modest life of a scribe and poet. Her half-sister declined to explain why she had left Kolchis, but, as Prometheus predicted, had shared with Athene a little of the precious allotment of Ambrosia her father gave her. Humbled and speechless, Athene had left resolved to never forget the kindness. She did not ask for Nectar, and Kirke did not raise the subject, much to Athene's relief and, perhaps, secret dismay.

On Atlantis, she buried her tainted sword and shield, the weapons with which she had committed such violence. Lest she ever need them again, she carved the rock above them to look like an owl, in honour of Prometheus who so loved birds. From there, he took her to his now neglected Aviary, and they spent a fortnight clearing away the overgrowth and finding a new caretaker.

"Does it bother you, the decay of what you built?" she had asked, cutting away lichen choking the windows.

"Impermanence is the one eternal constant in our world," he had answered.

At times, Prometheus would vanish for a day or a fortnight, sometimes longer, leaving Athene to her own devices. Perhaps he judged her now free enough of addiction to not need his constant supervision. In one such time, she checked in on Pandion, in Athenai. Though his Titan-blood slowed his ageing, the creases around his eyes revealed the first hints of his mortality, and never had a wrinkle cut more deeply than his cut her. Having no answer when he inquired about her despair, she had fled, only to find Prometheus awaiting her across the Strait of Korinth.

As a pyromancer, he could not directly instruct her in hydromancy or the harnessing of her Sight without use of Nectar, but still, he gave her exercises to calm her mind and focus her abilities. Whether the Nectar had wrought lasting changes or his advice helped, she saw more and more in flashes in still pools or in the shifting of tides. Hints of a youthful Herakles she would train, though she could not understand how she had seen him as a grown man upon Olympus years back, in the Gigantomachy.

Others, too, came and went from the cavalcade of her prescience, some with names, some with but faces. Bellerophon and Perseus and Theseus and Jason and Odysseus ... so many Men and demigods the future bid her tutor and shelter.

In Kemet, the land ruled by the god-king Ra, she walked with Prometheus along the great river toward Osirion, musing on the myriad lives she saw herself touching. "How am I to be worthy to mentor heroes? I, who wrought chaos and blood across Elládos?" And though she had left such things decades behind now, screams and pain still crept into her visions. For an Oracle saw not just future but past, and sometimes present too.

"Worthiness is a choice," he said, the simple words filling up the silence between them and stretching out to ring through her for hours.

In the evening, before a campfire he had ignited with a spark from his snapped fingers, they stared up at the stars together. "If you are to follow the path set before you in these visions," he said, "if you are to walk among Men and guide them, it may behoove you to sometimes conceal your identity."

Such had occurred to her, as well. Her presence, a famed Titan, a former Olympian, would draw attention away from those Men she tried to make heroes. "I could hide my face with a hood," she said, though some memory of an old prescient vision tugged at her, just beyond her reach.

"You can guard your face other ways, as well," Prometheus said, and she looked to him now. His once auburn hair had turned black as onyx, his skin tone deepened to match those of the Kemetians they had met in Memphis. Even his garb had shifted in hue and pattern.

Only his crystal blue eyes remained the same. Perhaps he noted her stare. "One aspect peculiar to a choice I made long ago, which makes shifting my irises impractical for me."

Athene felt her mouth go dry. "Glamour." She had seen herself, in a vision, changed in appearance. "This is glamour."

"Yes. The Titan blood in your veins, the Ambrosia, it will make it easier to access the part of your mind needed for such illusions."

"Sorcery?"

"No, though a bit of arcane lore most oft studied by those of sorcerous predilections."

"Teach me." She no longer cared that her voice sounded of begging. She had to know this.

"Yes, granddaughter." He reached over to cup her cheek. "Because you are worthy."

As the centuries rolled by, she saw less and less of Prometheus. The Firebringer no doubt had many of his own burdens to attend to. Athene could empathise, for her visions, when they came, prompted her to set in motion events across Elládos, some she scarce understood but felt must be needful.

In time, her visions pulled her to Neritum, where she helped the fisherman Diktys find a princess locked in a chest. Years later, she returned to the island, knowing young Perseus must at last make up for Athene's misdeeds with Medusa. Hephaistos's daughter had suffered long enough, and, if she could not break the curse, death would at least offer release.

Not bothering with a glamour for now, she waited outside Polydektes's palace for the demigod until he emerged, spied her, and dropped to his knees.

"Rise," she told him.

"My Lady," Perseus answered, bowing his head.

"Enough, Perseus. I've come to help you in your quest. To slay Medusa, you will need special weapons forged of adamant. Such tools were hidden in the Garden of the Hesperides following the Gigantomachy." Because Athene could not bear to hold them, and yet Prometheus had bid her keep them until they had come to Atlantis. Had he known, even then? "Follow the river to find the garden, then dig beneath the shadow of the owl-shaped rock to uncover the weapons. Once you have claimed them, you must find the Graeae. They alone can tell you where to seek for Medusa."

Behind Perseus, a woman rose. The same woman who had been with Herakles, in the Gigantomachy. "The Garden of the Hesperides. On Atlantis."

How was she with him? The woman, too, clearly knew her. But Athene hardly knew what to say—she did not have enough information to understand Perseus's companion—and so, instead, offered a nod, leaving them to their adventure. Her visions revealed enough to know Perseus would succeed, and Athene could not interfere too much.

WHEN KING IOBATES sent Bellerophon to slay a chimera, Athene helped him tame a pegasus to aid him in the task at hand. Perhaps Zeus would have objected to any mortal, even a demigod, having such a steed, but Athene doubted her father would punish her.

Later, when Perseus had slain Medusa and, Athene dared to hope, made right her mistake, she returned to him on Neritum, and he turned over the hateful head in its blood-stained sack. "I've no desire to ever wield such a thing again," he had told her, and she had taken it from him, and buried it deep. Perhaps Gaia would hear the prayers she whispered for the soul she entombed within her womb.

In the balance of things, Athene wondered if enough heroes aided, enough monsters slain, enough misdeeds corrected amounted to redemption. Once, she had asked Prometheus such a question.

"I hope so," he had answered, in uncharacteristic candour and reticence.

Again and again, she came to Perseus, over the years, offering her advice, directing his life and hoping her vision-born nudges would lead him to happiness. He did as she bade and named Elektryon his heir. Elektryon married Anaxo, herself a descendant of Pandion.

When their daughter was born, a child they named Alkmena, Athene came to bless the girl, her touch light upon the child's head. "She will be mother to the greatest hero in all Elládos," she said, for she had heard herself uttering such a prophecy in her own visions.

Perseus, now sixty-five years old and rheumy-eyed, chuckled his still charming laugh as he looked at his granddaughter.

Flickers tantalised Athene's mind, images of Herakles, growing up beneath Athene's own tutelage, fighting against Minyans, slaying monster after monster while she watched from the shadows. Though she could not reconcile her visions with the events upon Olympus long centuries back, she knew they had to be true. It left only the impossible conclusion that Herakles, grandson of Perseus, would somehow find himself transported back in time. Along with the same woman who had aided Perseus.

In the demigod's stories of those days, he named her Pandora and spoke fondly of her. The maze of past and future boggled the mind, but Athene had no doubt she would one day unravel it.

"Ah," Perseus said, falling into step beside Athene, "Andromeda and I have spoken of it, and I think, as soon as Elektryon settles into fatherhood, we shall abdicate our thrones. We've minds to travel once more, see the lands beyond Mykenai, before our knees grow too stiff for long walks."

A premonition that she would not see this man again struck her like a blow. Casting propriety aside, Athene swept him up in an embrace, then kissed the startled demigod on the top of his head. "You perhaps think you have served me these long years, but I owe you more than you know." Perseus had lifted burdens from her heart, and that demanded eternal gratitude.

"Yes, well, I might have preferred the hugging when I was still young and ... Ahem. Alas, now I belong to Andromeda, and we are not meant to be, my Goddess." A wan smile. "You'll ... watch over my kin?"

"Have no doubt of that." They would need her, almost as much as she suspected she would need them. "Farewell, Perseus."

The shock of a tear in her eye when she left had her faltering, looking back at the walls of Mykenai. She had wept when Pandion had died, long back, until she had thought she could no longer weep for the snuffing out of mortal lives. In her centuries of life, Athene had witnessed the births and deaths of more mortals than she could count. But not like him.

Not like him.

21

ARTEMIS

2399 Golden Age

*P*oised upon the balls of her feet, Artemis watched Nike circle, kopis in one hand, hoplon still awkward in the other. The woman lacked warrior instinct, and yet, she proved a quick study. An *astonishingly* quick study, in fact, as though she could absorb lessons imparted but once. In an afternoon, she had gone from holding the curved sword with an improper grip to having a mastery of basic footwork.

Should anyone have asked her—not that any in Helios's court would have approached her as she trained Nike in the gardens, the very day after Father married Perse—Artemis would have admitted she did not much favour fighting with a shield herself. Pneumatikoi-born agility allowed Artemis to evade most blows and, forced to it, her other Pneumatikoi could harden her skin to ward off those she could not dodge. Still, it had seemed prudent to train Nike in the use of a shield, as so many warriors relied upon one as their first defence.

The woman's shifting weight announced her lunge too soon, and

Artemis batted the kopis aside with her own hoplon. The clang of bronze upon bronze rang out, Nike's prodigious strength setting Artemis's arm throbbing.

From what she'd seen thus far, Nike would not much rely upon a shield, either. "Maybe we should try pankration," she said, tossing aside the shield to wring out the ache in her left arm.

"Why not the bow?" Nike asked, and Artemis favoured her with a wan smile. Indeed, she loved no weapon more, but Nike's case was unique.

"From all I have seen," Artemis said, "few Titans across Gaia can match you in the Pneumatikoi of Potency. Atlas, yes, and probably Zeus and Kratos, but I cannot imagine many others."

"Potency is your term for physical strength?" Nike asked.

"Indeed, and it gives you a great advantage in such conflicts. Given that you also have a Firewalker's talents, the extensive training necessary to use a bow well seems time better spent on other techniques."

With a shrug, Nike set aside her weapons, seeming not the least put out at finding herself switching fields of study once more. In their sail across the Thalassa, she had learnt Nike could sing, play numerous instruments well enough to make Apollon jealous, and spoke damn nigh every tongue Artemis had ever heard of. Were she honest, she would have to admit Nike engendered a flavour of jealousy in *her,* too.

With a twist of her wrist, she sent the other Titan tumbling headfirst into the grass. "Brute strength counts for a lot," she said. "But timing and leverage can help offset such advantages." And if Artemis experienced a flare of satisfaction at seeing Nike toppled, well, it was only to be expected.

"Abusing our guest?" her brother asked from off to the side. He stood with the setting sun limning his figure, turning his golden locks lambent while shadowing his face. The corona that framed him made him seem the very image of their father, his radiance belying his relationship to Artemis. Once, Eris had called him the most beautiful man on the face of Gaia, though with Eris, one could never be sure if such things were spouted to draw a rise from others. Still, from the way Apollon posed, Artemis half expected the praise had reached his ears.

Offering a hand to Nike to help her up, Artemis turned her back on her twin. "I'm training her. I'm certain some mirror in this palace is now in desperate need of your attentions."

"You drove Themis away from Delphi," her brother said, his words so abrupt Nike caught her off guard with a grab and a sudden attempt to bear Artemis down. Wriggling under the woman's arm, Artemis caught Nike's ankle and sent her stumbling to the dirt once more.

Backing away from her pupil, she joined her brother in strolling the periphery of the glade she and Nike had claimed. "What of it?"

"The greatest Oracular powers come from the drakon, Python, who lurks in the catacombs beneath the city. Were I to take the puissance in its heart, I could become as strong an Oracle as Koios had been, Artemis." He hesitated, glancing about the garden to check for eavesdroppers. From the way she watched, Artemis imagined Nike could hear them, but besides her, only a few girls bearing amphorae of wine occupied this area, those too far off to overhear. "Not even Father's alliance with Zeus may prove enough to overcome the remnants of the Ouranid League if we cannot find a means to counter the Hekatónkheir. Our last hope may lie in Oracular vision strong enough to overcome any advantage the Oracle Mirrors bestow upon Kronos, and in using that vision to hunt him down before he uses the monster to destroy us all."

"Python too is an Old One, some say born of Echidna, or perhaps even Gaia herself. You plan to slay such a creature?"

The look Apollon cast her way held such grim purpose she could not doubt his seriousness. His intent swept her up like a drowning undertow, held her breathless, compelled into its course. "With your help, I shall become the greatest Oracle left alive, find Kronos, and put an end to this."

"Not from the inside of a drakon's gut, you won't." Artemis folded her arms.

"I am asking you to aid me, though I will go with or without your support."

Nike had approached now, her visage wracked with as much desperation as Artemis's twin. "He's right. This has to happen. If he slays Python and takes Delphi, he may gain access to information we need to bring down the League."

Scowling, Artemis looked from her brother to her friend and back. She could not imagine this ending well.

THE LONG TREK to Delphi provided Artemis abundant time to further Nike's training, and while the woman had made great strides in passing days, descending into the welling gloom beneath the surface of Gaia, striving against Python, would end her.

"Remain outside and keep watch," Artemis ordered Nike as the three of them approached the cave temple that had once held Themis's Oracles.

"You may need my help," Nike protested. "I didn't spend all these days practicing with a kopis only to sit on my arse, ruminating upon philosophical debates I might raise in a symposium."

"And I didn't spend those days teaching you to watch you get eaten by a creature beyond your ken," Artemis snapped. "Remain outside, Nike. We intend to catch the drakon unawares, regardless."

Nike rolled her golden eyes. "And if you both plan to use bows, who will carry a torch for you to see with?"

Artemis opened her mouth, then, not knowing what to say, looked to her brother, who snorted.

Apollon offered Artemis's arm a reassuring squeeze before unshouldering his golden bow. Hephaistos had wrought the silvery arrows they both now bore, claiming them strong enough to pierce even the rock-hard scales of a drakon. While Artemis remained dubious, they would soon learn whether the smith Titan's claims were boasts or truth.

Mirroring her brother, she nocked an arrow, its tip glinting in the afternoon sun.

Taking her silence as permission, Nike set to lighting a torch.

"Don't die," Apollon said before striding into the gloom framed by the cyclopean arch. Did he speak to her, or to Nike? Either way, Artemis wanted to offer some answer, to tell him she could not bear to lose him either, despite all the weight of envy and the innumerable slights that lay between them. Those words, as ever, refused to pass her throat, forcing her into silence as she followed into the antechamber.

Beams of fading sunlight fell through the gable to highlight an altar set at the heart of a hexagonal chamber. Beyond, more arches led off into other branches of the catacombs, all thick with darkness that barely retreated from Nike's torch.

"This way," Apollon whispered, choosing the central tunnel with only a hint of hesitance. Her brother paid little heed as they passed a procession of sarcophagi set into alcoves, but Artemis could have sworn the dead lay wakeful within, vexed at the intrusion of the living.

The heat of Nike's torch radiated over Artemis's shoulder as the other woman crept close behind. The sense that Nike wanted to give voice to some thought filled her, but whatever plagued the woman, she kept it to herself, and Artemis dare not breach the silence to ask.

A break in the worked walls of the catacombs led into rugged lava tubes, before which Apollon paused. Her brother beckoned Nike forward, directing the woman to hold her torch across the threshold. The light played along ridges cut through the pyroduct, evoking the memories of the burning mass that must have carved these passages out of the mountain. Illumination vanished into the swallowing depths of gloom beyond. Peering into that tenebrous expanse, Artemis flooded Pneuma into Perspicacity, enhancing her senses, and still, she could make out naught save an inexplicable weight to the shadows.

Apollon met her gaze a moment, then entered the lava tube, his steps slow and muffled. Following close—not so close they might interfere with each other's shots, though—Artemis trailed him, Nike's light slowly spreading further, spilling over the walls, driving the shadows to draw up around them like curling wings.

A sudden churning in her gut—and a tingle along her limbs—had Artemis grimacing, casting about the tunnel for sign of their prey. As if they were the predators here. Instinct raged in her mind, demanded she fall back, pull her companions from the danger of this mad plan. Another step forward, and a wave of dread swept over her. From the stiffening of her brother and Nike's shuddering breath, they felt it too. The growing apprehension of their own insignificance.

Deeper into the tunnel, and it branched, passages winding left or right, some descending into the unknown depths of the mountain, boring perhaps so deep into Gaia as to scrape against the Otherworld.

An impression brushed over her, burgeoning into a certainty. The touch of a mind so vast as to defy constraints of space and time, so onerous as to render even Titan pride laughable. A crushing weight of an existence beyond comprehension stole the wind from her lungs. Had they imagined catching it unawares? Had they thought themselves here to slay a monster?

That word, *monster*, belied the truth of a timeless, devouring *god*.

An earthy stench of snakes and rot seeped into the air.

Within the murky depths of a side tunnel, shadows rippled, the Veil heaving in protestation, or so Artemis imagined, as a momentous, squamous bulk seemed to lurch into existence, mocking Man and Titan alike with its foul enormity.

... SACRIFICES ...

The unvoiced word rampaged through her mind, and Nike and Apollon too tensed, whirling upon the emerging Old One. Scales grated over stone, the sound of pulverising rock resounding through the lava tubes until it seemed to come from all directions.

Artemis dared a look back and beheld with a dread gasp that a saurian bulk now threaded across the path they had followed, emerging from one side tunnel and vanishing into the next. A veritable, slithering wall of dark scales, the top of which rose so tall even her enhanced eyes could barely make out the hints of ridged spines arising from the drakon's back.

The *twang* of Apollon's bow sounded, almost imperceptible beneath the echoing movements the serpent made. Artemis spun to see a silver arrow vanish into the pyroduct ahead.

An irate hiss saturated her consciousness until she could not have said whether it had been audible or not.

Incandescent wells tore open ahead, their foul radiance adumbrating a serpentine head rimmed by a maze of jutting horns and spurs. Even from this distance, Artemis gauged either of those eyes large enough she could have bodily fit inside the pupil. Its gaze fitted her with fetters strong as orichalcum, paralysing as it lacerated down to the pith of her soul, pulling from her every hidden thought and hope. It left her trembling, naked, and desperate to beg mercy but lacking permission to even utter a whimper in her defence.

THE HUBRIS ... TO STRIKE AT THAT ... YOU CANNOT BEGIN TO FATHOM ...

Those hypnotic, lambent eyes held her, growing larger as Python slithered closer. Artemis's bow slipped to her side, the arrow she'd held clattering upon stone.

SUBMIT ... TO THE WILL OF ETERNITY ... FEED ONCE MORE THE WHEEL ...

A sensation of monumental heat washed over her. Those eyes drank her in, swallowing her soul even as the colossal maw opened, exposing fangs longer than she was tall. Rank putrescence poured from the abyssal void closing in around her, and all Artemis could think, in the fragment of lucidity that broke through the soul-gnawing terror, was that all life must end thus. The delusion that the edifices of Man held any import must give way to the unabating hunger lurking just out of sight.

The heat raced past Artemis, scorching her tunic as it streaked over her shoulder, casting for Python. The scent of burning hair shattered the mental chains that had bound her. A single heartbeat of scorching, scouring wondering, and then she managed to dilate her perceptions with Alacrity. Even as she looked back, instinct had her shoving Apollon to one side and diving to the other herself.

A roiling conflagration erupted from within Nike, flames limning her arms and face, immolating her peplos as they swirled and danced. The inferno peaked, lancing out until an impression of flaming wings brushed the wide-spread walls of the lava tube. A current surged forward, vaguely avian, shrieking over Python's gaping maw with heat so intense it left stone gleaming red in its passage. That torrent of fire engulfed the drakon's head, charred its forked tongue, blackened its gums. A saurian eye ruptured and melted, even as a wordless screech of anguish bombarded Artemis's mind, mingling with the hissing roar that filled the cavern.

Python thrashed, its bulk colliding with the roof, setting the whole of the catacombs to trembling. Stones tumbled down around them, falling—to Artemis's dilated perceptions—as though through water, drifting down amid showers of dust and debris.

Behind her, Nike lay prone upon the ground, tendrils of smoke rising from her naked but unmarked back.

Apollon recovered faster, dashing to the cavern wall, leaping upon it, and launching a streaking silver arrow in a single motion.

With Nike helpless, perhaps unconscious, Artemis could not leave her. A surge of Potency lent greater speed to her legs, and she bent, sweeping Nike up and over her shoulder as she made a break for the tunnel they had emerged from.

Python's mass surged through the tube ahead and behind. Everywhere Artemis turned, the serpent's coils scraped over stone, cutting off any means of egress. Pausing just long enough to heave Nike in an alcove, she nocked her own silver arrow and joined the assault.

Her missiles punched through drakon scales, as Hephaistos promised, though they seemed mere thorns jutting from such a colossus. Not with a thousand arrows could they bring down this abomination. Not launched at the body, at least.

Even in her desperation, she spared a glance for Nike. The woman had saved their lives, and she hated to leave her here alone, but her brother faced off against Python's head even now. A mad dash returned her to the other tunnel, where, indeed, Apollon continued to puncture the serpent with his rapidly diminishing supply of silver arrows.

"The brain!" Artemis shouted at him.

Not waiting to see if he had heard, Artemis dashed to the opposite side of the tunnel. The drakon's remaining eye tracked her. The sudden, coiling surge of it came like lightning, even with her dilated perceptions. As she flung herself to the side, that enormous maw passed within a foot of her, the lower spurs of its jaw riveting stone as it passed. Its fangs tore a chunk out of the tube wall. The drakon spit it out, and twisted around for another lunge.

Flooding all the Pneuma she could into Alacrity, Artemis nocked another arrow. Please let this work. Let her not end her long life being slowly digested within the belly of this drakon. She had no chance to see if her brother would take the opening either. Only to act.

The lunge came fast once more. She could not slow it down enough. But she sighted into the putrid opening closing in on her, focused upon the soft palate at the roof of its mouth. Loosed, and cast herself to the side without bothering to see if she connected. The abrupt jerking of the serpent's head told her she'd hit something, though whether the arrow had punched through into brain matter, she didn't know.

Python recoiled, smacked its head against the tube wall, and gyrated wildly, hacking. Apollon's silver arrow streaked through the cavern, punching into the incandescent gleam of that remaining eye. Molten fluid sprayed out from the wound, sizzling as it splattered the cavern. Another arrow lanced through before the light died.

Only then did Artemis realise Nike's torch was out—had she used those flames to ignite herself?—and they had only been able to see from the radiance of Python's own eye.

An instant later, she caught her brother's screams, muffled by the dying convulsions of the drakon.

"Apollon!" Artemis stumbled toward the sound, but the hissing and thumping dominated, and every noise echoed through the darkness, seeming to emanate from all directions. "Apollon!"

His wordless, inarticulate cries deepened, pierced through with such anguish Artemis could not help but envision him crushed beneath Python. Or pierced upon its spearing fangs? Or ... Or ...

A dance of light spilled into the cavern, even that faint illumination sudden enough Artemis blinked, looking to where Nike stumbled in, flames coiling about upturned fingers. With her other hand, she held the singed remnants of her peplos about her waist, though she seemed more concerned with the state of the battle than anything else.

With the light, Artemis soon pinpointed the source of Apollon's cries—now moans of agony, in truth. Upon the stone floor he lay curled into a foetal ball, hands closed like claws against obvious pain. Once she drew close, the source became clear. Caustic spray from Python's eye had jetted over his arms and torso and splashed his face, corroding away skin and leaving weeping wounds wherever it had touched.

"Apollon!" Wailing, she dropped to her brother's side. Could even an immortal Titan die from such injuries? Though his jaw clenched in a rictus of torment, his ragged pants didn't seem to be weakening.

"Heart ..." he rasped, almost without moving his mouth.

The intent of his demand settled upon her, and she gazed about the cavern, feeling once more small in the scope of this behemoth. Hundreds, perhaps thousands of feet of coils ran through these tunnels, and she needed to find the heart, cut it free, and bring it for her brother to eat from.

And she would. She would do whatever it took to lend meaning to the horror the three of them had borne witness to, deep within the bowels of Gaia.

"You saved our lives," Artemis said to Nike while the pair of them watched Apollon thrash upon the ground, wracked by the tremors that had claimed him upon eating even a small piece of Python's heart.

Nike sat beside the small fire she had kindled. They had so little to burn, it had already dwindled to embers and would soon flicker out.

Artemis had lost track of how long she passed her vigil over her brother, unable to help him, wondering if the corruption of the drakon would finish the work its acidic blood had begun. But Apollon had come here for this, insisted it would render him at least as strong an Oracle as Themis, and that they must have such. Was it for their cause he made such sacrifice, or for his own pride? Perhaps she would never know for certain.

Hours, at the very least, she had watched Apollon writhe, dreading that he might have doomed himself. While she had whispered some invocations to Thoth, she could not say if the Moon God could hear her while she remained beneath Gaia, nor whether he could or would do aught to save Apollon. Perhaps she ought to have invoked Hyperion, though she suspected the Sun God would care little for her pleas.

"I wish I could do more," Nike said, fingers outstretched toward Apollon as if she envisioned waking him with a wave of her hand. "I came here because the Ouranids must fall."

A resounding groan erupted from Apollon as he rolled over onto his stomach. His eyes shot open, golden irises glinting in the light of the embers. "I know where you can find Kronos." Despite obvious pain, he described a pass in the Olympian Mountains, a ledge that, if followed, would lead to a cave where Kronos had a hidden sanctum.

Though it defied reason, Nike seemed to have some idea of the place Apollon spoke of, nodding grimly.

"I can't leave him like this," Artemis said when Nike looked to her.

"Of course. Try to get him back to Phlegra if you can, or at least to refuge in the foothills east of here. But I cannot delay. If there is a chance for me to find Kronos, I must take it, even alone."

Given the awe-striking flames Nike had unleashed, perhaps she could burn away Kronos before he could bring her down. Under any other circumstance, Artemis would have denied the woman, demanded she wait for more training. It wasn't enough, and sending her to battle with someone like Kronos was beyond reckless. Yet even as Apollon languished in agony for the sake of victory, so too must they all.

Python had been right. They *were* sacrifices, though not to the drakon, but rather to Ananke.

Jaw set, Nike rose, offering them both a grim nod, before setting off into the dark tunnel.

"I feel its taint saturating me," Apollon gasped when Nike had gone. "It thrums through my veins now, in liquid damnation."

"We'll find a way to cleanse it, then," Artemis promised, planting a kiss upon an unburnt spot on his brow.

When shuddering unconsciousness reclaimed him, Artemis eased him into her arms. She needed to get him far from this wretched place, give him time to heal. Too much had been lost for this Titanomachy, and she would not sacrifice her brother.

INTERLUDE: AUTOLYKUS

765 Bronze Age

*D*awn broke over the mountain, and though bleary eyed, Odysseus showed himself ready and present for the hunt. Autolykus could admire that, a man who did what needed doing, hungover or not. So, they set forth, hounds racing ahead, bounding off amid the trees. The morning breeze carried the scents of aspens and dew, a freshness Autolykus loved, though most days he favoured sleeping in until Hyperion stood well overhead rather than burning upon the horizon.

Out onto the wooded escarpment they trekked and beyond, into the highland valleys, bursting with purple hyacinths and dense with oaks and cypresses. Before midday, the baying hounds had cornered something in a thicket of brambles and underbrush. Odysseus, brave almost to the point of folly, brandished his spear ahead, pressing inward to the undergrowth, whilst Autolykus took up a more cautious position.

"Boy ..." Autolykus warned.

It happened fast.

Even with Autolykus's demigod reflexes, by the time he recognised the snorting of the boar, already it was crashing through the brush. Odysseus lunged for the beast, but the animal twisted aside. One of its tusks took the boy in the thigh, ripping upward from the knee. Despite his agony, the boy drove his lance clean through the boar's shoulder. The spearpoint burst out the animal's other side with a crimson spray, the shaft snapping in twain from the dying beast's weight.

Racing forward, Autolykus caught Odysseus as he toppled, shrieking from the wound he bore.

"Boy! Boy!" Autolykus hefted the young man in his arms, hurrying back toward his estate. Hot blood streamed over his forearm as he scrambled through woodlands and up the escarpment. "Stay awake, boy."

But already, Odysseus had begun drowsing, his words a tumbling mess of nonsense.

WHEN AMPHITHEA HAD STITCHED and dressed the boy's wound, she came to Autolykus, golden eyes stern and flashing with grief and vexation. "You had to take him out there, didn't you? You men, always wanting to prove yourself by killing one thing or another. Oh, and if it's something that has a chance to kill you back, more's the better, no?"

Autolykus didn't dare meet her eyes, so he decided it better to keep his gaze fixed upon the hearth. "The boy's a prince. Princes don't get to keep their thrones if they can't defend them with spear or sword. He'll have to fight other Men, too. Men can be as fierce as any boar."

Amphithea huffed, making plain she found his mumbled excuses even less convincing than he himself did. What was he to say, really? That he'd expected to find a deer or rabbit? A hunt that got out of hand made a man look a bit of a fool. Cornering a boar without intending to, that would make the pair of them look like the Gods of Foolarsery.

Once, maybe, his silver tongue could have bedazzled the woman. Now though, she seemed to see through his every deceit with the wisdom of a grizzled owl.

"He'll be all right?" He had wanted to make it more statement than question, but with her, even such efforts seemed forever thwarted.

"Oh, he will," she confirmed. "And you, you'd best see him kept that way from now on. There's ..." Her gaze settled upon the hearth fire, her face going slack.

"What?" He rose to her, taking her by the elbows.

Sometimes, without warning, Amphithea would get this far-off look and she wouldn't answer for a spell. Maybe it was Apollon's blood in her. Maybe her insights were some sort of latent Oracular gift. Maybe it was just intuition.

"Thea?"

She looked at him, lids now drooping, and shook herself. "There's great suffering ahead for our grandson. You were right before. He cannot escape battles, and worse. Much worse."

Autolykus's stomach churned. Much though he pressed her, no further answers were forthcoming. And not knowing exactly what trials Odysseus would face, all Autolykus could do was endeavour to prepare him to rely on his wits to overcome any possible challenge.

"SO THEN ..." Autolykus said, sitting beside the divan upon which Odysseus rested, sipping on watered wine, for Amphithea would not let him at the strong stuff so soon. "Where was I?"

"You married Grandmother."

"Hmm, and thought myself quite fortunate to have her, yes. I, no doubt, could have made myself king of Leukophrye, but having Tenes as an ally served better, and I had my sights set upon greater prizes."

"Or rather, making her brother a king endeared you to Grandmother."

Autolykus shrugged in acknowledgment of the boy's point. "That may have played a role in my thought process. It was long ago ... Either way, I had two daughters, born ten years apart. The elder was Polymede, your aunt, who married Aeson of Iolkos."

Odysseus shifted, no doubt seeking a position where his leg would not throb quite so much. "Wasn't that the father of famed Jason? Leader of the Argonauts? My father followed him to far Kolchis."

"Indeed, indeed. I went with them as well, as it happened." Autolykus snorted at the memories, though there was more bitterness than joviality from those days. It had not gone how any of them had hoped. "That was how I met your father, and thought him fitting for my younger daughter, your mother. Antiklea is something special. I wanted a safer world for her, removed from the politics that had troubled Polymede and her husband.

"I'm getting ahead of myself once again. Between the birth of Polymede and your mother's arrival, I had wearied of Leukophrye, the island by then named after Tenes as Tenedos. It was too small for my tastes and, though Amphithea doted on her twin brother, I found him brash and not half so grateful for his throne as I might have liked. In any event, you recall I grew up under the care—if you will call it that—of Helios's sister's son and found myself with a more than passing dislike of the whole genos.

"And yes, boy, before you object, I know well we've all got some Heliad blood. It doesn't make Helios any less of a blazing arsehole, does it? Helios was famed, you know, for his herds of cattle and sheep, too, though he kept them well away from Helion. Some of his greatest prizes he considered them. Amphithea, though, she knew somewhat of them. You see, her father Kygnus had, before marrying Polyboea, dallied with the Nymph Phaethusa, one of Helios's innumerable bastards. Phaethusa would hardly have mattered, save she was in charge of Helios's sacred cattle and had let slip to Amphithea where they dwelt: on the island of Thrinakia off the coast of Rassenia.

"So, I got it in my head that I was going to claim a share of that famed golden cattle for myself and make my fortune thus. So—"

"Ah," Odysseus interrupted. "So that's the real reason you married Amphithea."

Autolykus nigh choked on his wine. "What?" It had been a great many years since he'd felt himself flush from more than drink. Somehow, one never quite forgot that hot, queasy feeling of being caught out and cornered. "What in Hades's dark domain are you on about, boy?"

"You knew who Amphithea was before you helped her brother claim a throne. And you married her afterward because you knew she was a road toward the prize you wanted. It was all part of a long deceit."

Autolykus frowned. "Were that so, why would I still be married to her so many years after the fact?"

Odysseus considered a moment. "Because after it all, you decided you actually did love the woman. Snared within your own trap, the only recourse left to you was to convince one and all it had been your plan from the first."

The boy danced closer to truth than Autolykus cared to dwell upon. "Pain is addling your wits, boy," he said. "Perhaps I ought to finish this story another night."

"No, do go on."

Would cutting off here make him look more guilty of that which Odysseus had accused him? Probably. Eh, damn the clever little whelp, anyway. "Ahem. Well, so I set off for Thrinakia, intent on making my fortune and enjoying a little revenge on the pretentious Heliads."

"Fine," Odysseus said, after they'd paused for more wine and fresh olives to snack on. "So, you got yourself to Thrinakia, the edge of the known world." The boy's wound kept him from rising from the divan for aught more than the use of the chamber pot, and

Autolykus settled himself beside his grandson, intent to keep up his spirits.

"Indeed, and it was a voyage fraught with storms and worse perils still. To reach Thrinakia, one must thread the waters between Skylla and Kharubdis, those monsters of the deep. Tales say only the immortals know the safe routes to venture those seas, but I found the way and set foot upon the blessed shores of Helios's western isle.

"There, in pristine meadows rarely seen by mortal eyes, roamed herd upon herd of oxen and sheep, the former thick and straight-horned, covered in golden fur. Some believe it was from this very island whence Aeëtes's golden ram had first flown, though it was before my time, and I can say little of that. Regardless, something about these cattle had a touch of the divine, one could see it plain in the sheen of their coats and the glistening of their ebony eyes."

"And the guardians of the isle?" Odysseus asked. "Was it not protected by Helios's Nymph daughter, Phaethusa?"

"With her sister, Lampetia, yes, though Phaethusa was the more dangerous of the two, Amphithea had warned me. Named a Nymph but nigh powerful enough to be called a Titan, stories claimed. But as I said, once, years back, she had been a lover of Kygnus, dear Thea's benighted father. With my wife's instruction, I had forged a letter in mimicry of her father's hand.

"Phaethusa came upon me, swift as the wind racing over the hillocks, appearing with a *whoosh*, dire threat glinting in her golden eyes. Her palm sat lightly upon the hilt of a xiphos, and I knew, for all my own quickness, if I tried to overpower her, that blade would find a new sheath in my heart before I could so much as draw a weapon of my own.

"I fell back a step, hands raised in warding. 'Peace, Daughter of the Sun. Peace, I come bearing a letter.' When such a gaze fixes upon you, your heart races and you feel cunning and confidence leeched from you all at once. In her eyes, such a fire did I behold, I might have broken then, had I not met so many of her kin already. Thus, I kept the tremble from my hands as I drew a papyrus scroll from the folds of my khiton.

"One hand yet on her sword hilt, Phaethusa took the scroll and read my forgery, her face slowly dissolving from its granite mask to something fragile as ancient ostraka. Now, I thought, a strong breeze might blow her over, shatter her upon the hillside. And indeed, she crumpled the letter against her breast and bowed her head.

"Amphithea did not have every last detail of her father's broken relationship with this Nymph, nor did I. But some things I did know. Kygnus still mourned the loss of his connection to her, even years later, even married by then to vain Polyboea. There was a story I had of Phaethusa though, where she tried to tame her father's prized pegasus. Tried and failed and disrupted a visit of Zeus in the process. For the affront of interrupting whatever his supreme twiddle-fuck-headedness had wanted to say, he'd blasted the pegasus with a bolt of lightning.

"Phaethusa, some said, got herself all but banished to Thrinakia, allowed only occasional respites from her governorship of the isolated island." Autolykus shrugged. He had, of course, heard other reasons Phaethusa had wound up bound there, too, and clearly, she had ruled Thrinakia in her father's name before the incident. But it might have explained why she cut off contact with Kygnus back then.

"So, the lovesick Nymph pined for her lover," Odysseus said, "allowing you to steal a few head of cattle."

Autolykus levelled a heavy gaze upon his grandson. "Pined? Boy, take heed of this. Few forces in the World have more power than the heart. It can be a source of pity, yes, but scorn? For the heart, Men will challenge Titans. For the heart, Men will challenge Ananke itself. The heart is more than longing, boy. It's memory and thought and the grief over what was and what we imagined might have been. And we—people like you and I—when we must, can use this to our advantage.

"So no, I don't think she pined over Kygnus. She did, however, lose herself in wistful musings. She wandered far from where I had moored, and dove into thoughts I will not guess at. And just as well, because I could not have claimed any of the cattle otherwise. I herded some few onto my ship and made sail with all possible haste, hoping never to lay eyes upon Phaethusa again."

"You played her emotions like a harp."

Autolykus shrugged. He could not deny that. "I sold the cattle for a fortune, then returned to Tenedos to claim my family. I used the money to build this palace in which we sit, and I—"

Odysseus held up a finger. "Just like that?"

"What now, boy?"

Autolykus's grandson swung his legs over the divan to sit, heedless of any pain it caused him. "You returned to Tenedos to claim your family."

"Clearly."

"Leaving out the part where, having completed your original con, you intended to abandon your wife and daughter and abscond with more drachmae than you'd ever dreamt."

"I never imagined doing so." Autolykus had sought to foster a discerning mind in Odysseus. One capable of seeing through trickery even whilst formulating his own. There was, however, a point in which a boy might become *too* astute.

"Did Grandmother ever know about this?" Odysseus asked, mischief in his eyes.

"There's naught to know."

"I see what you mean about becoming a masterful liar." The boy reclined once more, winking. "Thank you, Grandfather, for the lesson."

For a time, Autolykus watched the boy, uncertain how to answer. Then, slowly, a smile spread over his face. Odysseus would go far indeed. Whatever challenges Amphithea had foreseen for him, he'd overcome them. Of this, Autolykus had no doubt.

"So," Odysseus said after a moment more. "Is that the end of the story?"

Autolykus chuckled. "Boy, you ought to know ... when a man has a need, there's always another tale to be told."

PART IV

Though some yet dispute the truth of this, it was in these final days, when Kronos had released the odious Hekatónkheir, that the Titan Nike arrived at Zeus's side. Her very name meant Victory, and indeed, she led the rebels against Kronos and his abominations, slaying the greatest of them single-handedly. Nike, though, demurred glory or title and thus became a mere protector of the Olympian order, rather than counting herself among their number.

— Polyhymnia, Analects of the Muses

22

———

PANDORA

2400 Golden Age

*I*t ought not have surprised Pandora to learn Kronos lurked within the shadow of Mount Olympus, wallowing in the corruption that must even now have seeped from the Tartarian Gate. Little surprise, yes, for through such he must have drawn the Hekatónkheir, or so she imagined in the dark of night, when she mused upon how the demon had crawled forth onto Gaia. But the place Apollon had described lay not upon the summit Zeus would soon claim as his own, but rather below it, beyond a narrow pass that banked around the far side of the mountain.

In days to come, the Olympians would restore the weather-beaten stones of the staircase climbing this mountain; Pandora had seen such with her own eyes, though never had she imagined the stairs themselves predated Zeus's reign. Avoiding the staircase for fear Kronos would have it watched, Pandora stuck instead to the rugged mountainside itself, though in places she had to drop to all fours, using her hands to maintain even her abortive ascent.

Rime crusted the lower rocks, and though the Phoenix inside kept her warm enough, her fingers stung from the cold. Higher on the peak, snow drifts piled, bits of powder billowing upon the mountain gales that swept over the ridges. A sense of wonder and despair pervaded upon seeing the summit of Olympus free of the eternal storm clouds that encircled it in her own time, as if all else she beheld so far had not quite driven home how out of place she had become. But to look upon the bare, snow-swept terminus of this blighted mountain, to see the soaring Skystone islands unobstructed by the black roil, it laid it all out before her. The very land itself would soon change at Zeus's behest, and she would be accomplice to it.

Jaw set against the filthy feeling that thought brought over her, she climbed still until, at last cresting onto an empty plateau. Here, in the not distant future, the Olympians would erect their agora, a town of worshipping sycophants and lesser Titans to serve as their voices. With the pristine height as yet undespoiled by Olympian temples, it took her a moment to recognise the spot where the temple of Apollon would later stand. Beyond that space lay a slight shelf wrapping around Mount Olympus, creating the pass he had described.

Perhaps he had chosen—would choose—to build his temple here because of the very vision that had led Pandora here. Perhaps Apollon wished to block access to whatever lay beyond, for his temple had utterly obscured the path in Pandora's time.

Pressing herself up against the freezing stones, Pandora shimmied around the cliff, admonishing herself not to look down at the precipitous drop that would send her spilling hundreds of feet below. Not that such a reminder stopped her from looking anyway. Vertigo churned her gut, had her leaning her head back against the rock, squeezing shut her eyes.

Deep breaths.

When the waves of dizziness abated, Pandora edged onward until the shelf opened onto a larger platform turning back into the mountain. Jutting rocks barred the way, save for a narrow opening between them. Beyond, she could make out light, but that offered little guarantee she would not find herself stuck, wedged between stone and screaming for help that would never come. If Kronos could fit through the gap, so could Pandora, and yet, if she had misjudged and this was not his route ...

But she had not come so far, braved the currents of time, and fought monsters to allow fear to stop her now. Fear served as but the reminder she had something worth living for. The very same reasons she *had* to do this. Prometheus and Pyrrha depended upon the unfolding future, which forced her hand into bringing down Kronos. As if she needed justification for destroying the man who had unleashed the Hekatónkheir. The pity she had once spared Kronos had evaporated like mist in sunlight upon the realisation of the horror Kronos had permitted.

Seeing no other path save forward, Pandora eased her way against the rocks. Behind her, her kopis scraped over stone, its clattering protests a counterpoint to her own grunts and strains. The passage proved not so tight as she had feared, though, and she managed through with little more than bruises before finding herself upon a jagged path descending at more than a forty-five-degree angle. Her sandals skidded over scree even as she steadied herself against the rock wall, once more trying to keep from looking down at the drop-off to her left.

The path descended perhaps two hundred feet thus before twisting round into a cave. Across from the entrance to it, crumbling stairs overhung the empty expanse. Where had those once reached? Though the cave looked natural, the remnants of carved columns flanked it. So much of the workmanship had broken away, melding with rock from the mountain in piles of debris upon both sides. What remained of a pointed archway featured an intricate carving of stone in an almost lattice-like pattern, parabolas crossing over themselves in a style unlike aught Pandora had ever heard of.

Flickering light emanated from within, obviating any need for a torch, so Pandora stepped inside the cave. The ceiling vaulted upwards, running in waves toward more pointed arches, less worn away from the punishing weather of the mountainside. Carved abut-ments—unnecessary given the supporting cave walls, she thought—

trimmed the sides every so often, these too featuring faded grooves of work more intricate than she had ever imagined. Well, save perhaps for the work Prometheus had created in the Box.

Light spilled out of flames housed within glass cases, these attached to the walls by slate-grey metal frames. Unable to help herself, Pandora traced her fingers along the strange material, finding it unwarmed by the lamp within.

"Gas lamps," a voice said, burbling up from the shadows just beyond her vision.

Pandora jerked around, hand going to the hilt of her kopis. With determined strides she advanced until, at last, she made out Kronos standing upon the threshold of a greater chamber, hands behind his back, position unthreatening. As she drew close, he stepped back, into the main chamber.

Within, the ceiling vanished into a greater vault that swallowed light, denying her the ability to tell how far up it went. And too, rents in the floor exposed dark chasms that might have plummeted off into eternity for all she knew. At the heart of this chamber rose a pedestal, as ornate as the rest of the architecture, standing in stark contrast to its contents: an unadorned stone Tablet carved with markings she could not read from this distance.

"I knew you would come," Kronos said, strolling the chamber with obvious intent to draw Pandora's eyes to its alien grandeur. The Ouranid lord took up a metal pole which he hefted to another of those metal lanterns he called gas lamps. A click sent a spark leaping from the pole, igniting the lamp and sending shadows retreating back from it. "Your ally slew Python, I knew, too, and fancies himself now so well versed in the future. Yet he remains a child stumbling in the dark, grasping for shreds of the Ontos beheld by those who have witnessed the breadth of the past, veritable gods of time."

Pandora eased the kopis free of its sheath at her back. "You have profaned this world."

Burn.

The heat rose in her breast, the rage at the death and carnage he had wrought.

A twinge of, perhaps, genuine regret creased his features then passed. "You of all people ought to understand the weight imposed upon us by the future, by our desperate need to change the aspects of it we cannot abide. Here we stand in a vault preserved from the gloaming, a place out of the Time of Nyx, as you name it." He jerked an accusing finger at the slab upon the pedestal as if she had missed it or it might answer her questions. "We stand in the presence of the very Tablet of Destiny! And you, who place ever so much trust in your Firebringer, fail to grasp his true nature. Oh, I see it now, Pandora ..." He knew her name? "I thought you like-minded, perhaps even primed for the Gnosis, but you remain mired in the same delusions that ensnare the whole of your race."

Uncertain how to react to the torrent of his words, Pandora fell back a step, keeping her weapon between them, but not raising it. "What do you know of Prometheus? And what, exactly, is Gnosis?" The word implied knowledge, but knowledge of *what*?

"Prometheus ... as if that were more than one title among so many. Here, it was Amirani, you know. Hmm. Oh, I do not doubt he loves you, and still, you cannot begin to imagine how much he has withheld from you. Perhaps he thinks it a kindness, sparing you the burden of the Ontos." Kronos strode toward her, paying no mind even when she hefted her kopis. "But I offer you my hand." Indeed, he reached for her. "I offer you the unvarnished Truth, and with it the hope we might change Fate at long last."

The temptation of his words shot through Pandora, set her sword trembling in her grasp until it slipped back down to her side. The Ontos, the Truth of all she was missing, it called to her like a siren song, beckoning her closer. As Kronos had said, Prometheus had never laid plain all he knew, and though she cherished the game of unraveling his mysteries, still Pandora *ached* for the answers, a pain so deep it saturated her bones. The need to solve every mystery thrummed through her very soul. Try as she might, she could not deny she wanted Ontos, even as she *needed* the means to thwart Ananke and create the future she so desperately sought.

And could Kronos offer such things? Perhaps his offer was a trick, lulling her into lowering her guard, yet the despairing need that emanated from him felt real enough.

"I—"

The clank of metal upon stone behind her had her spinning about, blade raised in warding against an intruder. Lamplight glinted off the aureate plates of Nemesis's panoply, while beneath her mighty helm, her eyes gleamed like sapphires caught aflame.

"No," Kronos fair spat and broke off toward one side, intent to escape the agent of Ananke.

Pandora agreed. No. No more interruptions by this servant of the Moirai, forever blocking any attempt Pandora made to break free of Fate. No, for now, Pandora was not what she had been when last she had encountered Nemesis. Now, she would no longer run.

"All you've seen," Kronos spat at Nemesis, "and still you are *blind*! Blind by choice, mired in your self-delusion, a pawn to the Unseen!"

Closing in, Pandora lunged, swiping with her kopis. The blade scraped over Nemesis's vambrace, the blocking arm knocking aside her weapon so abruptly Pandora had not seen it move. Her weapon clattered away into the recesses of the chamber. A hand seized her shoulder even as a knee collided with her gut. The blow hefted her off the ground, blasted wind from her lungs, and sent her flying backward.

Landing hard, unable to soften the impact, she rolled, tumbling to the very edge of a chasm, her hair spilling down into the dark void. A moment she lay there, vision dimmed with pain, struggling to even suck down a breath. When she caught one, it rasped free in a moan.

It would seem, even as the Phoenix avatar, Nemesis would not present an easy foe.

Teeth gritted for the pain, Pandora climbed to her feet and raised her hands in a pankration stance Artemis had taught her. Behind Nemesis, Kronos scrambled out of the vault, down some side passage. The gold-plated warrior cocked her head to the side, focused on Pandora. A single beat of her wings brought her up close once more.

The woman's fist shot out, like a bolt of golden lightning racing for Pandora's head. Practice rounds with Artemis had Pandora raising her own arm to block—barely—and pain shot through her arm, though she managed to knock aside the blow. Nemesis faltered a moment, taking a step back. A shame Pandora couldn't see her face beneath that helm; she'd have liked to have seen the shock to know Pandora could now match her strength.

The next blow came even faster, sending Pandora stumbling to block. The attack turned, however, and Nemesis caught her wrist and twisted it around behind Pandora's back. Even having seen Artemis use the same move, Pandora saw no counter. Which was all she had time to think before another blow fell like a hammer between her shoulder blades, sending her careening across the chamber, spilling onto the floor for the second time.

When she looked up, a man stood over her, staring down at her with vibrant emerald eyes. His skin was a shade darker than hers, as if he hailed from far off, though lighter highlights shot through his brown hair, perhaps indicating some fair blood. The stranger stepped around her, interposing himself between her and Nemesis.

"Assassin," he said, accent unplaceable.

Another beat of Nemesis's wings flung her toward him. When he moved, he did so with an easy grace, twisting out of the way of her furious blows with such profound economy of movement it seemed a dance. The foreigner did not block her strikes, not until the last, when his forearm knocked aside her vambrace and his other palm shot out, colliding with that golden breastplate. The clang that retorted could have come from a gong, and Pandora saw golden plate warp inward from the force of the blow, even as it sent Nemesis shooting backward more than thirty feet.

The winged assassin collided with the pedestal—which teetered —flailing to steady herself, even as a hand went to her injured sternum.

More astounding, the stranger spread his arms and leapt forward. Sheets of flame—*wings of flame,* in fact—burst from his back and sent him shrieking after his prey. Wings exactly the same as Pandora had seen erupt from her own back, soaring pinions of the Phoenix, hot enough to turn his shirt to ash. All she could do was gape, aghast at seeing someone else with her power, and indeed, the sense of burning fury inside only intensified, resonating with the stranger.

Burn, burn, burn. A conflagration that raged in her, seeming to leap from her core to his, as if the whole of the World might become cinders between them.

The instant before he landed, light bent around Nemesis, folding in around itself, and she vanished with a faint pop. The stranger's impact burst through the pedestal. The Tablet upon it tumbled free, one of the sigils upon it now lucent with blue radiance. The man didn't seem to notice, and then Kronos's precious stone hit the ground, spun, and toppled into a chasm, vanishing into the darkness.

Staggering to her feet, Pandora raised her hands in a defensive position, though when the stranger looked to her, he made no threatening move toward her, save the clenching of his fist at his side and the grim set of his jaw.

"Where is Kronos?" After the clamour of battle, his words sounded a mere whisper.

"Who are you?" she demanded.

"Where is the Gnostic?" His voice, though quiet, had adopted a dangerous edge now, an undercurrent that ran deeper than mortal threats of violence, tending toward something so primeval Pandora faltered.

"Gone already, fled at the approach of Nemesis. Who in Hades's dark Underworld are you?"

The closed fist opened. If her answer had frustrated, it did not show upon his visage, which relaxed to impassiveness. The heat scorching inside her receded, as if in response. "I am Kala." His confident stride may not have threatened, but Pandora fell back regardless until she stood within the vanishing beams of sunlight from outside. "I've no quarrel with you. Rather, I am of long acquaintance with one close to you."

"A friend of Prometheus." Because, of course, if someone else possessed the Phoenix, if he showed up in a time and place that defied reason, refusing to enlighten, who else could he be save a compatriot of her beloved?

Kala folded his arms over his chest. "It is not given to us to embrace so easy labels. We, who sail the sea of time, acknowledge all things, all relations, as transitory. Perhaps even mercurial." A strange reluctance to call Prometheus a friend, and yet he did not quite reject the idea, either, implying rather that his connection to her beloved lay within some unnameable middle ground.

Beyond that, the stranger had said 'sea of time.' "You, too, move through time." Though she had, perhaps in vanity, assumed herself the only time traveller, it stood to reason there were others. Perhaps many others?

A silent struggle waged behind his emerald eyes, an internal war over how much to tell her. That he knew of her, knew of her connection to Prometheus, did not seem enough for him to offer blind trust. His eyes scraped over her in a fashion that evoked memories of Prometheus, of his soul-scouring gaze. When at last he turned, he swept up a discarded satchel and withdrew from within it a metal box, holding it up before her face.

Its presence stole the strength of her legs, left her dropping to one knee as her mind whirled to reconcile yet another mammoth expanding of her perceptions. "He made two ..." Though, of course, she already knew better.

The Box that Kala had was not a duplicate of Pandora's, it *was* Pandora's Box. "Like the Phoenix itself, the Box came to me long after your death."

"You're from the future."

"An Era long after this one. After the surging waters swallow the lands, after the shifting currents at last give rise to continents torn into new shapes. As the World wanes, the span of Eras stretches too thin until it must snap under the strain."

The import of his words struck her as a blow to the gut. The unfolding Eras he promised ... They gave interpretation to this otherwise inexplicable ruin cut beneath Olympus. Because the world had ended before and would end again.

"The cleansing flame lurking within our breasts, the inferno it unleashes, it offers the chance for new life to rise from the ashes of burnt-away corruption. And thus we perpetuate the sick cycle, the obligatory carnage, in our attempts to forestall utter Khaos by unleashing bursts of it, by becoming tools of destruction."

"We?"

Pain creased his face. "Myself, in manifold incarnations, damned to forever destroy." It was hard to judge how much he believed his own words, though the anguish they caused him hunched his shoulders. Now, he set to adjusting the Box. "I shall see you again." She had spent enough time around Prometheus to recognise words spoken with prescient certainty.

Unwilling to risk getting swept up in the collapsing bubble that would ensue once he activated the device, Pandora fell backward. "I have so many more questions." Burning, aching voids that seared her soul. Coming here had not elucidated aught but had rather unraveled all she thought she understood of the World, of Kronos, of everything. Even of Prometheus.

"Beware the answers."

The sudden bending of light offered the only warning before Kala vanished, leaving her to gape in wonder at the myriad implications of his presence.

23

KIRKE

626 Bronze Age

Knosós lay upon the north shore of the island of Atlantis, its outline defined by the Palace of Elektra upon the acropolis hill. In the six hundred or so years since Kirke's sister Pasiphaë had married King Minos, Kirke had visited that palace perhaps a dozen times. Though the city remained a tributary of the polis of Atlantis, Zeus's bastard son ruled the north for miles around, as if this hill had become his own personal Olympus.

Luxuriating in the hot bath, steaming water lapping over her shoulders, she found she could pretend she had come here to see Pasiphaë, rather than flee Phaethusa and the shame cast upon her in her other sister's visage. Maybe she would never be able to look Phaethusa in the face again. Maybe Kirke would spend the rest of eternity compiling place after place where the ravages of her guilt left her unwelcome until nowhere on the face of Gaia could serve as home.

Yeah, and maybe she ought to have learnt to control her temper.

Tartarus! Why had she needed to spite Skylla? Why couldn't she have just denied Glafkos and sent the mer away empty-handed? With a groan, Kirke swept the hot water over her face, then sank down and swam about the bath house seeking release from the tension welling inside her taut muscles.

When she rose, hair plastered to her form, water streaming from her, a servant raced to her side and began patting her down with a towel. Kirke snatched it away. "It's a challenge, but I bet I can find my own arse to dry it, thank you."

The girl flushed, bowing as she backed away and certainly not deserving the bitterness Kirke lavished upon her. But then, if Fate cared who deserved what, the inequities of the World would not have so propagated, would they? The Olympian few would not prance about above the rest of Mankind, pissing upon the masses and demanding thanks for the rain.

Once dressed, Kirke stalked the halls of Elektra's former palace but paused before one of the frescoes displaying Zeus's victory during the Titanomachy. The son of Kronos stood atop a mountain, lightning crackling upon his arms, a storm raging above while the Ouranid League gathered in the distance, awaiting destruction. There, beside Zeus, stood the archers, Artemis and Apollon, Kirke's half-siblings through her father. And too, Poseidon and Hephaistos and that pair of fiery wings upon the mountain slope she had to assume represented Nike. The bitch who'd helped Artemis convince Father to betray the Ouranids.

This alliance had brought down the hegemony with a promise of a better world.

Kirke snorted.

The promises of those in power were worth almost as much as their golden rain.

Forcing herself to tear her gaze away, Kirke pressed on through the halls. This palace had its own amphitheater and a private lake for the aristoi, but she found Pasiphaë in her chambers. One had but to follow the screaming and the sound of priceless artefacts crashing against priceless Phoenikian furniture. Before she even reached her sister's rooms, a young slave came scurrying out, hands over her head and tears welling in her eyes as she fled her mistress's paroxysms.

Kirke twisted aside to let the girl pass, then slipped in through the door she'd left ajar but had to duck when a vase soared at her head. The ceramic explosion showered her in dust and shards of pottery, and Kirke shuddered. "Was that imported from Babilim?"

"It was imported straight from Minos's arse!" Pasiphaë spat.

Kirke huffed, cast about the room for a place to sit not strewn with debris, and settled for leaning against the wall beside the window. From up here, one could see the terra-cotta aqueducts that brought water all the way down from the mountains to the southwest. The whole of Knosós unfolded in impressive panoply beneath Pasiphaë's gaze, though Kirke had to wonder if her sister had ever seen it.

"So ... is Minos dallying with another pallake? Yeah, whew. Who would have thought the son of Zeus would be guilty of infidelity. I mean, I could *not* have seen that coming. It's almost as if—"

"Shut up," Pasiphaë snapped. "This isn't the time for your castigations."

Kirke clapped her hands in mock drama. "Oh. Oh, wait, you mean because I might have said something ... or other ... about not marrying Zeus's bastard? I think I did." She raised a finger. "Not the time? Of course. Sure, but you will let me know when the time arrives, yeah? I mean, I'd hate to miss it." She'd been waiting a while, after all.

The glance her sister cast at a golden chamber pot had Kirke tensing, ready to dodge if something else came flying her way.

Instead, Pasiphaë collapsed onto her sleeping kline with a huff and let her chin fall into her hands. "No amount of threats, promises, or cajoling seems able to keep his cock from straying. I think he rejects me because I have not given him a son."

Kirke rolled her eyes. "He has affairs because he's a tremendous arse who thinks with his stones, as seems to run in his family. It wouldn't matter if you had given him ten sons—and by the way, I rather imagined him an equal participant in the—" Kirke laced her fingers together and wiggled them for emphasis, "—production process—he would still be a randy toad chasing after every last cunt in the Thalassa. It has naught to do with you and it never did."

Her sister moaned. "I hate him."

"Then what do you care whom he ploughs? Take a lover of your own."

"He's my husband!" The second part of what Kirke said seemed to settle in on her. "And you think I, a *wife*, could have an affair and not wind up beaten, maybe unto death? What world do you live in, Kirke?"

Yeah, about that ... Kirke swallowed. "I actually, uh ... I wanted to talk to you about some things that have happened to me of late. I mean, I was on Thrinakia last year, and I—"

"It's not about you!" Pasiphaë shrieked. "I'm sitting here telling you my husband shames me, over and over, and you want to talk about whatever misadventures you managed on an island full of naught save cows and rocks? I cannot tolerate this any longer, Kirke, I *cannot*."

Grimacing, Kirke pushed off the wall. Why in Gaia's darkest crevices she had thought her sister might have half a moment to consider Kirke's plight, she had no idea. It wasn't as if *any* of her siblings ever offered her such concern. Not when Kirke flitted from one to the next, solving everyone's problems but her own. *Kirke, make a potion. Kirke, give me a poison to use on my enemies. Kirke, make my son a king. Make* me *a king. Make some fucking monsters, Kirke.*

Could she have so much as a kind word and a warm embrace when life left her bereft? Yeah, no.

"Can't tolerate it?" Kirke said. "Don't worry, I'll take care of it, little sister. I take care of everything."

AS A RULE, Kirke avoided sorcery, preferring to rely on alchemy whenever possible. Sometimes, however, one needed an effect no potion, tonic, poultice, or poison could produce. Sometimes, one needed to kick reality in the stones and spit in its face while it doubled over in pain. That doing so meant abrading her own soul and risking possession, well ... everything came with a price.

Thus Kirke knelt in the darkness of the woods beyond Knosós, incanting in a circle demarcated by glyphs drawn in sheep's blood. In a bowl before her sat a sampling of Minos's seed, which had proven ridiculously easy to obtain, though she doubted much Pasiphaë would have approved of her method. Of course, Kirke had taken a grim satisfaction in drawing her sister's husband to her, almost as much as she did in wiping his seed from her leg.

Her cants rose in volume, distressing the Veil. Kirke's mastery over that aspect of the Sight, over seeing into the Penumbra, had always been somewhat wanting, much to Mother's disappointment. All she perceived now was a haze, a flitting intimation of wispy shadows wafting about the periphery of her circle, seeking a way in. Still, even she could see the reverberations her sorcery wrought upon the World, shockwaves rippling the cosmos like stones cast upon a still lake.

Birds took flight in the distance, sensing the unnaturalness as Kirke's Art brought the Otherworld too close. Animals, people, they couldn't see such things, but the sense of malaise sometimes overwhelmed and drove them to flee as far and as fast as they could manage.

The dryad Sinoe came, crawling down a tree trunk headfirst like some lizard, its lithe skin bursting with moss and bark, twigs and detritus tangled in the mess of her hair. The creature leapt from the tree to land within the circle. Slowly, it inclined its head up, peering at Kirke through that mop of wild hair, a faint virescent luminance radiating from its eyes. The dryad licked its lips with an overlong purple tongue, leering at Kirke.

Oh, was that what it would want from her? Pneuma drawn out—stolen—through a liaison? Always a price, she knew. Always.

"Curse this seed," Kirke said, hefting the cloth with which she'd stolen it. "Should it spill in any womb save Pasiphaë's, let it become a blight of skittering scorpions to tear apart the adulteress from the inside."

The dryad slithered forward, placing a rough, bark-lined palm upon Kirke's thigh. With that purple tongue, she lapped at the seed, forcing Kirke to grimace in disgust. An instant later, the dryad was atop Kirke, pressing her into the ground, though it happened so fast she had not seen the creature move. Sinoe wriggled, pressing its— her—mossy breasts against Kirke's chin.

That tongue was brushing against Kirke's ear now. "Flesh." A whisper, sensual and so full of need.

"I will lay with you," Kirke agreed, "if you offer your oath to carry forth my curse."

"Done." The dryad wriggled around so her face was over Kirke's nethers and began ripping away at Kirke's khiton.

The creature's own crotch smelled of lichen. Suppressing a shudder, Kirke leaned into it.

&

WORD CAME TO HER, later, even in Atlantis, of the screams of abject horror that had begun to fill the Palace of Elektra at night. The madness and blood of a macabre curse that would, in the end, ensure Minos no longer strayed, though it had cost a handful of lives.

Alone in a room granted to her by an Atlantid family, Kirke sat before a candle and wondered at what she had done. It had taken her a fortnight to recover the Pneuma the dryad had drained from her. In all that time, in every night since, her dreams were haunted, plagued by oneiromantic visions of women whose wombs burst with venomous arachnids.

Waking in cold sweats, she would ask herself, over and over, if she was truly so much better than the Olympians. If Ambrosia poisoned her mind as well as theirs. The answer left her wracked in bouts of self-loathing so profound as to defy words.

24

ATHENE

687 Bronze Age

Seventeen years after Perseus had left Mykenai, Athene once more returned to the polis, pulled by prescient intuitions and a no-longer resistible urge to check in upon his kin, as she had sworn. The grasp of autumn gave the air a crispness one had to savour, promising long nights gathered around crackling fires, flush with the simple pleasures of spiced wine and old tales. The contentment that the season engendered faltered, however, when Athene stepped through the gates and caught wind of the disquiet that had settled like a noose upon the city.

Furtive glances stolen from behind half-closed shutters scraped over her, so laced with suspicion she found herself double-checking her glamour. She had come here disguised as an old woman, clad finely enough to belong to the aristoi, but not regal enough any should know her for a Titan. And still, vendors eyed her with looks reserved for strangers only in times of war.

When she came to call upon Elektryon in his palace, she found her answer, for it was not Perseus's chosen heir who received her and sat upon the throne but his older brother, Sthenelos. Athene's own visions had prompted Perseus to pass over Sthenelos and choose Elektryon, and she had trusted she had seen it for good reason, though as so oft with Oracular insight, she could never know for certain.

"Who are you?" Sthenelos demanded. While haughtiness crept into his tone, the sense of weight upon him all but smothered it. Beside him sat his queen, a woman Athene did not know but took to be Nikippe, a descendant of Pelops, of the accursed line of Tantalus. She had heard tale of their grand wedding, and, in fact, that they had a son now as well.

The time for pretence and subtlety seemed to have passed, and Athene let her glamour fall away like water streaming off her form. Her hair changed, her height rose almost a foot, and her silver peplos replaced her blue khiton. A collective gasp rang through the great hall, with many courtiers dropping to their knees in obeisance.

Sthenelos and Nikippe did not, though both bowed their heads in respect.

"Goddess Athene," the apparent king said, face grim.

"Where is Elektryon?" Athene demanded. These people had best have some better explanation for her than the firstborn having come to claim what he thought his due.

"Dead," Sthenelos answered, and Athene's mouth pressed into a thin line. Perhaps he realised into what treacherous waters he now waded, for he spoke quickly. "Slain by our nephew Amphitryon, though the painful tale of it is aught but straightforward."

"Speak," she commanded, suppressing the urge to scream. Amphitryon was the son of Alkaios, Perseus's third son. That he should slay his own uncle, Athene's chosen king, *Perseus's* precious blood ... it cleft through Athene's breast like an axe. Was this why her prescience had driven her to choose Elektryon as king? So that he might fall victim to *kinslaying*?

Effecting a put-out sigh, Sthenelos called for wine. "Mestor, you know, married young, into the royal family of Krokylea, one of the more insignificant of the Ionian islands. My brother, sadly, died young as well. His sons, though, chief among them Taphios, got it in their heads a portion of the kingdom of Perseus should come to them, as Perseids. Elektryon, of course, refused and ordered them to return to their island and content themselves with what Fate had given them. This did not, as you can imagine, go over well with Mestor's brats.

"In spite, they stole a great herd of royal cattle. Elektryon sent his sons to retrieve the pilfered animals, only, Taphios and his lot ambushed the boys. Now, I found no living witness of the battle that ensued, though I spoke to a goatherd who came upon the aftermath. Nigh as I can see, everyone there died, save—as I later learnt— Everes, a brother of Taphios, who got the herd onto one of his ships."

Athene blanched, and only Titan pride kept her from stumbling back, looking for something upon which to steady herself. "The whole of Elektryon's line has perished?"

"Well, no. Likymnios is but a boy, so he didn't go, and Alkmena lives too, so far as I know, though that's its own sorry side to our tale." Sthenelos sniffed and spread his hands as if to ask if he ought to continue. When she waved him on, he did so. "My brother Elektryon, livid, decided to avenge his sons himself. So he sends for Amphitryon, who was off in Thebes but betrothed to Alkmena. The girl swears she'll not marry until her brothers are avenged, loyal sister that she is, so Elektryon commands Amphitryon not to despoil her virginity until they are wed. Seemed a simple request, to me." His shrug, as if to say, 'what can you do with boys?' made Athene want to slap him into a stupor.

But thus far, she could not yet judge his part in all this. If she learnt Elektryon had come to harm at his instigation, Sthenelos would pay dearly, yes, but not until such a time. "Continue."

The new king cleared his throat. "Well, either way, my brother comes home with the herd, or most of it, and he's only just arrived amid the animals when Amphitryon hurls a club at him. The blow cracks his skull and he falls down dead."

Athene suppressed a wince. "Why would he murder his future father-in-law?"

A groan. "According to him?" Sthenelos wrung his hands. "About this time—I was in Delphi prior to this—word came to me of the death of Elektryon's boys, so I was headed this way to offer him my sympathies. I arrive just after the murder and seize control of the situation, as I cannot well let little Likymnios handle it, and Alkmena is just a woman." The king missed the further darkening of Athene's expression at that and plowed forward with his bleak tale. "So I brought Amphitryon before me and demanded an answer. The young man claimed that one of the bulls was about to charge, that he threw the club to stop the bull, but that it bounced off the horns and struck down Elektryon."

"You don't believe him."

"Outlandish as the claim is, I might still have given it some credence, if not for the fact Alkmena was thick with child on my arrival. Seems fair obvious to me the boy couldn't wait for a proper wedding, took her to bed, and couldn't risk the king's judgment for his broken oath. I couldn't well kill my nephew, though, whatever his crimes, so I had him banished from Mykenai. I hadn't expected Alkmena to go with him—nor take Likymnios—but so she did, which makes me think she went willingly to his bed too."

Athene couldn't hold back the frustrated sigh that blew out of her. Was this cavalcade of death and tragedy why she had seen herself telling Perseus to name Elektryon heir? Was it her fault? But Alkmena would be mother to a hero, to Herakles, and Athene had thought her meddling intended to ensure that outcome. Had she known the price, would she still have set such things in motion? Maybe.

But blood now stained even her attempts at redemption. Perseus forgive her. "Where are they?"

"Amphitryon won renown fighting for Kreon of Thebes, so I'd wager he'd return there, if I had to guess."

Much as she wanted to—needed to blame *someone*—she could not well condemn Sthenelos for any action he had taken, at least not as he told it. Perhaps Amphitryon's version of events would clarify. Either way, Athene was bound for Thebes.

THEBES WAS RULED by young Kreon, a descendant of Pentheus, the famed—or perhaps infamous—grandson and successor of Kadmus. Upon her arrival in the vaulted royal halls, glamoured as a middle-aged noblewoman to blend amid the bustle of courtiers, Athene found Amphitryon and Alkmena, sheltering with the king. Kreon had offered him ritual purification for his crime of involuntary kinslaying. That such absolution would have invoked Olympians who would neither hear the prayers nor in any way benefit from the sacrificed animal offered a sad irony Men would never grasp. They sought the comfort inherent in believing someone heard their entreaties and might interfere in their lives for good or ill, because it appealed more than facing the reality that the arbitrary whims of Ananke cared not a whit for them nor was there any authority to which they might appeal their circumstances. That they, and they alone, held responsibility for their misdeeds, and for any redemption thereof.

Thus, in atrabilious musings, Athene shifted amid the court, drinking in rumour and gauging the mood that ran through the elite of Thebes. Some claimed Amphitryon had promised his own young sister, Perimede, in marriage to Alkmena's brother Likymnios once the boy came of age. Others insisted Alkmena would agree to naught until the deaths of her brothers stood avenged and Krokylea made to suffer for the crimes of its princes. Much and more the crowd whispered of, some tales laced with fragments of truth and some thick with fancy engendered by the boredom of aristoi with too much wealth and too little desire to attend to the needs of those who worked the land and hoisted these nobles up on their shoulders.

How very like them Athene had once been, she now saw with a

pang of self-recrimination. Shallow and absorbed in her petty obsessions, long before her feud with Hephaistos. Once, she had claimed Prometheus had saved her from spending eternity blind to the needs of common Men. Holding her with his sapphire gaze, he denied it, swore her enlightenment had unfolded not because of him but as a result of passing through her own crucible. "That ability to, at last, peer into your reflection and glimpse the truth of your soul, and face it, sets you apart from so many of your fellow Titans."

How easy, how tempting to persist in the languid belief that she had *deserved* the lofty heights to which she had been born. As if the whole of a polis did not stand dependent upon the constituent pieces, stones of an arch supporting the whole. And Titans, the keystones of the arch, sneered down from their perches at the same imposts keeping them aloft.

"You seek my aid in avenging your cousins," Kreon said, his lounging posture upon his throne incongruous with the stern set of his face. "A voyage to Krokylea to seek recompense would prove a fair undertaking. Still, I am prepared to aid you, if you can solve a tricky problem for me, oh grandson of the *great* Perseus."

Athene found she misliked the way Kreon invoked Perseus's name, a man better by far than most she had met in her millennia of life. The temptation to shrug off her glamour, reveal her Titan nature, and castigate the king of Thebes as she had done with Sthenelos proved overpowering. But then, to give in to such whims without dire need for it was to fall back into the same hubris she had fought so long to climb free from. Would Prometheus smile with pride at her restraint?

"I am already in your debt for the purification you offered, my king," Amphitryon stated. "You have but to state your request and I will see it done."

Kreon's perverse smile almost concealed the depth of his desperation. "A fox plagues my palace and the lands around us."

"A ... fox?" Amphitryon asked.

"A great fox, with cunning beyond the ken of Man, stalking the halls, stealing food and—" Kreon grimaced, looking at the courtiers, who, by their stiffened silence, knew well the woe. A girl, perhaps nine years old—the only child in the court—clung trembling to the skirts of a governess. "Children."

Nascent intuition tugged at Athene's awareness, a pull toward any source of still waters into which she could fall into trance and understand the import of Kreon's words. For they held import, of that she felt certain.

"What fox steals *people*?" Amphitryon asked, while some of the gathered court looked away in shame and others fell into angry mutters.

Kreon leaned forward in his throne, no longer bothering to affect the casual air he had worn when Athene entered. "A blight sent by Dionysos, or so my soothsayers claim. A further plague set upon my house over his grievances with my ancestor, Pentheus. The fox they say cannot be found, cannot be tracked, cannot be caught, and thus we have suffered its predations almost from the moment I took this throne."

With gritted teeth, Athene folded her arms over her chest and shut her eyes for a bare moment. Tale had come to her how, some six hundred years prior, Dionysos had prompted a madness in the women of Thebes, one which had induced them to rend King Pentheus limb from limb. The story had so discomfited that Athene had planned to seek out this Dionysos and confront him over his crimes. Prometheus had dissuaded her, uttering Oracular warning that something primal lurked within the breast of the new god, something she could not understand or combat. In the intervening centuries, she heard passing tales of the miscreant, spreading debauchery and chaos in his wake like a trail of snail slime.

"Find the fox and slay it," Kreon commanded, "and my army will aid your campaign against the kin of Taphios."

"You cannot find the fox," Athene said to Amphitryon, when the two of them were alone in the chambers granted to him by Kreon, "because it is not a mere fox. The king had the right of it, for this is a curse visited upon his bloodline, perhaps by Dionysos, or perhaps by some other source."

Athene's visions within the water basin, even now sitting upon the floor, had revealed much. Too much, she thought, for she had beheld things unsought after. That her own father, mighty Zeus, had come to Alkmena in the night and taken her, though the girl had not known who the man was who forced her. In shame, she had begged Amphitryon not to speak of it, and thus her betrothed had allowed Sthenelos to think the child his, in violation of his oath to Elektryon. A sad state of affairs, and one that did not leave Athene well disposed toward Alkmena for demanding her beloved avenge her brothers. Still, Athene of all people knew the ravages such violations of self-determination wrought upon a mind.

Too, Athene had seen that Hera had learnt of the bastard child and would not tolerate it. Rather than risk displeasure from the Queen of Olympus, Alkmena would leave the babe in the woods, exposed. All this the waters had shown Athene, before revealing the truth of the fox that haunted Thebes.

"The fox lives within a person." The very girl Athene had seen in the hall, watching with intensity beyond her years. "Kreon has a sister, tiny Jokasta, the real victim of this curse."

Amphitryon paled. "You'd have me slay a child?"

"I am not convinced she even realises her crimes." Some shifters, like Artemis, knew of their condition and even learnt to control it, though Athene's former mentor had admitted at times she could not entirely curb the animal instinct that suffused her. Others, though, she had heard, were overtaken by the base nature of the entities lurking inside themselves. Stories of the werewolf, Lykaon, had long dominated the Minyan heartlands, and his descendants still haunted those hills. "And if not, she remains but a child. It falls to you to set a trap for this werefox, catch her, and prove to Kreon his prey lurks within his own beloved sister. Once he sees this, I am certain he will rescind his command for you to slay her."

Perseus's grandson groaned. "How am I to do such a thing?"

Beleaguered by her divinations and none too pleased with what she'd seen, Athene allowed a hint of her irritation to limn her face. "I came here to guide your efforts and give you the chance at heroism and greatness, not to solve your problems myself. Or perhaps *I* ought to marry Alkmena, too?"

His abrupt, obsequious retreat gave her time to linger once again upon the soul-shifting vision she had beheld. Amphitryon would need to attend to Jokasta and Kreon, and Athene had no doubt he would, for the pieces of her vision had begun to fall into place.

It was a future that she, too, must play a part in.

THOUGH PROMETHEUS HAD NOT SHOWN her such uses—perhaps had not mastered them—Athene found she could use her glamour to become translucent enough that most people would look right past her. Thus hidden, she watched as Alkmena bounded, weeping, through the dark of the woods beyond Thebes, fleeing the site of her affront to motherhood. That it ravaged the woman—as well it ought to—did not abrogate her from her crime of exposing a child.

Still, Hera had sent her threats—had reached a breaking point with her husband's infidelities, it seemed. Visions beheld in water months back guided Athene's steps now, threading between trees with confidence despite the deepening twilight. An owl hooted from the boughs above, and still, the babe did not cry.

When she came into the glade, she spied the swaddled bundle, nestled between the protruding roots of a great beech tree. A pair of black serpents slithered toward the abandoned child. Instinct took over and, flooding Pneuma to Alacrity, Athene dashed forward like the wind. Even with her enhanced speed, the snake that lunged moved fast. A hair later, and she'd have not snared it behind its hissing head. Athene broke both their necks and dropped them amid the roots before sweeping up the babe.

It was him, she had no doubt, not only because of the fulfilment of her Oracular visions, but from the pellucid look in his eyes. "I name you Herakles," she said, hoping that calling the child in honour of Hera might appease Zeus's justly vexed wife. Athene stroked her forefinger along the infant's soft cheek. "And I will see you find the grandest of destinies, little one."

25

PANDORA

2400 Golden Age

While a thousand questions she might have asked Prometheus burned through Pandora, in knowing she would not find the answers forthcoming, she found herself left with another, more scorching query for herself: was her love, however all-consuming, enough to excuse his reticence? That Prometheus strove to uphold the timeline for fear of the cost of acting otherwise explained his actions, for indeed, Pandora herself had oft found herself powerless to make her own choices. Perhaps, the more he saw, the more he became a slave to Ananke and the Moirai. Perhaps his failure to offer up the answers was not by choice, and yet, neverthe-less, she could not deny the bitter disappointment that soured her stomach, looking at him across the fire.

"Kronos has claimed the summit of Olympus," Apollon said, the sun-loving Heliad now clinging to the shadows beyond the firelight. It would have been easy to condemn his vanity, hiding his acid-burns in the dark and pretending himself yet the beautiful man everyone had long worshipped. Pandora might have even sympathised, though she suspected Titan Pneuma would eventually heal the Oracle. "After his encounter with Nike, he must have called up Atlas, for all forces now seem to converge upon that mountain range."

The rebels remained camped on the Phlegra side of the Olympian Mountains, where Pandora had sought them out after Kala and Kronos had both vanished. Perhaps she ought to have known it would always end upon the slope of that accursed mountain. The Moirai, wretched spinners, did so love their vicious ironies.

"Then our chance to crush them all at once has come," Zeus said. Did it cross his mind in the least they might fail? Did the future king of all these lands imagine how many lives might be lost to gain his throne? Pandora doubted it. No, Zeus would not have given a moment's consideration to any life save his own, and, in his gargantuan hubris, he could not fathom the idea of himself losing.

One day, in the distant future, Pandora *so* hoped she might glimpse his face when crushing defeat wrapt its greedy fingers around his neck. When, caught in its suffocating squeeze, the man realised, at long last, he had never been a god.

"One more thing," Zeus amended. "I want Kronos taken alive. For his crimes, I will see him cast bodily into Tartarus."

"*What?*" Hekate demanded.

"Nike told us Kronos has a gate to Tartarus up on that mountain," Zeus insisted. "He called that monster down on us from it. Justice demands he be cast through it."

Pandora's gut churned with such violence she feared someone might hear it, even if she did not retch. Was it *her* fault Zeus had bound his father rather than slay him?

"The Hekatónkheir will converge upon your own gathered army," Prometheus said, his gaze locked upon the shifting tongues of fire. "Unless someone fells it, you cannot claim victory against Kronos."

"I'll stop it," Pandora said, the words escaping before she realised she meant to speak them. Now, every eye turned toward her. Here, in the starlit hills of Phlegra, sat most of the future Olympian Pantheon, along with Hekate and Prometheus and others she cared for. Much though she might have relished the thought of allowing the demon to destroy the Olympians, she would never abandon her daughter. Besides, however cruel the future king was, if Zeus did not win, Pandora's daughter would not exist.

Everything always came back to that.

"I'll be by your side," Prometheus promised.

The look she cast him held gratitude, yes, but something more, something he would have read in her without doubt. A promise of her own, that one day soon, she would have her answers. In acknowledgment, Prometheus inclined his head.

Given the flicker of firelight, Pandora could not have been certain, but she thought … his eyes held a trace of … pity.

CROUCHED in the predawn shadow of Mount Olympus, caught in the maelstrom of fear and doubt—the obdurate certainty that no one, least of all *she* could challenge the Hekatónkheir—Pandora turned once more to Prometheus. In the sapphire depths of his gaze, she saw such humbling confidence it left her faint. The Titan watching her now believed in her, absolutely. She didn't think it some prescient foreknowledge of events but, rather, uncompromising trust.

How could one be worthy of this? How could she earn that which he freely bestowed? Perhaps only by fulfilling what they had set out to do. Further up the mountain, Zeus and Artemis and the others led the final assault upon Kronos and Atlas. The last two members of the Ouranid League had banded together, attempting to draw Zeus's rebels here, to the tainted peak, where they could unleash the demonic abomination. A desperate ploy born of a mind unhinged by its straits, of course.

Pyrrha was with Zeus and Artemis, and thus, she and Prometheus had conspired to save their daughter.

When Pandora had met her future self, she had received the warning Nike must fight alongside Zeus, or Pyrrha would die.

So.

They would intercept the Hekatónkheir and slay the Old One, just as she had helped Apollon slay Python. Or so the plan held, and the time for doubts had come and gone, swept from her by the chilling mountain winds. Prometheus had claimed the demon would lose some portion of its might beneath daylight, and thus the rebels had planned the very assault that must now unfold.

Her rage would immolate this abomination and put an end to this accursed war.

The chittering, discordant cries of dozens of mouths announced the presence of her dreaded prey, even as grasping arms yanked it free of a shadowed chasm below in a mockery of birth. Flowing like a centipede, the Hekatónkheir tore from the depths of Gaia, a chitinous mass of clattering limbs and Etheric visages forming into masks of torment. Prometheus had surmised the faces were those of victims, their souls subsumed into the monstrosity, slowly feeding it, their agonies stretched out over eons.

Oblivion, perhaps, was the most Pandora could offer them. Kopis in hand, she rose, shedding the tunic Artemis had given her, for it could not survive the flames she would unleash. By her side, Prometheus too stripped to the waist.

Some of those obscene faces locked upon them, fastening them with gazes of hatred—perhaps underlaid with pleas for release—though the demon continued its skittering ascent toward Zeus and his allies. Toward Pandora's precious daughter.

Never. A kick from the precipice sent her hurtling skyward even as her wrath-born flaming wings erupted from her back, tendrils careening toward the demon. A vague avian aspect shrieked from her torso as Pandora dove, faster and faster, closing in.

She landed hard upon a chitin-plated limb and lashed out, kopis passing harmlessly through an Etheric visage that, in the last, she thought might have been someone she'd seen in Athyras, an unnamed woman. Before she could ready another strike, the Hekatónkheir bent backward, twisting its profane form almost into a circle, bringing to bear a dozen grasping claws.

Artemis's training helped Pandora react faster than normal,

perceive the impending strikes as though they came mired, and thus twist out of the way of one and then another, kopis biting into demon flesh. Mostly, the blade clattered off chitin, but a few blows broke through, calling forth burbling ebony fluid. Too many limbs to dodge came at her, though, and one snared her in its chilling grasp, pinning her free arm to her side. A sense of putrescence washed over her at its touch. An awful force tugged at some ephemeral, eternal part of her.

It had begun drawing out her very soul, she realised in abject horror. Instinct screamed in her to beg for mercy, to call for aid.

Her sword hand remained free, and though the position was awkward, she managed to reverse her grip and hack at the digits wrapt around her torso. From this angle, her strikes lacked force, and dread sapped her strength further. An Etheric face burped into existence a foot from her own head, its slavering, distended tongue lapping out, reaching for her. Intent to penetrate her skull and feast upon her soul.

The primal scream of defiance ringing out from below cut through the riotous cacophony that enveloped Pandora, pierced even the absolute horror clawing at her mind. As the Hekatónkheir twisted, she was jerked upside down, pulled onto the arc of its obscene circuit, but given view of Prometheus the instant before his flame-drenched fist struck the ground. The land shuddered beneath his blow, leaving her to wonder if he had somehow wounded Gaia herself. The tremor roared, drowning out all other sound, stone grinding upon stone as pieces of the mountain jerked apart.

A jet of sulphuric vapours preceded a geyser of liquid flame, lava erupting beneath the demon, washing it in sizzling, searing heat. Fifty mouths at once shrieked, the demon scrambling to one side to evade the incandescent shower now raining down from the sky. In its sudden motion, Pandora tumbled free of its grasp, rolled, and caught herself on one hand.

Revelling at having emerged from a fall of a hundred feet or more without injury, it took her a moment to realise her palm rested in a cooling pool of lava. She jerked her hand free, gaping at unburnt flesh. Was she immune to all heat now? Pausing just long enough to wipe the lava off on a rock, she rose, then spotted Prometheus. Her beloved knelt in the same spot where he had struck the ground, panting upon his hands and knees, wracked by shudders of pain or some unseen struggle within himself.

He had done what he could, and with the demon wriggling back into an upright position, it now fell to her to finish this. She had dropped her kopis somewhere, but then, it had little aided her so far anyway. Charred flesh blistered and peeled away from one side of the demon, some of the limbs dangling useless. Along those reaches, no further Etheric heads rose up to glower at her, though others looked back to Prometheus, laced with wrath.

If it sought revenge upon him, though, it would first have to go through Pandora.

BURN!

The searing heat within her core rose, burst to living flame in her hands, answering her own scream. All of her rage, her years of torment—the innumerable stolen moments of her life—she poured in the flames in her core. The anguish of a child torn from her by the uncaring Fates, and grief of separation from the one she loved, over and over. Her wings once more hurled her airborne, but this time, Pandora made no attempt to land upon her foe. Rather, she shrieked down like a flaming missile. Limbs twisted back upon themselves, trying to snare her once more, but the speed her flames propelled faster than the demon could react. Her searing fist punched through an Etheric head and a conflagration exploded out of that face, fires washing over demonic flesh even as she soared by.

Pandora landed in a crouch, momentum causing her to skid along the escarpment, throwing up loose scree. Dust ignited in the heat of her flames. She twisted, staring defiance at the hideous abomination that now fixated upon her with all its remaining heads.

Offering it an obscene gesture it would never understand, Pandora rose once more. "One down."

The searing Phoenix within rose, her eyes becoming its eyes, her flesh melding with its flame.

As if it somehow apprehended her challenge after all, the

Hekatónkheir launched itself toward her, flung by a sea of grasping limbs, swarming over rock and crevice like a flood. Instinct sent flames spurting from her feet, scorching off her sandals as they aided her jump, then her wings carried her to a higher rock, and another.

Agile despite its bulk, the demon twisted around like a snake, darting up the slope in pursuit. One flaming leap after another, Pandora scaled Olympus, gaining ground on her pursuer. Every glance over her shoulder revealed more loathing from the surging dark mass. Its fury—and perversely, a hunger so deep it mirrored lust —bombarded her mind. The assault caught her just off guard enough her ankle twisted upon a rock, and Pandora slipped, tumbled back onto the slope, and rolled end over end toward the monster.

It reared up, awaiting her plummet. Her hand snared a stone, jerking herself to a stop. The raging, scorching fury within her breast threatened to immolate her, even if the demon did not swallow her soul. She could not sustain much more of this. But Prometheus, Pyrrha, all those she loved depended on her making an end of the horror Kronos had unleashed. And she would.

A heave sent her skyward, fingers reaching for a ledge high over-head. She caught it, pulled herself atop it with a roll, and peered down at the demon. Hideous waves of craving and wrath slapped against her consciousness, mingling with the Phoenix's fervid rage until she became a roil of emotion, one coalescing into the next. If there was a person, one who was yet Pandora, beneath the tide of sensations, that person had begun to falter, swept away.

Fire. She needed all the fire, enough to burn clean the World, reduce it to the purity of ash.

One last, shrieking leap skyward, the Phoenix bursting from mortal flesh, given form in streaking flames breaking across the dawn, almost to the very peak of Olympus. A turn, a twist in midair, and the climb became a plummet, a searing eagle become a meteor, wind stripping away Pandora's screams.

The conflagration slammed into the Hekatónkheir with explosive force, fires leaping in swirling arcs, dancing upon the unfurled depths of her fury. And it wasn't enough. Crashing demonic limbs surged down, sweeping toward her. Lacking the strength left to dodge, all Pandora managed was to catch one with both hands, keeping it from crushing her. The Pneumatikoi of Potency allowed her to stall its momentum, but the creature shifted, flowing around her, a mountain of charred, seething horror bearing down upon her.

In the end, not even her rage had been enough.

Pandora's knees cracked the stone beneath them. Her limbs trembled, her Pneuma dwindled. Pinned within a cage of fingers, darkness creeping in, she beheld Prometheus's agonised face as he dragged himself toward her, reached for her in desperation. "It's not about rage," she thought she saw him mouth.

But what could possibly burn hotter than her bottomless fury at all Ananke had stolen from her? The depredations—the *ravages*—that had broken her, again and again, she had already poured all of them into her flame, fed it with the depths of all anguish.

Unbidden, a memory flickered through her mind.

With Prometheus's *arm around her shoulders, the pair of them in their cottage looked out over the sea painted by the setting sun, while Pyrrha wriggled in her lap. A tiny hand grasped, snaring Pandora's finger, tugging upon it with surprising strength.*

"I never imagined such joy possible," she whispered.

"You're alive, Pandora. The churning Wheel of Fate must spin, bringing us soaring highs after plummeting lows."

Offering such precious moments.

In moments, ahead and behind, something lay past all the anguish. What burned hotter than rage?

"Hope ..." she whispered, choking under the strain of the demon's bulk.

Beneath her palms, incandescent sparks flared, melting stone, searing her eyes with their glare. The demon broke off her, shying away from such resplendent heat. In the instant of her freedom, Pandora jerked her hands together, and the air detonated with a force that shook the mountain, hurtling up dust and embers, flames erupting into arcing infernos that would scour clean all life. A shrieking eagle of flame blasted through demonic flesh, her immolating fires burning away black blood. Its pinions scorched the sky, burnt away clouds in a flash, flaming wings wrapt around the mountainside.

Arms spread in shuddering release, screaming until her vocal cords felt ready to rupture, Pandora stood amidst the writhing demon. Head after Etheric head burst apart, turned to billowing cinders sucked into the blazing tornados.

Exultant, the Phoenix shrieked in affirmation of life and purifying fire, and Pandora could not have said whether it was herself or the spirit in control. Only that, even as her vision dimmed, beholding the sizzling corpse of the demon turned to ash offered such ebullient satisfaction she could have lost herself and gone with a smile.

As darkness closed in around her, Pneuma expended, the inferno dwindled, and still, her smile persisted.

26

—————

ARTEMIS

2400 Golden Age

Lucent afterimages from Zeus's lightning danced across Artemis's vision, obscuring her attempts to draw a bead upon Atlas. The turbulent mass of bodies exacerbated the problem, Gigantes on both sides crashing into one another, Cyclopes' clubs cracking upon skulls. The remnants of the Ouranid-loyal Titan forces broke apart, scattering like startled crows from the coruscating fury of Zeus's onslaught.

Another of Artemis's shots flew wide and she cursed her impaired vision.

As if hurled from a catapult, a boulder screamed through the dawn-streaked sky. Alacrity slowed the missile's apparent momentum, but the projectile sped not toward her, but at Zeus. Though the roar of stone pulverising on impact seemed faint in the wake of repeated, deafening reports of thunder, Artemis knew it would have otherwise sounded like an avalanche. The galvanic assault ended with the same abruptness with which it had begun.

Had Zeus fallen beneath the crushing stone?

Slowly, the miasma of light before her resolved into Atlas, the Titan's heaving posture making clear he had flung the boulder. Beyond him, Kronos waded amid Zeus's forces, adamant sickle cleaving limbs and heads from bodies as though threshing wheat. The expert precision of his strikes bespoke a man steeped in countless centuries of violence.

The mountain rumbled, and while Artemis's balance let her keep her feet, many warriors fell to their knees an instant before a geyser of lava erupted on the lower slope. It took a moment for Artemis to tear her eyes from whatever madness unfolded with Nike and Prometheus. She could not afford to let herself worry over them, not now.

Spying her, Atlas closed in with a perverse grin marring his features, a promise of finishing the battle they had begun in Phrygia. And indeed, she owed him for the devastation he had wrought—and the death of Aidos. Her arrows streaked for him. Fast for his size, Atlas sidestepped one and blocked two more upon his burnished vambraces, before breaking into a wild, bull-like charge. The club he bore above his head looked more like the fallen trunk of a tree, and Artemis had no doubt not even Steadfastness would save her should it strike home.

Nocking one of the last silver arrows Hephaistos had forged to slay Python, she loosed. Atlas jerked his vambrace around to block that one as well but stumbled, gaping as the argent missile punched through bronze plate and flesh, wedging between the bones of his forearm. The Titan lord staggered, dumbstruck, the pain having perhaps not yet hit. In his shock, Artemis launched again, this missile snaking in for the Titan's eye. Atlas managed to twist aside enough the arrow gouged his temple rather than dropped him, but still, he fell back with a howl.

Nocking once more, Artemis prepared to take him in the throat—

The eruption of a towering conflagration on the lower slopes stole all other senses, left her spinning, trembling in awe. For wings of fire wide enough to encircle almost half the mountain streaked the sky, effulgent even against the radiant dawn. Wildfires scorched the spaces below, fit to burn away an entire battlefield should they run free.

Though she heard naught over the roaring flames, Atlas's scent forewarned of his resumed charge an instant before his one-handed swipe of that club closed in with her head. Alacrity alone allowed her to drop out of the way, releasing her bow, and rolling to the side. Another blow cracked down upon the escarpment even as she vacated the spot. Unable to use one arm, Atlas's sweeps, though mighty, lacked control. Trusting to her enhanced agility, Artemis shoved off the ground in a handspring, flipping over another wild swing of that club.

Her foot, cracking against Atlas's temple, barely seemed to faze him, though it gave her the chance to gain her feet and draw her knife. "I owe you," she growled at him.

Whether he heard or not, a mad, overhanded swing of his club brought it straight down. The manoeuvre might have pulverised a slower opponent, but Artemis, dancing out of the way, found it clumsy. Lacking the advantage of foreknowledge Koios had provided, Atlas no longer represented an impossible foe. All she needed to do was—

His knee came up faster than she'd expected, caught her in the gut. Steadfastness blunted it, but still, it sent her flying, spinning end over end, to crash down upon the slope. Momentum carried her onward, rocks and scree scraping her limbs as she gasped for breath and the chance to slow her tumbling fall. An instant of gripping fear shot through her. Her hand caught a jutting stone, jerking her to a rough stop that ripped a breathless groan from her. Only her Pneumatikoi kept her shoulder from yanking out of socket.

Where in the Underworld was her damn knife?

She had only managed to pull herself to her feet when Atlas's shadow fell over her, rapidly growing as he descended from a forty-foot leap down to her. Flooding Pneuma to Lightness, Artemis kicked off the ground and flitted away, floating back through the air, caught in a mountain current. While faster than him, she'd not want to engage Atlas empty-handed. That sounded like a recipe for a crushed skull.

Though he seemed to lack the Pneumatikoi of Lightness, Potency lent the Ouranid lord such strength in his legs that his leaps sent him bounding across the vast spaces between them. Artemis sprang again and again, directing him back toward the main melee, where she might claim a weapon.

Spying a spear, she landed beside it and bent, jerking it up, though she might not be able to pierce his Steadfastness with its bronze tip.

Without warning, a new fulguration split the sky, scorching the air, leaving behind a burning taste. Zeus's lightning streaked over Artemis's head, seeming almost instant despite her Alacrity. The blast caught Atlas mid-leap, and the towering Titan convulsed, flipped around, limbs flailing akimbo, before slamming down upon the mountainside in an uncontrolled, smouldering heap that vented a cloud of dust.

Did he live?

Either way, Artemis waded back in. Zeus had saved her, and the least she could do was aid in his conquest of Kronos. For if the last Ouranid lord should fall, the war *must* end. She dare not even imagine the cost if their followers refused to submit to Zeus after that. Ten years of blood and loss and betrayals ... it had to be enough.

Spear in hand, she felled a dozen Ouranid warriors and a Gígas before claiming a kopis from a fallen soldier. Then Kronos stood before her, head cocked in a posture of profound judgment and yet pitiful resignation—as if the lord knew how this must end. Perhaps he did. Perhaps the Oracle Mirrors had forewarned him how this was always going to end.

"You will regret, before the end," he said, voice almost lost in the moil of battle unfolding around them.

Not giving her time to mull over his meaning, he lunged, adamant sickle surging in with a vicious, measured swipe. Artemis parried with the kopis. The sickle dug into bronze as though her weapon were little more than decaying wood. Kronos's sudden shift yanked the ruined blade from her hand and sent her stumbling toward him. Her hand shot out for a pankration grab for his shoulder. Kronos's crossed wrists came up faster, caught her wrist between them, and stole her momentum. Before she could react, his fist cracked into her sternum. Blows rained upon her body in moves unlike any she had ever seen or trained against.

Steadfastness blunted each but warding against so many strikes began to rapidly drain her Pneuma, leaving her gasping as breath fled her. Though she staggered backward, Kronos advanced with her. His next blow sent her stumbling away, just enough he could swing that adamant sickle, her blade still stuck on the end. Alacrity allowed her to drop to the ground before the dark tip of that vicious weapon eviscerated her.

And she was lying on the ground, almost helpless. The dread of her situation closed in, a vice upon her heart, squeezing what little air remained in her panting lungs. Kronos could well kill her, and she wasn't sure she could stop him from doing so, much less overcome him.

Another blast of lightning split the air, slamming into Kronos's chest and sending him tumbling away from her. The lucent burst blinded her once again, leaving her blinking in a white haze. Twice now, Zeus had saved her from Titans mightier than herself. Rapid, uncontrolled—shamefully undisciplined—breaths ravaged her. Lightheadedness begged her to close her unseeing eyes. Pneuma depletion threatened to drive her into unconsciousness.

Still, Artemis forced herself to her knees, shaking through the grogginess and the blurred sight, to behold a mountain littered with corpses and those soon to join them. Zeus had mounted the dazed, smouldering form of his father and begun raining down wild, powerful blows upon the helpless lord.

A thought rose up, a question to which she well knew the answer: when the smoke cleared over Olympus, would Zeus claim to have won this whole war nigh single-handedly? Would he deign to offer the least credit to all the others who had fought, bled, and died for his cause?

Bitter, exhausted laughter spilt from her, too quiet for anyone else to hear over the tumult. Helios had kept her forever chafing in the shadow of her brother's golden glory. And Zeus ...?

Oh, Thoth, it all seemed so blisteringly clear now, and she ought to have seen it from the first.

Artemis let her head fall back hard upon the rocky slope.

27

———

HEKATE

1357 Silver Age

"*B*ecause," Persephone said, her fingers trailing along the flutes of a column, moonlight dancing off her ebony hair, "Mother insists upon a grand symposium, the sort to awe all the self-important Titan lords, and what symposium would be complete without you there?" The woman's half-Inumiden blood gave her skin a richness that, Hekate knew, had induced more than one Titan lord to ask Demeter for her hand, but Persephone ever demurred, preferring her independence.

Who could understand such sentiments better than Hekate?

Distant rumbles warned of impending winter storms. A wind whipped at Hekate's himation, but the crisp night air refreshed rather than chilled, a welcome relief, and thus they strolled the portico outside Demeter's palace.

"I don't favour parties overmuch," she admitted. Demeter had always offered Hekate solemn welcome in Thebes, the animosity between them buried centuries back, in those final days of the

Titanomachy. Perhaps their children had brought them together, though Athene and Persephone had not maintained their friendship past childhood. Or perhaps, surviving the ravages of that ancient war had forged bonds of pain and terror stronger than blood—fellowship in the commonality of wounds.

While Demeter offered Hekate no scorn, neither did the Inumiden Titan hold Hekate in special regard, despite the friendship Hekate had developed with her daughter. Once, centuries back, Persephone had beseeched Hekate to teach her sorcery. That Hekate had demurred to train even Athene had not dissuaded the girl until, at last, Hekate had related some hint of the demonic nightmares that still, on occasion, plagued her dreams. Some nights, she could not block the onslaught upon her soul. Some nights, a cavalcade of horror skittered through her mind, siphoning away bits of the *depth* of Hekate, hollowing her out until she feared one day but a shell would remain.

A hint of the Ontos, and Persephone had crinkled her nose and squinted her eyes, while no doubt trying to deny in her own mind the import of what Hekate had told her. Because no one who grasped that import would sleep well. And Hekate found herself left with sporadic reminders that the price of her hubris would yet come due, and Titan immortality but delayed a descent into eternity.

"Would you have me beg?" Persephone whined. "Anyway, there's something I need to speak with you about." The way she stood, palm braced on her abdomen for a hair too long ... She must have followed Hekate's gaze, for Persephone jerked her hand away, the act serving more to confirm suspicion than allay it.

Sometimes, Persephone acted like she thought herself one of Hekate's own daughters. Sometimes, Hekate could not help but feel Persephone *was* like one of her own, for it became so hard to deny the girl aught she wished for. And if Zeus's daughter had got herself with child out of wedlock, Gaia alone knew what Zeus might do with her. Was that why she had really sent for Hekate? "Fine, I will—"

A violent reverberation thrummed through the Ether, setting the Veil trembling with such fervour Hekate felt it without even having called upon the Sight. Clouds rolled in front of the moon, even as shadows around the portico deepened of their own accord, pooling into wells of darkness. Flames within the distant brazier retreated within themselves, the light becoming a candle in a sea of gloom.

A fell susurration accompanied a wind that abruptly swept in, not from the mountains but from two opposing directions at once.

"What the ...?" Persephone began, starting for the corner, where she could pass back around to the palace's main entrance. Before her, the shadows redoubled, hissing and whispering overlapping madness.

Hekate seized the woman's arm and yanked her toward the dwindling brazier. Even a candle offered some refuge, paltry though it seemed. Once Persephone stood within the fragile circle of light, Hekate looked about, embracing the Sight.

Sometimes, in moonless nights or gloamings experienced far from city flames, the shift between Mortal Realm and Penumbra seemed less pronounced. Now, she almost didn't notice, save for the slight warping and twisting of the columns. That, and the precipitous appearance of a half dozen dark figures, wrapt in tattered shrouds, bits of their ephemera billowing in the nether winds.

Wraiths.

Hekate sucked in a sharp breath, an instant before skeletal claws latched onto the back of her shoulders.

"*Hekate* ..." A hiss that somehow managed to add sibilance to even her name, a profane intimacy that had her shuddering whilst shreds of her soul bled from her.

"Keuthos?"

The claws tightened, a chill deeper than unmelting snows upon the highest peaks seeping into her, scourging her with each slowing beat of her heart. Her knees buckled. The coarse fabric of that shroud scraped her cheek as Keuthonymos leaned close. His fraying essence brushed against her, the stench of decay choking, though his words came without breath, somehow more horrible for being uttered thus.

"*My beloved* ..."

Persephone's scream, when it reached Hekate, seemed to come

from underwater, blunted now with Hekate's soul on the far side of the Veil. She could not shed the Sight with Keuthos attached to her, though, and so spied Persephone as she looked from this side. A bright shadow flush with Pneuma, her life force enticing but untouchable—or so it should have proved—by those in the Penumbra. A faint vibration in the aura could have indicated a second, nascent source of Pneuma within her, a growing child.

Even the candle flame of the brazier sizzled out as the assembled wraiths flitted about the darkness, searching for prey, and another figure emerged from the depths of shadows. Perhaps it had wormed its way out of the Roil beyond the Penumbra, or perhaps it had stood just out of sight. Either way, the figure resolved itself, and Hekate choked upon her own wail, too drained by Keuthos to mount any defence.

The despoiled neck still wept Etheric fluids, and within the core laid bare by splayed ribs seethed a mass of shadows. A crown of interlocked finger bones bedecked Hades, his eyes wells of onyx as he glared at Hekate, hovering over Persephone in implicit threat.

Hekate's impotent hand reached for the girl, but even that took the sum of her remaining strength. She tried to call the names of those bound within her, but her mind refused to focus.

Hades lunged—skeletal claws not unlike those of the wraiths— seized Persephone by the ankles, and yanked her toward himself. Then her form—and her scream—resolved itself with sickening clarity. Her head slammed on the shadowy ground, and Hades dragged the girl, ignoring her useless flailing, until he stood just before Hekate.

"I wanted you here," he said, voice a rasping echo as if a dozen speakers lurked within. "You made me thus and condemned me to eternity in the dark. Fitting, then, that you should bear witness when I claimed my bride."

No, no, no.

Not Persephone. She was innocent. Hades wanted her only to punish his brother for his perfidy. Hekate's mind recoiled from the hatred that radiated out of Hades now. The weight of self-loathing stole her breath. For he spoke the truth—she and Zeus had done this to him, had tried to create a servant to control the Underworld on their behalf. And had lost that gamble.

But she could not imagine how he had breached the Veil from the other side nor claimed a person to drag her across whilst still alive. Questions and objections mingled and melted upon her tongue, though, as her vision dimmed.

Even memory faltered, and more of her flitted away, taken by Keuthos.

If he took enough, if he devoured the whole of her soul, perhaps she might even avoid the fate the demons had shown. Oblivion sounded welcome ... compared to ...

WHILE WAVE after cerulean wave broke on the bireme's prow, Hekate lost herself in the mesmerising play of sunlight upon the water, her mind worrying at a thought until it had been chewed to the bone. Until it became a pulverised powder filling the air around her. How could Hades have breached the Veil and entered the Mortal Realm, even for a brief instant? How could he have drawn in a girl without the Sight and pulled her down to the Underworld?

Had he, driven to madness by the curse she had inflicted upon him, turned to the denizens of Tartarus not so unlike she had done in the Titanomachy? Oh, how many mistakes she had made in those days. How much dark sorcery she had unleashed in the name of efficacy, in her desperation to secure victory for Zeus.

Weakened though she was, on recovering her senses, Hekate had mused upon using Mormo to shift herself bodily to the Penumbra and chase after Persephone. Tithorea had pointed out that Hekate had neither the strength to confront Hades nor even knowledge of where he had taken the girl. She might search the Penumbra for years, let alone the Roil, without discovering his abode. And every breath she passed in the shadowy Realm risked her coming face-to-face with spirits and ghosts or worse, all eager to feast upon her soul or claim her flesh.

When at last the ship moored in Argos, Hekate could not well say she recalled the voyage. Not the crew, nor the taste of the salt air, nor much else, save a twisting impression of gloom, her mind flitting from imagined horror and remembered nightmare to envisage the fate in store for Persephone.

Persephone, precious daughter of Demeter and Zeus. Her abduction had broken the Inumiden Titan, Hekate knew, and part of her wished she could have done more to aid the woman, no matter how inconsolable Ananke had left her. But Zeus needed to hear of his brother's actions, and better he should hear of it first from Hekate, who might curb the worst of his violent excesses. If he could not strike out to punish Hades, he would assuage his wounded pride upon the people of Elládos. In her mind's eye, she could see the whole of Argos blasted apart by galvanic streams, the populace reduced to smouldering husks strewn about the streets.

Zeus, she knew, had come to Argos to negotiate with King Inachus about trade arrangements in the islands under Argosian control, ones in danger of falling under Atlantis's sway if things continued as they had been. While Hera ruled the polis in name, the Tethid Inachus arranged the daily affairs, and regardless, Hera would not have batted an eye to aid Zeus on her own.

Hekate found herself well-received by Inachus's servants and greeted by his daughter, Princess Io, who met her in the gardens. Rising from a graceful bow, Io offered a beaming smile. "For now, the King of Olympus is in private discussion with my father." More likely, this meant Zeus dictated terms he expected the demigod king to acquiesce to. "I can have him informed of your presence once he emerges. Before that, we have roasted game fowl if you like. Oh! And hazelnuts. I love those, and traders brought barrels full of them from Rassenia a few days back."

Though Hekate didn't know Io well, Kirke considered her a close friend, and Hekate could see why. The girl had a vivacity that filled up the room like an overflowing fountain. Under other circumstances, she'd have accepted the princess's implicit invitation to socialise. Other circumstances indeed. "I could use a place to rest."

They granted her a guest room, and Hekate sat with her legs folded, staring at the olive wood furniture and seeing naught at all while awaiting a summons from Zeus. The negotiations—assuming such a word applied—must have pleased him, though, for he called upon her, his ice blue eyes gleaming.

"Why the dour look?" he demanded, seeming more irate at any spoiling of his mood than concerned with her reasons.

"Something has happened."

ZEUS HAD SPUTTERED and raged at the indignity his brother visited upon him—upon *him*, not his daughter, of course—and Hekate had seen murder in his eyes. Only when she had convinced him that lashing out at innocents would make him look weak had he bridled his fury. Doing so cost him, however, and he withdrew into sullen silence that persisted even unto the finalising of the negotiations in the morn.

Hekate accompanied him into the court, more to keep an eye upon Zeus than out of any care for maritime trade disputes. Inachus sat his throne, his beautiful daughter beside him, and Zeus seemed to see neither of them. Forcing Hekate to take a hand in their tedious discussions, though she'd sooner have bathed in sewage than partici-pate in such a thing.

After bringing the discussion to an end with all possible haste, Hekate returned to her chambers. She'd have little choice but to remain in Argos so long as Zeus did to ensure he kept his temper contained, then, perhaps, she could return to Demeter. As if aught she could say would ever help.

Could the grimoire hold any answer about how Hades had done this? Could it tell her how to reach Persephone? Maybe, buried within the thousand, thousand riddles, the answer lurked upon those pages.

It seemed she had only begun to peruse the tome—it still seemed to swallow time when she dove into it—when a faint rap sounded upon the door to the guest chambers. She had never known Zeus to be so timid ...

Hekate opened the door, and outside stood not the King of Olympus, but Hekate's own daughter.

"Kirke?" she asked, drawing the girl into the room, embracing her. "I thought you'd gone to see your sister in Kronion." Hekate felt ready to burst apart over what she'd seen in Thebes, and somehow, having Kirke here offered a rock upon which to steady herself.

Some unspoken weight gripped Kirke, though, that much Hekate could see. Had she heard about Persephone? Her daughter held a phial in her hand, and as soon as Hekate noticed it, Kirke passed it to her.

"What's this?" Hekate asked.

"Yeah, um. It's a lust potion."

"I don't have need of—"

"You have to give it to Zeus and get him to lust after Io."

Oh, Gaia's great arse, she did not have the patience for this now. "Why would I do such a thing? Is Helios behind this?"

Some war waged across Kirke's visage, intimating a burden Hekate could not understand. "Zeus will abduct her and rape Io," she said, the words seeming torn from her, "and she'll wander the world carrying his child before coming to Tyros where her bloodline forms a new dynasty, all right? And ..." Her daughter choked on a sob. "And if she's not abducted, she won't do all that, and her descendant, Europa, won't exist to raise Pandora, who's actually your own mother after she travels back in time, but that will only happen if you and Zeus abduct her and Europa, in uh, about two hundred years' time, repeating this whole thing. And if you don't, you and I and Athene and *everyone* just crumble!" Kirke snatched Hekate's hand as tears flowed down her cheeks in rivers and snot ran over her lip.

Hekate extricated her hand so she could wipe Kirke's face with her sleeve, then grasped her shoulders. "Travels through *time*?" Her words bespoke madness ... and yet ... Pandora had vanished when

Hekate was a child, appeared again during the Titanomachy—as Nike!—then disappeared again. She claimed she was taken far away ... Naught about the woman had ever made sense. Was Kirke daft, or could there be real truth to her words?

Kirke fished through her satchel and pulled out a metal cube formed of interlocking panels and gears—a puzzle box, it seemed, more complex looking than any Hekate had beheld. Her daughter held it up in front of Hekate. "With this."

The sheer preposterousness of the claim ... Hekate took the box from her, turning it round, tracing her fingers over gears, shifting panels. If this did what Kirke claimed ... But it belonged to her daughter—and perhaps her mother—and Hekate had no idea how to use it. She returned the box to Kirke. "I know who Pandora is," she admitted.

Kirke broke down into sudden sobs, and Hekate could do naught save hold the girl and try to keep her from coming apart at the seams. What had so ravaged her child to reduce her to this? Had this box wrought such a thing?

If all Kirke had told her was true, she had no choice save to give Zeus the potion Kirke had made. Could refusing to betray Kirke's friend thus, to condemn Io to Zeus's assault, in fact result in Hekate and Kirke and Athene all coming undone? The weight of the burden churned Hekate's stomach.

Long ago, Enodia had prompted Hekate to lay with Zeus and birth Athene. To sacrifice Hades, too. How many of Zeus's affronts must fall at Hekate's feet? This was more than Oracular prophecy, though. This was the very shape of Ananke, manifested before her, *daring* her to step aside and destroy herself and her own children. What mother, faced with the potential loss of her offspring, would not sacrifice another in their place?

Hekate laid a trembling hand upon Kirke's head. Yes, she would do it. Of course she would. She would prompt Zeus to abduct Io and ensure the bloodlines continued as they must.

What was one more abrasion of the soul to one already damned?

28

PANDORA

2400 Golden Age

"You nigh killed yourself," Prometheus said, easing Pandora back into a sitting position. Her throat felt scorched raw, her flesh ravaged and trembling, all her Phoenix puissance sapped from her. "Or worse, yet, you might have let the spirit within become *you*."

She suspected not even Prometheus realised how very close she had come to such an end. Nor could she quite deny the shameful spark of relief the idea had lit within her. If she could abrogate the responsibility to fight against Ananke, if in surrendering her mind she might cease her struggles and yet feel no guilt, how could she not find herself at least tempted?

As so oft happened, her emotions must have played out upon her face, for Prometheus took her hand, face writ with consternation. "I cannot bear to lose you." Simple words, given weight by the, for once, unguarded emotion on his visage.

Guilt brought a flush to her cheeks. Had she just imagined

walking away from the desperate, piercing, soul-caressing love he offered her? Even if love proved a blade, boring down toward her heart, spilling her blood until her heart ceased to beat, still she would embrace it. *That* was the hope that had fuelled her. To never give in, to always strive for better. Kronos could harp on about Ontos, but unless his conceptions accounted for the depths of the human heart, his Truth was but pretence. A fragment of a greater whole he failed to grasp.

Still ... still, the things he had said had shaken her, taunted her, alluring with forbidden secrets that demanded rapt attention.

"Kronos?" she asked.

"Captured by Zeus." She followed his gaze to the summit of Olympus where, even now, dark clouds roiled, churning into a storm that would rage for at least another two thousand years. "If you would speak with him, you should take the chance before it slips through your fingers."

Prometheus knew what fate soon lay before his erstwhile friend. And while her lover—face contorted in anguish over what he knew impended—would not elaborate on the relationship between himself and Kronos, perhaps Kronos himself would do so. Her lover had the right of it, of course. Kronos would soon find himself banished to Tartarus, a place that must erode his already fragile mind with its ceaseless torments and unbounded horrors.

Beside her, Prometheus had retrieved her discarded tunic, which Pandora donned before scrambling up the mountainside, toward the summit. Despite the Box giving her ostensible control over time, she found herself perpetually without enough of it. The climb gave her just long enough to brood upon dark thoughts, but Pandora dare not try to call forth her wings again. Burning through her Pneuma had, as Prometheus said, almost cost her life, or worse. In her mind's eye, she saw herself, a living conflagration wholly given over to the Phoenix's imperative drive, to cleanse Gaia in purifying flame. A nightmare, and one she might make all too real if she pushed herself too far.

Atop the summit, wind from the growing storm whipped her hair while flurries of snow dusted her clothes. She found the harrowing location over which Zeus would build his palace, his self-aggrandising throne. Did its proximity to the Tartarian Gate contribute to his madness in later years? As if he were not a brute already. A savage who had slain his own mother, brother, and countless others, and now damned his father to eternal torment. But Kronos had unleashed a demon upon the Mortal Realm. This war, Ananke itself, had made wretches of them all, and any attempts she might have made to ascribe morality to either side of the conflict had become little more than self-indulgent wastes of time. There was, in the end, only what Ananke permitted and what desperation required, and the hope for some small overlap there betwixt.

Styx's daughter Bia, guarding the cave entrance, saw her, and though she opened her mouth to offer some witty remark, Pandora's expression forestalled comment. Below, down the winding descent, Pandora found her daughter, slumped against the wall, head hung in exhaustion and, perhaps, some other emotion.

"Your perfidy smears the records of history!" Kronos's voice boomed after Hekate. "Your name shall become a curse, a woeful invocation. The dark witch with loyalty to *none!*"

Weary eyes peered up at Pandora through disheveled auburn locks, but Hekate made no comment, neither about Pandora's victory over the Hekatónkheir, nor about Kronos's accusations. What relationship had Hekate and Kronos shared? She had not realised her daughter knew the Ouranid lord well enough for him to have taken her part in this personally.

"Are you all right?" Pandora asked.

"The king demanded we unleash a storm in honour of his victory. Aiding the use of his abilities comes at a cost. Soon I will sleep, and ..." Pain laced her voice. "Dream." The last word almost seemed to break her, and Pandora tried to draw her daughter into an embrace, but Hekate edged around her, refusing contact.

Damn it. Damn Ananke for the myriad ravages it inflicted upon Pandora and all her kin. They were made playthings of Fate, and still, she had not seen the full scope of the board on which the game unfolded. Perhaps Kronos could help with that, though.

In the centre of the great chamber across from the Tartarian Gate, Kronos knelt, bound with chains of orichalcum, his platinum mane spilling over his shoulders and obscuring his face. At least until he looked up at her with those pale blue eyes.

Even knowing this had to unfold, knowing she would, in fact, lead to his later release, part of her wanted to grab the fetters and free them from the spoke pounded into the stone. To spare Kronos the agony ahead. Perhaps that was why Prometheus had not joined her now. He could not bear to stand by and allow this to happen, knowing he had the power to stop it—if he could have borne the price.

"There are things you wanted to tell me, back in that vault," Pandora said, kneeling before the fallen Ouranid lord. "If aught still weighs upon you, say it now, before Zeus arrives."

Kronos huffed. "My faithful son, eh? He wishes to have Atlas and Arke brought up first, to join me in my fate, but yes, I cannot imagine them too far off. Still, why should I share aught with you now? I tried to offer reason and knowledge, the very gift of Gnosis, and you refused it, timewalker. Why should I trouble myself now?"

"What is Gnosis? What is the Gnostic Cabal?"

A pained, hopeless chuckle answered. "An idea, a dream perhaps, ephemeral as dew upon spiderwebs, and yet more real than the scope of the World itself. A hope, however vain, for an unbounded future. An existence belonging to *Man*, free from the predations of the Wheel." A deranged laugh escaped him now. "Where did it begin, you perhaps wonder? In Vulgeth, we might have said, huddled in dark vaults and ruminating over the vagaries of our fragile, immortal existences, so precariously perched upon the edge of the Abyss."

How easy to dismiss his ravings as utter madness, and yet the force of his conviction seemed to fill up the cavern with a physical weight. Ananke had ravaged him as much as her, of that, Pandora had no doubt. Whatever he had seen in his Oracle Mirrors had broken him. Was his descent born from a frenzied struggle to break free of the same ouroboros that trapped Pandora? "What is Vulgeth?"

Even as she asked the question, her mind whirled, drawing up the unfamiliar word. For Prometheus had once invoked it, asked her if the Box's design was based ... upon that of the Time Chambers of Vulgeth.

"Where is it?"

Kronos sneered. "Where? Do you really think the Unseen Order will allow you access?" His bitter snort held such condemnation she recoiled. "You sacrificed your single chance for free will when you hesitated to join me. Deviate but a hair, and the Order's assassin shall disabuse you of any notion that you may write your own destiny."

"Nemesis." Pandora swallowed. She was so close to cutting through the haze of fear and madness that plagued him, of finding the answers she needed. "Fine. What is the Unseen—"

Voices echoed from the tunnel, and soon Kratos and Zelus guided bound Atlas and Arke into the chamber. Behind them, Artemis aided a still-burned Apollon, and others slowly filed in, all come to witness the foul judgment Zeus would visit upon his own father.

She couldn't leave him like this. Not in the grips of such all-consuming despair. Though she ought not to have—if they had tried, Artemis and others might have overheard—Pandora leaned in close to Kronos's ear. "One day, I will get you out of this. Cling to hope and thus what remains of your mind."

With that, she fled the cave before anyone could intercept her and ask what she had discussed with the prisoner. As she emerged, she caught Hekate watching her, reclining upon a rock. Her daughter's gaze darted up the storm-washed peak above, from which strode Zeus, fair shining with vain pride, as though the whole of this victory lay at his feet. Perhaps history would record that, though Pandora quirked a smile to think Men would build statues of Nike.

How strange the weavings of Ananke. Much though she loathed the Moirai, still, she had to admit a grudging admiration for their Tapestry.

Not wanting to speak to Zeus—him least of all, always—about her fight against the demon or aught else, Pandora scrambled down the path before he could catch her. She made her descent, mind whirring with Kronos's ravings. Unseen Order, Gnostic Cabal,

Vulgeth ... this Wheel, whatever it implied. So many things he had known to make her wish she had sided with him. To make her wish Ananke would have *permitted* her to side with him, strike down vile Zeus, and learn of the Ontos he had offered her.

As she climbed lower, toward the falls that poured down over the side of Olympus, she spied Prometheus now making his own slow ascent. She need not ask why he had taken his time, for pain ravaged his face, and he made little effort to hide it. When she reached him, she stopped, part of her longing to grasp his hand. But the weight of secrets pressed upon her, making that impossible.

Though he had his reasons, she had no doubt, still he refused to make plain the game she found herself playing, the shape of the ouroboros, or the nature of the Ontos with which Kronos had first tempted and now taunted. The distance that cleft between them would pain them both, but it was real, despite the soul-consuming love she bore him. The wind tore at her hair and clothes, worse now since Zeus and Hekate had given rise to that storm.

"Did he say aught?" Prometheus asked, voice just audible over the raging cataract nearby.

"He said a great deal," she admitted. "Not all of it made sense. Some of it made too much sense." She hesitated. Were she to ask him about any of the things Kronos had said, would she get more than evasions? Perhaps, but only if she posed the right questions at the right times. He made her work for answers until it became equal parts pain and pleasure. "Will you speak with him?"

His posture grew more rigid. "I must."

Well then, perhaps, once he came down again, he might offer *her* the chance to probe. Maybe he knew well she would soon press, for he inclined his head in acknowledgment before heading on, up the path, to bear witness to Kronos's wretched sentence.

Groaning—her weariness both physical and mental—Pandora resumed her descent back toward the base of Olympus. She had done as her future self had implored, fought alongside Zeus, saved Pyrrha, and overthrown Kronos. But then, sooner or later, would she not have to *become* that same future self, saving herself from sinking Atlantis?

Kronos had all but confirmed that, in the ancient past, in the Time of Nyx, others had existed who had witnessed the invisible cage wrapt around the World.

The Moirai had tied threads to every life, plucking each to weave their Tapestry, giving neither weight nor pity to any mortal whims. They made mockery of free will, enslaved the ambit of time, and ground Man into the dust.

For such an affront, Pandora could see but one response: she would burn the Moirai to ash and forever break the hold of Ananke. She would free the very World.

EPILOGUE

Gloaming Era, Golden Age

Much as Amirani had feared, the creation of the Veil and the end of the last Era had created a World darker still than what had gone before. While one no longer had to fear entire cities of faeries drawing Men into their games, nor had he seen evidence that the Wild Hunt yet rode in the Mortal Realm, the sorceries that had created the Veil had scarred the World, aborting its rotation.

Men could not venture into freezing expanses of the Nightlands for fear of those that stalked the eternal dark, while the Daylands offered blistering death to any unprotected travellers mad enough to cross the boundary. Only in the Gloaming did the few cities of Man yet survive, huddling against hidden predators just beyond their borders.

The desperation that had given rise to the Veil had, he mused, driven Mankind to its darkest hour.

Or maybe the Wheel of Fate turned and turned and all he saw was the shadows it cast, differing in hue, but still reflections of the same obdurate Truth.

Amirani found himself plodding along the dirt path between the outlying villages and the ominous metropolis of Vulgeth, dust caking his boots and surtout. The leafless branches of twisted trees overshadowed the road like clawed fingers, as if in testament to some rot that had settled in on the land. Even after passing years in the Gloaming, still some part of him revolted at the perpetual twilight. Even after adapting, he balked at the need for constant vigilance against threats out in the gloom. Whether or not aught that stalked these regions could have caused him permanent harm, given his immortality, he did not wish to endure the hardships they might foist upon him.

Perhaps he should have refused Vorsanos's invitation to join him in the Cathedral City. Still, Vorsanos—as he called himself these days—had ever been close to Sequana, and maybe they would have learnt from their errors. So much had passed, yes, but still Amirani somehow found himself hoping they might understand. Or at least part of him hoped it, given that the damning Ontos might crush his old friends if they ever fully grasped it.

He could not say he had done them any favours by showing them hints of Gnosis.

Too soon, his boots fell upon the cobbled streets of Vulgeth, just outside the iron gate. The growing city rose up around him, all pointed arches and buttresses, as if the metropolis was some spiked denizen of the deep woods. An army of gas lamps lined the street, struggling to push back the omnipresent dark that held the Gloaming in its relentless grip.

Some few citizens still about stared at him with suspicion and fear in their eyes, even as they finished bringing inside their wares and began bolting their doors. One sketched some kind of warding gesture at Amirani's regard. Without a cycle of day and night, the city never slept, exactly, but much of the populace rested at the same time by unspoken accord, trusting to strength in numbers to offer some protection.

A foulness poisoned the air, here, smoke of too many fires mingling with a fog that wafted over the streets, rising from the river.

But the foulness ran deeper than the smog.

From the shadows of an alley, Vorsanos strode forward, his aspect altered just a bit. Little surprise Sequana would have taught him her glamour as well, given their pull upon one another. Amirani's old friend wore a black top hat and he walked using a cane he could not have possibly needed, its butt clacking upon the stones. Affectations, yes, but then Amirani understood well enough the need to blend in with the locals.

These days, he even wore a smallsword at his side, after all.

How, exactly, had Vorsanos known he would arrive at this very moment? His friend had no Oracular insight, unless something momentous had changed in the long years since last Amirani had seen him. Still, he did not pose the question, instead offering a nod of respect.

"We must move quickly," Vorsanos said. "Even for us, it is best not to tempt *them*."

"Best," Amirani answered, "would have been had Erlik left the ruins of Falias to rot rather than erecting a city upon it."

Vorsanos beckoned, leaving Amirani no choice but to follow as the man darted back through the alley, guiding him through the maze of Vulgeth. "Ah, well, the cathedrals actually serve to mitigate Naamah's influence upon our world. Erlik thought it wise not to let any trace linger. The Veil has proved less total than he had hoped."

Of course, Amirani had warned him about that, too. "Is Erlik still himself?"

"He is …" Vorsanos shrugged. "He is less, and he is more." A pause. "He told me you warned him he would pay a price for the Veil, but still, he did not understand it."

"Yes, he seems to have recurring issues with taking actions before apprehending the consequences. You claim to be mitigating Naamah's power, but I rather think Erlik imagines to harness it."

Vorsanos stiffened but continued to lead him, leading him from an alley and onto the main street, then up the steps of one of the numerous cathedrals that created the skyscape of Vulgeth. This one boasted a stained glass window depicting an angel falling from the sky, and Amirani couldn't help but falter, staring at it.

His companion allowed him his brief pause, then rapped upon a door three times his height. It creaked open, allowing them ingress, and the moment they entered, it was pushed closed by servants and set with a great bar.

Rings of candles around each column served to adumbrate the cathedral's vaulting ceiling and great halls. Their footfalls echoed noisily as Vorsanos escorted him toward the heart of the place. There Sequana reclined at ease upon a stone bench, feet kicked up upon the back of it. Rather than the frilled dresses popular with ladies these days, she wore men's garb similar to Amirani's own, right down to the smallsword dangling from her hip.

Her aspect had not much changed from when he had last seen her, millennia ago. "Who are you these days?" he asked.

"Remiel," she said, then looked to her perpetual paramour. "Did you tell him?"

"Ah," Vorsanos said, clearing his throat. "Not as such."

Amirani looked back to him. Pyromantic visions had hinted at this meeting, true, but still he was not certain what they wished of him. Content to let them take their time, he settled onto the bench beside Remiel's propped-up feet.

Vorsanos worked his jaw. "Hmm. Four of us have now cast aside our rings, as you did. We are no longer bound to the Archons."

Amirani folded his arms. "Welcome news." Even if they were decisions taken eons after they should have been. "Who are the others?"

"Erlik, of course," Vorsanos said. "And Veles."

"Who?"

"Narada. He and Erlik will be meeting with us soon."

Amirani struggled to keep the shock from his face. He'd have expected another answer—Kadru perhaps—but he supposed any of them rejecting servitude to the Archons should count as a blessing. "But why am I here?"

"The Dodecadic Circle is broken," Vorsanos said.

"I was there," he said, unable to keep the bitterness from his tone. He was there when it broke and he lost everything. But then, Vorsanos had saved him that day. It *almost* made up for none of them trusting him when he came to them before. When he warned them of their masters' nature.

"We have formed a new order," Remiel said. "One dedicated to achieving Gnosis and, through it, breaking the Wheel of Fate."

"We believe you now," Vorsanos said. Needlessly. And nigh ten thousand years too late.

"You cannot change Fate," Amirani said simply. These people had glimpsed a fragment of the Ontos and thought it the whole. They still had no idea of the nature of the World, nor the bargain he had made with the Fates.

Vorsanos glanced at Remiel before turning back to Amirani with a sly smirk. "I have something to show you. Something which proves that, perhaps, despite all we have seen, Fate *can* be changed."

Author's Note:

"That bird the mighty son of pretty-ankled Alkmene,
   Herakles, killed, drove off the evil affliction
   From Iapetos' son and freed him from his misery—"
—Hesiod, Theogony

The Titanomachy. The Gigantomachy. The Trojan War. These are the greatest wars in all Greek mythology. It seemed only natural that they would demarcate the boundaries between ages, ending the Golden, Silver, and Bronze Ages respectively. And in this book, we see the culmination of two out of three of these great wars.

Many fantasy novels depict war, often focusing on the large scale —the clash of armies. But for *Tapestry of Fate*, I wanted to show the struggles and the psychological effects of the violence at ground level. The veneer of heroism with which we see single combat and martial prowess is there, yes. But a veneer, because underneath that warrior aesthetic, those affected by violence—on any side of it—suffer for it. They lose a part of themselves.

In the same vein, Hekate loses part of herself not by physical violence, but the violence against order that sorcery represents. In attempting to command spirits and demons, in domineering over other wills, she too destroys her own soul. With each act of desperation, the price she pays compounds, driving her invariably toward a tragic end.

Pandora spent her whole life with a comparative lack of power. Now, gifted with might for the first time, she's forced to come face to face with the aftereffects of all she's suffered.

The end of the Titanomachy and the freeing of Prometheus shifts Pandora's aims and perspectives, and now she's forced to confront the bigger picture: can she have free will at all? Can she claim a life for herself? There's a lot more ahead for her.

If you've enjoyed this book, I encourage you to join the Skalds' Tribe newsletter and get access to exclusive insider information and your FREE copy of *The Moments of Kadmus*. **I generally send every week or every other; I promise not to mail more often than that.** No spam, no selling your email address to marauding warlords, none of that.

Join me here to grab a free novella and stay connected with me: https://www.mattlarkinbooks.com/skalds/

Thank you for reading,
Matt

PS Pandora's journey continues in the *Madness of Herakles* …

https://books2read.com/madnessofherakles

Join the Skalds' Tribe newsletter and get access to exclusive insider information and a selection of free books to kickstart your Matt Larkin library.

https://www.mattlarkinbooks.com/skalds/

ALSO BY MATT LARKIN

Tapestry of Fate

The Gifts of Pandora

The Valor of Perseus

The Inferno of Prometheus

The Madness of Herakles

The Threads of Theseus

Heirs of Mana

Tides of Mana

Flames of Mana

Queens of Mana

Gods of the Ragnarok Era

The Apples of Idunn

The Mists of Niflheim

The Shores of Vanaheim

The High Seat of Asgard

The Well of Mimir

The Radiance of Alfheim

The Shadows of Svartalfheim

The Gates of Hel

The Fires of Muspelheim

ABOUT THE AUTHOR

Matt Larkin writes retellings of mythology as dark, gritty fantasy. His passions of myths, philosophy, and history inform his series. He strives to combine gut-wrenching action with thought-provoking ideas and culturally resonant stories.

Matt's mythic fantasy takes place in the Eschaton Cycle universe, a world—as the name implies—of cyclical apocalypses. Each series can be read alone in any order, but they weave together to form a greater tapestry. Want a place to start? Check out *Darkness Forged.*

Learn more at mattlarkinbooks.com or connect with Matt through his fan group, the Skalds' Tribe: https://www.mattlarkin books.com/join-the-skalds-tribe/

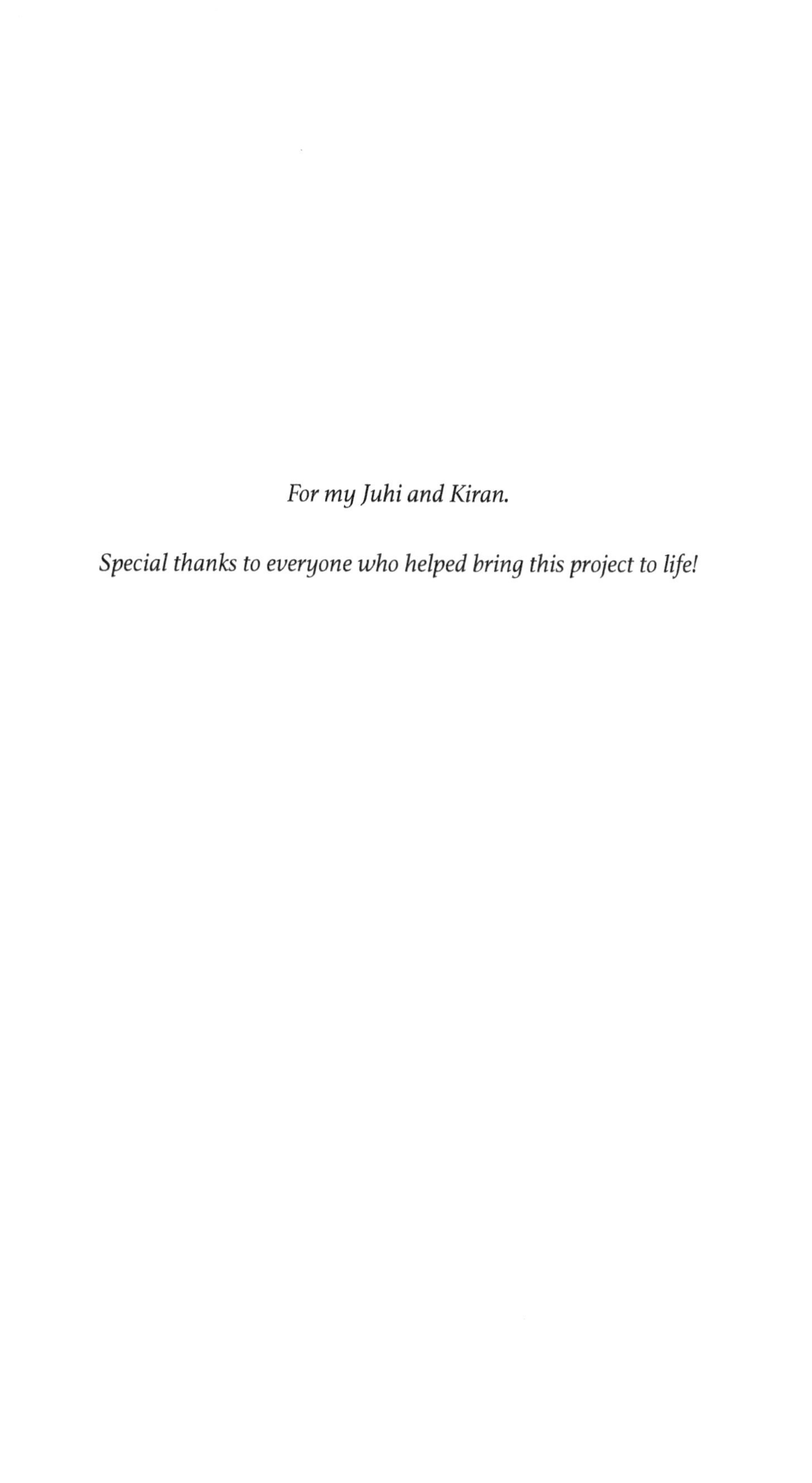

For my Juhi and Kiran.

Special thanks to everyone who helped bring this project to life!